# THE TRICKSTER'S DAUGHTER

Others' Child closed her eyes and opened them again. Coyote was sitting in front of the fire, its light turning his coat red-gold.

"If you human people are going to keep making rules about what you can and can't do," he said, "you are going to have to think further ahead. I have more sense than to make rules."

"That's all very well," Others' Child said crossly. "You have no morals."

"That is a fine way to talk to your father."

"*You* are not my father!"

"How do you know?" Coyote inquired, grinning. "All people are my children when they go into the wild places."

He looked at her for a moment more, and then he was gone. She thought she saw the yellow eyes gleam behind the flames. Then they vanished, too.

# THE DEER DANCERS

## BOOK TWO

# Wind Caller's Children

# AMANDA COCKRELL

AVON BOOKS ◆ NEW YORK

THE DEER DANCERS, BOOK TWO: WIND CALLER'S CHILDREN is an original publication of Avon Books. This work has never before appeared in book form. This work is a novel. Any similarity to actual persons or events is purely coincidental.

AVON BOOKS
A division of
The Hearst Corporation
1350 Avenue of the Americas
New York, New York 10019

*For Felix*

# Author's Note

There are older stories, always, embedded in the tales we hear, of the old times, of the old ways, of when the world was young. Stories within stories, like nesting boxes, from the panorama of creation and flood, of disaster and repentance, to the core of the story, to the men and women who lived, or might have lived, or maybe still live at its heart. Look through the surface of mythology and you will find them.

If you lived among the People, five thousand years ago in the Valley of the Rio Grande, where New Mexico is now, you would find those stories just beginning to be made. The oldest gods have been with humankind always—the Great Mystery Spirit, the Feathered Serpent who is the breath on the water; and Coyote, who is chaos, and keeps good and evil balanced. But the tutelary deities, the ones who teach humankind to plant, to make music and art, to weave—those the People must make for themselves.

Often it is from the animal people that these gifts come, and from the animal people's human side that the gods are born. In the old days, human and animal people lived and talked together, and the animal people might take human form and human mates.

The borders between the worlds are thin in this early time into which you have fallen backwards. You might meet Coyote around a bend in the river, nose deep in clear water. You might see Grandmother Spider weaving a pattern that looks too familiar, and catch a glimpse of your life in it. For we are all at the heart of our own myths. That is why even the most unlikely tale of walking mountains and talking snakes, and heroes' journeys to the underworld, has at its heart a first true story.

# Prologue

*The red stone house in the cliffs looks as if it has swallowed up the sun. It pulses with light at the day's end, a fire going out, burning itself to ash. And as the sun falls down behind the western mountains, dropping a blue-gray shawl over the world, the cliff house begins to glow with another kind of light. The yellow beacons of fires stud its walls, like a handful of stars that Coyote threw against the sky. They flicker, making the shapes of doors and windows waver.*

*The people of the cliffs pad across the flat roofs of their aerie and step down the ladder that descends through a hole to a room below. They are bundled in furs and blankets to ward off the cold. The old woman who sits beside the fire is bundled even more heavily. Her gray head sticks up above her blankets like a magpie out of its nest, and her hands are buried in the folds. Two young men sit beside her, adding sticks to the fire and heating her a drink of cactus liquor. To be that old is to be very important and powerful. One who is that old remembers things that hap-*

pened before birth, things that happened on the edge of time.

A person that old can remember how the gods came, and becomes the people's memory.

"In the old days," the old woman tells them, laying aside the threads she will need to weave her story, "before the People came to the cliffs to live, they did not know how to do many things. They did not make pots yet, only baskets, and no bows, only long spears, and they hunted as they always had since the Great Cold and the Wandering, and since the Great Game went away, leaving only the little animals that we have today.

"They did not plant maize but gathered wild grass seed and broke their teeth on it and were altogether not as we are now.

"And then the man with the flute came from the south and brought maize to the Yellow Grass People, and they began to make a god of him and of the woman he took, who could draw pictures in the dirt to call the deer. The man brought Coyote with him—or perhaps they were both Coyote, the man and the beast together—and there began to be a great many of Coyote's children among the dogs of the People; and also there were two of the man's and the woman's children.

"Now, it is not a good idea to have Coyote too much among you, but Coyote himself thought it was a very fine thing and began to brag. Most people brag a little, even though it is a very unpleasant habit. But Coyote brags all the time and can make a stone shout at him to keep quiet.

"And then he brought another child to the Yellow Grass People—or he made the woman bring her; it amounts to the same thing. This child was also different. She had been stolen from or maybe just left behind by the Others, the stranger people, when the Yellow Grass People learned to make war (and that was Coyote's doing, too) to drive the Others out of their caves. Coyote had only to sniff her to know what she was, and then he bragged louder than ever.

"When Coyote brags, everyone has to listen to him because there is no choice. The Sun hears him and the Moon hears him, and Rattlesnake goes down into his hole, trying not to hear Coyote yammer on about his many fine children, not to mention his great potency. As everyone knows, Coyote will stick it in anything.

"Grandmother Spider heard him, of course, sitting in the middle of her web. Grandmother Spider's web stretches across the Universe, its watery strands moving in the Feathered Serpent's breath. Grandmother Spider is as old as Old Man Coyote, and although Coyote may claim to have invented art, and to have brought music and maize, it is Grandmother Spider who did the work. Grandmother Spider taught the people to weave baskets, and later to make pots. She taught them to sew clothes with threads of sinew, and to make ropes and sandals, and later to weave cloth. Everything that is woven or knotted or braided or twined is the gift of Grandmother Spider. She knows everything because she hears everything, and although she is generally kindly disposed toward people, it doesn't pay to anger her. What Grandmother Spider weaves, she can unweave.

"So Grandmother Spider wove the girl called Others' Child into the fabric of the Yellow Grass People. Coyote brought her, but Grandmother Spider heard him yowping and bragging, and as soon as she took a look she knew that this one was hers, and what she had to do with her.

"'I never thought I would have a child with you,' Grandmother Spider said, giving Coyote a sidelong look that he thought was amused and therefore didn't trust. She shifted on her web, and her long legs hung over the slender gray lines. She looked young today, and hungry. Coyote edged away a little.

"'I have children everywhere.' He grinned when he wasn't so near the web and lifted a back foot to scratch behind his ear. 'All the girls like me. I can make it as long as I want to.'

"'You're faithless,' Grandmother Spider said. 'And you have fleas.' She scooted a little farther out on her web, and in one corner of the Universe the stars bounced. 'My husbands are always faithful.'

"'The more fools they.' Coyote could see the husk of an old husband dangling just below the Great Bear.

"Grandmother Spider scuttled toward him. She was very beautiful, with long dark legs and golden arms, but Coyote danced just out of reach. Coyote has some sense.

"She hung off the edge of the web then, and saw the human child below, asleep on a bed of brush and deer hide with one of Coyote's numerous offspring in a ball between her knees and her stomach. Outside the cave, the man with the flute stood among the maize. The flute notes fluttered in the air above him, and Grandmother Spider saw that he had almost become a god."

The cliff people ring the fire in front of the storyteller, their faces burnished by it, like pots of light. The old woman, who may even be Grandmother Spider herself, begins to weave the threads of her story. . . .

# I

# The Rain Stopped

The flute notes beat upward in the hot, dry air, carried on the updraft above Wind Caller's head. To his children, watching from the greasewood bushes, the repeated notes seemed to tumble down like raindrops, kicking up puffs of dust at his feet. But no rain fell after them, no clouds massed in a sky that was as hot and empty as a baked blue stone.

"It's not going to rain," Mocking Bird said pessimistically. "It isn't working."

"The song isn't *for* rain," Follows Her Father informed him. She was Mocking Bird's twin, and inclined to be scornful of him because she had been born first, a circumstance to which she attributed superior knowledge of almost everything. It helped make up for his being a boy. "It's to make the maize grow." Singing up the maize, Father called it.

"Well, it won't grow without rain," Mocking Bird said.

"Sssh!"

They sank lower in the greasewood bushes. Father had said not to come with him while he was trying to talk to the Maize God. Apparently that was like when he was trying to talk to Looks Back, the old shaman. Children were not allowed to interrupt.

Others' Child peered over the heads of her brother and sister, pushing them down. She was three years older than they were and felt that her advanced age gave her privileges, so that they were all reasonably content with their positions in life. "If the Maize God wants it to grow," she said, "and it needs rain, maybe he'll send it. If he doesn't, we'll have to move early this year. The deer will leave if all the streams dry up."

"Oh, no." Follows Her Father looked horrified. She had helped to plant the maize, and envisioned the tiny ears shriveling in their husks, withering for lack of water. The land had been dry all summer, and they had dipped water from the steadily shrinking river to keep the maize alive. "If we go, it will die." She could feel herself drying up like the maize.

"Looks Back is going to try to make it rain tonight," Others' Child said. "And Mother."

The twins nodded solemnly. Even the Deer Dance and their mother's magic were beginning to fail at calling the game. There were no turtles in the river, and the fish people died when their streams sank into the sand. The Yellow Grass People were living close to hunger, and they expected Looks Back and Mother and Father to make that different. The twins felt very important about that. Others' Child was beginning to be afraid.

The children watched their father again, silhouetted by the low sun against the yellow tufa cliffs where the Yellow Grass People lived. He was muscular but more slender than the other Yellow Grass men—as if his bones were smaller, Others' Child thought. He was magically different, from his slightly slanted eyes, which were vaguely like Others' Child's, to his aquiline nose. It was not beaky like those of the men of the Others—Others' Child silently fingered the small bump in her own—but it was arrogant, as if it knew more than anyone else. Bent over his flute, his body had the curved shape of a cupped hand, and his nose jutted out fiercely, the way that Cat Ears's chin did. When Wind Caller and Cat Ears argued, which was always, they seemed to Others' Child to be standing nose to chin.

Wind Caller stuck his flute in his belt and pulled his hunting knife from it. He lifted his arms upward, and the looped braids in which he wore his black hair, unlike those of any of the Yellow Grass People, crisscrossed the dark pattern of his arms like a spiderweb. While the children stared, he pricked both thumbs and squeezed them until they dripped blood. Onto each of the hills in the maize field he squeezed a drop, bending and straightening rhythmically, up and down, his voice rising and falling in a chant the children didn't understand, in a language that Wind Caller no longer spoke.

"That's what the Children of the Sun do in the south, where Father and the maize came from," Follows Her Father whispered. "They give the Maize God blood."

"Mother says they are uncivilized," Others' Child said. Deer Shadow, their mother, still found her husband's gods incomprehensible.

"No, it's what they have to do," Follows Her Father said somberly. She was slender, but with the compact muscularity of the People, and she moved inside her skin like a small cat. Once again Others' Child, angular and bump-nosed, was aware of her Otherness.

She watched Wind Caller bending, straightening, turning through the rows, doing what the men of the Yellow Grass People could not: calling up the maize that would feed them. He turned sideways to the slanting flame of the sun, and it licked at the old scars on his breast, rows and rows of them like silver raindrops against the red-brown skin. Others' Child saw fresh blood there, too, to feed the maize. . . . All to feed the maize.

"He has to do it," Follows Her Father whispered, "because the maize says it's time."

Others' Child felt the skin on her arms tingle. Mocking Bird shifted under her hand, coiled like an impatient russet snake, his round face turned toward his father. They both knew that Follows Her Father was right. Wind Caller was a god, a gift-bringer for the People. They all knew that to be a god meant also to be a sacrifice.

At night he sat silently by the fire with his scarred hands folded in his lap and watched the rain-calling. The children were relegated to the far side of the dance ground with people of lesser importance, and Deer Shadow was with Looks Back, conferring in whispers. Wind Caller sat wrapped in isolation, self-exiled from the Yellow Grass People by his own difference.

The children craned their necks to see past the brightness of the flames. When they were grown—which would be when Mocking Bird was thirteen, and when the girls had their first flow of blood—they would be permitted to sit with the elders and maybe even take on some of their parents' power. But tonight they were children, held firmly in their place by the tribe. There was a sense among the Yellow Grass People that Wind Caller and Deer Shadow held too much magic between them as it was, although certainly a child did not always inherit that power. Cat Ears, the chief of the hunters, was the son of old Looks Back and had wanted to be shaman like his father. But everyone else had sense enough to know that Cat Ears was ill-tempered and prideful, and that to give him that power would be bad for the tribe.

The children of Wind Caller and Deer Shadow

would not have to have their parents' power conferred upon them, and they knew it. They had it already, held it wrapped around them like a secret blanket, a shield against the cold loneliness that sometimes shrouded them when the Yellow Grass People looked oddly at them or spoke behind their hands, or when strangers at the Gathering pointed at them and whispered.

Mocking Bird was the freest of them. He could make his small flute sing to anyone, even to Follow the coyote, his father's companion. But because there were others among the Yellow Grass People by now who had learned to play, there was less magic in that. It was Follows Her Father who, from the time she could walk, had padded behind Wind Caller to the maize field and sat and talked to it as if it were someone she knew.

"You have to let them have what they have," Deer Shadow had said, shrugging. When Others' Child had picked up a stick and drawn a puppy in the dirt because she wanted one, a small bitch from one of the litters that Follow had got on Aunt Four Fingers's dog had nosed its way past the hide over the cave mouth. Deer Shadow had given Others' Child an odd look and let her keep it. She watched closely now to see what Others' Child drew in the dirt.

Bitch sat with them at the rainmaking, her yellow-gray nose in Others' Child's lap. Follow was lurking somewhere outside the firelight. He was old now, and he had gotten wilder as he aged, as if he were preparing to move out of this world into whatever Coyote arranged for his children after death. He stayed at Wind Caller's heels only when there were not too many people around. Although his dealings with Deer Shadow had mellowed somewhat with age—she cooked him mush and stews that he could get his teeth through—and he still slept in the cave, he was leaving them; they all knew it.

Too many people had left since the dry years

started. Others' Child was twelve, and she could remember when the maize grew over her father's head, the streams were full of turtles, and ducks flew over each spring and fall. Since the Yellow Grass People had driven the Others from the People's caves and killed many of the Others' men, the Others hadn't troubled them, and the deer had come back to the People's hunting runs and grown fat. Others' Child and Deer Shadow's babies had grown fat with them, although Deer Shadow had had no more children. The twins had taken all the life she had to give, Looks Back had said when her only other pregnancy ended in cramps and bleeding. That, he said, was why she had been given Others' Child.

Then had come the start of the dry years. Since then Aunt Four Fingers had died, and Deer Shadow's father, Found Water, and one of his wives and more of the oldest among the bands of the People.

It wasn't only the land of the Yellow Grass People that was drying up. The other bands of the tribe—the High Rock People, the Smoke People—all of them were growing gaunt. Even the maize didn't save them. It was withered and dry the first year and stunted the next. If the People stayed to tend it, they couldn't hunt because the game had moved; if they followed the game, the maize died for lack of water. It was a gift they would have done better not to have taken, Cat Ears had said angrily last winter after the Yellow Grass People moved up the hills to their winter caves without enough meat to see them through the cold months and eight of them died.

But Others' Child, chin on her hand, watching the rainmaking, knew there was no place to go where the deer were plentiful. That was just Cat Ears being angry. The old chieftain, Blue Stone Man, had died in the winter, too, of the lung sickness, and the new young one, Wakes on the Mountain, was willing to listen to Cat Ears complain because Cat Ears had voted for him.

Others' Child cuddled Mocking Bird and Follows Her Father closer to her, an arm around each with Bitch between them. The rain dancers were coming, the sparks flying over their heads like red birds. Others' Child could hear the faint thin drumming the men made with split twigs on stretched hides. The women's feet pattered on the packed earth. Strings of shells were sewn to their deer-hide skirts, and the sound of a hard rain moved with them over the dance ground. There had been an ocean here once, Looks Back said, and shells dug from the earth had power to bring water back again.

The women danced in slanting lines like the rain walking across the purple mountains. The lines crossed and recrossed, splattering against each other, black hair flying like thunderclouds over the shell rain. It was women who could talk to the rain, sing to it with their own fertility. Deer Shadow began to dig at the earth in front of her with her drawing stick, carving droplets in it, marking out the lines of rain above the shape of Red Rock Mountain. Line on line of drops like the scars on Wind Caller's chest, like the flipping tails of fish people deep in the river.

Deer Shadow wasn't sure she could call rain. Once she thought she had called Coyote when Wind Caller had first come to the Yellow Grass People. She still did. But Wind Caller said he came from the south, where his people had exiled him for thinking he knew better than the chieftain-priest. A common failing of adolescent boys, he had said, amused, watching the new men strut with new spears at last year's Gathering. But the People suspected him of being at least half a god anyway. He had brought the maize, and who but a god could tame Coyote?

Deer Shadow was the woman who could make deer in the earth and summon them from it. She could watch that gift flowing into Others' Child, who wasn't even born to the People. Surely that meant that the magic came from outside. Surely that meant that it would work with rain.

Behind her, Looks Back lifted his arms, burned-dry grass tied about his wrists, showing it to Rain God in case he had been too busy with matters in the sky and hadn't seen, telling Rain God how great was their need. He wore his rain mask, which had snakes painted on it with the red dye that came from the mountains. Tied among the tufts of burned grass were snake's rattles that buzzed as he swayed.

Deer Shadow cut her digging stick deep into the ground, made soft by a basket of precious water from the river, carving droplets, bigger and bigger, shaping their curves like gourds, like pregnant women's bellies, like the fat husks when the maize was ripe. The women danced wraithlike to the rain drums. They were thin, their legs as fragile as the legs of deer. A faint wailing of a hungry child rose over the rain sound.

That night Deer Shadow and Wind Caller lay in their cave in the tufa cliffs and listened for the sound of rain. The children were asleep; Deer Shadow could hear faint snores from the other side of the cave. They had learned to sleep through hunger.

"What if it doesn't rain?" she said fretfully. "I don't know if I can make it rain. We've tried before. If we ask too often will it not come at all? I don't know these things."

Wind Caller sat up creakily, one hand braced on the cave floor. These last years his bones had begun to grow stiff so that he woke in the morning feeling like a turtle encased in a hard shell. He touched Deer Shadow's hair. A streak of gray ran through it. Wind Caller secretly liked it. She was still beautiful despite the lines that cut from her nose to her stubborn chin. She had a fierce beauty, like a pine tree or a wind-carved stone. "What does old Looks Back say?" he asked her.

Deer Shadow bit her lip. It was dry and cracked, and she licked the blood off it. "That the gods will send rain when they understand how much we need it. That we must not be speaking to them in the right way."

"And in what way does he suggest?"

Deer Shadow's head drooped, her chin in the furs wrapped around her. "I don't think he knows."

Wind Caller made a noise that might have meant anything. He didn't think the shaman knew, either.

"Some are saying there may be some evil here we don't know about. That someone may have done something wicked."

"Someone of the Yellow Grass People?" Wind Caller inquired. "Or someone of the Smoke People, or the High Rock People? Or the Buffalo Leap People? Or of the Others? They are starving, too. They sent men to try to trade us red dyestone for meat. Or for maize. Cat Ears and Found a Snake drove them off. Most Wise, it is not just on our heads that it is not raining."

"Tell that to Cat Ears," Deer Shadow said. "And Runner. Her baby died."

"Cat Ears likes to stir up trouble to be important. Tell Cat Ears that the gods told *you* the evil is in him, and see what he does."

Deer Shadow looked horrified. "I can't say that the gods have told me things. They would do something to me."

"I recall a time," Wind Caller murmured.

Deer Shadow snorted with amusement in spite of herself. She had informed her people that her new-found husband *was* a god, shortly after his arrival. "It was that or let Cat Ears kill you," she said. "And besides, I *thought* it was true."

"I think it's true now," Wind Caller said. "About Cat Ears."

"You don't. You just don't like him."

Wind Caller put a hand into the shadows. Follow

was there, nose on his paws, dreaming. They could hear faint whining sounds. Wind Caller felt his ribs through the rough coat. "Follow doesn't like him, either."

"That coyote doesn't like anyone but you and the children," Deer Shadow said. It was still a sore point. *I am still jealous of a coyote,* she thought, and snorted with laughter again.

Wind Caller stopped scratching Follow and put his arm around her. He pulled her head onto his shoulder. "If you can keep laughter," he said, "then we will live."

"I am afraid for the children. I don't know anyone but us who hasn't lost one." The children of the People always died easily, and now there was drought. "I am afraid Death will notice them and remember."

"We only have three," Wind Caller whispered.

Deer Shadow ducked her face away from him. She had always felt wrong in some way because she hadn't been able to have more.

"Stop that," he said. "Perhaps that is why we can keep them. And why they sent us Little Coyote."

No one called Others' Child that except Wind Caller. Deer Shadow wouldn't let them. And she didn't like it when Wind Caller did it. Deer Shadow was going to see to it that her daughter had a proper place among the Yellow Grass People, because there had been something feral about Others' Child when she had come to them, and Deer Shadow was afraid of it, for her. Maybe it was only her Otherness, but Aunt Four Fingers had called her a coyote, too, and made a crossed-fingers sign at her. The People had been wary of the Others then, and angry at them.

Then Looks Back had had a dream. He had dreamed that Grandmother Spider had come to tell him about Others' Child. Spider had been beautiful, he had said: pale silver like moonlight, slender-legged and graceful with the vast expanse of her web behind her. She had told him that the stolen child should be of the Yellow Grass People, of Deer Shadow's house and Found Water's clan.

"Did you send her?" Looks Back had asked.

"No," Spider said, "Coyote did. And the fool that snatched her from her mother. But now that it is done, I can see how it should be." Since Grandmother Spider could see backward and forward and even sideways, Looks Back hadn't argued. He had told his dream at the fire on the dance ground that night, and after that Spider had come to him several times to talk about this and that. Sometimes it wasn't Grandmother Spider herself but Listens to Deer, who during his life had been a soft man, a man/woman, and hence was considered to be very holy in the tribe and very wise. He always appeared to Looks Back in the spider form, but the old shaman recognized him, as one does in dreams.

These visitations and his own great age gave Looks Back much standing. So if *he* didn't know why the rain had stopped, who could?

"Lie down," Wind Caller said. "Sleep. You won't make it come by listening for it."

"How do you know?" Deer Shadow said stubbornly. Surely she could make something come by wanting it. She had done it before.

He pulled her under the furs. "I can think of another thing to do." He put his mouth on her breast and grunted happily at her reaction. "Some things still grow when I want them. See there?" He nuzzled her other breast with his lips. "And maybe this will make it rain."

It might, Deer Shadow thought. Sex was a powerful force. It didn't matter that babies wouldn't come of it. Who knew what else might? The urge to life was in everything, in the rain dance, in the fish gasping in their shallow waters, in Bitch's first litter—which would be three parts coyote if they didn't keep her away from Follow. It was all part of the same dance.

It was all part of wanting, and believing that wanting would make things happen.

The children heard their parents rustling in the darkness in the furs on the brush bed. There was very little the children of the People did not know about at an early age.

"What do you think it's like?" Follows Her Father whispered to Others' Child.

"I don't know," Others' Child whispered back. "Nice, or why would anybody do it?"

"It looks funny," Follows Her Father said thoughtfully.

"Well, it's rude to watch."

"Aunt Owl said that with her husband it was very bad, and he beat her. But Squirrel's wife says it's fun if you have the right husband."

"Women don't know anything," Mocking Bird said because he was embarrassed.

"We know more than you," Follows Her Father said, and she and Others' Child both giggled at him. Mocking Bird turned his back on them in disgust.

Bitch wriggled her way deeper into the pile of furs and children, and they drifted to sleep again.

They woke in the morning to the thin sound of rain, the soft rain called female rain, soaking the rocky talus below the cliffs.

"Wake up!" Follows Her Father grabbed her mother by the hand and prodded Wind Caller in the back. "There's rain!"

Outside, the children were dancing in the water, their bare red-brown skin gleaming with it, polished as river stones. Others' Child spun in circles in the rain, the piece of blue stone that she wore on a thong around her neck spinning out as she whirled. Mocking Bird hopped on one foot, flute to his lips, singing to it.

Deer Shadow went to the cave mouth, her hand in

Wind Caller's, and looked at the sky. Already the rain was slackening. She laid her head against his chest with a murmur of despair.

Always it was this way. Sometimes Rain God would send rain when they asked, but never enough, and it never lasted. This rain would dry up on the dusty ground as soon as the sun came out.

"It will fill the water holes a little," Wind Caller said.

"A little," Deer Shadow echoed. The little that kept them from death was always so small. She saw Looks Back standing in the rain, carrying his great curved tooth with him, taller than he was. It was from the time when the Great Game had roamed the land and one of them would feed a band of the People for a whole moon. Now the Great Game were gone, only the spiral of Looks Back's tooth to show that they had been. Looks Back stood inside its curve as if it would hold magic in, make the rain stay. *He is old*, Deer Shadow thought. *He will go from us, too. Maybe to wherever the rain has gone.*

As she thought it, the rain slowed. The people turned their faces up to it openmouthed, letting it run down their chins, but it stopped, and the sun flared through the clouds. Deer Shadow could almost hear it hiss, like Rattlesnake, the water drying up on hot stone.

Looks Back shook his head, shaking off his trance, and stepped out of the circle of his tooth.

"With respect, old man," Cat Ears said, looking as if he meant none, "this will do us little good." He stuck his chin out, and his flat, backswept ears made him look like a lynx.

Looks Back turned around toward Cat Ears, his gray hair straggling on his shoulders. It was hot already, and the shaman wore only a breechclout of braided rabbit skin. His own skin bagged and drooped from his ribs, and stiff gray hairs sprouted in his nose. His hands were mottled, with thick, ropy veins that stood out when he clenched the great tooth. He shook it at Cat Ears, and everyone stepped back a pace. There was no love lost between the shaman and the chief of the hunters, never had been since Cat Ears had been old enough to toddle and quarrel with his father. "There are times when it is a mistake to say things that everyone knows," Looks Back said. "If a thing is true, it is true. If it is not true, you may make it true with the telling."

"Yah!" Cat Ears said. "You are an old man. Maybe it is time another talked to the gods."

Wakes on the Mountain, the new chieftain, watched warily. A little knot of younger hunters was gathered behind Cat Ears. It was always the youngest who followed Cat Ears, the youngest who were impatient. Age conferred great power, but it also meant you were walking toward an end of things, when younger men would have their turn.

Wind Caller let go of Deer Shadow's hand and stepped between Looks Back and his son. Two of the other men, One Ball and Squirrel, joined him, their feet planted apart, crouched a little, as if ready to fight. Hunger had made everyone as touchy as fire in dry grass. "The rain will keep the maize awhile," Wind Caller said. "If we have to move after the game, the women can stay here and tend it until it ripens."

"And let the Others come and take it," Cat Ears said. "Like they did before. Yah, you are stupid."

"The Others are starving, too," Wind Caller said. "I saw the men who came to trade. You can't eat red dyestone, and they have no meat, and all the wild grasses are dying. Only the People have maize."

"All the more reason the Others want to take it from us!" Runner said. She cradled her older son in her arms. "Are we going to lose *all* our children?" Wind Caller couldn't tell whether her face was streaked with tears or rain, but it looked fierce, and her ragged teeth were bared.

"They haven't the strength," Wakes on the Mountain said. "I sent men to spy on their camps and see if they had meat, if they had found better hunting runs than we have. They are dying, too. They are worse than us. You know that, Cat Ears, you saw."

"It is not the Others we have to fear," Looks Back said. He gazed at the sky, eyes narrowed.

One Ball looked exasperated. They needed better answers than that even if Cat Ears *was* a fool. Cat Ears could track game if there was any game to hunt. He could find deer when no one else could. He breathed their breath. You couldn't discount him completely. If there was no food for the winter, it wouldn't matter who was right. "Then what, Old Uncle?" One Ball said. "Then what?"

"I will speak with the gods," Looks Back said. He closed his mouth with the mumbling motions that the nearly toothless make, and went back into his cave. The deer-hide flap fell behind him, and the people milled uneasily outside in the drying mud.

"The gods never say anything we understand," One Ball said irritably.

"Hush," Deer Shadow said. "That is why we have a shaman. To understand for us."

"Does he?" Runner demanded. "Does he? *Someone* must tell us the reasons for things." She looked agonized, and her bewilderment was mirrored in the rest of their faces. If the shaman didn't know, then the world had become unstable, sliding beneath their feet.

Looks Back lay down on his bed again, its dry grass crackling under the deer-hide blanket. He pulled his tattered wolfskin robe over him and closed his eyes. When it came to talking with the gods, he could see better with his eyes closed.

He yawned. Now that he was old, he liked to sleep. That way he could see things beyond the world of the People. Once he thought he had even seen the world where Wind Caller came from. It didn't matter if Wind Caller's first home was truly where the gods

lived or was only a place full of different kinds of
men. The gods had lived with people when they felt
like it ever since they all came Up From Below together.

Looks Back yawned again; he turned on his side
and burrowed under the wolfskin. The cave was
quiet. With the rain smell still in the air, he might
have been in a piece of a different year altogether,
when the rains had still come and his old wife had
not died. . . .

At first he didn't see Spider. But then he noticed
that his eyes were open and his hands, folded in his
lap, were young again. He shifted his shoulders experimentally, clacked the teeth in his mouth, and
grinned. That was nice. Spider hung from her web on
the far wall. She had a fall of black hair and the man/
woman Listens to Deer's face.

"Ho," said Looks Back.

"Ho, yourself." Listens to Deer was weaving a basket. Looks Back didn't try to figure out if it was Listens to Deer or Spider. There was no reason it couldn't
be both, just as Listens to Deer had been a man and
a woman at the same time. People like those were
messengers, the ones between worlds, and did not
have to be only one thing. Therefore they understood
many things.

"We are starving," Looks Back said. "The rain has
stopped."

"Stopped altogether?"

"The female rain comes, sometimes," Looks Back
said. "But never enough. The water holes are drying
up. And never the male rain. Do you know why?"

"I know a story," Listens to Deer said. Spider's legs
moved across the basket, threading in and out, in and
out. It was a water basket, with a dark band across
the top like storm clouds. She held the dark grass in
one hand, the light in another, and the reeds for the
ribs in a third. Looks Back couldn't tell what her

fourth through eighth hands were doing, but the story seemed to grow out of their motion and take shape like the basket.

*Rain Boy, whose mother was Frog Old Woman and whose father was Lightning, had a beautiful wife. Her name was Weaver, and she lived with him under a rainbow bridge in the desert badlands. Rain Boy was very jealous and kept her to himself out in a brush hut where no one would see her. She didn't have anything to do all day, so she wove baskets, and plaited sandals, and made rope, and any other thing you could think of to weave. She made fur robes for her husband—he was always damp and cold, not so nice to live with, and much resembled his mother—for she was a dutiful wife, though she had never seen any other men. She never bragged about her weaving. That was not a safe thing to do, for Grandmother Spider does not take kindly to it. Weaver was most respectful, as befitted a good daughter.*

*Still, word got around, especially when the woman was beautiful and the husband was away making rain in the mountains. One day Butterfly Boy came to her brush hut, and Weaver found something to be interested in besides her weaving. Butterfly Boy was very beautiful, even more beautiful than Weaver. Beauty is the strongest spell of any and causes more foolishness, but Weaver didn't know that. I know that, and Coyote knows that, and Weaver would have known it if Rain Boy hadn't been such a fool as to be jealous before he had any reason to be and kept her shut up in the desert with no one to talk to but Horned Lizard.*

*At first Weaver didn't look at Butterfly Boy because she was paying attention to her weaving.*

*"If you would take your eyes off that basket a minute, I would show you what you're missing," Butterfly Boy said. He is very vain, and he has a right to be.*

*Weaver looked up, and even the dry, humming cicadas went quiet. Butterfly Boy gleamed like a handful of sun* and blue stones. Weaver set her basket down without even looking at it again. "What do you want?" she asked hopefully.

"I want you," Butterfly Boy said. "I want to take you to my house in the flowers and make you my wife." For a little while, anyway, Butterfly Boy thought, because he is not noted for his faithfulness.

And that was when Rain Boy came home. He stood dripping in the doorway and smelling of lightning. As we all know, Rain Boy is not only jealous but prideful, and he has a temper. He looked at Weaver and was furious with her, too. So instead of just trying to cut Butterfly Boy's balls off with his skinning knife, Rain Boy said, as if it didn't really matter, "I'll race you. Whoever gets to the top of Thunder Mountain first can have her." He pointed upward at the dark peak arched over with the rainbow bridge.

Butterfly Boy loved a race. And the woman would still be there when it was over. So he said, "That's fair," and took off, swirling up into the sky, wings flashing scarlet and blue, bouncing the sun off them and scattering colors farther than the rainbow. Rain Boy ran after him.

Weaver watched them go. She folded her arms across her beautiful rosy breasts and tapped her tiny, high-arched foot. She was in a temper with them both, Beautiful and Ugly giving no more thought to her than to make her the prize in a race. And she was not Grandmother Spider's daughter for nothing. "We'll see," she said, and she went outside with a coil of woven rope. She put a loop into it, threw it, and snatched the rainbow out of the sky.

The air darkened as Rain Boy flashed across the desert. Streams sprang up under his feet, and water poured down through the blackened sky. Thunder crackled, and when Rain Boy reached the peak of Thunder Mountain, Butterfly Boy was nowhere to be seen.

"Hah!" said Weaver, watching Butterfly Boy reel along a muddy road, his wet wings beaten and drooping.

"I won," Rain Boy said. He stood over Butterfly Boy,

arms crossed. "So I'll keep my wife." He got his knife out.

"Are you sure it was fair?" Weaver said. She touched her husband's arm. "It rained and he got wet. You wouldn't want people to say you were dishonorable and didn't race fairly."

"Certainly not," Rain Boy said. "Since you're properly repentant, I'll give him another chance before I kill him."

"Do that," Weaver said. "Your honor is more important than anything else."

"Let me get my breath first," Butterfly Boy pleaded.

"Very well," said Rain Boy.

Butterfly Boy winked at Weaver under one wing. He could tell she wanted him instead. What woman wouldn't? As the sun came out, Butterfly Boy flapped his wings, fanning its heat across the desert.

Rain Boy began to look a little pale, transparent as the false water that shimmers on hot sand. He ran, drawing the clouds around him like a cloak, trying to pull the water from them. Butterfly Boy was well ahead now. Weaver spun her rope and threw the rainbow back in the sky. The clouds paled, and Rain Boy staggered out of them into the hot sun. "Too bright! Too bright!" he wailed. He fell into a pool of sun, his wet hair drying up with a sizzle like water on hot stone.

Butterfly Boy touched the peak of Thunder Mountain and fluttered lazily back to see what was going on. "I guess you'll come with me now," he said to Weaver.

"I have to get my things," Weaver said. She went back into the brush hut, but she came out with a net of fine strands, woven with her own hair, as thin as light and as strong as spiderweb. She threw it over Butterfly Boy and held on while he floundered inside it.

Rain Boy staggered upright and stumbled across the sand to them. He lifted his ax while Butterfly Boy tried to shield himself with his torn wings. Rain Boy raised the ax and brought it down on Butterfly Boy's skull. It split right in two. Out of the split in his skull and

*through the rent in the net flew a funnel of little but-
terflies, tiny as a child's fingernail, red and blue and
yellow, scattering across the sky, too small to do anyone
harm with their beauty.*

*"There. Now he is useful," Rain Boy said.*

*"More useful than you know," Weaver said. "This is
what comes of your jealousy."*

*"Mine!" Rain Boy said. "And what of your faith-
lessness?"*

*She looked at his frog face and winced, for truly But-
terfly Boy had been very beautiful, but she was a good
wife and beauty is fleeting, anyway. "The little butterflies will scatter," she said, "and they will give many
faithless women a moment of pleasure. And then they
will become something else entirely and give those
women enough work to keep them from dreaming of
pretty boys while their husbands are not home."*

*And she went back in the brush hut and refused to
explain anything more to him. But the butterflies scattered across the world like seed, and wherever they lit,
they sprouted up, and Rain Boy learned to water them
when Weaver told him to. And he stopped trying to keep
his wife at home and let her wander where she would,
and so she taught the people many useful things. And
now the butterflies are the maize that grows, and even
when Rain Boy sulks, and Coyote comes sniffing around
to see what mischief he can make, it is Weaver's women
who tend the maize, and Weaver who holds the world
together with her net.*

Looks Back rubbed his eyes with his hand. "I don't
understand," he said fretfully to Listens to Deer's face
on Spider's body. "It was Wind Caller who brought
the maize."

Spider's long legs flexed themselves, and she
danced delicately along the lower edge of the web,
weaving. "I don't understand, either," Listens to Deer

said. "Not when I listen in this world. When I listen in other places, it makes more sense."

"Maybe I should listen in another place," Looks Back said. "I have grown tired of this one."

"And what of Cat Ears?" Listens to Deer asked.

"Cat Ears doesn't listen at all. *I* can't change that. I am tired of trying to change Cat Ears. I like it here, with my teeth back again. This is very fine."

Spider slipped loose a knot in her web. "Come along, then," she said.

# II

# The Flute Song

The land of the Yellow Grass People was very beautiful, even when it was as dry as old bones. Above the yellow volcanic tufa, where the People had dug out a string of wind-eroded caves, rose the deep blue corrugated crests of the mountain range. A stream sliced through it, cutting its way down from its source, and the rock on either side was striped in deep rose and brown and tawny yellow, like a butterfly. Hot springs bubbled in the high folds—a cure for the lung sickness, or for women's illnesses, or just for the pain of old age—and around them grew the juniper and piñon pine, a blanket of dark green blotched with stands of yellow aspens.

When Looks Back came out of his cave, he could see the thin lines of Spider's web, sharp as the horns of the moon, running south over the land, making him a road. To the southwest a pale blue mountain was set against a bluer sky, sleeping over the badlands at its feet, a black stone country that Looks Back could see now was not evil, only That Which Is. He wouldn't be surprised to find Coyote living there. To the east lay the great river valley where the People's stream fed into Water Old Man, and to the south more mountains, purple and azure above a red plain.

The burned trees and the shrinking stream opened and made a path for him, and he could see the shining spokes of Spider's web there, too, running through the branches. The path led upward through them, toward the sky, and he began to follow Listens to Deer along it. At first he was panting to keep pace—in his spider body Listens to Deer had eight legs. Then Looks Back's breath came easily, and the path grew solid. Like the trails the People's feet had cut in soft stone, going up and up the mountain, it spiraled toward the sun.

Runner found him at night when she went to take the old man his food and see if he had news from the gods. She sat back on her heels and gave a howl of terror that brought all the Yellow Grass People running to the cave mouth.

Deer Shadow pushed her way through and jerked Runner out of the way.

"He's dead!" Runner howled.

"Be quiet, you silly woman." Deer Shadow shoved her away again, but Runner kept pushing back, as if she thought that if she looked again, she might see something different. Deer Shadow bent her head and let her breath out slowly. Looks Back *was* dead. His mouth was open, and his lips pulled back from his gums. His hands were folded peaceably on the wolf-skin.

"He promised us the answer!" Runner sobbed.

"He may have heard an answer," Deer Shadow said, "but it was his."

Wakes on the Mountain pushed his way into the cave, too. "We must wait until the power comes to another of us," he said while Runner howled. He let his eyes run over the faces peering at him. Whoever the vision came to would be the next shaman. Wakes on the Mountain thought uneasily of the possibilities.

A dry wind rattled through the cave where the body lay. In four days it would be burned so that Looks Back's spirit would go to the Skeleton House, where it belonged. Even a shaman's spirit—*particularly* a shaman's spirit—had to be encouraged to leave. Otherwise, the dead might stay, and that was dangerous. No one would even speak Looks Back's name, lest they give him a reason not to go.

A man of Looks Back's power required a feast before his burning, too, but there was not enough food to waste by eating it all at once. Wakes on the Mountain thought about what to do while the people argued in frightened whispers.

"He will come back and live in our caves!" said Magpie, Wakes on the Mountain's wife.

"The old man knew we have no food," Squirrel grumbled.

"He isn't a man anymore," Dancing Bear said. He was a huge, lumbering man, but his wide shoulders were thin now, incongruous on his ponderous frame. "There's no telling what he might do. It isn't good to talk of him."

The children hung on the edge of the crowd, listening. "Do you really think Old—the one who is gone— would hurt us?" Follows Her Father whispered to Others' Child.

"I don't know. Mother says you change after you're dead. He might not know us. The dead get angry that they aren't living, and then they try to take you with them to the Skeleton House."

"There is plenty of food for the dead people in the Skeleton House," Mocking Bird said. He rubbed his empty belly. "If I were there, I would want to stay. I hope we're going to have a feast, though."

"Then what would we eat after?" Others' Child asked.

The men were breaking away from the rest, gathering into a knot around Cat Ears. Follows Her Father found Deer Shadow talking with Magpie and tugged at her hide skirt. In the heat of summer, that was all that most women wore, and she could see that Deer Shadow's ribs were beginning to show. She rubbed at her own. "What are we going to eat? Will there be a feast?"

"The men will hunt again tomorrow," Deer Shadow said. "Whatever they can kill before the burning we will cook to honor him. Maybe he will send us something."

Follows Her Father put a hand on her mother's arm. The skin felt hard and dry, like brushing stone. "All they killed yesterday was a rabbit and a burrow dog. And mice." She made a face.

"And you can eat mice when you are hungry." Deer Shadow slipped an arm around her and said to Magpie, "We must go farther afield. We are picked bare here."

Magpie nodded. Every day the women gathered greens and wild grass seed, dug camas bulbs, and searched for quail eggs and snails and turtles in the stream. But all of those were vanishing with the water.

Now they followed the dwindling stream far beyond their normal summer wanderings. Sometimes the men left to hunt and were gone for days, limping home at last with a deer if they had been lucky, with a handful of rabbits and squirrels if they had not. The big buffalo, which in good years wandered west into the People's land, were gone entirely.

This time the hunters came home, footsore and angry, with one deer and a dead dog, gored by the horns. The deer was old and hadn't wanted to be taken, which was a bad sign. When the hunters honored the game properly, it gave its breath willingly.

The women dressed the deer anyway, as well as the dog, and tanned both hides. Nothing was wasted, not even in good times.

"I always said that old dog had about enough brains to tan its own hide with," One Ball said. "Stupid dog." He kicked at the tree where the fresh skin was hanging. The dog had been his. There had hardly been enough meat on it to be worth eating.

On the fourth day, Wind Caller and Wakes on the Mountain carried Looks Back's body to the fire pit on the dance ground and laid it on a pile of dry wood, covered with his wolfskin robe. His great tooth stood beside the firepit but not in it, waiting for whomever the power might come to. The people cast covert glances at Wind Caller, who pretended not to see them, and at Cat Ears, who everyone knew had wanted to be shaman after his father and had had it refused to him. It was possible the power still might come to Cat Ears, but the idea made them uneasy.

Others' Child watched with the edge of her thumb in her mouth, biting it hard when Wakes on the Mountain and Wind Caller put the torches to the dry wood. Looks Back was the one who had said she belonged to the Yellow Grass People. Maybe they wouldn't think so anymore now that he was gone. The flames bit into the wood and roared like Storm Old Man, a dark, dry, hot, hungry voice. In a moment she couldn't see through them. The smoke stung her eyes. She watched her father put an arm around her mother and whisper something in her ear. Suddenly she wanted to be between them, huddled safe from whatever might come from out of the dark.

Since there was no shaman, Wakes on the Mountain was chanting the prayers that went with the burning. The fire's voice grew louder, and the smell of burned flesh began to clothe the air. It lifted the hair on Others' Child's neck. Her father said that burning left you with no body to wear in the otherworld. He had made Mother promise not to let them burn him when he

died. A sudden flare lifted the flames as if Looks
Back's body were trying to rise, protesting that.

Others' Child ran, pushing through the people
around the bier, and buried her face between her father and mother.

The power settled on no one through the rest of that
bone-dry summer and into winter. The trees dried up
and shed their leaves before the first cold moon, and
when the Yellow Grass People went to the yearly
Gathering at the autumn equinox, they saw how thin
the ranks of all the People were. Wakes on the Mountain conferred seriously with the chiefs of the Smoke
and Lightning and High Rock peoples, and all the
others. There was hardly a band among them who
had more than fifty adults, and they were thin and as
suspicious as starveling coyotes now, hiding with jealous secrecy any knowledge of a full water hole or a
salt lick where the deer still came.

"We are not supposed to be like this!" Deer
Shadow said disgustedly. "This is not the way the
gods have told us to be!"

"Then the gods had better send rain," Wind Caller
said. He looked out over the Gathering ground. Looks
Back's tooth marked the camp of the Yellow Grass
People, even though they had no shaman now. Across
the valley the standards of the other bands were
spread: coyote tails, eagle feathers, a brush of porcupine quills. The Gathering was the yearly
coming-together, when the bands of the People
crossed paths with one another in their autumn moving. News and gossip were exchanged, stories were
stored away for winter boredom, marriages were
made, children came of age: newly made men and
women with their first taste of adulthood. Wind
Caller remembered his first Gathering with a secret
grin. Deer Shadow had been pregnant with the twins
and short of temper, and he had found a woman of
the High Rock People to console him. Deer Shadow

had thrown rocks at him when she had found out.

Now she leaned her head against his chest. "If it were not for the maize, we would not be here at all," she said, watching a dozen women moving around the fire pits. The meager game that the hunters had brought back roasted on spits above the hot stones where maize cake was cooking. Only ten years had passed since Wind Caller had come with a handful of seed. Now they were dependent on those small fat ears. Truly her husband was the Gift-Bringer. *I have lain with a god*, she thought with satisfaction. *He will not let us starve.*

When the Gathering was over, the bands of the People moved on, higher into the mountains, where there were caves that caught the low sun and the piñon pines grew. Piñon nuts and dried meat and maize meal were their winter diet. Sometimes if the weather was clear, the hunters might make a kill, but mostly they mended spears and chipped new points, and told stories of old exploits that grew with the telling. When the solstice came, the men went into the secret cave, where the women were not allowed, and turned the sun around.

And then spring came, and the snow melted, and the People went down the mountain again to the tufa cliffs, and surely now the deer would come back. There was even a new shaman: A boy who had been made a man at the last Gathering saw his vision. His name had been Porcupine, but now he was to be called Hears the Night. That was the name Bear had given him in his vision, because it was the quiet of the stars that had called him out of his cave to see Bear in the first place. So Bear must be his totem, everyone said, and Hears the Night said that that was so. He looked at Deer Shadow grudgingly; he had wanted Spider to come to him as she had to Looks Back, but it was Deer Shadow who dreamed and talked to Spider now and told the stories that Spider told her.

"A woman cannot be shaman," he said sternly to her after he had had his vision. "It is not right that Spider talks to you."

"Tell that to Spider," Deer Shadow said. Hears the Night wasn't much older than her children. It made her irritable to be lectured by him. She went on grinding the handful of maize in her quern. It would go in a cooking basket with a few shreds of rabbit meat and the little bitter yellow squashes whose vines trailed through the scrub brush in early summer. This year the vines had shriveled, and the squashes had withered early.

"It is not right that you tell stories of the People around the fire at night, either," Hears the Night said. "From now on I will do that."

"Make it rain instead," Deer Shadow said, but she touched her breast in a gesture of respect anyway; Hears the Night was young, but he would probably learn better. And now that they had him to talk to the gods for them, now, surely *now* it would rain.

But no rain came, except for the thin short showers that barely kept the land alive. The stream shrank further, and even Water Old Man sank down between his banks. The people ate snakes, mice, and lizards and ladled water on the maize. That year the men and women had to separate so the women could remain in the tufa cliffs to feed the maize water while the men roamed into lands they had never hunted. Cat Ears could feel the tribe's hunger at his back, pushing him into a landscape he couldn't read and had to study to learn.

The coyotes were hungry, too. Their voices warbled up and down the valley, and Others' Child tied Bitch up when she pricked her ears at the sound. There was no need to tie Follow. He had grown too old to answer. He let Wind Caller go hunting without him and lay on the cave floor in the sun, as if even at midsummer he was cold.

He wouldn't live through the winter, Deer Shadow thought, but he did, and limped into another summer with his ribs protruding and his patchy coat coming out in tufts. That summer Others' Child began to bleed and had her initiation at the solstice.

"It would have come sooner if you hadn't been starved," Deer Shadow said, knotting up her daughter's dark hair with a pair of turkey feathers. "You are as thin as bone."

There were two other girls who had begun to bleed since the spring, and the women took them and Others' Child to a brush hut in the valley beyond the dance ground and left them there until darkness fell.

"What are they going to do to us?" Quail asked, trying to peer between the woven branches.

"You'll get your nose caught, sticking it where you shouldn't," Others' Child commented.

"My sister says they beat you with whips and make you eat a frog," Yucca Spear said.

"A live one?" Quail put a hand to her mouth, backing away from the brush wall.

"And when has your sister ever told the truth?" Others' Child said loftily. "She said the moon would fall out of the sky on you, too, if you took her necklace again."

Others' Child and Quail both nodded. So far it hadn't. Others' Child flopped down on the floor of the brush hut and folded her hands in her lap. She wished the others would be quiet. She wanted to think about being a woman, about what it would be like. It was the start of a different life, as if she were moving to a place never seen before. It was all part of the pattern, Mother said, but Others' Child knew her pattern was skewed, with pieces torn away. Her pattern began in the middle, like a basket with no bottom. Now that she was going to be a woman, would that change? Would the holes weave themselves closed, block out the feeling of not belonging, of Otherness?

"Sister says there won't be anyone to marry us." Yucca Spear was digging at the dirt floor with a twig. "She says the boys will want women who are more than bones."

"Yah, and where will they find them?" Others' Child snapped, irritated to have her thoughts interrupted with Yucca's worries.

"Father says it won't rain because there's a curse on us. He doesn't know who put it there, but he knows a curse when he sees it." Quail nodded at them, emphasizing her father's store of knowledge. "Father says by midsummer there won't be any water in our stream, either."

"If it's a curse, Hears the Night would have found it," Others' Child said.

Quail sniffed. "Maybe it came from outside the People." She looked pointedly at Others' Child. "Maybe that's why Hears the Night can't see it."

"And maybe the moon will fall on you," Others' Child said.

"Your father has been listening to Cat Ears," Yucca Spear told Quail. "Everybody knows Cat Ears doesn't like Wind Caller."

"That's because Cat Ears wanted to marry my mother," Others' Child said. "But she wouldn't have him, so he had to marry a woman who looks like a turkey hen." She gobbled at Quail. Cat Ears's nearly chinless wife was Quail's sister.

"Hush!" Yucca Spear said. "They're coming!" She stuck her nose to the wall again. Through the gaps they could see torches burning holes in the dark. The smell of pitch left the air acrid.

Others' Child, oddly dissatisfied, watched, too. She had wanted to have her initiation at the Gathering at the fall equinox, when all the bands of the People would be together and there would be a great feast, but not even a fierce concentration had been able to

put off her flow of blood past the summer solstice.
Mother said it would have come sooner if she hadn't
been half starved. Maybe she was older than they
thought. The Others, Mother said, had been hungry
when they had tried to drive the People out of the
tufa cliffs, when they had left Others' Child behind.
Maybe she hadn't been as young as she looked. It
irked her not to know her age, and now this initiation
at the solstice, with no one to watch but her own
band, seemed to her second best. *Yah, and I am petty
and wicked for thinking that when we have no food*, she
decided.

The women circled the journey hut, singing, their
bare feet rustling in dry grass. Others' Child could see
that two men, Dancing Bear and One Ball, had been
allowed near enough to the circle to stand ready with
extra baskets of water, in case flame dropped from a
torch. They were in constant fear of fire now in this
dry land.

There were only twice as many women as Others'
Child had fingers, ranging from two newly made at
the equinox, their hair still cropped, to Mother and
Magpie and Cat Ears's wife, Silent. *I remember when
we were more than this*, Others' Child thought, frightened. Eight of the women handed their torches to the
rest and came into the brush hut. The smell of smoke
came with them, and the torches flared outside, light
flowing through the woven walls, flinging strange
and twisted shadows on the ground. They circled the
three girls, singing, bunching them together, knotting
them into the pattern that was Woman—life, and
death, and birth—so that the People would always be.
They howled, a ritual mourning for the first death,
childhood's death.

In her hands Magpie cupped a stone with a nestlike
depression that cradled live coals. Deer Shadow
dropped something onto the coals, and a thick, res-
inous smoke wreathed through the torchlight and the
shadows. It made Others' Child think of Great Snake

hunting. Father had told her about Great Snake, who was greater even than Rattlesnake and who lived in the wet lands to the south where Father had come from. Now Others' Child thought she could see his broad, flat head in the writhing coils. She stared back at him, eye to yellow eye, while Mother took her daughter's long hair in one hand and a skinning knife in the other and hacked it off.

It spilled in a black pool at her feet, and her head felt oddly light, as if she might rise now with the smoke. Deer Shadow and Magpie tugged at her hide skirt and dropped it on top of the shorn hair so that she stood naked except for the blue stone on the thong around her neck. The women outside handed in baskets of water, and the women inside began to ladle it down the girls' bellies and thighs. The water had been dipped from the shrinking stream whose sluggish current ran only inches from its muddy bottom, and it was brown and smelled of decaying reeds. Others' Child wrinkled her nose.

The older women let out a new howl, this one a crescendo of yips like coyotes calling, and pulled the girls, shorn and wet, into the spiral of their dance, feet drumming on the muddy grass. Others' Child slipped into place behind Mother and watched the torchlight slide down her damp belly. They spun out the door of the journey hut, spiraling wide into the night, and Others' Child saw the Universe revolve around her, the wide slow sweep of the star road spilled across the sky like the paths that the People wore into soft rock from years of spring and autumn travels. The night sucked her up, and for a moment she danced on the star road and could see the shining web beneath it.

Then they were dancing their way through the men and boys, and the young girls, insignificant now, who were not women yet. Others' Child could feel their eyes on her, the men's especially, eyes sliding like hands over breasts and belly. She liked the way it felt, spinning under the stars, and the way that the two boys who had had their own initiation today watched her with new knowledge in their eyes. Beyond the circle of the dancers she could see her brother and sister, sitting cross-legged with Bitch between them, watching her whirl. Follows Her Father looked envious, hugging Bitch to her, but Mocking Bird's eyes flickered behind the torchlight so that she couldn't see into them. Others' Child spun past them, past the reflected flame of Mocking Bird's eyes, into her new dance. She didn't long for the Gathering anymore. There was enough for her here, among the Yellow Grass People.

The men and initiated boys came out to dance opposite the line of women, husbands reaching for wives with new hunger, the unmarried ones slipping into line opposite the few girls not forbidden to them. The People could marry only outside their clans, and the Yellow Grass People consisted of three clans that now numbered no more than forty adults altogether. Most had always looked for mates at the autumn Gathering. This year there would be an urgency behind that, not to go solitary another year.

Others' Child danced, her body weaving a pattern of its own, her shorn head feeling light as thistledown. Most of the boys who watched her so hungrily couldn't marry her. She found pleasure in that, almost spiteful, to sway in front of them, Great Snake looking for his dinner, daring them to come and be bitten.

"You had better marry that one away at the Gathering," Magpie said to Deer Shadow, watching her.

"She is too young," Deer Shadow replied.

"Pooh," said Magpie. "She is older than Coyote."

"She is young. Let her have it for a while." *Let the boys learn they can't have everything.* Deer Shadow slipped back into the line of dancers, looking for her husband, and saw Silent instead, watching Cat Ears nervously, trying to see if he wanted her or if he wanted to be left alone. Sometimes he beat her if she got it wrong. Deer Shadow looked at Others' Child again. *Let her find someone she won't wake in the morning wanting to run through with his own spear.*

She found Wind Caller and held out her hands to him. They slid out of the dance into the shadows and the dry grass that rustled at their feet and along the valley. It whispered of coming of age, of the circle that all life traversed, of the hard, bright, golden days when they had been young. *I have gray in my hair*, she thought, *and his teeth are bad. Soon I will be Deer Shadow Old Woman with grandchildren. That is not such a bad thing.* They sat under the skeleton of a barewood tree, the dry grass prickling through her skirt. Wind Caller took out his bone flute.

The music was like birds, floating up from the flute to sit in the tree. Deer Shadow could see them, lined along its branches, or maybe it was only the distant firelight that shaped their red breasts, cocked heads with bright eyes. You could weave things with music, she thought. She had always thought so, and the older she got, the more certain she was that Wind Caller wove something with his. Coyote broke things open, sent them spinning into the world to make change come. Grandmother Spider gathered up the shreds and wove them together into what was supposed to be. If you left it to Coyote, Deer Shadow thought, they would all be put together wrong, turkey heads on bears' behinds, fish in trees. It took both.

The flute song wreathed about the people on the dance ground without their knowing it. It stayed, singing in the air above their heads, long after Wind Caller had laid his flute aside and pulled his wife down into the whispering grass. The dancers heard it in their blood, in the red riverine channels where life still flowed, where the dance would go on and on, and deeper in their bones, from which the flute was made.

Hears the Night came out of his trance like Bear

waking, and saw Others' Child swaying to the sound
of hide drums and the rainfall patter of shell rattles.
In the torchlight, her skin had the luminous glimmer
of Red Rock Mountain in the rain and the sheen of
flute song. She could call images out of the earth the
way her mother could—a likeness that brought mas-
tery over the animal people. Clearly, she was going
to be a woman of much power—and she was *not* of
his clan.

Hears the Night took a place at the center of the
men's dance, between Cat Ears and Wakes on the
Mountain. One Ball and Squirrel made room for him
with gestures of respect. He was young, not even so
tall as they, but he was shaman. He looked at Others'
Child, and she lifted her shorn head and gazed back
with speculative interest. The circles spun, men's and
women's, overlapping, linking, until they moved in a
great wave like Water Old Man, flowing into each
other. Hears the Night danced chin to chin with Others' Child.

The drums softened. Others' Child felt the circle
slowing as if the wheeling stars dragged their feet.
The smell of cooking meat came from the fire pits,
and she stopped, perplexed, only half out of the
dance, while the valley spun around her. A warble of
hunting coyotes rose from its edges, a bright flare of
sound on the horizon. The dancers spread out toward
the fire pits. Hears the Night vanished and returned
to hold a stick with rabbit meat on it in front of her.
She blinked at it. Suddenly she was ravenous, her
stomach contracting. She bit hungrily into the meat,
her first in days, gulping and swallowing.

After the first few bites, Others' Child watched
Hears the Night out of the corner of her eye. It meant
something that he had brought her meat and she had
taken it. She didn't have to marry him, exactly, but
he wouldn't have brought meat to a girl of his own
clan, a girl who was taboo to him. He ate his own

portion silently and then wiped his mouth on the back of his hand.

"Do you remember the Others?" he asked her, as if they had already begun a conversation.

Others' Child swallowed, perplexed again. "No." *Did she? A woman who wasn't Mother? A woman who was screaming?*

"Now that you are a woman, these things are important," Hears the Night said. He threw the bone he had been holding to the thin dogs, and they fought over it.

"Why?" Others' Child demanded. The one who was dead had never asked her. She couldn't name Looks Back, not even in her head, because by naming the dead a person risked calling them, but there were ways to think of them. "I belong to the Yellow Grass People. It was said so."

"The gods might be angry if I took a woman with a taint still on her," Hears the Night said. "What is right for other men may be forbidden to me. If you are cursed, I must drive it off first."

"I am not cursed!" Others' Child said indignantly. "Father would have known, or Mother!"

Hears the Night looked important. "I am shaman. I am given the great magics to know, not the little ones. If I say to the gods that I want you, then they will tell me if it is permissible."

"Who said that I wanted *you*?" Others' Child replied. But she did. He was handsome, his adolescent body hardening into muscle, the line of his throat and shoulders suddenly strange to her, as if something new inhabited him. She could see his penis standing up under his breechclout from looking at her.

Hears the Night didn't listen to her. He was talking to the gods, explaining it to them. When he was through, he pulled a small smooth stone from the pouch he wore around his waist and touched it to her breasts and her mouth, and finally put it between her legs while Others' Child looked at him indignantly.

But it felt good. His fingers there made her nipples harden and something just below her belly ache in an odd way. She wanted him to leave them there, but he didn't, and Quail was giving her covert glances, and Yucca Spear was giggling. Hears the Night put his hand on Others' Child's arm and pulled her away from the firelight. She decided to forgive him for being self-important.

They slipped into one of the storage caves that pocked the talus slope below the cliffs. Too small to live in and barely big enough for them, it was lined with stone pits that would hold the maize when it ripened. Hears the Night put his otter-skin cloak on the floor for her to lie on and pulled his breechclout off. Watching him curiously, she lay down, counting up sensations: the otter fur soft against her back, the feel of his fingers tangled in the hair between her thighs, his mouth on one breast, almost swallowing it. Others' Child knew girls who had been doing this since before they were women, but now was her first time. She hadn't wanted to before, but now she wanted to fiercely, with a desire that wasn't so much for Hears the Night himself as it was for the thing they did, a demarcation, a stream to cross into adulthood and knowing. He pulled her legs apart, and in the dimness she could see his penis, stiff as a spear shaft, go into her.

It hurt, and she bit him in the shoulder. He didn't seem to notice. She pounded her fists on his back, and he didn't notice that, either. His breath came in steady grunting pants in her ear as his penis went in and out of her. It didn't hurt *quite* as much now. She shifted her hips experimentally, and it began to feel nicer. Hears the Night let his breath out in a moaning shudder and rolled off her.

The rest of her family was asleep—at least ostensibly—when Others' Child tiptoed into their cave. Her mother raised her head, gave her a long look, and lay back down. The deer hide that hung between her parents' bed and the rest of the cave had been pulled to one side, Others' Child noted, possibly to afford a better view of the cave mouth, but her mother didn't comment when Others' Child lay down stiffly beside Follows Her Father.

"I know where *you've* been," Follows Her Father announced, afflicted by no such discretion.

"Go to sleep," Others' Child said. "You don't know anything."

"What was it like?"

"Go try it yourself." Others' Child pulled the furs over her head. She could still hear the coyotes howling around the rim of the valley, and she wondered what they were hunting. Mice, maybe. Like people, coyotes ate anything and bred with enthusiasm even in the starving time. Others' Child wondered, feeling depressed now, if she would have a baby. If she did, she would have to marry Hears the Night. She would have to have someone to hunt for her and the baby. *I don't want a baby*, she thought irritably. *I don't want Hears the Night. He went to sleep.* That was not how she had imagined it. Bitch whined at the coyote song, her ears pricked. Others' Child reached an arm out and put it around her furry neck.

"You don't want them," she said. "You don't need more puppies. You couldn't make milk for the last ones."

Bitch looked at her, yellow eyes catching the thin moonlight. She hung out her tongue and grinned.

"Dirty coyote," Others' Child muttered. "Go with anybody, even your father."

Bitch lay down again, nose on her front paws, and yawned elaborately, an eloquent pretense at having no plans to go anywhere.

In the morning, it was Follow they couldn't find. Bitch was snoring innocently, curled among the children's furs, and she opened one yellow eye when

Wind Caller stood in the cave mouth and whistled, but she didn't get up.

"He's gone with them," Wind Caller said.

"Tchah! He is too old to go with coyotes," Deer Shadow said. "He's only bones. Coyote Old Man doesn't live in him anymore."

"Well, he's gone with them," Wind Caller said. He tied his breechclout on.

"And where are you going?"

"To find him," Wind Caller said.

"Bah! So they can eat you, too?" Deer Shadow said. "No!"

Wind Caller picked up his spear. Mocking Bird sat up in the furs, scrubbing his eyes. "I'm coming."

"To find a filthy coyote," Deer Shadow muttered, but she looked across the valley, eyes narrowed. The low sun made the barewood trees and the dying cottonwoods by the river into elongated runners racing over the ground. She couldn't see anything else.

Mocking Bird went out to piss and came back in for his spear. In another year he would be a man, Deer Shadow thought. Let him go if he wanted to. The two of them would be all right together. The coyotes might pull down a hunter caught alone, if he was injured, or set one of their bitches out to bait a dog into coming too close, but they wouldn't attack two healthy men.

"It won't matter, though," she said to the girls. There was something gone, some emptiness in the air that she thought she knew.

They found Follow not far out into the valley, sprawled in a dry wash. His throat was torn open, blood sinking through the patchy fur into the sand. He was already stiff.

Mocking Bird sniffled and bent over the battered shape. "Why did he go out?" he demanded. "He knew he couldn't fight anymore."

"Maybe that's why," Wind Caller said. "He was old and it was time to go Away."

"They didn't eat him," Mocking Bird said. "They killed him, but they didn't eat him."

"It isn't good for you to eat your own kind." Wind Caller knelt and cradled Follow in his arms, awkwardly, stiff legs jutting out.

Mocking Bird snorted. "Coyotes don't know that. Not when they're hungry."

"And when isn't a coyote hungry?" Wind Caller replied. He put Follow down and hunted for a stick to dig with. "They were afraid of him, then. He still had that."

Wind Caller dug a hole in the dry sand, pulling it away with his fingers when it trickled back. "It will keep the buzzards off him," he said defensively, as if someone had asked him why. Already flies were beginning to circle around Follow's muzzle.

When he thought he had gone deep enough, Wind Caller laid Follow's body in the hole and started to cover it up again. His face might have been carved out of red stone now, teeth clenched.

Mocking Bird stared at the gray form as it disappeared under the sand and tried to put life back in it, to remember life back into it. As babies he and the girls had feared nothing as long as Follow was pacing after them. For some reason, maddening to Deer Shadow, Follow had decided he owned the children and had bitten anyone who touched them. They had slept happily pillowed on his smelly hide. He was more than a dog, a kind of guardian spirit, and it had occurred to none of them in their babyhood that he would die.

Wind Caller covered over the grave with rocks. He looked at Mocking Bird's miserable face and ruffled his hair. "I found him before I found the People," he said, "and I liked him better a lot of the time. But Coyote doesn't let you keep the things he gives you. You'd probably better learn that now."

# III

# Where Coyote Lives

Among the Yellow Grass People, any news took wing, but especially this: Wind Caller and Mocking Bird had barely come home before everyone knew that Wind Caller's coyote half had gone Away, throat torn out by its own kind.

Cat Ears took the news to Wakes on the Mountain, and together they hurried to the shaman's cave to apprise him. Hears the Night considered the significance of what had happened.

"It was most unwise of Wind Caller to bury it and not consult me," he said. Wind Caller rarely consulted him about anything. "It may be that the ghost coyote will come and live in the man."

"Would that be dangerous?" Wakes on the Mountain asked.

"No!" Cat Ears said sarcastically. "No, it is good luck to have a man-coyote in your camp."

Hears the Night held up his hand. If he let Cat Ears

take over a situation this dangerous, he would never wrest power back from him. "Everyone knows that this man is a part of Coyote," he said. "And that the animal was the other half, dual natures imprisoned in separate bodies. The woman said so when he came to us."

"And I said he was a witch," Cat Ears muttered, "but no one listened to me."

"It may be that the woman did not perfectly understand the nature of this duality, being a woman. But it is true that the coyote spirit, having no living body to reside in, may now unify with the man spirit in the man's body."

"What does that mean?" Wakes on the Mountain demanded.

Slowly Hears the Night said, "Coyote is the Old Trickster. He is Gift-Bringer, but not to be trusted."

Cat Ears snorted. "What have I been saying? We should have killed him when he came here and let Coyote find some other place to bring his great gifts."

"He brought us the maize," Wakes on the Mountain commented. "We would have starved without it by now."

"And we would not be so tied to it that we cannot go into new country to hunt and take our women with us!" Cat Ears snapped. "Yah! Have we become plants, with our feet stuck in the ground? Shall we go and dig a hole and lie down in it, so that maybe we will sprout in the spring?"

"You are not someone whose opinions I would trust to be unbiased in this matter," Wakes on the Mountain said with a half smile, but also with a certain caution. Cat Ears was older than he, with gray in his hair and the craftiness with which age replaced muscle. Cat Ears was also chief of the hunters, and his word carried weight.

"There is no doubt that the man is magical," Hears the Night pronounced, "and thus capable of much. If the coyote spirit has returned to him, then he is possibly dangerous. Most certainly unreliable. It is necessary to ensure that the coyote spirit does not wake. It cannot be driven out, but it may be kept sleeping. I, Hears the Night, can do this."

They watched impatiently while the shaman gathered his power about him: his bag of blue stones, his eagle feather, his cloak of wolfskin and turkey feathers. In another bag he put dried sage, a handful of juniper berries, greasewood leaves, and a magical stone with an eye in it that he had found by the river the day after he had had his vision. "With the eye stone I may see the cure for this man," he told the chieftain, his voice low and important.

"You had better cure him before we hunt," Cat Ears said caustically, "or I may drive the coyote spirit out with a spear in his back."

Hears the Night lifted the great curved tooth that had belonged to Looks Back, and wished that he hadn't been so quick to lie with the coyote man's daughter the night before.

"This is a matter for the shaman, Cat Ears," Wakes on the Mountain said. "It is a bad idea to anger Coyote before a hunt."

Cat Ears subsided, grumbling, and Hears the Night said, "I will go now and make a magic so that Coyote will sleep. Wakes on the Mountain will come with me, but Cat Ears, you will not."

Wind Caller was sharpening a spearpoint on the cliff wall outside his cave. Years of using the stone for that had gouged out overlapping striated hollows in the soft rock so that it looked as if someone had carved a giant basket from the cliff wall and taken it away. The forepart of the spear shaft lay on the ground by Wind Caller's feet, split and ready for the point. He was bending to pick it up when he saw the procession approaching.

Hears the Night, wrapped in his wolfskin-and-feather cloak, carried the giant tooth with authority.

Wakes on the Mountain walked behind him. At a respectful distance behind them followed the rest of the Yellow Grass People, alerted by the shaman's attire that something interesting was about to happen.

Wind Caller turned slowly, put the spear shaft down, but kept the blade in his hand. He made a gesture of respect at Hears the Night. "What important thing brings the shaman here?"

"The coyote spirit that has died," Hears the Night said. "I have come to keep it from settling in you and making you crazy."

Wind Caller balanced the spearpoint in his hand. "That is kind of you. So far I do not feel crazy."

"It is dangerous," Hears the Night said. "With the animal dead, the spirit has no place to go."

Wind Caller chuckled. He pointed at Bitch, panting in the shade, waiting for them to take her hunting. One or two more of Follow's get could be seen among the dog pack that followed the curious. "He was very potent," Wind Caller assured Hears the Night. "He left many pieces of himself. If I were a coyote, I would stay in them. They have more fun, even Bitch."

"It is not a matter for joking," Hears the Night snapped. "The animal's death makes you dangerous. It is only through my power that we may all be protected."

Wind Caller fingered the spearpoint. He narrowed his eyes at the shaman. "I am not half so dangerous now as I could be. Coyote and I feel most disinclined to have demons driven out of us."

"He has gone back into you already," Hears the Night said. "It is worse than I feared."

Wind Caller looked at him thoughtfully. "What do you propose to do about it?"

"There must be a ritual, a cleansing. The spirit must be made to sleep."

"And how must this be done?" Wind Caller inquired. He glanced at Deer Shadow, who had come out of the cave and was staring angrily at Hears the

Night. How quickly could she hand him his other spear? he wondered.

"*I* will do it," Hears the Night said. "Immediately. We must not wait."

"If we don't hunt *now*, early in the morning, we will catch nothing," Wind Caller said. "Then we will all be hungry, and you will not care quite so much about where you think Coyote may be as long as he isn't in your belly."

"It is impossible for you to hunt with the People before you have been made safe," Hears the Night said.

Wind Caller scowled at Wakes on the Mountain, who stood imposingly beside Hears the Night but had said nothing. "Then we will all go hungry because someone thinks he is seeing ghosts. It is easy enough to know where that idea came from." He looked beyond Wakes on the Mountain to Cat Ears in the crowd of the curious. "Yah, maybe I will go crazy, Cat Ears, and run through the camp biting at your feet."

"Tell your wife I must have a basket of fresh water," Hears the Night said.

Deer Shadow glared at him and spun around on her heel, pushing past the children into the cave. Others' Child stepped out from the cave mouth and fixed a discomfiting gaze on Hears the Night. When he looked away, she crouched and began to draw a brushy-tailed shape in the hard-packed dirt. Hears the Night walked over and stamped it out with his foot, chanting the Keeping-Away Song.

As Deer Shadow came out again with a basket, she cuffed Others' Child's head.

"My wife has gone to fetch you water," Wind Caller said unnecessarily while Deer Shadow pushed the onlookers out of her way, shouldering through them in a fury. Cat Ears stepped out of her path.

Wind Caller looked at the Yellow Grass People peering curiously at him from behind the chieftain.

They wouldn't settle down until it was done. If Follow was in him somewhere, he couldn't feel it. He felt unpleasantly alone. "Very well," he said grimly. "The shaman may do what he thinks best."

Hears the Night nodded solemnly.

"Yah," Others' Child muttered in disgust, nursing her sore temple where her mother had smacked her. "What the shaman does doesn't last very long."

Yucca Spear, standing on the edge of the spectators, heard her and gave a muffled snort of amusement, which she immediately tried to turn into a cough.

Hears the Night reddened and fixed a gaze on Yucca Spear that reminded her of his power. She clapped a hand over her mouth and, frightened, hid behind her mother. The shaman turned the look on Others' Child next, but she didn't lower her eyes or move from where she crouched outside the cave mouth. Hears the Night put on his sky mask and turned away from her, shielding his face from that baleful glare.

The sky mask was inlaid with crushed pieces of blue stone, and it had hair of buffalo grass, carefully cured so that it was springy and soft to the touch. The hair around the blue face rustled, and Hears the Night's eyes looked out through dark-rimmed slits. It made him taller somehow, and older—much older. With the sky mask on, it wasn't only Hears the Night before them but also Sky God, and anyone in his right mind was afraid of Sky God.

He began to lay the juniper berries in a circle around Wind Caller, while Wind Caller watched him uneasily. Others' Child envisioned her father leaping from the circle and running, swift as a shadow on all fours, before Hears the Night could take the coyote half out of him.

He didn't run, though, and when Deer Shadow came back with a water basket, he stood docilely while Hears the Night chanted and poured it around his feet, around the circle of juniper berries, and then threw sage and greasewood leaves on top.

*Yah, and I can throw leaves on my feet, too,* Others' Child thought. She marveled at her dangerous impiety and then thought sullenly, *I don't care. He doesn't know everything he thinks he knows.* She drew in her breath in a gasp and looked up at the sky. The notion that the shaman might *not* know everything was suddenly terrifying to her. What if nobody knew anything, not really?

Hears the Night spoke to Sky God through his blue stone mask, reminding him of how Sky God had split the coyote spirit in two when it had angered him, and that now one of the two bodies was dead. It was the telling and retelling that made a thing true and thus manageable. Hears the Night told Sky God that he, the shaman, was going to make the coyote spirit sleep in the man, as trees slept in winter, so that it could not run loose among them and bring evil. Then he told the eye stone to watch Wind Caller by holding it in his face and chanting.

Wind Caller's teeth were clenched and his eyes blazing by the time Hears the Night finished. Cat Ears wore a look of smug satisfaction.

"With respect," Wind Caller said through the clenched teeth, stepping through the opening in the circle that Hears the Night had made, "I am going hunting. If you wish to speak longer with the gods, perhaps you can find someone to make your kill for you." He picked up his new spear shaft and began fitting the point into it.

He said nothing more, and the shaman watched him uncertainly, to see if the spells were going to stick, or so Others' Child thought. There was an uneasy murmur from the crowd, and Wakes on the Mountain lifted an authoritative hand.

"It is all well now," he said. "Go and get your spears. Cat Ears has found a deer trail." He looked at Deer Shadow as if he might order her to call her creatures, and then thought better of it. They had danced the Deer Dance only two nights ago, and besides, Deer Shadow looked vicious, holding her drawing stick as if she might stab someone with it or call up things that Wakes on the Mountain didn't want.

The hunters left, and Wind Caller set out with them. One Ball and Squirrel slapped him on the back to let him know that *they* weren't afraid of him, particularly not now. Bitch padded at his heels, tongue lolling. Follow's get were valued among the People's dogs. They were sneak thieves who stole food out of the fire pits, but they made the craftiest hunters.

The hunting party came upon only one deer on Cat Ears's new trail. It was an old buck, drought-thin, with a backbone like a knifeblade, and they ran it down together, dodging the wildly swinging horns when it turned on them at last. Wind Caller notched his new spear into his spear-thrower and cocked his arm back. Cat Ears was between him and the deer, and for a moment he thought about which one he should make his target. Then the moment passed, and he stepped wide around Cat Ears and threw his spear into the deer, along with three others, and the deer went down in a bloody froth and a flailing of legs.

When they spread out on the way home, Dancing Bear killed a rabbit with a sling, and Wind Caller waited by a drying water hole to spear a badger that Bitch ran to ground. He slung the badger over his shoulders by its forepaws and a sinew thong. The water hole had shriveled to nothing but a cracked mud flat with a murky hollow at its center.

The river that ran by the tufa cliffs, the summer place of the Yellow Grass People, was drying, too, Wind Caller saw when he came to it. For a year it had been no more than a stream, flowing sluggishly with the scant spring runoff and shrinking to almost nothing by summer's end. Then the winter had been dry and freezing, and this spring there had been less runoff than before. Now the stream had shrunk again to no more than a trickle down its exposed channel, rocks bumping against each other in the bottom and the moss on the dusty stones burned up. The turtle people were gone, and the fish people must have swum downstream into Water Old Man, where there would still be cool holes in the deepest places.

Wind Caller knelt on the edge of the stream and took the badger off his shoulders. It smelled of death, as if it were holding on to his back. He looked up at the sun, hot as a stone, and at the maize drying out in the field that had once stood at the river's edge. Now the river had shrunk away from its banks, and the water that kept the field green was gone. The mud was cracked into ragged pieces, fissures splitting them apart like parched skin. Wind Caller picked up one of the baskets that the women had been using to water the maize and scooped muddy water from the dying river channel. But when he poured it on the plants, the water drained into the caked sand at his feet so quickly he hardly saw it. The few drops that dampened the surface turned to air.

He fingered the leaves that sprouted from a stalk, and they crackled in his hands. A husk felt stiff and empty. Wind Caller rubbed other husks between his fingers and found some of them still hard. He scooped up more water while the badger lay on the creek bank among the dead reeds and began to stink.

When he went back to the caves, he shouted at the women for not giving the maize more water.

"There is not enough for that," Magpie said, hands on hips, ready to shout back at him. "If we take too much it will dry up altogether, and then there will be none for us, and none in the water hole. We give it all we can afford to give it."

"You are a stupid hen," Wind Caller muttered disgustedly, but he said it in his native language, which he no longer used, because Magpie was the chieftain's wife. Then, in her speech, he asked her what she was going to eat this year.

"We have given the maize all that we can," Deer

Shadow said, taking his arm and pulling him away from Magpie. "The stream is nearly gone."

"We should be gone, too," Magpie said. "To somewhere where there is water. Downstream to Water Old Man."

"The men go there already to hunt. If we don't stay, we will lose the maize," Deer Shadow said.

"It is an evil magic," Magpie replied. She looked at Wind Caller and added, "There is a witch somewhere."

Deer Shadow sniffed. "It is easy to blame your troubles on witches. If it were not for my husband, we would not *have* maize."

"My husband says," Silent whispered, looking a little away from Deer Shadow, of whom she was afraid, "that when Coyote gives a gift, he always steals it back again. That is what my husband says."

"Your husband is Rattlesnake's brother," Deer Shadow said viciously. "May he step where his brother will bite him."

Silent crossed her fingers, middle over forefinger, at her.

Wind Caller dragged Deer Shadow away this time.

"I'll smack her face the next time she says that," Deer Shadow told him.

"She's only a rabbit, and her husband beats her," Wind Caller said. "Leave her alone. She can't do you any harm, and it is beneath your dignity to argue with her."

All the same, the idea that Silent had put in their heads, even though everyone knew it came from Cat Ears, spread like a vine through the camp, thicker and stronger as the maize died. It was the only thing that grew. They watered the maize with what could be coaxed from the creek, and twice a day, when no one was looking, Wind Caller himself went to water it some more and to talk to the Maize God. But even if he had emptied the creek for the maize, it would have done no good. Each drop that touched the ground was sucked up by the hot earth as if it had been thrown onto a fire.

No rain fell, not even when they danced the rain-calling, not even when Deer Shadow drew rain with a sharp rock on the cliff face, not even when Hears the Night went into a trance and spoke to Rain God. Rain God said he could do nothing: Something was holding the rain back so that it could not fall. At that, everyone gave each other uneasy looks. They knew of only one person who never listened to Rain God and was known to play with the seasons. Coyote had been responsible for rain once, but he had been capricious with it, and the Great Mystery Spirit had taken it away. Now he was jealous, Hears the Night said. He felt satisfied with that explanation, for it meant that it was not the shaman's fault that he could not make it rain.

Then Wakes on the Mountain came to him and said that if Coyote was to blame, the shaman must fight Coyote. The people must have food.

Hears the Night burned one of his precious red feathers in a hollow stone, mixed it with mud from the drying rivulet, and sewed it in a snakeskin. This made a great magic. Snakes, because of their shape and movement, could bring water. That was why the feathered serpent represented the breath on the water of Great Mystery Spirit. Also, Rattlesnake could overcome Coyote with his bite. Hears the Night explained all this solemnly to the people. At sundown he went to Wind Caller's cave and, with the Yellow Grass People following, began to build a fire outside it.

Wind Caller had seen them coming. He stepped out into the last of the light with his fingers balled into fists. "The shaman honors us," he said, although he made it sound as if that were barely possible. "Why is this so?" He bit off the words with a snap of his teeth, and Hears the Night looked at him warily.

Hears the Night made a warding-off gesture intended to forestall any magic of Coyote's as well as any more straightforward approach. The spell robbed all muscle of its strength and made the one upon whom it was laid too weak to stand.

It did not appear to work on Wind Caller. He folded his arms across his scarred chest and showed no signs of falling down. Hears the Night snatched up his eye stone and set it to watch Wind Caller. "Coyote is eating the maize," Hears the Night said. "I will drive him out."

"You drove him out the last time," Wind Caller said.

"The magic may not have been strong enough," Hears the Night muttered, irritated at having the subject of his spells argue with him in the people's hearing.

"How is it that the shaman knows so very much and not this one thing?" Wind Caller inquired.

Hears the Night laid the snakeskin on the ground at Wind Caller's feet, and Wind Caller stepped away before he saw that it was dead. "Hah!" Hears the Night said triumphantly. "Coyote is afraid to be bitten. Now I will drive him off." He lit a pile of resin and dry grass in a cupped stone and stuck it in Wind Caller's face. Wind Caller coughed and pushed him away.

"Go away, Little Uncle," Wind Caller said furiously when he had caught his breath. "Go find what is really holding back the rain."

"There was always rain until you came!" someone shouted.

"Witch!"

"We are dying!" They stamped their feet, and even Squirrel, who was kin to Deer Shadow, looked frightened and angry.

"There was rain for a long time after, too," One Ball spoke up gruffly, but no one cared. Everything was dying, and someone had to take the blame. The stranger had brought a magic food, and they had all gotten fat eating it. Now he was taking it away again, and that was not fair. Someone threw a dried husk of maize at Wind Caller, the shriveled ear rattling inside.

"Be still!" Hears the Night shouted. "I will make a magic that will drive Coyote from us."

"The only way to drive Coyote from something is to kill it," Cat Ears shouted.

Deer Shadow pushed her way past Wind Caller. "You will be sorry you came here to my cave, telling tales against my husband," she said into Cat Ears's stubborn face. "You can't drive Coyote out of anything. Coyote is in everything. Coyote is in you, Cat Ears, right now, biting at your liver." She spat at him and lifted a hand as if she were about to hit him.

"Get the woman out of my way," Hears the Night said. "This is not a business for women."

"Yah bah, it is a business for fools!" Deer Shadow snapped at him, but Dancing Bear grabbed her by the arms and pulled her away.

"Let her alone!" Wind Caller screamed at him, but they closed in around him, blocking his path.

"This is not right," One Ball stubbornly insisted, but no one listened. He was old but not important.

Out of the corner of his eye Wind Caller saw the children coming up from the midden, where they had been throwing out the pieces of a grinding stone that had cracked. He pushed with his hand at the air between them, motioning them to stay away. Others' Child stopped, staring. She grabbed Follows Her Father and Mocking Bird by the shoulders.

Another dry husk of maize hit Wind Caller in the face. He realized that they had been down in the maize field, cutting it, while he had been arguing with Hears the Night. The dried end of it left a gash at the corner of his eye. He could feel warm blood trickling down. He snatched the husk from the ground by his feet and threw it back, fury getting the better of him.

"Be still!" Hears the Night roared. No one listened.

Wakes on the Mountain stepped forward, shouting, his open palm cradling a split ear of maize. The cob was twisted and studded with only a few kernels, which were shriveled and empty. The rest had never begun to grow. "Why is this so?" Wakes on the Mountain demanded of Wind Caller.

"Coyote has taken his gift away again," Hears the Night said. "It is as I said."

The crowd pushed forward. Deer Shadow struggled to get free of Dancing Bear's grip.

"We must make him give it back!" Cat Ears yelled. No one remembered that it was Cat Ears who had said the People should not plant maize in the first place. That was too many years ago, and they were too accustomed to having it. When it was gone, it was as if the giver had made a mockery of them, made them small and powerless. Someone must be to blame. Now a few rocks were mixed with the maize husks being hurled at Wind Caller. One struck him in the forehead, and he caught Hears the Night by the throat with one hand and snatched up the snakeskin fetish in the other.

"Nothing will bring back the maize but *rain!*" Wind Caller spat at him. "Do I look like I can hold rain in my hands?" He flung the snakeskin away and spread his empty hand in the shaman's face as Hears the Night gasped.

"We know who plays with the seasons," Dancing Bear said. He shook Deer Shadow as if he thought she, too, were responsible.

Hears the Night pushed Wind Caller away from him, his eyes wary. The eye stone skittered across the ground, and he scooped it up. Hears the Night's spells should have made it impossible for Wind Caller to lay hands on him, and since that was not the case, great magic must be at work here. Maybe it was even as Cat Ears said, he thought, frightened.

"We are starving!" someone shouted. In the dusk, no one could tell who spoke, the anonymity making vengeance easier.

"It is *his* fault!"

"Witch!"

It was so easy to be certain that it must be someone's fault, so incomprehensible that it might be no one's. If it was no one's fault, then things could not be made right. That in itself was terror beyond understanding. If that was so, then all was unknown. They began to throw rocks at the black gulf of uncertainty that had widened in just the spot where Wind Caller stood.

A spear flew by his ear. Deer Shadow screamed with fury.

The children started forward, but hands reached out and caught them on the run. Others' Child thrashed wildly in Runner's grasp.

"My baby died!" Runner screamed in her face. "Coyote took my baby!"

Wind Caller leaped past Hears the Night, knowing he only had one chance, scrambling and sliding down the talus slope beyond the caves. The Yellow Grass People howled as they went after him. One Ball tried ineffectively to stop them, put his hands up and shouted at them, but they pushed him aside, battering him against the cliff face. Squirrel ran past, eyes like stone, any indecision gone.

Wind Caller stumbled, and for a moment in the dusk he appeared to go down on all fours. Then he straightened and ran, feet pounding across the valley. The dying light lengthened his shadow behind him, stretched it out across the sand.

"Kill him!" they screamed. "It *is* Coyote!"

"*No!*" Deer Shadow clawed at Dancing Bear's eyes, and he knocked her down and held her face in the dirt. Someone tied her hands behind her with a piece of yucca rope. They dragged her into the cave. Four or five more pushed and shoved the children in, too, tying them while they howled and thrashed.

"You!" Dancing Bear pointed at old One Ball, standing there beaten with his mouth agape. "Keep them here."

They started down the slope, picking up loose rocks as they went.

"You are *cursed!*" Deer Shadow shrieked after them.

# IV

# Digging a Hole

Her curse was the last thing Deer Shadow said, the last words she spoke aloud, and the Yellow Grass People were to remember that afterward.

The children screamed and pleaded to be untied, thrashing in their ropes while One Ball looked at them like a man who had just been handed a bag of snakes to tend. But Deer Shadow sat silently, her back against the cave wall, and stared at him, eyes like two burned places in her face. She didn't turn her head when he moved away, but wherever he walked, he felt as if she were still looking at him. It was worse than the children's pleadings and threats.

"I can't let you go," he said to her, even though she wasn't the one who was screaming at him to do it. "I know you. They'd throw stones at you, too."

"Cat Ears had a spear!" Others' Child screamed. "So did Found a Snake. Let us *go!*"

"You little ones stay here," One Ball said, trying to

sound avuncular. "Whatever's happening—"

"They're going to *kill* him!" Follows Her Father cried, trying to get her hands loose by rubbing the rope against the stone edge of the storage pit. She looked at Bitch, sitting in the shadows of the cave. "Why didn't you go *with* him?" Bitch flattened her ears.

"It's not her road," Others' Child said, defending her. "It was Follow who belonged to Father. Uncle One Ball, let us loose."

"I can't do that," he said heavily. "You wouldn't be safe." They weren't children anymore, he could see that. Others' Child was a woman, and Follows Her Father was close. Mocking Bird was small, but there were beginning to be muscles in his forearms and a new definition in his face, a bony, birdlike look. Just now he looked uncannily like Wind Caller, and the realization made One Ball take a step away from him.

"I think we've all gone mad from the hunger," One Ball said wearily. He sat down with a thump and put his head on his knees so he wouldn't think about letting them loose. "Whatever's happening, you can't stop it now."

"You *know* what's happening!" Mocking Bird said. He thrashed again, kicking his feet, trying to stretch the rope loose. There were dirt and tears on his face.

One Ball grabbed Mocking Bird's feet and tightened the rope. "I know you can't stop it," he said. "I know they'll go after you next if you give them the idea. We did this once before when we were frightened." He made himself say *we*. He hadn't stopped that one, either. "When it's over with, they'll be sick with it. Don't you go near them."

"What are they doing? How can they think it will help?" Follows Her Father turned her face into the dirt and tried to put her hands over her ears so she couldn't hear the howling and baying in the distance.

"They think what they have to," One Ball said miserably.

Now they could hear the sound of the Yellow Grass People, like hunting coyotes ripping the throat out of something they had caught.

Deer Shadow didn't close her eyes or stop her ears. She listened, as if there were some secret message for her in the sound. Her skin was pallid, blood drained away so that her cheeks and forehead were ashy. Her dark eyes stared out into the dusk, waiting for whatever came back. One Ball crossed his fingers behind his back.

By the time the Yellow Grass People came home, the children were still. Deer Shadow had never moved. Follows Her Father lay with her head on the cold stone of the storage pit lid, her eyes closed. Others' Child had curled her angular body around Mocking Bird even though their hands were tied, and he rested his head on her shoulder.

One Ball stood up. He could see shapes coming through the late dusk like shadows, moving on the thin edge of twilight vision. They had no shadows of their own; the light was gone now. He thought he saw something walking with them, something big that went on all fours, but he couldn't be sure. When he looked again, it was gone, and where it had been he could see the stars beginning to come out behind the people, spattering the darkening sky.

They carried Wind Caller with them. One Ball had wondered if they would, but he thought that Hears the Night would be more afraid of leaving him in the valley to walk in his dreams. Some things you didn't want in your dreams.

When they reached the edge of the dance ground, they dropped the body on the packed earth and stepped away from it. Squirrel ran panting up the slope for a torch, turning his head away from Deer Shadow's cave as he went by. *That won't do you any good*, One Ball thought.

Women began to poke their heads out of other

caves. Some, and Runner was one, had gone with the pack that had run down Wind Caller. Runner had been a friend of his once, but that was before her baby had died. Many other women had said that it was men's business, and busied themselves at their hearths, not listening to the noise outside.

Squirrel trotted back with a torch in his hand, and One Ball moved heavily away from the cave mouth. "I'll untie you now," he said to Deer Shadow. "You'll . . . want to bring him back in here."

Deer Shadow didn't answer. When he cut the rope around her wrists and ankles, she bent to rub them, flexing her fingers. Then she went to the grass-and-deer-hide bed she had shared with Wind Caller and folded herself cross-legged on it.

One Ball cut the children free. Bitch came out of her corner and shivered against Others' Child's leg. Others' Child turned to Deer Shadow and said, "Mother?"

The other children looked at her and then at each other. "Mother, we have to go bring him home."

There was no answer. There wasn't going to be. Mother had gone somewhere, too. Others' Child looked at Mocking Bird and Follows Her Father. The name broke her heart now. "We have to go get him," she said. She was oldest. It would be up to her.

Mocking Bird picked up his father's spear. One Ball took it away from him. "No. Don't make something worse happen. We are already sick with this one." He made it sound as if it were a disease. Others' Child thought it was.

They went slowly down the slope in the darkness, away from the sullen glow of the untended fire on their hearth, out toward where the torches wavered and flickered on the dance ground like tongues licking at the air. *Tasting death*, Others' Child thought. *Licking it up*.

Her father lay on his side where they had thrown him, back and legs curved inward a little, like a thin

moon, as if he had tried to curl himself into a ball.
Dark bruises mottled his face, the blood already pooling, twilight-colored under the skin. Fresh blood had
run from a cut over his eye and from the corners of
his mouth. But it was the gaping hole in his chest that
had killed him. A spear had run up under the breast-
bone to the heart and been jerked viciously out again,
pulling any hope of life with it. Others' Child saw
other wounds besides, so many that no one would be
able to say whose hand had finally killed him.

Follows Her Father knelt by Wind Caller's lacerated
feet, cut and bloodied in flight, and put her head in
her hands, whimpering. Mocking Bird compressed his
lips into a thin slash, forehead knitted, trying to put
life back into his father's body the way he had tried
to put it back in Follow's.

Wakes on the Mountain and Hears the Night
looked at the children stolidly. "You may take him
now," Wakes on the Mountain grunted. They weren't
going to admit fault.

Hears the Night had just finished a chant over the
body. "I must go and think of which magic to make
at the burning," he said. "You may have him until
then." His expression suggested that he believed they
should be grateful for that concession. He looked at
the Yellow Grass People and raised his arms. "Now
it will be different, and the rains will come. That
which stopped the rain has gone back to its belonging
place. It was very difficult to do that."

The Yellow Grass People nodded, reassured. They
were justified in what they had done to save themselves. They looked at each other with satisfaction.

"He will walk in your sleep if you burn him," Others' Child hissed. Her father hadn't wanted to be
burned; his people needed their bodies afterward, he
had said.

Runner slid behind Squirrel and crossed her fingers
at Others' Child.

"We brought him so that you could do what is

proper," Wakes on the Mountain said severely.

"Better to have left him for the coyotes," Cat Ears said. He seemed satisfied with himself, almost exultant. "For his own kind."

"We could have done that," Hears the Night said to Mocking Bird. He didn't look at Others' Child. "But out of respect for your mother—"

Follows Her Father looked up finally. "My mother cursed you," she said.

Mocking Bird put an arm around her and one around Others' Child. "Help me with him," he said to them. He took Wind Caller by the legs, and the girls lifted his shoulders. The crowd moved away from them quickly, holding out crossed fingers again.

"Tell your mother to get the body ready to be burned," Wakes on the Mountain said.

The children didn't answer him.

"Pah, if they don't want to burn him, let them dig a hole and put him in it," Cat Ears said. When Runner looked shocked, he snapped, "That's what to do with a witch!"

There was a murmur of agreement. It was important to establish that the dead man had been evil. Otherwise . . .

"Hear me," Hears the Night said. They clustered around him, pulling close, as if whatever might be out there beyond the torchlight with Wind Caller and his children was slavering to get close, too.

"That one was not one of us. He came from stranger people, brought us a gift, and stole it away. The People have taken back the gift that is ours, which was ours to do, and now we must send the stranger away in the proper manner. If the stranger people do not burn their dead, then we must not burn him. It is as his daughter says: If we send him in the wrong fashion, he may not go."

They shifted uneasily at that. The fierce heat of the hunt had worn off, and now they were alone with its image burned into their eyes.

"We will let his children send him," Wakes on the Mountain said. "That way, if it is not done right, it is their spirits he will follow home, not ours."

There was another murmur of agreement.

"What about the woman?" Cat Ears's wife, Silent, cast an apprehensive glance toward the faint glow of the hearth fires in the caves. They could see a shadow moving across the light of Deer Shadow's fire. The figure crossed and recrossed, weaving who knew what vengeance.

"Leave me to see to the woman," Hears the Night said. It would be ill doing if they killed her, too. Hears the Night had not meant to kill the man—now dead, that one could not be named again—only to deflect his magic. Because it had happened, no doubt it was necessary and meant to be, but one killing was enough. Now it was important that he keep his hold over his people and the woman both. Again he wished that he had not lain with the woman's daughter.

He started back toward the caves, moving solemnly, emphasizing his fitness to be a barrier between the Yellow Grass People and what they feared.

Deer Shadow didn't move when the children brought Wind Caller back to her. She sat motionless and silent, her impenetrable eyes opening until they were all pupil, as if to take him in all at once, whole. Then she turned her head away to face the cave wall, her hands open in her lap as if something would fall into them. They couldn't tell what she was seeing, or if she was; maybe something on the other side of the rock.

"Mother?" Follows Her Father tugged at Deer Shadow's hair, but Deer Shadow didn't look at her. Follows Her Father gulped down a sob. "What's *wrong* with her?"

"I don't know," Others' Child said. "I think she's gone Away."

"She's still here!" Mocking Bird said fiercely. "She's not dead!"

"No, not like Fa—" Others' Child couldn't imagine her father's spirit as a vengeful ghost—not to them, anyway, though maybe he would walk in Cat Ears's sleep. Nevertheless she couldn't make herself say his name. Hears the Night and the others had taken that away from her, too. "Not like him. But she's gone somewhere."

"What are we going to do?" Follows Her Father sniffled.

Others' Child looked at Mocking Bird. "We're going to dig a hole. And if Hears the Night wants to come and make magics over it, he is welcome. But I won't let them burn him. Mother promised him."

"How can you stop them?"

"They won't try." Others' Child stuck her chin out. She knew that to challenge the shaman that way was audacious of her, perhaps even reckless. But she knew a thing about the shaman that Follows Her Father did not—had done a thing with him that Follows Her Father had not. It gave her a certain power over him, and she was pretty sure that Hears the Night thought so, too: He had stayed as far away from her as he could get since the first day he had tried to drive Coyote out of Wind Caller. *Come and see what your spells bring you now*, Others' Child thought viciously. *See what comes out of the night for you.*

"We will do what Sister says," Mocking Bird said tightly. He had been fighting back tears and had won. He was almost a man, head of his family now. It behooved him not to howl like a baby. He glanced at his mother. She might have been one of her own pictures, or a wind-carved stone that only looked like a woman.

She didn't move when they lifted Wind Caller and carried him out into the dark again.

\* \* \*

"We will sit with him until it is light enough to dig. I don't trust them," Others' Child said. She scowled over her shoulder at the flames that flickered at the foot of the cliffs. The children had left Bitch to stay with Mother and had taken their father's body to a place their tribe would be afraid to come, in case they changed their minds. Out here in the tangled scrub it was cold and dark-of-the-moon. The Yellow Grass People would not like looking for them here.

"I'm hungry," Follows Her Father said.

"We're always hungry," Others' Child retorted. "What would we eat if we went back?"

Follows Her Father opened her mouth as if she were going to argue, then closed it with a snap, biting off whatever words had been coming. They were raw with grief and the sudden shocked sense of loss that might come with having a hand or a leg cut off. Tomorrow it would hurt even more. Others' Child pulled the twins to her, one on each side, the way she had done when they were little. With both arms she wrapped the three of them in the fur blanket they had carried their father in. Even in summer the dry nights were cold, but Wind Caller wouldn't need the blanket now. Furs wouldn't warm skin without the heat of life inside.

They began to dig at first light, prizing up the earth on the edge of the maize field with flat-bladed digging sticks. There was something fearful about a hole that deep, Others' Child thought. But Follows Her Father said that he had to go there, and Others' Child knew she was right.

The sun was a streak of crimson along the blue mountain to the east, staining it bloody as the hole went deeper. How far could you go into the earth? Others' Child wondered, nursing blisters. And what would happen if you just kept going? If you stepped into the hole with Father and began to cut steps down into the dirt, would you come at last to where the dead lived under their lake in the north?

She sank the stick into the dry earth and shoved more up the sides and out of the hole. The ground here had been turned over into hills for the maize, but not everywhere and not so deep as they needed to go. *What if he wanted to come up again?* Others' Child wiped her bloody fingers on her bare skin and looked at Wind Caller, perfectly still as the sun ran down the mountain. They had laid him out properly, with legs straight and hands folded on his chest because they knew that he would stiffen in a while. All dying followed the same pattern. And after his body was stiff, it would relax again, and his spirit would go. That was why the Yellow Grass People burned their dead, so that the spirit couldn't come back to the body again.

Others' Child liked the idea of putting their father in the maize field so he could come back and haunt Cat Ears and Hears the Night. She had said so to Follows Her Father, who just shook her head and said, "No, he has to go to the maize."

Others' Child decided that she would think of it however she wanted to think of it. Follows Her Father was the one who talked to maize, not Others' Child. Had the maize wanted him? Was that what had happened? She suspected that Follows Her Father thought so. As for Others' Child, every time she saw her father's battered face, she wanted to howl, bury her face in her blistered hands and scream.

"Dig," Mocking Bird said tersely, and she went back to the hole.

The dry sandy soil slid into the hole with them, whispering like a snake on stone. Mocking Bird cursed with frustration as he wiped his forehead on his arm. Follows Her Father got their water basket and filled it with handfuls of loose sand, then carried it to a pile beside the hole. The sun was hot and high up now, and Others' Child feared that it would shrivel her up the way it had the maize. Above them, she could see the black wingspan of a vulture, and she spat up into the sky at it.

Along the cliff face three or four people were always watching them, but no one came near.

When the hole was as deep as his waist, Mocking Bird declared it deep enough, and Others' Child didn't argue with him. She lined it with the fur blanket because she couldn't bear to put him into plain dirt like something on the midden.

"We need that," Follows Her Father said. "The maize doesn't care."

Others' Child clambered out of the hole as if she would smack her. "I care. And the maize died. It killed him!"

"Maybe," Follows Her Father said. "He knew it would. He told me that once."

Others' Child hugged her arms around herself.

"He didn't want it to," Mocking Bird said. "He was just afraid of it."

"Help me lift him," Others' Child snapped. She looked at the maize and thought that it murmured something with its dry leaves. *We must be fed*, they whispered as the hot wind brushed them.

The children lowered Wind Caller's body into the hole, letting it fall with a thump on the furs. Blindly, crying again, they pushed the dirt back in on top of him with their hands. It seemed even less than had come out, Others' Child thought, he took up so little room. She began to carry river stones up the bank and pile them on top. Mocking Bird and Follows Her Father did, too, and they wore a little path in the riverbank, bare feet powdering the cracked mud.

All the while the Yellow Grass People watched them through the thin trees that grew between the maize field and the cliffs.

When they trudged slowly uphill again, they found their cave empty, the fire sinking into ash. Deer Shadow had gone. Others' Child spun back out of the cave, furious, looking for Hears the Night, screaming curses at him. Mocking Bird grabbed her arm.

"Look." He pointed to where a little knot of people were standing, their voices hushed for once, outside the cave where Wakes on the Mountain and Magpie lived. It was one of the best caves, as befitted the chieftain. Once it had belonged to the man/woman Listens to Deer.

Deer Shadow was sitting halfway into its cool depths, on Magpie's best fox-skin blanket, the one with the tails for tassels at the corners. Her feet were bare and folded under her, her hands lying open again in that odd gesture in her lap. She looked out of the cave at them, but Others' Child could tell right away that she couldn't see them. Bitch saw Others' Child and came slinking out of the cave to stick her nose between Others' Child's knees and whine.

Magpie was pulling at Wakes on the Mountain's arm. "She just came in and sat down," she said between her teeth. "I don't want her in my cave."

Hears the Night turned slowly from the cave mouth, where he had been talking to Deer Shadow in a low voice and receiving no reply. He spoke to Wakes on the Mountain now. "The chieftain will have to find a new place."

Magpie yelped.

"Be quiet!" Wakes on the Mountain said.

"You did this!" Magpie said. She pointed a finger at Others' Child. "You told her to come into my cave. Now there is something bad in there. I'm afraid to go back in."

"It is not good to go back in," Hears the Night said. "It is hers now."

Magpie looked as if she were going to argue some more, but Hears the Night grabbed her wrist, hard, his fingers sinking in. She glared at Wakes on the Mountain.

"The chieftain's wife does not wish to go in there

anymore," Hears the Night said. "It is not good to go in there anymore. That woman is mad."

Where Deer Shadow was, it was raining. The water wriggled down from the sky like snakes, shimmering and opalescent, and she could see the droplets hung in the web of the spider who lived at the cave mouth and ate the flies that the people's leavings drew. It had been easy, it seemed to her, to stretch time like sinew, to go back into this old country. It also seemed to her that now she could not go forward again. But that was all right because Wind Caller was beside her now, stretched faceup in their bed, snoring. Not loudly, just enough to tell her how tired he was and how much fermented berry juice he had drunk because it was summer solstice and a festival, and you had to get drunk enough to stagger at a summer festival or you might be tempted not to turn the sun around, just to let it go on being summer forever under the warm stars. And there had to be winter, of course. Everything had to be born and die, had to turn all the way through its pattern.

But whatever was outside could not come in here, where she lived now, in Listens to Deer's old place. Neither winter nor death could cross her threshold. Here behind the warm rain she could live with the man at the heart of their lives, with years to go before they spun out into the blackness, into whatever came next, into bones on the fire. The rain and the heat of the man were a room around her that she could inhabit always, a space within the cold dry years where it would be wet and love would stay.

"Is that what you want?" the spider over the door asked her, and Deer Shadow saw that it was Grandmother Spider herself. "You are a woman, not a moth to live in a cocoon."

Deer Shadow put an arm around Wind Caller's sleeping head, to make sure he was really there. Sometimes when she looked at him, she could see through him. "Did you not teach the moths to spin, too?" she asked Spider. A cocoon felt safe. She could feel feathery moth wings form around her, floating on the heat currents from the fire.

"If you have decided to be one of the moth people," Spider chuckled, "then you'll have to come out in the spring, when you will mate and die. You won't even get to see your eggs hatch. If you don't burn to death first," she added.

Deer Shadow could feel the flames move a little toward her, red and seductive as skin. "Then I am not a moth," she said sulkily. "I will be a ground squirrel in my burrow with my mate." The wings dissolved. She could feel her body round and fat and furry, curled in the darkness.

"Then that one will eat you," Grandmother Spider said. She jiggled her web, and Deer Shadow could see Coyote dancing on it at the far end. When he saw her, he stopped and scratched, then trotted along the dry strands that ran toward the center, the way Grandmother Spider had taught him. He hopped off into the cave.

He nosed Wind Caller. "Your people are fools," he said.

"You let them," Deer Shadow said.

"I let everything happen," Coyote said. "Sometimes I make more things happen. I don't *stop* things." He looked as if she had misunderstood him entirely. "I am always hungry," he said, as if that explained things.

Deer Shadow shrugged off the ground squirrel's fur, splitting it down the back. Coyote looked mildly disappointed. "Go away," she said to him.

"I sent you the man," Coyote said. "Aren't you grateful?"

"You don't ever do anything right!" Deer Shadow flung at him. When she looked down at Wind Caller, she could see through him again. She concentrated until he was solid and she could hear him snore.

"I made art," Coyote said. "I made pictures."

"I don't want them."

Coyote lolled his tongue out in a toothy grin. "You don't have to. Others' Child has them now."

Deer Shadow peered at him, puzzled. "Who?" The soft murmur of the rain enclosed them.

"You have children," Grandmother Spider said, and now Deer Shadow could see that Spider was Listens to Deer as well. He did that sometimes. "Don't you want to see them?"

"They are grown," Deer Shadow said, remembering them now. "They don't need me. Not like—" She put an arm around Wind Caller's head. "If I let them in, he'll go. I can't hold on to both." Wind Caller stirred in his sleep, an arm flung outward. She closed both her own arms around him frantically.

"Well," Grandmother Spider said to Coyote, "what shall we do now?"

"I only came here because you wanted me to," Coyote said huffily. "It's as much as my life is worth, traveling that way." He looked at his paws as if they might be sticky, and eyed her web with mistrust. "I only came because of the young one that can make pictures. This one—" He nosed Wind Caller again, and Deer Shadow smacked his muzzle with the empty bowl that someone must have brought her dinner in. "This one is on the way to being a god," he said, backing up with a snap at Deer Shadow's hand for good measure. He didn't bite her, though. Even Coyote is afraid of madness. "This one won't do anything else interesting," he said. His yellow gaze lingered on Wind Caller only a moment.

"Go away," Deer Shadow said, her eyes narrowed. She knew they were trying to take him away. Even Listens to Deer was trying to pull her forward again.

It was hard to hear the rain now. She closed her eyes tight and made them go, listening until the sound of water and Wind Caller's slow breathing filled the cave.

\* \* \*

Madness was a sacred condition. Unlike craziness, which was evil and made a person unreliable, the madness of one who had gone to live inside her own head was the inexplicable work of the gods, and must thus be holy. Deer Shadow stayed in Wakes on the Mountain's cave, her cave now, and not so much as a bone spoon was removed from it. In a fury, Magpie demanded that everything she had owned be replaced, and gave Wakes on the Mountain no peace until he did so, but Deer Shadow never touched the cooking baskets, the grinding stones, the needles and awls.

She ate what they brought to her and spoke to no one. Obviously she was very holy, but Bitch refused to go back into the cave with her again, flattening her ears to her head and making the singsong growl she used when she was angry, as if there were something else in there with her.

Her children would not go in, either. They had tried once, but Deer Shadow had seemed more of a stone woman than their mother. Follows Her Father had cried all that night until Mocking Bird and Others' Child were howling, too, but those were their last tears.

The children of the People grew past tears early. They turned to stone, Others' Child thought in the morning. Like Mother. Clear stone, that splintered from their skin.

"You must go and see if she will speak to you," Hears the Night said gruffly to Others' Child in the afternoon. He looked angry at having to be there. Others' Child enjoyed it. She looked at his crotch.

"I must know what she says to you," the shaman said. His young face was painted with mud in stripes like a chipmunk's back. It made a mask from behind which he could look at Others' Child.

"Go and ask her yourself," Others' Child told him. She had been grinding grass seed in a quern. A basket of yucca root for soap bubbled beside the fire, and she stopped to scoop a hot rock from the coals with a spoon and drop it in, wanting all the while to heave it instead at Hears the Night. Mocking Bird had gone hunting with the men, because there was no one else to hunt for Follows Her Father and herself. The People would feed anyone who had no one to hunt, but in these times they would get scraps when everyone else was done. And all the people were afraid of Deer Shadow's children now. Follows Her Father had gone to look for camas bulbs and berries in a thicket half a day's walk away. "We have all we can do to see to ourselves," Others' Child said bitterly.

"The woman does not speak to me," Hears the Night complained, reluctant to admit that he could not compel her. She must be very holy indeed. It was aggravating that her daughter was not more malleable.

"Nor does she speak to me!" Others' Child snapped. "And now we are alone, and it is your doing."

"It is the doing of the gods," Hears the Night said stiffly. Others' Child sniffed at him.

"I thought once that you were a suitable woman for me," Hears the Night said, losing his temper. "Now I think there may be a curse on you."

"No," Others' Child said astutely. "You think there's a curse on you. You think Mother cursed you, and you want to undo it."

"That is not becoming talk from Coyote's daughter," Hears the Night said.

"Yah bah, you do not frighten me," Others' Child spat at him. Nothing could frighten her now. What worse thing could come? "And you have not made it rain," she threw at him also.

"It will rain," Hears the Night said stolidly. He pointed at the sky.

There were clouds, heavy black ones, hanging on the horizon. Pressing down, Others' Child thought.

She yearned toward the rain and felt it coming to suffocate her at the same time. If it came because Father was dead, because Hears the Night was right, she didn't want it, she thought venomously. The air felt thick, the way it did before a lightning storm. She felt the hair prickle on her arms. A streak of lightning split the black clouds, like Rattlesnake striking at the ground, his tail alight. Hears the Night looked triumphant.

But it didn't rain where the Yellow Grass People were. It rained on the High Rock People, and probably on the Smoke People, judging by the direction of the clouds. It would make more water in the dry washes, but from the dusty cloak that enveloped Wind Caller's people there would be no surcease.

When the clouds blew away at morning, Hears the Night came to the mouth of Others' Child's cave again and stood there with his most serious face. "The game has all gone away to other people's water holes," he said. "You must call them back."

Others' Child swallowed the last of the thin mush that Follows Her Father had made of grass seed and half-green berries. She wiped her mouth on her hand and demanded, "Why?"

Bitch got up from her place at the fire and growled at Hears the Night's feet as she sniffed them. "Make it go away," Hears the Night said.

"This is her place. She belongs here," Mocking Bird said. He and his sisters sat in a row in front of their fire, blocking Hears the Night's way.

"The woman who was your mother can no longer call the game," Hears the Night said. "Her gift went into you even before she went Away. I have seen it."

Others' Child scratched a deer in the dirt with a half-burned stick from the fire.

"That is not the way to do it," Hears the Night said. "You are not doing it right."

"I saw how her mother did it," Runner said from behind Hears the Night at the cave mouth. "Make her come out and do it the way her mother did it, while the men dance."

Others' Child could see the men ranged behind Runner, spears and atlatls in their hands. They carried what little journey food the women could gather in packs of deer hide or in bags made from bladders. Beside Others' Child, Mocking Bird was fitting a new point to his father's smallest spear. The pouch around his neck held what meager food he had found, and his father's rope sandals, too big for him but too good to waste, were laced to his feet. "Maybe you should show us how it is all done," he grunted at Runner, pulling the thong tight on the spear shaft.

"I never said *I* could do it," Runner said. She looked halfway proud of that now, as if it were a suspect talent. "But it has to be done on the dance ground."

"She is supposed to fast first," Magpie said.

"And she is forbidden to men the night before," Squirrel's wife said. She cast a suspicious glance at Hears the Night, who flushed and stepped back from Others' Child, asserting distance between them.

"How do we know she will do it right?" Silent said, looking frightened. "What if she drives the deer away instead?" Her chinless face quivered.

"Why would she do that? She is hungry, too," One Ball said from the midst of the waiting hunters. He sounded exasperated.

Silent clutched her arms around herself. "We don't know what she might do."

Cat Ears gave his wife a look of disgust. He said to Hears the Night, "I will find the game when that one has called it. Make her come out on the dance ground and do it properly. Now we will dance." He brushed past Silent and stalked down the hill, moving heavily, as if his joints ached. There was gray in Cat Ears's hair now, Others' Child saw. She didn't remember it being there before. Maybe Mother had put it there. Or Father. It was satisfying to think that.

Others' Child stood up, unfolding her young bones from the cave floor with deliberate grace. *Yah, and can old Cat Ears do that anymore?* She had seen him trying to get up from the council fire in the morning, creaking and cursing. The thunderstorm that had missed them had made it worse. "I will go to the dance ground and call the deer," she said to Wakes on the Mountain—the only one who had not been nattering at her. She took her mother's sharpened drawing stick and jabbed it at Hears the Night to make him get out of the way. Follows Her Father, Mocking Bird, and Bitch fell in behind and beside her, an escort to guard her from further advice.

"That one needs to be married," someone muttered as she passed. "Those children need watching."

"Their heads are getting too big, and they have no manners."

"What do we expect from a witch's brats? I said when they were born that we let too much power into that family."

"Hush, they lost their mother, poor babies. She can't even see them. And it wasn't their fault about their father."

"Then you mother them. Teach them how to behave to their elders and important people."

"Yah, only Old Woman Rattlesnake could mother those three."

The three walked stiffly, backs erect, pretending they didn't hear. Mocking Bird's knuckles were white. Others' Child thought the people sounded like a tree full of birds chattering I-told-you-so as she sat down in the dirt of the dance ground, in front of the dead fire. The other two pressed themselves beside her, daring anyone to tell them they didn't belong. Bitch fastened suspicious yellow eyes on the people ringing them.

Others' Child smoothed the dry earth before her with her hand. This was where Mother had made her magic, had made the deer run up out of the earth, their slender legs flashing in the early light. Could she do it? She had never tried, and now she felt the people pressing around her, their hot breath like a cloud, until she couldn't breathe herself. *I never tried to call anyone*, she thought, *only to put bugs in someone's bed.* That had worked well enough when Quail had made fun of her and called her skeleton bones: Quail had run shrieking out of her cave, shaking a tarantula from her blanket. But that wasn't like calling the deer. The deer people were the human people's counterpart, sustenance and magical totem at the same time. If they were not addressed properly, they would not come or give up their breath to the hunters. That was what the Deer Dance was for, to speak rightly to them: to say, *We know you. We are one with you.*

Others' Child blinked. While she had been thinking, the hunters had vanished, and the deer had come in their stead, out of the blinding dawn onto the dance ground, antlered heads solemn, bobbing to the sound of Hears the Night's skin drum. The deer hides hung down their backs, and they carried sticks in their hands, mimicking the brittle forelegs of the quarry. The Deer Mother in a white skin pranced in front of them, stately, shaking her deer-hoof rattles. It was Magpie, Others' Child knew, but for this morning it was Deer Mother, and even though Magpie didn't wear a mask, Others' Child could see the deer face anyway: wide dark eyes and black nose at the end of a pale muzzle, ears spread wide, listening to the chant. Before, there would have been Father's flute to guide her steps, but this morning Mocking Bird sat obstinately still, his hands bunched into fists in his lap.

Others' Child took her drawing stick and began to mark the deer in the dirt, giving them shape and grace to come flying out of it, joining them with the deer on the dance ground. For a moment she thought she saw them come, saw their bounding shapes leap across the air. And then she could feel hot breath on her neck again, and the deer faded from sight.

"Go away," she said to Runner and Hears the Night, who were peering over her shoulder. "You are spoiling it."

"Yah, we will go on watching you, Most Important," Runner said. "In case you think to draw evil things instead."

"That is not the way Deer Shadow did it," someone else said, pushing closer. "When she made them, they faced into the dance. You are sending these away instead!"

Others' Child snapped the drawing stick between her hands. Fury was a small lump boiling in her stomach like a hot rock in soup. She flung the stick onto the dance ground among the dancers' feet. A hiss of shocked anger came from behind her.

"Go and get me another one," she said over her shoulder to Hears the Night without looking at him. "You have spoiled this one."

Hears the Night hesitated. All the people were looking at him. He grabbed a small boy who had ventured closer to the adults than he was supposed to be. "Go and fetch a stick from this woman's cave," he said from between his teeth. He looked at the back of Others' Child's head. "The one who came from the stranger people like her father would do well to remember it, and to remember her manners."

The back of Others' Child's neck twitched under her cropped hair.

When the boy came back, she put the stick between her breasts for a moment, trying to warm it, trying to will life into it. She thought she could hear her mother's voice, and she forced that other voice, the voice of her anger, into silence. It was not right to take petty squabbles to this place. This place was holy. She drew now with fierce concentration, trying to shut out the hot, heavy air, the scent of mistrust choking her.

But although Hears the Night edged back this time, she could still feel him there, feel all of them peering at her, muttering, telling each other what was not right. And the deer, when she drew them again, were flat in the dirt, only pictures. They lay on their sides, dead of some poison or of disbelief. She stared at them, frightened, but they wouldn't move.

Could anyone else tell? She brushed them out swiftly with her hand, stood up, and said, "It is done."

Mocking Bird trailed behind the hunters, panting to keep up. Old Cat Ears had lungs like a lion, he thought, watching Cat Ears trot down the deer trail. He changed his sweaty grip on his spear and trotted after, Bitch at his heels. A few other hunting dogs ranged beside them, and Bitch gave one of her half-brothers a sniff. His tail waved like a gray plume, but she carried hers low, the way Follow had done. Somehow she seemed more coyote than the rest.

Mocking Bird felt like one himself, outcast from the other hunters. He trailed behind, partly because he knew no one wanted to be near him on the trail. Before the bad time, he had been made much of: one of a pair of twins, magical, certain to be holy for the tribe. What was that worth now?

"Move up!" Squirrel shouted at him over his shoulder, because no one wanted him at their backs, either.

The dusty water hole was empty when they reached it, with only a few tracks to mark that deer had drunk there.

"Days ago!" Cat Ears said and spat.

"The water is foul, full of mud," One Ball said. A rain after a long drought always washed bad things into the water. "We should go down to the Place Where the River Runs Backward."

"That is a hand and three days' fast travel," Squirrel said. He held up eight fingers. "That is where the Gathering hunts in the fall."

"Too far," Cat Ears said. He thought. "We will go

back and get the women, and go that way. We will move on."

"Early?" They looked uneasy. The pattern of their wanderings lay on the year precisely, aligned with the seasons. To shift it was to venture onto unknown ground.

"We will go," Wakes on the Mountain said. "We will find new hunting grounds. We were fools to stay only for the maize, anyway."

They turned in their tracks and brushed past Mocking Bird, leaving him standing in the trail.

Others' Child was packing the family's possessions into baskets, tying as many of them as she could to Bitch's travois. What the dogs couldn't drag, the Yellow Grass People would carry in packs and on their heads, or load them in a hide to drag them. Their possessions were those of a nomad people: lightweight baskets and turtle-shell bowls, bone spoons and needles and scraping tools, stone axes and adzes, spears and flint knives. One change of clothes apiece, perhaps; a pair of extra sandals, woven from yucca leaves; and jewelry—blue stones looped around necks and arms, a prized eagle feather, a polished agate. It would take two men just to carry Hears the Night's bags of spells and medicines, and his great tooth. A prized grinding stone, worn into a perfect bowl, made weight but could not be left behind. What food had been saved would be added to the load.

Follows Her Father watched the packing, the sorting of things easily replaced that could be left for next summer and things that must make the journey—if they came back next summer. What if they did not? What if they went on and on? Would Mother know? The people would make a litter and carry her because she was sacred. Would she know if they carried her into strange lands? Mother loved this place. She had fought the Others for it.

Follows Her Father stuck her thumb in her mouth,

biting the edge of it. What if they never came back?

She glanced at Others' Child to make sure she wasn't noticed and slid out of the cave into the blue dusk. She would tell Others' Child where she had been later. Since Cat Ears and Mocking Bird and the hunters had come home, all the women had been howling in protest and packing as they howled. Only Others' Child was silent in her fury. The People would leave tomorrow to hunt at the Place Where the River Runs Backward, out of season, and the women would have to find a place to live there. It seemed a fearsome and dangerous thing to do.

Follows Her Father saw Mocking Bird standing outside their cave, not doing anything, just staring into the dusk. She shook him by the arm.

"There was nothing to hunt," he said to her. "Whatever she did, it didn't work the way Mother's magic did. They all thought it was my fault."

"It didn't always work for Mother, either," Follows Her Father hissed. "Magic isn't like that. They will be sorry."

"How are you going to make them sorry?" Mocking Bird asked. "I would like to."

"I will not be called Follows Her Father anymore," his sister said. "I will be called Maize Gone Away, and they will be sorry."

"Yah, you don't make sense," Mocking Bird said. "Where would you go? And they won't let you, anyway. They are afraid of us."

"I have something," she said. She tugged at his arm. "We will all go. You and me and Sister and Bitch."

"I don't know where we're going now." He fell over a dead tree jumbled among the stones that ringed the midden.

"Be quiet!" She led him by the midden and along the dry bank of the river, past their father's grave with the dead maize rustling over it. Mocking Bird looked around him uneasily.

"Here." She bent and pried at stones half buried in the ground.

"You are crazy," Mocking Bird said. "What have you buried here?"

"I didn't," she said. "Father did."

"What?" He pushed at her. "What?"

There was a storage pit dug beneath an overhanging rock—almost a small cave in itself—that kept the rain off. When she pushed away the lid, he saw that it was lined with flat stones, shaped with an adze to fit. Inside was a basket wrapped in hide and tied with sinew strings. She took it out and shook it so that he could hear the rattle.

"What is in there? And why was it a secret from me?" Mocking Bird demanded. He was insulted.

"It's seed. He knew there might be drought."

"Maize seed?"

She smiled at him fiercely, the sudden secret smile that twins share. "I was Follows Her Father. He only told me, so it would come to me to plant it." Her face fell. "When they killed him."

"He didn't know they would kill him!" Mocking Bird said.

Maize Gone Away whispered, "He knew."

# V

# A Hole in the Sky

"It is not for the Yellow Grass People's teeth," Maize Gone Away said as she put the basket of seed among the things that Others' Child had tied to Bitch's travois.

Others' Child looked up, exasperated, from where she knelt on the cave floor. "We can't take all that. Not if we're going alone. They'll catch up to us."

"They won't let us go, anyway," Mocking Bird said pessimistically. "They want you to call the game for them. And if they find out about that seed . . ." He thought about it and added grumpily, "I'm the only one they don't need."

"It is not important to me in this world what the Yellow Grass People want," Others' Child said. "Maize Gone Away is right, and she has given herself a true name, which doesn't happen often, so it's a sign. While they are arguing like ducks quacking whose fault it all is, we will go somewhere else, and they can find someone else to blame. Maybe they will all blame each other and everyone will kill someone else until there isn't anyone left. I would like that."

"How will we eat?" her sister asked, suddenly frightened now that Others' Child had adopted the idea so easily.

"We will hunt," Mocking Bird said. "We have Bitch to help us. And there are three of us. Our father did it, and there was only one of him, when he came north to our people."

"There was no drought when he came north." They had all heard the story of Father's adventure, told and retold it to themselves. Maize Gone Away looked at the other two, eyes wide. "Do you think it was the old chieftain's curse that killed him? Remember how his old chieftain cursed him before he left? How he used to say Jaguar might come for him one day?"

"If you think Cat Ears is Jaguar," Others' Child said scornfully.

"Nooo . . ." Maize Gone Away said. "But—"

"What about Mother?" Mocking Bird said. "We can't take her with us."

"Mother isn't with us now, anyway," Others' Child said. "She may be somewhere with him, I think, but she isn't with us. She never talks to me, not even when I dream."

"Hears the Night thinks she does," Mocking Bird said. "Were you going to marry him?"

"No," Others' Child said shortly. She padded to the hide that hung across the cave mouth and peered around it, taking care not to be seen. They could hear the commotion of packing up all along the cliff face, women shouting for their children, men cursing as they fumbled for spears and dog harnesses in the growing dark. A few fires burned down by the riverbank—families who had moved closer to the water as the river receded, to sleep in brush huts where the faint night breeze might bring a fleeting dampness. Tonight they seemed blurred to her, as if the flames had been smudged by a damp hand. Others' Child looked at the sky, and her eyes widened. She beckoned the other two forward.

"Coyote," Mocking Bird whispered. Across the sky, the stars were winking out as if someone had poured water on them. As the clouds thickened the three could smell thunder on the air. The skin on their necks prickled. The clouds were heavy, throbbing like drums. Why had no one else seen? Mocking Bird wondered if it truly was Coyote's storm and only they could see it.

"This time it will rain," Maize Gone Away whispered.

"Not if we stay," Mocking Bird whispered back. He knew that suddenly. It *was* for them. It was to set them free from this place where they were no longer honored. Or to drive them out.

"Quick, before it starts," Others' Child said. "If we get across the river before it fills, it will run too deep for a while for anyone to chase us." They were desert children and knew about flash floods. There was a cave where old Looks Back had gone to see visions. They could wait out the storm in that.

She began pulling things off Bitch's travois, emptying their packs and rearranging them. "Only what we can carry. The travois makes tracks, and it's too slow."

Maize Gone Away put the maize seed in the bottom of her pack and jutted her chin out at Others' Child.

"Yes," Others' Child said. "No," she said when Maize Gone Away tried to put in her mother's grinding stone. She spread out what they would take: three bone spoons and two needles, pincers, a roll of sinew, water baskets that would nest inside each other, a gathering basket, and all their knives and chopping tools, fleshers and scrapers. Mocking Bird's and Father's spears and atlatls, Mother's skinning knife, the woven nets and snares. Winter furs and deer-hide blankets that could be tied to Bitch's harness without the travois. A coil of rope, clothes that they could wear, and extra sandals that could be hung around their necks. All the food: the handful of withered camas bulbs; a hoarded fist-sized sack of dried meat; cactus leaves; a sack of grass seed that compared to maize tasted like sand. Three turtle-shell bowls. The fire drill. Father's flute.

Others' Child snapped her fingers at Bitch. They shouldered the packs and slipped past the hanging hide into the thick air. At first she thought the other caves were still, that they had been hushed into silence by the air. Then she heard voices, but very far away, inside something, as if already some invisible wall divided the three of them from the rest.

Others' Child pushed Mocking Bird and Maize Gone Away down the slope toward the midden and the river beyond. Above them the sky shuddered and drowned the faint voices.

Before it was quite dark, Caught the Moon bustled into the cave that had been Wakes on the Mountain's. "I brought you food. Some berries that haven't quite gone bad. And elder tea. It's bad for your digestion just sitting like that. But of course you won't listen to me." Caught the Moon cocked her head at Deer Shadow, studying her. "I'm not sure you *hear* me, if it comes to that." She clucked her tongue and fussed with the dirty turtle-shell bowl that had held a thin soup of wild grass seed this morning. "You eat right enough."

Caught the Moon knew that Deer Shadow wouldn't eat until she left, though. No one ever saw Deer Shadow eat, but as far as they could tell, that was all she did, that and get up to piss and defecate. No one ever saw her do either thing. To Caught the Moon she wasn't frightening, just someone who had turned her back on everything. Caught the Moon could understand that. She and her sister, Give Away, had both been married to the same husband, and when he and

Give Away had died in the starving time, and the children, too, Caught the Moon hadn't seen much point in staying here herself. But here she still was, apparently not going to die, and the People had found a use for her, tending the madwoman. "She is too stupid to be afraid," Cat Ears had said of her, and Caught the Moon had overheard him, and knew that he meant also that she was expendable.

Yah bah, what did Cat Ears know? The madwoman wasn't going to hurt Caught the Moon. And if she wanted to hurt Cat Ears, it wouldn't matter how far away he was.

"Your hair needs combing," Caught the Moon said, reluctant to leave her only company. She got a bone comb that had been Magpie's—Magpie had made a great to-do over it—and began working the snarls from Deer Shadow's long black hair. "I'll braid it for you and tie it up. You don't want it down your back in heat like this." Deer Shadow sat silently, hands in her lap, while Caught the Moon tugged at her hair.

"You won't know," Caught the Moon said chattily, "because you never come out of this cave—and you'll be blind as a mole soon if you don't, but of course you won't listen to me. But anyway, the men came back with nothing tonight—*nothing*—and after your girl made a picture magic for them, too, and now they're saying we have to move on early, and go hunt near the Place Where the River Runs Backward. I don't know how the shaman or all the gods he talks to thinks we're going to find a decent place to live there. Six days in journey huts at the Gathering is one thing, but two whole moons! Only there has been rain that way, and the hunting runs don't belong to any-one else. People have always been allowed to hunt there if their game trails go dry, so I suppose there's nothing else to do." She made an exasperated noise. "Well, I'm going to have to cut this knot out. What do you do when I'm not here?" Caught the Moon sawed at Deer Shadow's hair with her flint knife and said suspiciously, "It didn't look like this yesterday. But of course you don't pay any attention. If ghosts are snarling up your hair, I'm not going to come in here anymore."

Deer Shadow didn't answer.

"There, now." Caught the Moon put the snarl on the fire so that no one could find it and make a spell with it. The fire needed tending, too. "They're making you a litter, you know," she went on, "to carry you on. If you ask *me*, there's some of us would just as soon leave you here, but Hears the Night said no. What is it like to be sacred, I wonder?" She stopped talking and sniffed the air. "Do you know, I do believe it's going to rain."

The roar of the storm came on the heels of her voice. Water poured down outside the cave mouth, running in rivulets from the hanging hide and across the floor. A flare of lightning lit up the night outside, framing the hide in white fire, and the thunder banged while it was still glowing. Caught the Moon felt the lightning in the air and screamed, flattening herself on the floor beside Deer Shadow's bed. It felt as if the lightning were in the room with them.

Deer Shadow didn't move. Caught the Moon wasn't sure she even heard it—there might be no storm wherever Deer Shadow was. But there was definitely one here. It banged and rolled above them as if someone were pounding rocks together, and Caught the Moon could hear shrieks and curses all up and down the cliffs as the people dragged their journey goods inside, slipping in the instant mud. The brush huts on the riverbank flattened under the driving rain—not the soft, soaking female rain, but a wind-driven gale of water: male rain, vicious and angry.

The sky cracked open again. Caught the Moon climbed onto the bed with Deer Shadow and clutched the madwoman to her, burying her face in Deer Shadow's shoulder. This wasn't just rain, this was the

voice of the gods, bellowing down at them. The stones
beneath them quivered, and Caught the Moon let go
of Deer Shadow and flattened herself again in the dry
grass that padded the bed. It was musty and smelled
of mice but not enough to block out the lightning
smell outside. Caught the Moon grabbed Deer
Shadow again, wrapping her arms around her waist,
face in the mouse-smelling grass. If she was holding
on to the sacred woman when the gods came, surely
they would leave her alone. Unless it was the woman
they were coming for. . . .

Caught the Moon flung herself away and crouched
by the door this time, gibbering with terror. The hide
flap swung in the gale, battering itself against the
wall.

Wakes on the Mountain waded through the storm.
They were his people, and thus it was his business to
let the storm take him if it would save the rest.

Water poured from a hole in the sky. Runner and
her husband were struggling in the swirling knee-
high current to pull from the wreckage of their brush
hut the baskets they had packed for the moving on.
Runner held her son by the hand. His head was nearly
under the water.

"*Go!*" Wakes on the Mountain shouted at her. "Get
the boy uphill!" He got one hand on a basket pinned
beneath the center pole. As he pulled, the pole came
loose from the debris that had floated against it and
spun, catching him behind the knees. Wakes on the
Mountain tumbled facedown in the muddy river,
breathing water. The channel roared above him, past
flood stage in an instant, roiling down what had been
an almost dry wash.

He flung himself upward, fighting the river, spitting out mud. He could see nothing in the darkness
but the sheets of lashing rain illuminated by lightning.
It flashed three times in quick succession, and the
gods roared, their voices shaking the earth. The river

threw him against the fallen trunk of a dead cotton-wood, and he clung to it, hoping the water wouldn't pull it loose, too, and tumble him like a stone until he fell into Water Old Man.

A basket floated by, bumping on the crest of the water, and a spear, tumbling end over end. What might have been an arm lifted an instant from the current and vanished. Wakes on the Mountain felt his arms growing numb, his body battered by the flood-borne debris that swept against him.

Above the flood Runner crouched with her boy in-side Deer Shadow's cave, the first dry place they had blundered into. Her husband was somewhere in the storm, and Caught the Moon was howling beside her, rocking back and forth on her heels.

"Be quiet!" Runner reached out her free hand and smacked her. Caught the Moon hiccuped, her sobs fading under the sound of the rain. Behind them Deer Shadow sat silently while the rising water floated to-ward the cave mouth.

Outside, Hears the Night was looking through the sheets of rain for something. He knew the gods were speaking, and he tried his best to listen, letting them roar their message, batter him with it as he stood be-side the rising water. But he could not understand. They spoke some language that Bear had not taught him. He stood in the driving rain and prayed for vi-sion, or knowledge, or something that would tell him he was not abandoned.

One Ball and his wife scurried back and forth across the wet floor of their cave, pushing baskets and bags higher onto the stone ledge that jutted from the back wall. Their sons and sons' wives had dragged their own possessions up from the riverbank—it took years of drought to make a man fool enough to build on the riverbank—and now they were out looking for the baby that was missing. If she was in the water, One Ball knew it was too late. Her mother splashed fran-tically along the dark cliff face, hoping that the child had found her way into someone else's cave. This cave, one of the lowest, was filling up with water, which was ankle-deep on the floor now. The rest of the children huddled in the driest spot, barely visible in the cold darkness. All the fires had gone out, and One Ball wondered if the gods were going to drown them.

The lightning split the sky again, and Wakes on the Mountain, still clinging to his tree, saw the child in the water. He let go and lunged toward her, kicking himself away from the detritus of dead wood uprooted by the current. The water tumbled him, slapped him under, but he caught her by the hand before the current slammed them against the riverbank, forcing them outward again, spinning them like brushwood. With his free hand, he clawed at the slick bank, but the river cut it away from under his fingers.

Runner's husband staggered past the cave mouth and knelt, vomiting water. Below them, all their possessions sank in the flood surge. Teeth chattering, he put a hand on Runner's back and pulled the boy between them. They could hear One Ball's daughter-in-law wailing.

The rain lashed the cliffs and the parched land for most of the night. Just before dawn it stopped, leaving a sodden countryside under a flat gray lake, drowned in too much of what it had yearned for. Had the yearning itself been so strong that it had done this? Hears the Night wondered. Everything was askew. The swollen river carried bushes and dead animals on its muddy back, banks overflowing, the water lapping at the talus slope. The water had dropped a little since the flood's crest, but it still covered the dance ground, the midden, and the maize field, familiar landscape blotted out. The sky was overcast, sullen as the river, and the air was dank and cold.

Wakes on the Mountain staggered up the talus slope with the dead child in his arms. Magpie came out of their cave to meet him, her arm around One Ball's daughter-in-law. Hears the Night ran his hands through his sodden hair, untwisting the bedraggled eagle feather that had been knotted into it. He smoothed the feather with his fingers, over and over, face bewildered.

Caught the Moon slipped out of Deer Shadow's cave and stared at the sky. Behind the wet curtain of clouds over the eastern rim the sun was a dim glow. She looked over her shoulder. The madwoman had never moved all night, even when the water had begun to lap at the cave floor. Caught the Moon had wondered how she would get Deer Shadow out of there if it rose. Now the water was sinking again, back toward the riverbank, leaving dead mice and ground squirrels in its wake, along with the oddly limp body of a rattlesnake caught in a barewood tree. Caught the Moon pictured herself like the snake, hung on the dead-appearing limbs, hidden in spring by an explosion of red flowers.

Her stomach cramped, and she thought despairingly that there wouldn't be anything to eat now. Magpie and Silent were spreading the sodden remains of squash and cactus fruit and half-cooked rabbit left from the rabbit drive three days ago on flat stones to dry. All the rabbits would be drowned, Caught the Moon thought. They should go and find them before the meat went bad.

She looked at the sky. They had needed rain. All the rain dances and rain prayers had asked the gods for it. But it seemed now that whatever came to them came hurled by a furious hand.

"We will not move on today," Wakes on the Mountain said heavily. His teeth were chattering, and Magpie put a half-dry fur robe around him. "The Place Where the River Runs Backward will be flooded." He looked out over the water. "It may be that now the grass will grow and the deer will come back."

The cloud cover burned off a little and the air warmed, as if in answer. The ground began to steam. Wakes on the Mountain looked over his people, counting the dead. An old man who had lived down by the river and the dead child were laid out on the wet ground, with the women wailing over them. He listened to names in his head as they came to him. "Where are the children of Deer Shadow?" he asked.

There was a sudden silence. The people looked around them, looked at each other, as if the children might be disguised.

"Well, I never saw them all the night," Caught the Moon said. "As if they cared if she drowned, leaving me alone with no way to move her."

"*They* are drowned, then," Magpie said, looking at the roiling water.

"No." Hears the Night knew that much for certain. It was one piece of the voices that he was allowed to understand. "They are gone."

"Gone? Gone where?"

"The storm took them," Hears the Night said heavily.

"That's what I said," Magpie retorted. Wakes on the Mountain, shivering in his furs, gave her an admonishing look. She rolled her eyes to indicate exasperation with men in general and went to get the fire drill and some dry grass from her bed in the cave. The wood was wet, and it was going to take some doing to get a fire started.

Hears the Night turned around and went into Deer Shadow's cave. He hesitated, picking her out of the darker shadows around her. A thin beam of sunlight crossed her bare foot. Maybe she would know. Maybe she would tell him how they had lost the young one who could call the game, and the twins whose paired natures held magic between them, even if they were in disgrace. He wished Deer Shadow were not a woman. They were shadowy creatures to him, like the seasons, one moment compliant, the next sneering for reasons he couldn't grasp. It was easier to talk to the gods. He knelt before Deer Shadow, pleading. "Revered, we do not understand."

Deer Shadow couldn't see the boy kneeling in front of her, or the shaman, either. They were two versions of the same face, one bewildered, one solemn, one washed clean by the rain, one marked with mystical signs. But they were transparent like the rain. It was easier to see Spider hanging in her web over the door.

Something had told Deer Shadow that her children were gone. But she didn't have children, just fat babies who couldn't talk yet. And the man. She looked at the man sleeping beside her to make sure he was still solid. If she didn't watch him, sometimes he faded into rain like the ghost faces that kept trying to talk to her.

"I am wet," she said to Spider, noticing that for the first time.

Spider chuckled. It was an interesting sound, like a cat purring. Deer Shadow had heard that once. She had come upon a lynx chasing a butterfly through the dry sage. When it had caught the butterfly, it had rolled on its back to play with it, and then stretched out on the hot sand and purred, rumbling somewhere in its throat, butterfly wings sticking out of its mouth. The lynx had been a big one, and Deer Shadow had been small, and she had tiptoed away.

She looked to see what Spider might be eating now.

"You are wet because the world is flooded," Spider said, not eating anything, but there was something hung ready at the back of her web. "Even where you are you will be wet. There was a storm. Your children have gone away in it."

"Gone where?" Deer Shadow asked, seeing them as battered bright wings, pursued by the wind's teeth. She knew that Grandmother Spider could weave storms if she wanted to. "Did you make that happen?"

"No. They made it happen, I think. Maybe you should come out and see about it."

"No," Deer Shadow said. After a moment she asked cagily, "Where have they gone?"

"There are more humans than just the Yellow Grass People," Spider said. She looked complacent. "I told you that a long time ago," she added, but in Listens to Deer's voice.

Deer Shadow sniffed. "The Others. They aren't human. They steal from us."

"What about the child?" Spider sounded crafty.

"She is human because she belongs to *us*. Hah!"

"And your husband?"

"He belongs to Coyote," Deer Shadow said resentfully. "I spend all my time trying to keep Coyote from taking him."

"Then maybe that is a sign," Spider said. "I will tell you a story—"

"I don't want to hear a story!" Deer Shadow said. "Your stories make things happen. Go away if you aren't going to tell me about the children."

"What children?" Spider said. "You don't have any, just babies, remember?"

Wind Caller sat up beside Deer Shadow and yawned. Deer Shadow turned her back on Spider, putting her arms around her husband, patting his hair, touching his chest, making sure he was solid. Only a sliver of her, a piece flaked from her outermost layer, could hear Spider telling her about the other ways there were to live in the world, the other people who lived them.

*A band of wanderers hunted a little to the north on higher ground, where the game was scarcer in the summer but where, as it chanced this summer, the floodwaters did not come. They called themselves the Kindred and thought of themselves as the first and only people*

*on the land. The inhabitants farther to the south, like
the far-flung tribes with whom the Kindred sometimes
traded, were not truly people at all, and so, because the
gods had given this land to the Kindred, it did not matter who had been there first. In this reckoning the Kindred were of one mind with the Yellow Grass People.
The only difference was in their view of who was real
and who was not.*

The Kindred, whom Deer Shadow's people called
the Others, knew they were the real ones. They knew
the right way that things should be done, and the
Trespassers did not. Also, the Trespassers' faces were
flat, which was a sign of a lack of spiritual power. It
was up to the Kindred to inhabit the land properly.

The Kindred hunted deer and antelope and
sometimes made a trek west to hunt buffalo. The
women gathered piñon nuts and cactus fruit and
camas bulbs, and the men set snares for turkeys,
which for some inexplicable reason the Trespassers
did not eat, although they dressed in turkey feathers.
Among the Kindred were traders as well as hunters
and warriors, and these traders had seen many curious things among the tribes of False People. There
were as many strange ways of doing things as there
were stars in the sky, said Night Hawk the Trader,
and the rest of the Kindred shook their heads and
clucked their tongues and marveled at his stories.

When the great storm came, the Squash Band of the
Kindred hid in the caves and narrow rock shelters
where they summered on their high plateau and
watched awe-stricken as the lightning danced across
the sky. They could see it strike to the south, illumi-
nating the desert. The headmen of the Healers, the
Rainmakers, and the Deer People got together and
said that finally the prayers of the Kindred had been
answered. Now the grass would grow again, the water holes would fill, the deer and antelope and rabbits
would come back, and all would be as it had been.

And as an added favor from the gods, the Trespassers in the floodplain would drown.

*Maybe*, Night Hawk the Trader said skeptically. Although he was young, he had been more places than most and was inclined to disbelieve everything. Fire God and the Two War Gods had spoken once before, when Night Hawk was a child. They had given the Kindred the yellow tufa cliffs in the lowlands. The Kindred had listened and taken them from the Trespassers, but not much later the Trespassers had tricked the Kindred and driven them out again. That had rankled ever since. Most of the young men of the Kindred could not remember the cliffs, which had taken on a mystical aura, a land of promise, shown and withdrawn.

The Kindred yearned after it; even in good years they were a little hungry. Their upland valley was not as thick with grass as the country where the Trespassers hunted. With the drought the Kindred had died easily, their numbers shriveling until there was talk of the Squash Band hunting with the Turquoise Band, all the Kindred together.

"We will wait and see," the head of the Deer People said. "That is what Healer Old Man and Rain Old Man and I have decided. The storm spoke many things. We must not decide what was addressed to us until we hear the voices clearly. That will take much listening."

"And first," said Healer Old Man, who with Deer Old Man and Rain Old Man governed the Kindred, "we will thank the spirits of our ancestors for the water that runs in the rivers now."

The Kindred turned their gaze from the Three Old Men down the red sandstone slope to where the sun pooled on the rock, luminous as daybreak.

*For the rain we thank you.*
*For the rain that feeds the grass we thank you.*
*For the grass that feeds the deer we thank you.*

*For the deer that feed the people we thank you.*
*For sun on stone and wind on water we thank you."*

Night Hawk the Trader lowered his arms and then spread them out again, stretching. The world looked very fine suddenly. Clouds were still drifting above the mountains, and that might mean more rain. Even if not, this storm would break the desert open like the barewood tree bursting into blossom. In no more than days, yellow and scarlet flowers would carpet the valleys, and soon there would be fish in the rivers again, swimming upstream from the depths of Water Father where they had hidden.

"It will be a better life now, eh, Aunt?" He patted an older woman on the shoulder.

Leaf Fall wasn't of his clan. "Aunt" was a term of respect. She sighed, a voluminous breath of air escaping into the bright, wet day. "There will be meat, maybe. In time, not right away. Nothing is ever right away. Young men are too impatient."

"We don't have much time," Night Hawk said cheerfully. "There are too many ways to get killed."

"Angry husbands are one of them," Leaf Fall said.

Night Hawk patted her cheek. "All the pretty girls are married."

"And I am not a pretty girl," Leaf Fall said with a snort, "so don't play your tricks on me. I am an old woman and smarter than pretty girls. I am older than most, and you should give me respect and bring me some willow tea for my aches before you hunt. *If* you are planning to lend us your great skills this morning, and not go blundering into a hole in the ground where monsters will eat you." She gave him a sidelong glance. He was too old not to be married, as old as her own dead child would have been. That memory still twisted Leaf Fall's heart, made her mother young fools like Night Hawk who wouldn't settle down but wanted to tramp all over the land with a pack, trading with monsters and False People.

"And who brought you the necklace of shells, oh most gracious old Aunt, all the way from the edge of the world?" He bent down so that he could look her in the eye.

"You haven't been to the edge of the world," Leaf Fall said, but she patted the necklace with pride.

"I have," Night Hawk said. Leaf Fall had never been willing to admit that that was possible. "I bought the necklace from a man there, for red dye-stone, which I nearly fell off the mountain getting."

Leaf Fall shook her head. "You should settle down and be a headman like your father was." She knew he wouldn't do it, though. A hawk had flown up from its kill right at his mother's feet when she was carrying him. Leaf Fall remembered. And now he had a wandering foot. It made it too easy to tumble another man's wife and then hang his pack on his back and walk away. That and the rakish set to his shoulders, the handsome strong-boned face like the hawk that had marked him. It was weather-worn already, but the long eyes danced, and the long mouth covered white teeth and, Leaf Fall knew, a wheedling tongue.

Night Hawk shook his head back at her. "The gods don't talk to me. The land talks to me. All the wonders there are to see. I can bring you red and blue feathers from the great bird that lives in the south, or greenstone, or bones from a fish bigger than you are. But don't ask me to tell you when to move to winter grounds, or whether it will rain, or how to bring the spring back each year. So far I have always left that to the Three Old Men, and they have always done it."

"Hummph!" Leaf Fall said, and he went to bring her willow tea.

Night Hawk dipped water out of the stream that bubbled down the mountain. This morning it had been thick with mud, but already it was clearing. It had never gone entirely dry in the drought. There had been little enough food, but they had never been thirsty, so Leaf Fall had said. But she was thin, he thought. He would stay and hunt a few days with the Kindred warriors and make sure she got a share of it. Much of the year Night Hawk was foot-to-trail, seeing what the Turquoise Band was doing in the spring, and whose pretty daughter had come of age; going east toward the Buffalo Hunters in the summer, or west over the mountains to meet traders from the coast. He usually came back to trade with the Trespassers at their autumn Gathering, but lately the Trespassers had driven him away with stones.

The Trespassers had a food that had become part of the Kindred's legends by now. The Kindred had seen it growing when they had taken the southern caves from the Trespassers—Aunt Leaf Fall remembered it—but the Trespassers had driven them away before it was ripe, and although Night Hawk had seen it in their camps, too, they would never let him have any. Now they threw rocks at him as soon as he got near.

He took the water to the fire where the women were cooking and picked a hot rock out with his bone spoon. He immersed the rock, and the water steamed around it. He put another and another in, taking the old ones out as they cooled. When the water was bubbling, he put in a handful of willow bark and let it steep.

What was the seed that the Trespassers kept to themselves? he wondered. They had been jealous of it even at the beginning and had always taken it away whenever he was near, even before they had begun to drive him off. It must have been another trader who had brought it, he thought. But where had that one come from? Strange and wonderful people that Night Hawk had never seen, maybe: a village of gods. Or perhaps they were False People from a land where the plants were as strange as the fish bones were at the coast. He decided with arrogant certainty that the Trespassers had not learned how to make this grow for themselves.

A daughter of the Rainmakers looked at him curiously while he stared into the tea. "Is that for you? I never heard that willow tea would cure an itch in the foot." She tossed her long black hair at him. "*You'll* be gone again as soon as the mud dries, I suppose."

"Why does everyone want me to leave?" Night Hawk said plaintively. He shook his short-cropped head and inspected her while her friends giggled behind their hands.

The Rainmaker girl was no kin to him, even though he was a Rainmaker himself. Everyone belonged to one of the three groups, but membership had nothing to do with which clan you were born to, and everything to do with what headman your parents had promised you to. This girl was safely of another clan and had grown up a lot since his last time among the Squash Band. She had small breasts that tipped up jauntily. They seemed to be saying something to him—and nothing he could repeat to Old Aunt.

He smiled at her, stirring the willow tea. "This is for Aunt, but maybe I will take it for heartache."

"It's no good for heartache," she said gravely, with a dancing light in her eye.

"Oho. And what do you prescribe for that?"

"I suppose you would have to go see the Healing Men," she said demurely, unwilling to carry the game any farther.

*You're too young for me,* Night Hawk thought. Maybe it wasn't a good idea to stay and hunt. Maybe he should take his pack and make one last trip east to the Buffalo Hunters before he found himself with a wife.

He stuck a finger in the willow tea and tasted it, screwing up his face. It was right. He got a turtle shell from his small store of possessions, well protected under the overhang of the rock shelter where he lived, and dipped tea out in it. Most of what his two packs contained were trade goods: shells and beads and flint knives, red dyestone and beaver furs and deerskins.

His personal possessions consisted of spears, tools, two baskets—one for water and one for cooking—a bone spoon, and a bowl. The women collected everything else: grinding stones and gathering baskets, piles of furs for bedding, cradleboards and combs and hair ornaments. All those things Night Loon traded but did not own. And anything he *did* own he would have traded for an object rare enough to interest him.

Old Aunt was still sitting on a warm rock looking out over the valley when he took her the tea. Just below where her feet rested, a yucca plant grew, struggling to push its roots through the stony ground. "I never cut this one," she said, sipping her bitter tea in little slurps. "I always like there to be something beautiful when I look out at my day." The yucca fruit was edible, the roots made soap, and the fibers of the leaves made sandals and rope and cradles and anything else that could be woven.

Night Hawk looked at the stunted plant. It wasn't worth cutting.

Leaf Fall smacked her lips over the tea. "Now I feel young again," she said with a half-smile to let him know that he was in her favor. "I will go and look for birds' eggs."

Night Hawk was staring across the valley southward where they had seen the lightning storm playing across the horizon.

"What are you looking at?" she asked sharply.

"I don't know. Do you ever feel as if something is just beyond where you can see it? Just past the corner of your eye?"

"My daughter is there," Leaf Fall said. "The one that is dead. Is that what you mean?"

"No," Night Hawk said. "And I am sorry to make you think of her."

"I would anyway. Now that Antelope has gone to live with her husband with the Turquoise People, I have no one to take care of."

"So you take care of me." Night Hawk chuckled. "And tell me how to behave."

"Most certainly," Leaf Fall said. "You need to be told. And what were you almost seeing, if it isn't our dead ones?"

"I don't know," Night Hawk said. "Maybe it's the storm. Storms uncover things. I remember one big one, when I was foot-on-trail. It washed a whole skeleton out of the ground, of a big cat, bigger than I have ever seen, with fangs like a snake in its mouth."

"Did you pick it up?"

"I couldn't have carried it. And I was afraid of it." He raised an eyebrow at her. "I wondered if there were more of them there. What I did was hurry through that country, but since, I have thought about storms and what they wash out. Now I keep thinking about that cat."

"You think it is out there?" Leaf Fall looked at him accusingly. "That is a fine thing to tell an old woman to worry her at night."

"Not the cat," Night Hawk said. He chewed on his lip thoughtfully, still looking south. "But something is out there."

# VI

# Claw Marks

When the storm broke, the water came down on Others' Child, Mocking Bird, and Maize Gone Away like a thick, cold hide, driven on the wind. The thunder beat at their ears, deafening them until Others' Child thought she might never hear anything again but the angry voice of the storm and Coyote's barren howl, echoing off all the desolate places, the untamed, unruly places, the frenzied, furious places where fear lives.

Hearts pounding, the three stumbled toward the river with Bitch lumbering beside them, ungainly under her load of hides. Bitch stopped and looked suspiciously at the water in the river. Already the current was flowing. A sheet of lighting cracked the sky open, showing them the water, ankle-deep all across the bottom of the riverbed.

"Hurry!" Others' Child shouted over the thunder. Mocking Bird and Maize Gone Away stumbled down the bank, and she gave Bitch a shove. "Now!"

The rain flailed at them, the charged air lifting the hair on Bitch's neck. The storm was silent for an instant, and then they heard a thin crackle like someone stepping on brush. Lightning flashed, enveloping them. It hurled them for an instant into the next world, thunder clamoring in their ears—frozen in white fire, tumbling back into water.

Others' Child was floundering in slick mud, rain in her eyes. She looked frantically for Mocking Bird and Maize Gone Away, for Bitch. Lightning flashed again, farther away, but bright as daylight, and she saw them struggling in the current, saw that she was on the other side of the river. She couldn't remember getting there.

"Run!" she screamed. "This way!" Shouting over the storm, over the roaring of the river, over a dark sound that was growing bigger, growing nearer. They slithered through the rising water, Bitch fighting to keep her footing. Others' Child saw her go down under the load of wet hides. Then it was dark again. Above the riverbank Others' Child slipped her pack loose and fumbled toward them in the deepening water. Reaching blindly in the darkness, she grabbed Bitch by the pack and Maize Gone Away by one hand.

"Mocking Bird!" No answer, only the river's roar. Others' Child spit up water, gasping, trying to pull Bitch's pack loose. It slipped into the water, and Bitch vanished. The roar upriver was louder now, gathering force, hooves drumming like buffalo pounding down the channel.

Maize Gone Away, still struggling with her pack, stumbled against her, and Others' Child caught her arm and pulled her toward the bank. They climbed the slope frantically, fingers digging into slick mud, the smooth river-washed stones breaking away under their feet.

"Get higher!" Others' Child pushed Maize Gone Away up the bank. "Higher!" Slipping, she groped around for her own pack, her face in the mud.

*"Sister!"* They heard the voice thinly through the rain.

"Here!" they shouted, but there was no answer.

Others' Child's hand closed on her pack, sodden and half buried in the mud. Her fingers clenched around it. They would die without what they had brought, as easily as they would die without each other. "Here." She gave it to Maize Gone Away. "Get away from the river. Hold on to these."

"What should I do?" Maize Gone Away whimpered.

"Can you find Old Uncle's cave? The place where the old shaman went to see visions?"

She looked around her into the wild night. "I don't even know where I am," she wailed.

"Then wait for us. Just get away from the river. Go!" Others' Child pushed her, and she stumbled off, lugging both packs.

Others' Child waited for the lightning to show her the drowned world, and when it flashed again, she saw the river running full and the wall of water that roared down its channel. She screamed and ran downstream, angling away from the bank, shouting for Mocking Bird. The water tumbled over her, knocking her down, rolling her head over feet, crashing its way down the channel. Gulping water, she flailed in the drowned chaparral for something to hang on to. A thornbush lacerated her arms and face. The crest passed, sucking the water back with it, thundering downstream. Others' Child found herself in ankle-deep eddies, her hide skirt torn off, her sandals long gone. Rain plastered her hair against her face as she looked frantically into the darkness.

*"Sister!"*

She heard it again and stumbled toward the voice, rain battering her back and sides. "Mocking Bird!" she screamed into the dark.

*"Here!"*

The wind howled and tore the sound away. She shouted again and cocked her head, hand cupped around her ear. The lightning had moved on across the valley, the flares fainter. Finally she saw him for an instant, frozen under a smoke tree, clutching his pack and Bitch's.

She felt her way toward him, the wet rocks sliding under her feet. Far away now she could hear the roar of water in the channel. The river that surged by them here was over its banks, undercutting the ground, breaking off chunks of clay bigger than a cooking basket.

They had to get to higher ground. If the rain kept up the river would grow more swollen yet. She dropped in the mud under the smoke tree. "Can you walk?"

"I tried," Mocking Bird said, teeth gritted. "But I turned my ankle."

"Get up. Can you put weight on it?"

"I think so." He got himself to his feet, hanging on to the wet branches, crushing the drowned, feathery blooms in his grip. "It hurts."

"I know," Others' Child said desperately. "I know it hurts. Can you *walk* on it?"

"I have to," Mocking Bird said. "Don't I?"

Others' Child picked up his pack and slung it over her shoulder. She tugged at Bitch's load.

"Where's Bitch?" he said.

"Didn't you find her? You found her pack."

"It nearly drowned me. I was trying to get out of the water and it hit me. That's when I turned my ankle in the rocks."

"Bitch!" Others' Child screamed into the rain.

"I called her," Mocking Bird said. The lightning lit the sky again. They could see only the rain and the river.

"Come on. We have to get Sister. I left her alone."

"What about Bitch?"

Others' Child grabbed his arm. "She's a *dog*. We

have to find Sister." A twinge of loneliness stabbed her. They might all be left alone in the black rain. She pulled him out from under the tree and picked up Bitch's load. Carrying the wet furs and hides was like carrying rocks, but she knew better than to leave them. Tanning skins took time, and that was only if they caught something big enough to skin. They weren't going to kill a deer, especially without Bitch. She staggered on toward where she had left Maize Gone Away, going slowly to let Mocking Bird keep up with her. Her arms ached like fire, and the rain and hair ran down in her eyes so that she couldn't see even when a flash lit the landscape.

They followed the riverbank northwest, calling her name, and found Maize Gone Away near where Others' Child had left her, perched on a slope above the flooded river. She stood with her pack at her feet, howling into the rain.

"He's here. I found Mocking Bird."

"I thought you were gone." Maize Gone Away sniffled. "I saw the water come, and I thought you were gone."

"We have to get dry," Others' Child said, realizing that it was up to her to tell them what to do now. "And we have to take all these things with us or they'll be ruined by morning, so don't argue with me."

"Where's Bitch?"

"I don't know."

Maize Gone Away began to sob again.

"We can't go back," Others' Child said. "Even if we wanted to, we can't get over the river. We have to get out of this storm. So you have to carry your pack." She hung Mocking Bird's over his shoulders, fighting the knot in the wet sling. She got her own up on her back and saw to it that Maize Gone Away had hers tied tightly. "Now you take the other end of this," she said to her sister, lifting one end of Bitch's load.

Maize Gone Away tried to lift the other. She staggered a step and sat down hard in the mud. "It's heavy."

Others' Child lifted her up again. "Then we'll drag it."

They inched north, cutting away from the river into the low hills, heads bent against the rain. When the lightning flashed, Others' Child took their bearings, nudged them slightly to the north or east, and they stumbled on.

Her feet hurt, and she knew if it were not for the cold rain washing over them she would feel warm blood between her toes. Her ribs were bruised and sore, and her arms ached from dragging the hides. Mocking Bird's breath came in painful gasps every time he took a step. Maize Gone Away was silent now. She took a step, dragged the hides, took a step, dragged the hides.

"We'll get there," Others' Child said between her teeth. As the oldest, it was up to her to tell them so. If she didn't, they wouldn't keep walking.

There was no way to know how long the storm had battered them, but finally they came to the jumble of rocks that Others' Child remembered. She set her pack down and began to climb, hoping that Rattlesnake had not chosen to wait out the storm in the same refuge. The water might have filled his underground nests.

The shaman's cave was as she remembered it—narrow and deep, running back into the mountain. She felt her way gingerly along the wall, listening for the sound of other inhabitants over the drumming rain outside, sniffing the wet, musty air. It was empty, she thought. The old shaman's spells might still guard it. If they did, he wouldn't mind their being here.

She went back to the cave mouth and helped the other two to scramble up and drag the packs inside.

"We'll never get a fire going," Maize Gone Away said, her teeth chattering. "I'm so cold."

"There is still some wood here," Others' Child said. As Looks Back had grown older, his bones had grown colder, and he had always had a fire. "Spread the packs out and let's try to find the fire drill." They had to keep moving, keep doing things. She knew that was important.

The fire drill—two sticks lashed with sinew so that they could be turned between the hands—had been buried at the center of Others' Child's pack and was still dry. She made a pile of some of the old dry wood from the back of the cave and a handful of the disintegrating grass that had been Looks Back's bed. She began to turn the drill, her teeth now chattering, too; they all sounded like people made of bones. She tried not to drip water into the thin thread of smoke that began to rise.

Shivering, the other two watched her. "I'll take a turn," Mocking Bird said.

"No. There it comes!" A tiny spark flew out and died in the grass. Others' Child turned the drill faster. Another. Finally it caught, and they crouched around the finger of flame, carefully feeding it bits of grass, then twigs, and finally small branches. The wood was rotten and crumbly, but it burned.

The children huddled around the fire, pushing more wood into the flames, coughing at the smoke. The wind blew the rain in through the narrow cave mouth. Others' Child spread her pack open and got out a hammerstone and her adze. She picked two short lengths of wood that seemed sound and sharpened one end of each. Then she made Maize Gone Away help her push the stone that Looks Back had used for the same purpose up to the cave mouth. Others' Child stood on it while Maize Gone Away handed her the wet hide from Bitch's pack. She hammered the stakes through each end of the hide and into crevices on either side of the opening. The hide hung down, flapping in the wind, but it kept most of the water out.

"Spread everything else out now." They opened the other packs and laid furs and baskets and clothes to dry beside the fire, huddling naked among their sodden possessions. Mocking Bird's ankle was swollen and puffy, and Others' Child looked at it and tried to think what the old shaman had done when Grandfather Found Water had twisted his.

Maize Gone Away took her seed and spread it carefully on a flat stone, turning each kernel over with a fingertip.

"Will it be all right?" Others' Child asked her, hacking a strip from a wet fur blanket with her skinning knife.

"I think so." Maize Gone Away sniffled. "I have to watch it. If it parches, it won't sprout, and if it doesn't dry quickly, it will rot." She sneezed.

"Yah, it's like tending a baby," Others' Child muttered. She wrapped the strip of wet fur around Mocking Bird's ankle and pinned it with her needle. "I need boneroot for this, I think." Suddenly her eyes filled with tears. "Mother used to dig it, but we haven't any now."

"It will get better without," Mocking Bird said, gritting his teeth.

"We have to have medicine," Others' Child said. "I brought what there was, but it isn't much. Mother hasn't paid any attention, and no one's been sick, so I didn't think. There's too *much* to think about!" she said furiously. "I can't think about it all."

Mocking Bird put his arm around her and laid his head on her shoulder. Maize Gone Away finished turning the kernels and came to sit on her other side. "We are all here," Maize Gone Away said, patting her sister. "Except for Bitch," she added mournfully. "But we belong just to each other now. Nobody else."

Others' Child pulled the half-dried fur robe around all of them. It was woven of strips of rabbit skin and edged with coyote fur. It smelled like wet dog. She tried not to think about Bitch, drowned in the wet darkness.

The fire warmed the robe; their bodies, huddled together, drew heat from one another. When Others' Child could see that Maize Gone Away's lips were no longer blue, she stood up and spread their other hide, stiff and mostly dry, on the remains of old Looks Back's bed. She lay down on it with a twin on each side, the fur robe over them all. Outside, the wind butted against the deer-hide door. When she closed her eyes, she could still see the red hands of the flames on her eyelids. . . .

The dream was as smoky as the cave, a thick smell of wet wood and fur and trampled grass. After a moment she saw that it was Coyote she smelled, sitting in front of the fire, brushy black-tipped tail curled around his paws.

Coyote opened his mouth and closed it again with a snap. After a moment his tongue came out, and he licked his muzzle and nose. "I have just eaten a drowned mouse," he told her. "There are a great many of them out there."

Others' Child was a little afraid to talk to him. "Did you send the storm?" she finally asked him.

"Oh, no, it's your storm." Coyote never took the responsibility for anything if the results were bad. "Everyone is very upset about it, too. Like an anthill when you poke it with a stick. Your shaman is trying to wrestle with it, but it's bigger than he is. Do you want to watch?"

"Yes," Others' Child said. And then she could see Hears the Night, very small, just in front of the fire, wrestling with a gray-colored man who looked like river water. He fell, feet bumping against the air, and the gray-colored man sat on him. Others' Child giggled.

"Well, maybe that isn't exactly how it is," Coyote

said. "But it's close. When you make pictures, things aren't ever exactly. You know that."

"What's Mother doing?" Others' Child asked.

"I don't know." Coyote scratched his ear with his hind leg. "She won't let me in. She's trying to hold on to the man. Stupid woman. That's why I came with you." He yawned again, turned around three times, and curled himself beside her, his fur hot from the fire, smelly flanks close against her ribs.

Others' Child woke with his fur in her face, damp and smelling of river water. She sat up, scrubbing her eyes, and saw that it was Bitch, wedged between her own chest and Mocking Bird's. Her bedraggled coat stank of mud and decayed reeds.

"Bitch!" She put her arms around the wet neck, and Bitch opened one yellow eye and looked at her. For a moment Others' Child thought it *was* Coyote, and she caught her breath. Then Bitch yawned, just as Coyote had done, and buried her gray nose in Others' Child's armpit. Her tail thumped, the black tip flipping in Mocking Bird's face until he woke up, too. Others' Child stared at it, amused. Bitch never wagged her tail.

"Glad to be home, are you?" she said to the gray face buried in her arm. "Where have you been?"

Bitch didn't answer. Maize Gone Away woke up and hugged her, too. Sunlight was streaming through the gaps around the hide, and the fire had sunk to embers. Mocking Bird put more wood on it. Maize Gone Away prodded the kernels of maize, turning them over to be sure. She scooped them back into their dried basket.

"Now you have to promise," she said. "Before we do anything else. Before we try to go anywhere."

"What?" Others' Child said.

"We can't eat it," Maize Gone Away said. "No matter how hungry we get. We have to carry it with us until we find a place to plant it."

"Of course," Mocking Bird said. "We are not stupid."

"I know you when you are hungry," Maize Gone Away said. "Promise."

Mocking Bird sighed. "May Coyote eat my bones if I touch the maize without your leave. Will that do, oh Most Important?"

Others' Child thought about her dream. It wasn't a promise that *she* would break. She repeated the same words because they needed something binding.

"Very well," Maize Gone Away said. She put the basket away and got the water basket that she had set outside last night to catch the rain. She gave the other two a smug look because *they* hadn't thought of that.

"We have enough food for two days, maybe," Others' Child said while Maize Gone Away rubbed the dirt off some stones and put them in the fire to heat. "After that we will have to hunt. And we will have to put distance between us and the People before the river goes down."

They looked down into the valley at the churning gray water. They could see even from here that the current was still swift. Far away, across the flooded land, they could see the cliffs that had always been their summer home. It was too far to see if anyone was moving there.

"We should go north, upriver," Mocking Bird said. "That is where the game will go. And our people will stay to their side of the river because of the Others."

"The Others?" Maize Gone Away said, frightened.

With a shock Others' Child realized that she had cut herself free, sliced the rope that bound her to the Yellow Grass People. The people of her blood were in these hills somewhere, but she was afraid of them, too.

"There are only three of us," Mocking Bird said. "If we can hide from our people, we can hide from the Others. I am more worried about finding game." He looked at them disparagingly. "I will have to teach you both to hunt, I suppose."

"And we will teach you to tan hides," Others' Child said with asperity. "And I can already kill ducks with a sling."

"I killed a rabbit with a throw stick once," Maize Gone Away said importantly. "Our father said my aim was better than yours." She subsided when Mocking Bird glared at her.

"You are disrespectful," he said.

"We aren't your wives," Others' Child said.

"And we are older than you," Maize Gone Away said.

"Yah!" Mocking Bird held his hand up, thumb and forefinger a hairbreadth apart, to indicate how much older she was.

"I am older than both of you," Others' Child said. She rubbed Bitch's head. "And Bitch has more sense than any of us. She tracked us through the storm. We will make her chieftain, maybe."

The other two grinned at her, quarrel forgotten, sense of adventure rising with the spreading sunlight. "We should travel today," Mocking Bird said. "While we still have food to eat. We will be like our father when he left the Children of the Sun." No one mentioned that their father had had a hostile tribe baying on his trail. And a curse.

The sense of wonder and adventure lasted through the first day as they tramped northward through still-familiar land, sheltered at night by a rough-cut brush hut, with a roaring fire to keep any interested animals at bay. They found a rock with a water-worn hole at the center to carry a few coals in, and it worked almost as well as the buffalo horn that Wakes on the Mountain used during the moving on, even if it made one more thing to carry.

New grass and a scarlet blanket of flowers were springing up under their feet, and the air felt hopeful, not seared as it had been for so many years. All the same, they were footsore by the second day, trying to put as much distance behind them as possible. Others' Child gave up worrying about leaving tracks, and tied one of their two precious hides onto poles to make Bitch a travois, and after that Bitch dragged a larger share of the load. She ate more, too, and the food ran out before they'd thought it would.

They had veered from the Yellow Grass People's usual trails now, and wandered uncertainly into a long valley thick with sage and snakeweed, the higher slopes spotted with juniper, oak, and piñon pine. There was no sign of human habitation. Here, they thought, they might stay a little, find a shelter at the base of the mountains, and hunt whatever lived in the valley. Mocking Bird made much of telling the girls to stick with their slings and throwing-sticks. They didn't know how to handle a spear, he said, and it was unlikely they would flush anything big enough to need one.

A little creek ran down the valley, possibly to join the Yellow Grass People's river in the south. Where it flattened into a wide pool under a stand of willows was where animals would come to drink at dusk and morning.

Bitch sniffed at the water and lapped it up noisily. She sniffed again at the mud around the riverbank and slid into the shadows of the scrub that grew tangled among the willows.

"There are fox tracks," Mocking Bird said, "and badger and raccoon, and a big cat."

"The cat will be out at night," Maize Gone Away said. "We need to be away from here by then. I'm not going to compete with a cat for that badger."

"Then go eat field mice," Mocking Bird said. He imagined himself draped in a catskin.

"We have to *eat*," Others' Child said fiercely. "And there are three of us. Give me a spear, too." She crouched in the scrub beside Bitch, clutching tightly the spear Mocking Bird gave her, her stomach growling. They had found some juniper berries to eat this morning, no more than a handful apiece that weren't withered. Even Bitch had wolfed down her share.

Nothing would move in the heat of midday. The children lay in the shadow of the scrub, half drowsing. They were downwind of where the tracks led, Mocking Bird said. If they were very still, they would catch something at evening.

They had left their packs and Bitch's travois under an oak tree at the edge of the valley, having found no cave or shelter larger than the hole of a burrowing owl. Mocking Bird had tried to poke a spear down the hole, but either it had a bend in it or it was empty. Only a feather came back on the spearpoint. The only other animal they had seen was a turkey cock, flying up startled out of the sage. As everyone knew, such birds were poison to human people, although the coyotes ate them. Bitch had lunged after the bird with a snap of her teeth, but by then it was high in the air.

Now hunger became a sort of rhythm, like their breathing. As the sun slid behind the shelf to the west, they watched the water hole avidly.

At dusk a snake slid out of the brush to drink. Maize Gone Away stirred, but Mocking Bird laid his hand on her arm. If they made a noise killing the snake, nothing else would come. The snake whispered away again into the grass and went down an owl's burrow to look for eggs.

Bitch lifted her head, ears up. Mocking Bird put his other hand on her neck and looked upwind. A badger waddled down to the water. Mocking Bird leaped to his feet, spear in hand, and the badger bared its teeth, bracing itself on heavy claws. Bitch rushed at it. The badger snarled and swung its head, snapping at her throat. She jumped back and up, nearly over it. The badger's jaws came together with a snap on air, and it suddenly lumbered back into the scrub. Mocking Bird flung his spear after it, impaling it through the hips. Pinned, the badger swung around and snarled at them, its pointed teeth glinting. Bitch danced around it, looking for an opening. Mocking Bird pushed the spear into the soft ground, mindful of the heavy, snapping jaws, and Others' Child ran the second spear through the badger's throat. It spit out a choking growl and lay still, blood running out onto the spear shaft.

The three of them fell on it, slitting open the belly and cutting the entrails out for Bitch, licking the warm blood off their fingers. Others' Child cut the liver in three and they each ate a piece, gobbling with the urgency of the starved. They dragged the carcass through the scrub and stunted grass to the oak tree and set about skinning it, impatient to get at the meat.

Once the skin was cut loose, the head was taken off and the brains saved in a bag made out of the bladder. When the skin side was tanned, the mashed brains would be rubbed in to make it supple. Others' Child took the skin down to another part of the river and pegged it in the stream to soak while Maize Gone Away put the carcass on a spit over the fire. She had already roasted the heart when Others' Child came back, and they shared it, the juices running down their chins.

The badger was tough and the meat was rank, but none of them cared. They gave Bitch her share, and the bones to crack, and put the rest into a basket with a tight lid where she couldn't get hold of it. It would feed them another day, giving them time to learn the ways of the game in a valley this small, Mocking Bird said.

It seemed as good a place as any to stay while the weather was warm. Before winter they would have to find a cave somewhere, a little higher up where the piñon pines were plentiful and the low sun would shine. But for now the little valley was home. Others' Child wove a brush hut together around the poles that Mocking Bird cut, using tall grass and fox-grape vines for lacings and aspen leaves, cut on the higher slope, for its roof. When the wind blew, the leaves rustled like voices talking, the gray-green looking silvery in the moonlight. They seemed always to have something to say, but she was never sure what.

The end of summer began to come more quickly than they had expected it. The aspens still on the hills turned yellow, like splashes of sun between the dark pines. Mostly they had been hungry since they had left the Yellow Grass People. The rains had not come again except for a few showers, and the streams shrank back down. The animals that came to the water hole were wary. The three caught a quail in a snare once in a while, and learned where the lean, long-legged rabbits had their burrows, but mostly they ate lizards and snakes and sometimes a ground squirrel. They saw one deer, but even between the three of them and Bitch, they couldn't run it down. Instead they looked for turtles in the stream and scoured the hillsides for juniper berries and yucca, always one step behind hunger.

At night they lay in their brush hut, the fire blazing just outside the door, and listened to the other things that hunted then: the fluttering wings of a bat, the booming of a nighthawk scooping up bugs with her big mouth, the passage of an owl, and the shriek from its prey when it swooped. They could hear coyotes singing in the foothills around the valley, and once the howl of the big puma whose tracks they had seen by the water hole. The black and white stripes of the badger's fur were now a bag to hold the plants that Others' Child cut and dug in case someone got sick, but they had acquired little else of value. Mocking Bird had made them each a new spear, and if either girl went out alone she took one with her, as well as a knife at her belt. They were too much alone here, and the voices of the coyotes lingered in their ears.

"Time to move on," Mocking Bird said. "Tomor-

row." He had appointed himself chieftain, but the
other two knew he was right. They thought wistfully
of the Gathering—it was almost that time—and hungrily of the piñon nuts that would ripen on the upper
slopes and keep them fed. If they could find a place
to be warm through the winter, they would live.

Maize Gone Away went to cut the last of the tall
grasses that the rains had brought, going to seed now
in pale dry patches, bent over in the wind. The foxtail
grasses were vicious, with barbed, burrowing seed-
heads that worked their way into ears and dogs' eyes,
but the drooping heads of buffalo grass contained
seeds that could be ground and eaten. She stripped
the tiny heads between thumb and forefinger into her
basket, thinking, in one of the sudden bouts of fury
that seemed to come on her unbidden, of the maize
and her father and the Yellow Grass People. It was
their fault she was here. The anger seemed to over-
whelm everything else until sometimes Maize Gone
Away thought, frightened, that she couldn't see what
was real under her hand. She looked uncertainly into
the scrub as if her own fury might lie out there watching her.

Others' Child was loading Bitch's travois and their
packs, and Mocking Bird had taken Bitch and gone to
try to kill a rabbit for journey meat. They had set
snares among the reeds in the little river for ducks,
and when she had stripped all the grass clean, Maize
Gone Away went to check them.

To call the real ducks down, Mocking Bird had
made false ducks from reeds and grass to float in the
river. They were lifelike, with bright stone eyes and
feathers saved from other kills. Tied with a line of hair
to a stone that sat on the river bottom, they bobbed
realistically in the water. Maize Gone Away took her
sling and a few smooth stones out of the bottom of
her gathering basket. If the snares hadn't caught any
ducks, she might get one with a rock.

She edged toward the water. It was almost dusk

and time to go back. Mocking Bird and Bitch would be home, and Others' Child would have something for them to eat, even if it was only grass and a handful of deerberries and mush. Again she thought of the maize and the Yellow Grass People, and her anger shivered along her skin, raising the hair on her arms. It felt like some live thing stalking her.

Maize Gone Away could see the grass decoy ducks bobbing on the river. They had drawn their likeness out of the air, a flock that she had heard overhead earlier. A drake flapped frantically in the reeds, one leg snared, lifting itself nearly out of the water and falling back again. Maize Gone Away set her basket down and trotted purposefully to the water's edge. She waded in, pushing the reeds aside, passing the snared duck to pick up Mocking Bird's decoys first. The live duck flapped and thrashed, beating up water into her face. Decoys over one arm, she grabbed it by the throat and killed it with a quick twist. Then she waded out of the water, and the thing that had stalked her, hidden behind the scent of her own anger, came padding out of the scrub.

The puma was the tawny color of the dry grasses, and its yellow cat eyes caught the last of the low sun. The three had heard it roaring its hunger in the hills at night.

Maize Gone Away had no more time than to drop the duck and the decoys and shriek before it leaped at her, the bunched muscles of its haunches springing it forward, claws spread. She ran and felt its weight on her back, rolling her across the ground. She tumbled, batted by those huge paws, its leap a little too short. Frantically she pulled her spear from its carrying strap and found that the shaft had snapped off short with her fall. She came up crouching, spear cradled in both hands, and screaming. Maybe Others' Child and Mocking Bird would hear her, she thought frantically, her stomach churning with fear as the cat crouched to spring again. Maybe screams would frighten the cat.

The puma looked at her, golden eyes ringing dark expanded pupils in the dusk. It took a slow, crouching step forward. She could feel the burning on her back where its claws had raked her, like a hand.

"Go away!" Maize Gone Away screamed at it. "Go away! I'll kill you with my spear! You can have the duck!"

The puma's eyes didn't stray from her. The duck lay where she had dropped it, a still pile of brown and green feathers. The puma's muscles bunched, and she could see the dark tip of its tail move behind it.

If she threw the spear and didn't kill it, all she would have was her knife—and the spear was broken off short, and she didn't have an atlatl to throw it with. Maize Gone Away tightened her grip on the shaft. The sweat of her palms made it slippery.

There was a crashing in the scrub beyond the riverbank. For an instant the puma stiffened, and then it sprang. She felt its hot weight tumble her down, pinning her this time, the teeth nearly at her throat. Others' Child and Mocking Bird came shouting after it, dancing around her, trying to spear the cat while Maize Gone Away thrashed in its grip. Mocking Bird's thrown spear pierced it in the shoulder, and it left Maize Gone Away crumpled in the dust and sprang toward him instead, snarling, spear shaft thudding against its forelegs.

Mocking Bird kicked at the puma's underbelly, trying to pull out his spear while it rolled him on the ground. Others' Child circled just outside the puma's reach, prodding it with her own spear, while Bitch snapped at its hamstrings. Bitch sank her teeth in, and the cat's back leg collapsed under its snarling weight.

Maize Gone Away picked herself up from the ground, still clutching her shortened spear, blood from the puma's claws running down her arms. She rammed the spear into the puma's neck. It had Mocking Bird half pinned under it now and was trying to get him by the throat. She pulled her spear out and drove it in again. The froth on the puma's mouth turned to blood. Mocking Bird got his belt knife free and buried it under the cat's chin. The puma thrashed on top of him while Maize Gone Away and Others' Child kicked at it and tried to shove it away with their spears. At last it collapsed, yellow eyes glazing, and Mocking Bird crawled free. He stood, chest heaving in and out, while Maize Gone Away clung to him and Others' Child and Bitch inspected each other for bites.

"You scream better than the cat," Mocking Bird said finally, his voice tight, setting Maize Gone Away back a little and rubbing off some of the blood to see the claw marks. "I heard you clear by the old rabbit burrows yonder."

"Those cuts need a poultice," Others' Child said severely, as if Maize Gone Away had been neglecting them. They were frightened into ferocity with one another. "Take the duck back and take Bitch with you. Mocking Bird and I will bring the cat."

Maize Gone Away cradled the green and brown feathers to her breast and dangled the decoys by their dark threads of braided hair. Others' Child's hair hadn't grown out enough to use yet, but Maize Gone Away and Mocking Bird had clipped theirs to use for the decoys, so that the new growth stuck up in tufts at their temples and the napes of their necks. The blood was running down her arms again. She walked carefully through the dry grass to their brush hut, feeling unbalanced now, as if she might tip over.

Others' Child made a poultice of plantain and greasewood and plastered it on Maize Gone Away's arms by firelight, trying to remember the right thing to say to go with it. Cat scratches were very bad, and she wished she had a shaman to suck the evil out of them, she said, even if it was Hears the Night.

Maize Gone Away sat very still, front teeth biting

her lip. After a while the poultice stopped the bleeding, and the fuzzy feeling in her head began to go away.

Mocking Bird, his own scratches dressed, was still skinning the cat, muttering about that being women's work but not loud enough for them to quite hear him. He took the catskin and a torch to the river and pegged the skin out in the current so the water would clean it and the fish could eat some of the flesh off. Then he would cure it in ashes for a while before they moved on—Others' Child said that Maize Gone Away shouldn't travel tomorrow anyway—and it would keep well enough until they found a winter place. He would take pains with it then, he thought, and make a fine skin of it for Maize Gone Away. He realized that he had decided to give it to Maize Gone Away before he had even skinned it. She was the one who had nearly got eaten. He felt proud of himself for that gesture, and older somehow. Next year he would be a man. Maybe that was it.

Mocking Bird pounded the stakes into the riverbed until he was sure they wouldn't come out. Maybe he would call her Cat Meat in private, he thought, and joke with her a little, and Others' Child would tell them the stories that Mother used to tell, and it wouldn't be such a bad winter. The cat's carcass would feed them for a long time.

In the morning, Maize Gone Away's arms were inflamed, but Others' Child put new poultices on them and said she could walk if she hung her bundles on her hips, or from a sling around her forehead. Mocking Bird looked at the sky, which seemed to have gone gray overnight, and said it was time. The rest of the cat was bundled on Bitch's travois, and they set out for the higher slopes to find a shelter from the cold that was coming.

The first one they found, a cleft among some jumbled rocks, smelled so loudly of Bear that they knew better than to go in, or even stay nearby. They wandered farther north, among deep canyons and steep, angular mesas jutting to the sky. They turned east but retreated again when they saw a band of the Others. It was a hunting party, or maybe raiders, the children thought while they crouched frozen in the aspen leaves behind a downed tree. The Others were known to raid such bands of the People as they thought were weakest.

The three made a wide swing around the trails where Mocking Bird saw more tracks of the Others, and around a second set of trails that they knew belonged to the High Rock People. "They are still hungry," Mocking Bird said with satisfaction, noting the direction of their tracks. "They are trying to find enough to last the winter." As far as the three of them were concerned, any band of the People was the enemy.

They went farther, into lands that the People had never ventured in, they thought, even the Buffalo Leap People, who were far wanderers. Another cave at the foot of a steep bluff proved to have Bear's brother in it, and a third to have housed wolves too recently to be comfortable. But finally they found a high canyon and near its upper reaches a narrow chamber, longer than it was wide, under a rocky overhang that would keep out the rain. A stand of piñon pines grew on the slope above, and there was water from a thin stream that wound its way through the rocks and made a little pool not far from the cave.

With frost in the air, they knew—as they had not entirely in the summer—what it was that they had done, how much they had to hide from the relentless wind and the bone-cold snow and whatever waited, winter-hungry, outside the cave. They dug a storage pit for the maize and lined it with stones to keep the damp out, and dug a fire pit at the cave mouth. They hung Maize Gone Away's catskin across the doorway to breathe its scent on anything that might think to come in. And one morning while Others' Child looked at herself in the pool, when she was getting water, she saw someone she didn't know—her hair had grown past her ears and hung in a tangled mat like brush on her shoulders. Her face was longer and thinner; her nose jutted sharply between deep-set eyes. Her hands and legs were scarred and scratched with brambles, like Maize Gone Away's claw marks.

*We are marked,* she thought then. *We are all marked now. These will not wash away.*

# VII

# Turning the Sun

At the winter solstice the low sun pointed like a finger through the crack in the outer wall of the Men's Cave, and the Yellow Grass People knew that it was time to turn the sun around. That was done by the men, deep inside the inner chambers of the cave, and it was a most important matter in which women were not permitted to participate because woman magic was always powerful enough to skew other spells.

Hears the Night put on his robe of turkey feathers and took his great tooth in his right hand. The old bone felt warm under his palm, as if something still lived in it. Sometimes Hears the Night felt that the tooth knew things he did not, if only it could be made to speak them. Bear had told him that bones that old spoke in tongues no one understood now, but Hears the Night hoped he might one day receive the proper hearing. The winter was already bad, and it had not yet properly begun; all his magic seemed to stumble over itself or fall away through cracks in the air, like breath escaping.

They had done evil. He had known it when the storm took the children of Deer Shadow and the dead man. But to speak it aloud to the People when he himself had set it in motion . . . well, Hears the Night was young and reasonably prideful, and that was not an easy thing to do.

Now he was afraid the sun might not turn. And he was afraid of the sickness that had started with the cold. First one man, and then another, and then three of the children and two women, all coughing up thick phlegm, coughing up some spell inside them. Hears the Night had tried to suck out the spell with his sucking tube on the skin of the chest, and he had shown the people the little red stones and the dead spider in his hand, but he was not sure that they had really taken the evil with them. It was like floundering in fog. He wasn't sure if they, if he, had done too much or not enough. Was the dead man's vengeful ghost at work, and if so, should it be placated or hunted down?

In his dream last night, Hears the Night had asked Bear. Bear wouldn't say, either.

In midwinter, Bear did not like to be awakened. Bear had looked at him sleepily and said, "Coyote is up to his tricks. You should never trust him."

"What can we do?" Hears the Night had asked his totem.

"Oh, you can't do anything about Coyote," Bear said. "No one ever has, since the beginning. We've all tried." He looked at the shaman's miserable face and relented. "But I will give you an amulet to keep him away for a while," he grunted. He padded away and paused, veiled with the drifting snow. Then he vanished into it.

In the morning Hears the Night picked up the bear dung outside his cave and spread it along the path up from the lower valley, and the trail up into the piñon pines above. He saved a little, mixed it with cold, melted snow, and poured the result along the ground in front of the caves, and twice around the fire pit.

One of the sick children got well, and one of the women died. Now he had to turn the sun, and the weight of its light felt heavy in his hands.

Deep inside the cave the torchlight painted all the colors red and black: red faces and hands, red eyes reflected in the flame; black shadow pooling on the stone, its fingers plucking at them from beyond the lit circle. A cold breath from the depths of the mountain curled across their feet. Hears the Night lifted his arms to the stone ceiling and then cupped them around the little torch.

"Sun Father, come out of the mountain and make new light." He clapped his hands quickly, plunging them into darkness.

As always, it was suffocating, unexpected. The dark enfolded them like a thick hide. There was a hiss of indrawn breath and the uneasy shuffle of feet. Hears the Night knelt on the floor, feeling Wakes on the Mountain and Cat Ears settle beside him. He sat back, crossing his legs, arranging himself deliberately while the men caught in darkness tried to hold themselves still.

"We kindle new light to guide you, Sun Father," the shaman said, and he heard the eager murmuring around him. Usually he made it take as long as possible to bring a spark. The effect of waiting was always salutary. But today he was afraid, like the men around him, that it would not come. It was a fear new to Hears the Night, and it settled in a frighteningly permanent and intimate way about his shoulders as he turned the fire drill.

Someone coughed in the darkness, tried to stifle it, and coughed again, racked with spasms. *One Ball*, Hears the Night thought, distracted, losing the rhythm of the fire drill. It slipped from his fingers. He righted it, feeling the sticks in terror that they would still be cold, that nothing would be waked from it by him this year.

His stomach lurched in relief as he felt their warmth—a faint heat like flesh. Hears the Night turned the drill again, driving it harder into the pine needles that lined the fire pit in the floor.

The darkness was complete. No faint thread of light showed in this deepest chamber of the cave. The spark, when it came, might almost have been imagined, a tiny starburst that winked and died. A collective breath was gathered in and let out. Another spark, another, then a quick spurt of flame, framing the shaman's hands.

"Sun Father returns!" Wakes on the Mountain proclaimed, voice echoing off the stone walls. The fire burned brighter, fed with twigs by Cat Ears. Hears the Night breathed his breath on it, and the flames quickened. It had come to them again, at the deepest point of the year—the New Light. "Go and tell the women," Wakes on the Mountain said.

Cat Ears thrust a new torch into the flames, and it caught, filling the cave with light, a bright piece of sun on the end of a stick. He made a gesture of respect to the shaman and the chieftain and set out down the narrow passage that led through three outer chambers to the daylight. The other men followed after, pleased with the strength of their magic.

"Light has come back," they told the women while Cat Ears thrust the torch into each cold fire pit, newly laid with kindling. Fire after fire blazed up. "We have turned the sun in his course," they told the women. "He is heavy, and look, our hands are burned." They held up soot-smeared fingers.

The women crowded around the new fires, warming themselves, stamping their feet, bundled in furs. It was bone-cold without fire in the high caves. Cat Ears stopped outside the cave that Deer Shadow had

taken for her own. She had stepped off her litter the
first day and sat down in it, never mind that it had
belonged to Hears the Night last winter. Cat Ears
looked in cautiously, then back over his shoulder at
Hears the Night.

"She'll put a curse on me, maybe," he suggested.

Hears the Night took the torch. He was beginning
to distrust Cat Ears. "Then I will take the fire in to
the woman. That is why I am shaman, to protect
you." There was only a faint trace of acid in his voice.
The torch felt heavy in his hands, like the sun.

He pushed his way past the hide flap into the icy
cave. The fires had been doused since midday, but
Caught the Moon had cleaned out the hearth and laid
new wood on it. She had wrapped a bundle of furs
around Deer Shadow, too, but Deer Shadow appeared
not to notice them. She sat as she always did, cross-
legged with her hands in her lap, looking at things
nobody else could see. Hears the Night wanted to
touch her to see if her skin was still warm, but he was
afraid to.

"The People fall sick," he said sternly, to cover that.
"One has died. Is this your doing?" He put the torch
in her fire.

The woman under the furs didn't look at him. He
couldn't truly be sure she heard him. Madness might
have taken her far away. Maybe she talked to the man
who was dead—that had happened before.

"Is it the man's doing? Does your husband curse
us?" he asked her.

There was no answer, only a look that might have
meant *I hope so.*

The flames leaped up in the newly laid kindling.
Hears the Night fanned them with his hand. "It is the
lung sickness," he said, thinking that she was hearing
him now. "The children have it, and old One Ball. I
don't think he will last the winter."

Her eyes might have moved toward him and away.
He knew he saw her blink.

"I have sucked the curse out of them," he went on, "but it may take more magic than mine. The sickness is very strong." He poked the fire until a spray of sparks shot up. He said accusingly, "You are a healer. The man/woman who died before your husband came to us taught you. I know these things."

Deer Shadow narrowed her eyes. For a moment he thought she was actually going to speak to him, but she didn't.

Hears the Night folded his arms on his chest. "We have no one now who is touched that way by the gods," he told her. *Except you*, he thought, and certainly that was a different matter, since the man/woman hadn't been mad. But still, the gods' touch was the gods' touch. It should give her powers. He had felt his own come on him like a robe settling on his shoulders when he had first seen Bear. He wondered what it had been like for the woman. "You are a healer," he said again. "You will displease the gods."

Deer Shadow's narrowed eyes glared at him. She made him think of a snake suddenly, and he retreated. It was not right that the woman was able to put visions like that in his head.

Deer Shadow waited until Hears the Night was gone. Then she got up slowly, unfolding herself from the bed. She saw Spider out of the corner of her eye, still hanging in the doorway. "Watch him for me," she said to Spider.

Spider looked at the man lying where Deer Shadow had been on the bed. Already he was growing thin. She could see through him. "You had better not take too much time," she said.

She had thought it was summer outside, with the warm rain she liked, but when she stepped past the hide over the door, she saw snow on the ground and fur boots, which someone had put on her feet. She paused, puzzled, and then decided it didn't matter.

The snow crunched interestingly under the boots.

Wakes on the Mountain and Magpie goggled at Deer Shadow as she went by.

"What is she doing?" Magpie hissed.

Wakes on the Mountain was silent, trying to decide that for himself. If she had come back to them, it might be a good sign. If not, were they going to wish that Hears the Night hadn't waked her? He looked at Hears the Night to see what the shaman thought about it. The shaman wore an expression of sardonic satisfaction, so maybe it was all right.

"You *can* hear," Hears the Night said thoughtfully.

Everyone else the madwoman passed got out of her way and crossed their fingers at her as she went by. She didn't seem to see them.

Deer Shadow went to the cave where One Ball lived and looked at him and told him to lie down. His old wife retreated to the corner and cowered there.

"You have the lung sickness, and you are an old fool to be walking around with it," Deer Shadow said. Her voice sounded hoarse, as if sand had gotten into it. She hadn't used it much to talk to Spider and Wind Caller.

"So you decided to wake up," One Ball said, coughing. He sounded as if he was trying to bring up something that wouldn't come.

"I decided you shouldn't die," Deer Shadow said.

"I'll try to oblige you," One Ball said with a grimace.

"You don't want to die," Deer Shadow said. "Otherwise I would have let you."

One Ball bent over, racked with the coughing again.

"Heat some water," Deer Shadow said over her shoulder to his wife, whose mouth was a round circle of surprise. "Yah," Deer Shadow said, "*move*, you stupid woman!"

"She's afraid of you," One Ball said.

"She should be. I'll make a rattlesnake to come and

live here. *She* didn't try to stop them when they killed my man."

"She hid in the cave. She didn't help them, either."

The wife was creeping around the edge of the cave with a water basket. She looked at Deer Shadow fearfully.

"She's my wife," One Ball said. "Let her be."

Deer Shadow inspected the stores at the back of the cave, rummaging in baskets and leather pouches, smelling their contents, and took a handful of willow bark. The wife filled a basket with snow and gave her a black look as she dragged it back inside.

"Tell her to make the water boil," Deer Shadow said to One Ball. She went outside into the sharp cold sun and looked around her. She went into Magpie's cave while Magpie screeched and Wakes on the Mountain grabbed his wife's arm. The chieftain's wife had a fine array of healing herbs. Deer Shadow appropriated some wintergreen and a bundle of greasewood leaves. Then she stalked into Cat Ears's cave, and Silent ran out, flapping her hands. Deer Shadow helped herself to a bunch of yarrow.

In Hears the Night's cave she found lizard-tail and mountain balm. She looked around the shaman's dwelling with a sniff for the fact that since there was no woman to keep it clean, it was not clean. He was standing in the doorway, but it was hard to say whether she saw him or not. She looked at something in the corner of the cave mouth, over his head, and said, "I won't be long."

By the time she got back to One Ball with her gleanings, One Ball's wife had the water bubbling in a basket so tightly woven that only a few drops seeped through the sides.

"Lie down," Deer Shadow said to One Ball. "And tell her to go away."

One Ball broke into a spasm of coughing. When he could, he said, "Do it."

His wife gave Deer Shadow a suspicious glare. She

was nearly as old as One Ball, gray-haired and almost toothless. She spat on her hands and rubbed them together and held them out toward Deer Shadow in case any curses emanated from her, and then she hobbled out.

One Ball lay down on the bed by the fire. His breath rattled in his lungs.

"Take your shirt off," Deer Shadow said.

"You've started talking. Now you won't be quiet, I suppose." He coughed and spat into his hand, leaning on one elbow. "Bah, I am dying."

"Maybe," Deer Shadow said. He pulled his deerskin shirt over his thin chest, and she laid her ear against his ribs. "Does it hurt when you breathe in?"

"It hurts when I do anything." He gave a weak chuckle. She thumped his chest and put her ear to it again. "Yes, it hurts."

"Chew this while I make you a tea." She gave him the lizard-tail root. "And stay under the furs. We will have to sweat the sickness out, since the shaman's sucking stick does not work."

Her tone was acerbic, and he shook his head at her, popping the lizard-tail root in his mouth. "You will make trouble for yourself. You are too spiteful to have a true madness."

"How do you know?" Deer Shadow asked him. "Madness feeds on spite, I think. And I never said I was mad." She paused, as if thinking about it. "Do *you* think I am?" There was somewhere else she was supposed to be, wasn't there? Why was she here in this cave with him? Where was Wind Caller?

"I don't know," One Ball said honestly.

Deer Shadow ground the dried greasewood leaves in One Ball's wife's mortar, then the mountain balm, wintergreen, and yarrow. She threw the results into the water basket and added two more hot rocks from the fire, fishing out the old ones. The willow bark went in on top of the rest. She stirred it all with a long spoon.

"This has to steep for a time. Till sunset, maybe. I will sit here with it." Deer Shadow folded her legs under her and settled into silence as if she were in her own cave.

At first One Ball thought she was slipping back into her trance, or whatever it was that she lived in. After a time he saw that her fingers were moving. It was hard to say what they were doing. Weaving something, he thought. Her long fingers plucked and pulled at empty air. "You look like Spider," he said, wheezing. It hurt nearly as much to talk as to breathe. His lungs had gotten worse since they had turned the sun around this afternoon.

"I am making you a new breath," she said, eyes closed. It was gray outside, the last of the red spilled sunlight soaked up from the snow by twilight. She lifted her hands and buoyed whatever it was into the air above the fire. Then she bent and tasted the medicine in the basket with the end of the spoon. "This is ready." She looked around her for a bowl. There was a turtle shell among One Ball's wife's goods, and Deer Shadow spooned the tea into it.

One Ball had been lying on his back, head propped on a bundled hide. He raised himself on one elbow and slurped what she had brewed. "Yah, that is vile." He wiped his mouth on the back of his hand.

"It would not drive out sickness if it tasted good," Deer Shadow said. "Sickness would stay just to taste it."

One Ball coughed.

"Drink some more. Finish the bowlful. And another bowl when you get up to piss at night." She looked toward the cave mouth and then toward One Ball, uncertain. "I will stay to see that you do. And to listen to your breath."

"Are you going to let my wife come back?"

"It is not important to me."

"It's important to the old woman," One Ball said. "And she's my wife. I am cold."

"Very well. If she comes back, she can stay." Deer Shadow sat down again on the cave floor. She looked around, saw a fur robe that wasn't being used for One Ball, and put it under her. When the wife crept back in, Deer Shadow seemed not to see her. Later, when she wanted to listen to his breathing, she rolled him over and put her head to his chest as if there were no wife there at all.

She stayed for four days, never speaking to anyone but One Ball. Maybe she decided that that was enough. If she spoke to too many people, they might pull her back into the world. To One Ball she spoke freely, and he wondered if that meant he was going to die after all.

But he lived. She roused him to listen to his breathing, to pour hot medicine tea down him or make him hold his head over its steam, or to make his wife boil more water. His wife fed her—that was manners—but One Ball wasn't sure Deer Shadow noticed what she was eating any more than she had when Caught the Moon fed her.

On the fourth day, whatever it was that had its fist around his lungs loosened its grip, and he began to be able to cough without pain. Deer Shadow made another dose of tea and had him make his wife watch her so that she would know how to do it, too.

"Keep drinking this until it's gone, and then some more that your wife will make. Put your head over the basket while it steams. Stay by the fire this season and tell big lies about the bears you have killed. The young men can go hunting for you now."

"Yes, Most Wise." One Ball smiled at her. "Are you going to live among us now?"

Deer Shadow cocked her head at him, perplexed. "Do I not?"

"I'm not sure," One Ball said gently. He thought that she would go where she needed to. Tomorrow she might see through him again if he came to her.

She gathered up the dried bundles of medicine and laid them in a neat row for One Ball's wife. Then she went outside and didn't come back again.

Caught the Moon found her walking down toward the winter dance ground. It was a cold, clear night with stars like icicles and a winter moon as bleak as stone. Caught the Moon took her by the arm and tugged her back.

"You don't want to go there. There's no one there. *He* isn't there." Caught the Moon was beginning to understand who it was that Deer Shadow saw when she wasn't seeing the live person in front of her. "I kept your fire burning. Come along back now."

Caught the Moon led her back to her cave and left her sitting there on the bed by the fire talking to someone Caught the Moon couldn't see. She didn't know whether it was Deer Shadow's dead husband or somebody or something else entirely. It gave her a creepy feeling on the back of her neck.

"I can't find him," Deer Shadow said accusingly to Spider.

Spider folded her arms. "You were gone four days. Wanting-magic doesn't last that long."

"I told you to watch him for me. Did you let Coyote take him?" Deer Shadow looked suspiciously around the cave for footprints.

"He just got thinner," Spider said. "I warned you." Personally, she thought it was for the best.

"Where has he *gone*, then?" Deer Shadow wailed.

Spider sighed. "Out where your children are, maybe. Maybe he remembers them even if *you* forget."

"I am a man now," Mocking Bird said. He stood in front of their spring house, one of the little brush huts that the People made during their travels down to the lower valleys in spring. "It doesn't matter if there are no other men to make the Men's Dance with me. I am a man." He folded his arms and scowled at his sisters. "You will not treat me like a child any longer."

"I wasn't!" Maize Gone Away said indignantly. She shook her shorn head at him to emphasize her innocence. Maize Gone Away had begun to bleed in the winter, and at the spring equinox Others' Child had cut her sister's hair off and recreated as much of her own initiation dance as she could remember. Ever since, Maize Gone Away had been inclined to give herself airs.

"You were," Mocking Bird said. "And I am a man. We were born in the winter, so I have been a man since then, so you will not tell me to fetch the water anymore."

"Someone has to fetch the water," Others' Child said, trying to be conciliatory.

"Women fetch the water," Mocking Bird said.

Maize Gone Away sniffed. She wore her catskin around her shoulders, lordlywise. "Men bring home the meat. If it takes the three of us to run down our dinner, it will take the three of us to cook it."

They glowered at each other, eyeball to eyeball. Others' Child giggled suddenly. They might have starved in the winter, and there had been times when she thought they would. They might have been eaten by wolves or the puma's mate, or fallen into a crevice on the steep slopes where they had scrabbled among the piñon pines for nuts. Any of these things might have happened, but they had not, and so now they were arguing over a water basket.

Others' Child looked at a soft spring sky. For a while, at any rate, while the snowmelt ran in the streams, there would be fresh cress and water snails, and spring greens in the meadow. When they got to the valley where they had summered last year, there might be ducks on the river, and geese, flocks of them flapping overhead, darkening the sky on their spring travel. The world just now was good, and she had

had a dream. Dreams always had meaning, so this one had been important. Others' Child laughed out loud and danced around the other two, wiggling her fingers by her ears to show them how they looked.

Eventually they noticed her. "What is it, Feet on Hot Coals?" Maize Gone Away said.

"Yah, you look stupid, like someone quarreling with himself." Others' Child danced around them again. She stopped in front of them. "Go away and be ashamed of yourselves. I will fetch the water. And then I will make deer in the dirt because it is a lucky day."

"I will get the water," Mocking Bird grumbled. "How do you know it is lucky?"

"I had a dream," Others' Child said. "There was a white deer, and it talked to me, but I couldn't understand the words. I think they were in deer language."

"Mother!" Maize Gone Away whispered.

"I don't know. I think so."

"Does that mean she's dead?"

"No. It was a live deer. But if I draw deer today I am sure we will get one."

"We might drive one over the cliffs to the south," Mocking Bird said. "I've seen tracks near there. If we come on them from the thicket on the far side of the water hole. It hasn't worked yet, though," he added dubiously.

"It will work today," Others' Child said. She wasn't sure where the certainty came from. She wasn't even sure that that was what the deer had been trying to say. The deer had looked more as if it was looking for something. But something had been telling her things since winter. At times she almost felt its hot breath on her neck. They weren't always good things, but they were usually true.

Others' Child sat down in the grass in front of the spring house and began to dig it up with a flat stick until she had a bare patch of earth about as long as Bitch, who was watching her with interest.

"No, we don't need any sneaking coyotes," she said to her. "I am drawing dinner." Once last winter, on a night when they could hear the coyotes singing under the moon, Bitch had slipped out of the rope that Others' Child had tied her up with and had come back with a bitten ear and pregnant. The pups had been born dead, which was maybe just as well.

"I am going to make a deer," Others' Child said, and she began to do so, marking the slim legs out in the dirt she had smoothed over. The head was high and branched with antlers. It bounded across the valley, and Others' Child made three small hunters run behind it, spears drawn back to throw. She put another spear in the deer, and it seemed to slow its wild leaps. Then she put a dog on the other side to turn it toward the cliff.

Whatever had promised her a deer gave them one. They ran the deer over the cliff as Mocking Bird had said they might. It flew in front of them, wild-eyed, a young buck cut from the rest by Bitch, turned toward the mesa's edge while the old buck and his does thundered down the plateau, away from the escarpment at its edge, leaping like shooting stars in the hot sky.

The young buck flew over the cliff without pausing, launching itself into air, feet paddling on invisible ground. It twisted, plummeting upside down, and landed with a thud they could hear from the top. The three and the dog ran for the narrow trail up the side of the mesa and scrambled down it, slipping in the red dust and the scattered, wind-cut rock, Bitch sliding on her haunches.

It was the first deer they had killed, and they danced around it triumphantly, and Others' Child knew that they should save the skin and the head to dance the Deer Dance in. Because they were outcast from the People did not mean that they would give up their ways. With only themselves for a clan, to keep to the ways, to keep the ritual, was more important than ever.

The buck was thin, bones showing through its hide, but they leaped up and down, whooping. Then they tied ropes around it and began to drag it to their journey camp.

"Mother sent it," Maize Gone Away said. "I know she did. It's a sign."

"Of what?" Mocking Bird asked, puffing. The deer was heavy, and his sisters had a tendency to let him pull the hardest.

"I don't know," Maize Gone Away said. "But we have meat to take down to the valley. And when we get there, we will plant the maize."

Others' Child looked uneasy. "I don't think it's time."

"Not all of it," Maize Gone Away explained. "But we have to see if it will sprout, and it is better to have fresh seed. That way we will make more seed, too."

"What if we can't stay in the valley? What if there isn't enough to eat?"

"We took it from the People. We have to plant it and eat it," Maize Gone Away insisted. "That is what it is for. It wants to be planted."

"Maybe some of the others of the People kept back seed," Others' Child said. "The High Rock People or the Smoke People."

"No, only our father," Maize Gone Away said stubbornly. "The rest are all as stupid as the Yellow Grass People, yah!"

Mocking Bird grunted. "It is their fault that I can't go back and be made a man properly. Do you remember the feasts we used to have? And the dancing? Even when there wasn't enough to eat?"

Others' Child's eyes teared suddenly. She wiped them with the back of her hand and pulled harder on the rope. "I remember coming back to the summer place every year. The first thing I always did was go and wade in the river and try to splash . . . to splash *Father*. It was a game. And I *will* name him. I want him to come back. I want him to come back and curse the Yellow Grass People." The deer's antlers caught in the tangle of a sage bush, and she jerked savagely on the rope. It was their fault, the People's fault, for the loss of everything she loved, for their exile here alone, blistering their hands on the rope, dragging a scrawny deer to a brush hut that wouldn't stand up properly.

*We will learn,* she thought. *We will learn to make a proper hut and to tan hides so they don't stiffen so, and we will not be helpless. We are grown now, and if we haven't died this year, we are not going to. And the Yellow Grass People will starve more than we. I will see to that.*

When they got back to the spring house, she left Maize Gone Away and Mocking Bird to butcher the deer and sat down again at the flat space she had smoothed in the dirt. She began to draw deer over and over again, lines of them, one following the next. When she ran out of room, she smoothed them away and began again.

"What are you doing?" Maize Gone Away asked her, bending over the dirt, holding her bloody hands away from it.

Bitch came up to sniff, too, her nose greasy with the offal, and Mocking Bird said testily, "Someone might come and help. I can't seem to get the head off."

"She's making deer," Maize Gone Away said, puzzled. "Where are they going?"

"Away from the Yellow Grass People," Others' Child said with satisfaction.

"Toward us, I hope," Mocking Bird said.

"Maybe," Others' Child said. "But they are going away from the Yellow Grass People."

Maize Gone Away planted the seed that summer in the little valley, and it came up. She watered it from the stream when the ground got dry. The rains were still sporadic, only coming, it seemed, when they could do the most damage: tear down loose rock or flood a dry wash and drown someone. All three of them had a sense of the world being slightly out of kilter, as if someone had tipped the seasons and run them all together, or twisted the sky just barely enough to notice, so that the land had a new form that could only be seen and recognized with a dreaming eye.

Maize Gone Away saved the seed from the new maize, and they ate only a little of it. When she had planted it, she pricked her finger and put a drop of her blood in each of the holes the way Father had done, and the other two had watched her, horrified. Was she going to die like Father, then? Would the Maize God want her, too?

They killed another deer that summer, but deer were still not plentiful, and mostly Others' Child's magic drew rabbits and smaller game to their snares or throwing-sticks, even though Mocking Bird had made a hood and robe out of the first deer's hide and danced the Deer Dance for each hunt. But they didn't starve. They grew tough and wary, and nothing ate *them*, either, because they had learned from Maize Gone Away's cat to know when something was walking behind them.

In the fall they hunted well clear of the Gathering. Others' Child wanted to go back and put scorpions in the caves at the bottom of the tufa cliffs while the Yellow Grass People were gone from them, but Maize Gone Away and Mocking Bird refused. It was too far, they said, and besides, it was an idea that Coyote had thought up, and not a good one.

It probably was, Others' Child admitted.

"Be content with driving the deer away," Mocking Bird said. "But you *might* try to turn them toward us."

But it had not worked that way. Maybe it was the rains being out of kilter, or maybe Others' Child's spell was indiscriminate. For whatever reason, the deer were not biddable. They moved away from the People's hunting grounds, but they did not come more frequently in reach of the three wanderers' spears.

By the time another winter was gone, it began to seem that the deer people were possessed of some deeper urge, driven by forces that the human people could only feel as something wrong in the ground. By late spring there was no rhyme or reason to the wanderings of either group.

The Kindred felt it, too.

"Something is wrong with the mountains," Night Hawk said. "I have just come from among the Trespassers, and they think so, also. *And* they are half starved."

"All that is wrong with the mountains is that the deer have come to *us*," Wing Foot said cheerfully, tightening the haft on his throwing spear. "As certainly they should, because Fire God and the Two War Gods gave us this country. If the deer have come away from the Trespassers, then that is right."

"That may be right," Night Hawk said, "but something *is* wrong with the mountains. They feel wrong when I walk on them."

"Have you told this to the Three Old Men?" Wing Foot asked him. He was nearly the same age as Night Hawk, but where Night Hawk was a wanderer, an adventurer, Wing Foot was a traditionalist. Things were simple except when they were not, and then they were matters for higher authority. All matters of importance were to be taken immediately to the Three Old Men. If they did not feel that aught was wrong, then it was not.

"Their wisdom is that the gods have supplied us with deer this summer because we are a holy people," Night Hawk said. He frowned at his atlatl and slid his fingers in and out of the hide loops at the grip end. A moonstone tied two-thirds of the way down its length added balance and a blessing. "But when I find deer where I have not found deer before, and the ground makes me feel sometimes as if one leg has suddenly become shorter than the other, then I am suspicious."

"But you are hunting with us," Wing Foot said, grinning, "instead of going out again to see if the mountains are walking around in the night. How is that?"

"Because I am hungry, fool," Night Hawk said. "I am lucky if I can kill a deer by myself, and I am tired of journey food, and when I trade with the Trespassers they feed me garbage: gristle and burned seeds." He nocked a throw spear into the notch at the other end of the atlatl and tested the feel of it.

"They have to feed you," Wing Foot said. "That is manners, even among such as they. They don't have to give you anything good."

"They don't. And they have nothing worth trading these days, either. I will go toward where the sun lies down and trade with the men from the coast."

"That is a long walk."

Night Hawk shrugged. "Who is waiting for me?"

"Old Leaf Fall," Wing Foot said. "She talks about you as if you were hers: 'When Night Hawk the Trader came home to hunt for me . . . ' You be careful, or she will marry you."

Night Hawk chuckled. "She only wants a son. She never had but the two daughters, Antelope and the one that was killed in the fighting. *She* gets the scraps, too, when the Kindred hunt. Besides, who would want me when they could have you? You are the pretty one. I will tell her so when I see her."

Wing Foot threw dirt at him and tried to rub it in his hair.

"Ha ha! All the girls love Wing Foot!" Night Hawk chanted.

"All right!" Wing Foot's handsome face flushed redder. He drew away. "They do not." It was not his fault that he was the most beautiful of the young men of the Kindred.

"The Three Old Men will have to decide who is to have you," Night Hawk said. "Or the girls will all pull each other's hair out. Like Willow and Foxtail."

Wing Foot glared at him. "Willow and Foxtail are not girls I would marry. They have no decorum."

"I will protect you," Night Hawk said cheerfully, his worry over strangeness in the mountains forgotten for the opportunity to annoy his friend.

"You will protect me by lying with all of them yourself. You will make trouble if you don't stop that."

"Then it's a good thing we are hunting tomorrow," Night Hawk said, unrepentant. "But I don't know what you'll do when I leave. It's a good thing you run so fast."

Wing Foot balanced his spear in his hand and looked southwest to where their high valley dropped down into a series of lower mesas and steep-walled canyons. "If you are going through the Trespassers' country again, and it is true that our gods have taken their deer, you may have to run faster yet. Maybe that's what's in the mountains—the Trespassers' hunger."

Night Hawk looked at him consideringly. Wing Foot didn't often think deep thoughts. And maybe there was something in what he said. "Maybe I will go and talk with the Three Old Men again," he said after a moment.

"What does it feel like?" Wing Foot asked.

"What?"

"Whatever is in the mountains. Whatever is wrong." He was beginning to look unsettled, as if Night Hawk had finally made him nervous.

"It feels like something moving. Not really moving, but as if something wants to. Something underground. The *wanting* is moving. I can't explain it better than that."

Wing Foot looked uneasy now. Wanting was serious business. Even he knew that. If you wanted something enough, you might get it.

# VIII

# The Mountains Walked

Geology moves slowly, a shifting here, a loosening there, like the slow metamorphosis of the human body. Whatever was wrong in the mountains, its urges were mirrored in the urges of the three children who were no longer children. They had been separated from their kind for nearly three years now, and in that time their bodies had shifted like the mountains stretching. They grew in their sleep and sat up in the morning, looking for—

"Where have you been?" Others' Child said suspiciously.

Mocking Bird dumped an armful of cut wood at her feet. "Getting you wood."

"With Maize Gone Away? She has work to do here."

"You always want her here," Mocking Bird said sullenly. "You talk about things you won't let me hear. And, anyway, she is fishing."

"Where are you going now?" Others' Child asked him as he turned away.

"To put out snares." Mocking Bird turned again, his face half angry, half puzzled. The tension between them hummed like a taut rope, but he didn't know why, or didn't want to, because that would demand answers. He was as tall as she was now, and would be taller. His body had gone muscular, all hard, un-expected angles and flattened curves. He wore his hair braided and pinned in a knot with a turkey feather stuck through it. Like everyone else in the heat of summer, he wore very little else.

Mocking Bird went down to the river. He took out his flute, stuck through the thongs that tied his breechclout, and blew pensive notes on it. He tried to think what was wrong. But since what was wrong was mostly youth, the music wouldn't stay thought-ful. It whispered around him, a kind of mental gid-diness suggestive of adventure, until he grinned. Maize Gone Away was fishing. He would sneak up on her and roar at her. She would think the puma had come back.

He tiptoed through the rushes, letting his move-ment follow the ripples of the wind so that when the rushes whispered together they wouldn't speak his name.

Maize Gone Away was standing over a pool, spear poised. She wore only the blue stone that she had had around her neck since babyhood and a rope belt to stick her hunting knife through. The breeze lifted the black hair from her neck and fluttered it out behind her like a dark bird's wing. She balanced forward on her toes, poised above the water in such a way that the flat rock on which she stood, her bare feet and calves, and the line of her thighs and buttocks seemed all of one piece, carved from the same stone. She had already been in the water. There was a fish in the basket on the riverbank, and her legs sparkled with myriad drops of water.

Mocking Bird slipped up behind her. Maybe he would be a water snake, he thought, and put his hand on her feet and make her jump. He slithered forward, like Snake Old Man looking for his dinner.

Maize Gone Away shrieked and danced backward on the rock, kicking at the air. But she didn't drop the spear. When she saw it was Mocking Bird, she pointed it at his throat, gasping. "I nearly stabbed you with this!" Her heart hammered under her ribs.

Mocking Bird fell backward in the river, laughing. He surfaced and spit a spout of water into the air. "If you thought I was Snake Old Man, you would have aimed too low," he sputtered. "You should have seen your face!"

Maize Gone Away dropped the spear and jumped in the water. She pushed him under again and tried to hold him there.

Mocking Bird wriggled out of her grasp and came up splashing. He flipped an armful of water in her face.

"I almost had a fish!" Maize Gone Away said, splashing him back.

"I am sorry," Mocking Bird said, not very contritely. "Shall I help you catch another?"

"With the noise you made," Maize Gone Away said severely, "they are all downstream in Water Old Man by now. Maybe we won't give you any of the one I caught, either." She glared at him in mock indignation, standing knee-deep in the cold, swift water.

"You made the noise." Mocking Bird put his arm around her shoulders. "I thought the puma had come back. But I am sorry I scared you."

"You didn't scare me," she informed him. Water dripped from her hair onto his arm, and rolled down her chest, bright drops pendant at the tip of each breast. He had a sudden urge to touch the drops, to let them run onto his own fingers. Embarrassed, he pulled away from her and splashed to the riverbank.

"I thought you were going to catch another for

me," Maize Gone Away called after him.

"No, you're right, they are all gone now," Mocking Bird said. He wondered if she had seen his cock stand up under his breechclout. His stomach lurched with shame. He went to set his snares, what he should have been doing all along.

He had made enough fine snare rope from Maize Gone Away's shorn hair to catch quail regularly as well as the ducks that came in spring and fall. Always he untangled it and rerolled it carefully. It took hair a long time to grow. Others' Child's hair was only now as long as it had been before her initiation. She fiddled with it at night, combing it out with a bone comb until it crackled, magic snapping like sparks off the teeth of the comb. Mocking Bird wondered what spell she made with it, but he never asked her. It made him uneasy, like Maize Gone Away's wet breasts.

Yah, he thought, they were women, and who ever understood women? He lay on his stomach, wrapping the fine snare rope around the stem of a sage bush, laying out invisible loops to catch thin bird legs where he had seen the quail's three-toed tracks in the dust.

For a swift moment he felt as if he were floating on water, and then the sensation passed. Mocking Bird gripped the ground with both hands. What was wrong with him? He could feel his heart flipping in his chest like a fish. He sat up carefully. Nothing moved. In fact the world was very still around him, as if it were frozen suddenly in amber, held motionless and expectant through who knew how many years. And yet there was a sense of motion just gone, motion to come. It made him queasy. He left the half-set snares and went away, back to their camp where it was safe.

Others' Child grumbled to herself as she laid new wood on the fire and put stones to heating in it. "We're a clan, just us to ourselves now. It's not right to spend all their time together and leave me with no company. Twins, yah! Like two pieces of the same branch. Yah bah, I have feelings, too. She promised she'd help me make soap, but she'd rather fish with *him*." Others' Child thought irritably of Mocking Bird and then, without meaning to, of Hears the Night, who for some reason had begun to cross her mind unbidden.

Mocking Bird came up the path to the juniper-roofed hut the three of them had built this year, scuffing pebbles in front of his toes. Others' Child saw how much he had grown this season.

"Maize Gone Away caught a fish," he said, flopping down on the trampled grass outside the hut. "But I scared the rest away."

"Playing games, I suppose," Others' Child said reprovingly.

"No." Mocking Bird got his throwing spear and began to tighten the wrappings on the haft. It didn't look to Others' Child as if they needed it.

"It's all right. There have been lots of fish this year." Others' Child dropped the rocks into the cooking basket. They hissed, making little threads of steam. "You needn't look so miserable," she said. His lip stuck out. It was funny. Suddenly she wanted to comfort him, hold him in her lap the way she used to. Images slid through her mind like fish swimming, startling, unbidden images, and flicked away again, leaving her flushed.

She leaned over and kissed him on the cheek to show that none of it meant anything. He turned his head instead and their lips met briefly. They pulled back as if they had kissed the hot stones. A voice screamed at them from the brush.

"Yah, you drove all the fish away and left me standing in the river!"

A fish smacked down on the ground between them, and they flung themselves to their feet, away from it and from each other, looking to see where it had come from. Maize Gone Away stood glaring at them, hands on her hips.

"That's why you drove the fish away," she said inaccurately. "So I would stay out by the river. Neither of you loves *me* anymore!"

"What are you doing crawling around in the bushes spying on us?" Mocking Bird demanded.

"You don't want me around!" Maize Gone Away shrieked. She put her hands over her face and fled, sobbing.

Mocking Bird looked at Others' Child, eyes wide.

"Go away!" Others' Child said, and he ran, too.

Others' Child pulled a loose piece of juniper from the roof thatch. Its scent bit at her nose. *I should have known better*, she thought. *I am the oldest. This was for me to see. I saw it the night I was a woman. I should have known.*

Bitch crawled out of the brush hut, stretching. She spread her toes and yawned. It was almost twilight, the time she liked to hunt.

"We will be no better than you," Others' Child said miserably to her. She picked at the juniper, deliberately pulling sprigs from it and flicking the torn-off pieces away with her fingers.

Bitch hung her tongue out with an expression that said being like her was not such a bad thing. She had had two more litters since the ones that had been born dead, but all of them were more coyote than dog and had taken to the wilds when they were seven or eight moons old. Bitch took her domestic responsibilities casually.

"Yah, you are a dirty coyote," Others' Child said.

Bitch whined. Others' Child thought she was protesting the insult until she saw that Bitch was looking at the ground. Then Bitch got up and began to pace, padding back and forth in front of the brush hut while Others' Child stared at her. She whined again. And then the low, growling, singsong voice that she used when she was threatened or angry came from her throat.

Others' Child stepped back a pace. The thought that Bitch might have gone mad flicked across her mind. "Bitch?" she whispered, frightened now.

Bitch swung her head around and looked at Others' Child. Her yellow eyes glowed. She began to turn in circles, as if she were trying to trample out a bed.

Others' Child backed up another step, and the ground twisted under her feet. She stumbled, righting herself with flailing arms. She felt as if she were standing on a log in the water, and her heart lurched with the ground. The earth shivered again and was still, deceptively so, as if it had not moved in the first place. Others' Child looked around for Mocking Bird and Maize Gone Away, and saw them running toward the camp, quarrel forgotten. They flung themselves at Others' Child, and the three of them stood, arms locked around each other, staring at the ground in terror.

Bitch had stopped turning in circles. She stood with all four paws braced until she was sure the earth was not going to quiver again, and then she trotted into the brush.

"She felt it," Others' Child said. "Before it happened. I thought she had gone mad."

"I felt it, too," Mocking Bird said. "When I was setting snares. I thought I was only sick to my stomach."

"What was it?" Maize Gone Away whimpered.

"I don't know," Others' Child said. "I have heard that in the old days the mountains walked about until they were in their proper places. Old Uncle told me."

"This isn't the old days," Maize Gone Away said, frightened.

The three of them looked about uneasily. Must they go someplace else again? This was home; they had made it so. But how could a place that moved under their feet be home? And how could it be home when

the things that crept into their dreams at night lately
lived there, too? Mocking Bird and Others' Child exchanged glances, wondering if their wickedness had
set the earth moving. Maize Gone Away didn't know
yet what evil had come upon them, but the other two
did, and it would be no wonder if they were sick with
it.

Incest was the greatest of the forbidden things. It
brought evil events and poisoned the whole land.
Marriages between members of the same clan were
not allowed, much less between sister and brother.
The intricacies of any one tribe member's relationship
to another were always remembered and could be explained by any old woman of the People, but this did
not even require explanation. And it did not matter
that Others' Child had been stolen from the Others.
She was of Found Water's clan now, and nothing else
made a difference.

Others' Child squeezed her eyes shut. This was her
fault, not to have known this would come upon them.
But how should she have known, before, when she
was still a child? Her coupling with Hears the Night
didn't count. It hadn't even been nice. (Then why was
she beginning to dream of it?)

Wordlessly, she picked up the fish that Maize Gone
Away had thrown at them and began to clean it.
Shamefaced, Maize Gone Away pulled the cooled
stones out of the water, put hot ones in, and tucked
the cooled ones under the coals to get hot again. "I
am sorry I shouted at you," she muttered.

"You are our sister," Others' Child said. "We love
you better than anybody." She pulled the guts out of
the fish and left them for Bitch to find when she returned from her wandering. Others' Child felt as if
someone were trying to do the same thing to her.

She wrapped the fish in a handful of summer
greens and cooked it in the water. After they had
eaten it, Mocking Bird took out his flute and played
for them. The music rose into smoky twilight. In a

while Bitch came home, licking her muzzle. She ate the fish guts hungrily and lay by the fire, breathing warm fish breath at them. Others' Child and Maize Gone Away had made drums from pieces of a hollow log and the deer's bladder, and they tapped them in time to the flute song, fingers fluttering on the drumskin. Slowly, as the darkness came down, the sense of wrongness slipped away, and they were as they had been. The earth was still. Its movement seemed a part of the other thing that had beset them. Surely now all was well.

When they lay down to sleep, though, something unspoken made them lie apart, still side by side but not flung across each other as they were used to doing. Bitch came and wedged herself between Mocking Bird and Maize Gone Away for their warmth, and Mocking Bird let her breathe fish entrails at him and didn't shove her away.

Others' Child, on Maize Gone Away's far side, lay stiffly, arms folded across her chest, listening to the night, wondering what they were going to do. The fire burning just outside the hut made slippery shadows on the brush walls. She kept thinking she saw something moving in the flames, like the girl who had married Fire. That girl had sunk down into her family's hearth to become one with the heart of the flame. Others' Child hadn't known what that story meant when Old Uncle had told it. She thought maybe she did now.

After a while her eyes closed, and opened again, and Coyote was sitting in front of the fire, its light turning his coat red-gold.

"If you human people are going to keep making rules about what you can do and what you can't do, you are going to have to think further ahead," he said.

"I have more sense than to make rules."

"That's all very well," Others' Child said crossly. Everyone knew that Coyote was shameless and would do anything. "But we have rules. And so what do we do now? Also, the earth is moving."

"It's just an appetite," Coyote said, ignoring movements of the earth. "Like wanting to eat a rabbit."

"Yah, you have no morals."

"That is a fine way to talk to your father."

"*You* are not my father!"

"How do you know?" Coyote inquired, grinning.

"Because our father was a proper man and didn't do it with his daughters," Others' Child said.

Coyote grinned more broadly. His shaggy hide was matted with burrs, and he smelled of old urine. He lifted his leg and made water on the door of the brush hut. She could see his penis, bright red. "You shouldn't have come into this valley, then," Coyote suggested. "If you don't like this way of doing things, you will have to go back to two-legged people."

Others' Child took a cold stone from the bottom of the cooking basket. "Go away or I'll throw rocks at you. We aren't your children."

"All people are my children," Coyote said. "When they go into the wild places."

"Then tell me why the ground is moving here."

"It's moving because something is moving it," Coyote said. "That is simple." He looked at her for a moment more, and then he was gone. Into the fire, Others' Child thought. She thought she saw the yellow eyes gleam behind the flames. Then they vanished, too.

In the morning, in the solidity of sunlight, he might not have been there at all. Bitch sniffed suspiciously at the place where Coyote had pissed on the hut door, but then she ignored it. Mocking Bird sat up and stretched, and Maize Gone Away crawled out from under the furs and began to poke up the fire.

The air outside was full of birds. Others' Child could hear their chatter in the trees and thought of the dawn voices at a Gathering—cheerful, sleepy, quarrelsome voices, blending together. How long had it been since she had been at a Gathering and watched the boys' initiation dance, and seen them beautiful and terrible with new power? And wanted them so that she ached between her legs? It was the way in which she had wanted Hears the Night. Or some boy.

Gold light pooled in the valley as the sun came up over the mountain. There was a slight breeze, and the grass flowed slowly in it, like honey. While she watched, it shimmered and changed so that it might have been a valley reflected in the still waters of a pool, motionless, enclosed in the water, with no voice to speak. She realized that the birds had gone silent.

She looked at the other two to see if they felt the silence and instead saw Bitch fling herself to her feet, paws scrabbling on the grass. She dived into the brush hut, circling and whining, and Others' Child knew now that it wasn't the madness but terror. There was only time to shriek to Mocking Bird and Maize Gone Away before the ground began to rock.

This time it rocked harder, heaving and buckling under them, and they could hear a roaring deep down below as if the First World were waking again. They clung to one another, cowering in the brush hut with Bitch while the earth swayed. A rumbling began high above them, and a rain of stones fell on the hut.

The juniper thatch came down under a big stone, pinning Mocking Bird's legs. Maize Gone Away and Others' Child clawed at it, fighting their way through the collapsed roof, the juniper scent thick in their throats. The branches raked against Others' Child's cheeks like hands. A broken roof pole, jagged-ended, protruded from the thatch and gouged her arm as she fell against it. Flung back and forth by the heaving earth, Others' Child shoved at the stone. Mocking Bird was thrashing under it, and under the thatch, pulling at the brush.

"*Help* me!" Others' Child screamed.

Maize Gone Away fought her way through the rubble and pushed, too. The stone rocked slightly. Mocking Bird groaned. They pushed again, and it rolled away with a thud. Mocking Bird limped to his feet while the ground kept shaking. Others' Child could feel the warm blood running down her face. Mocking Bird's lip was split open, his shins gashed by the roof poles and the stone. Bitch was limping on one foot.

Maize Gone Away staggered out of the wreckage, brushing twigs and thatch from her hair. Another stone fell beside her, rolling wildly in a circle as the ground heaved again. She looked up, and her eyes widened. Above them the mountain began to stand on end.

"Get away!"

They ran for the open valley, away from the rocks that tumbled and slid down the mountainside. It was hard to keep their balance. Mocking Bird fell on his face, staggered up, and plunged on. They splashed across the stream to the far side, and saw the water churning, the current roaring backward up its channel. The stones underfoot were slippery with old moss. Maize Gone Away fell to her knees and floundered, coughing up water. Others' Child grabbed her by the arms and pulled, feet braced against the sway of the riverbed.

They plunged through the sharp reeds that bordered the river, fleeing from it, convinced in their terror that it would suck them down, pull them into whatever maelstrom raged under the earth. On the open valley floor they stopped, breathing hard, and looked wildly back at the mountain. The earth had stilled, but their brush hut had vanished under a pile of stones, and more boulders still slid downward, bouncing and tumbling from a raw gash in the mountain's face. It was as if a giant hand with a fleshing knife had cut a piece from it, Others' Child thought.

The ground rocked again, and she screamed as it parted in front of them. A fissure like an angry mouth opened the length of the valley floor, cutting diagonally from a sinkhole near the river to the far mountains. Where it crossed the valley it had opened nearly at their feet. They stared into it in horror. An arm's length wide, it sank into the heart of the earth, who knew how deep. Bitch growled at it as if something lived there. The earth gave a final shudder and was still.

They backed away from the chasm, their legs like water, waiting for the ground to shake again, for the chasm to open and swallow them. Everyone belonged to Coyote in the wild lands, Others' Child thought. Was that what he had meant last night?

They looked backwards the way they had come. "Everything is *gone!*" Maize Gone Away said with a sob. A final stone dropped onto the hill of rock that had buried the hut. Its clattering progress filled the still valley.

The knowledge came home to the other two. Food, clothing, tools, weapons, all that they had painstakingly carried away from the Yellow Grass People and made in their years alone—all were buried in stone. Hungry, nearly naked, they had nothing left but the maize in the field, and it wouldn't ripen for a moon. If the convulsions in the earth hadn't torn it from the ground, Others' Child thought.

"We have to find a new place," she whispered. "We have to get away from *that* thing." She eyed the opening in the ground.

"We have to dig down to our hut," Mocking Bird said.

"We can't," Maize Gone Away said. "It's too much rock. And what if more of the mountain comes down?"

"What if you have no spear and nothing to eat?" Mocking Bird said.

Maize Gone Away started to cry. "It's too many stones."

"No," Mocking Bird said gently. He wiped away

some of the blood from her face. "It is only stones. We will move them one at a time."

Others' Child saw that he had decided. She felt too weary to argue with him, and maybe he was right. But the valley wanted them gone, she was sure of that. When they had their possessions, such as had not been crushed in the earth's mouth, then they would go. The valley would hurry them along, she thought. Nothing here was stable now, and nothing was safe.

Night Hawk had just time to run before the cave roof fell in. He dived beneath a falling shower of stone, tugging old Leaf Fall by the arm while the mountain rattled. Behind him he could hear screaming and the roaring of the rocks. A great cloud of dust rose up all along the sandstone cliffs while they shook themselves into a new shape. Cave mouths disappeared as if behind no-longer-open lips. New holes gaped, jaws wide. Wing Foot caromed into him out of the dust, his eyes wild. Leaf Fall pulled away from Night Hawk's grip and knelt on the heaving ground, her head buried under her hands.

"No, you can't stay here!" Night Hawk hauled her up again. The ground trembled and slid. A boulder as big as his chest rolled by. He yanked her out of its way.

"Get away from the caves!" Wing Foot shouted. He grabbed a shrieking child and pointed it away from the rubble.

"Mama!" it shouted, turning back.

"Run that way!" Wing Foot turned it around again, but the child stood paralyzed, face screwed up in fright.

"Take it away from here," Night Hawk said, pushing the child at Leaf Fall. She stared at the child as if it were a fish and then grabbed it by the hand and lumbered away with it. A stone shelf collapsed where she had been standing.

Whatever was beneath the earth was trying to get out. It shook the walls of its prison. The ground sank under their feet. Night Hawk fell, clawing his way out of a hole that had not been there before and was already closing up again. It would eat him if it could. He scrabbled frantically, his face in the rubble as he kicked against stones that slid away under his feet. A pair of hands lifted him under the shoulders and pulled him free. He fell against Wing Foot, and they staggered away from the caves, weaving as if they were drunk.

The ground continued to heave, and then with one last long shudder it was still. Dust choked the air, rising in clouds from the rubble. A wailing sob like a wolf howling pierced the screams of mothers and children hunting for one another. A woman clawed at the rocks that blocked her cave mouth. After a moment she sat back on her heels and howled again.

As the dust settled it coated everything, a fine layer of breath blown out of the earth and sifting down like dry rain. Night Hawk's hair was gray with it, his hands powdered with sand. The Kindred milled fearfully at a distance from their caves, asking each other what it meant, what had happened, who was missing. The roaring in the earth had certainly been the gods speaking, they told each other, but the Three Old Men must tell them what was said.

Night Hawk had felt the wrongness in the mountains. Now he stepped gingerly on the ground, from foot to foot, to see if it had gone away; if this had been its voice; if it were sated now. He didn't think so.

Behind him the woman was still wailing at the blocked cave. She had dug away enough rock to expose a small, still hand. Her own hands were bleeding.

The Kindred counted their dead but could not release them. Two children and their mother lay buried

in one cave, a third child, the one whose hand her
mother had dug free, in another. But no one could
move the stones that pinned the rest of the girl, and
finally they had covered up the hand again while the
mother wailed.

A dozen others were bruised and bloodied, one
with a broken leg that might or might not heal; the
Old Man of the Healers looked grim over it. At night
they huddled around fires out of reach of the cave
mouths, afraid to go back in. A stone had fallen from
the roof of Rain Old Man's cave as he went to get his
rain stone to look through—all matters of the earth
were the province of the Rainmakers—and had nearly
brained him. He had come from the cave puffing, eyes
wide, and sat down at a good distance. Others went
inside the cave and could see small stones dribbling
down from the hole in the roof.

In the morning the Three Old Men told the Kindred
how it must be.

"There is a wound in the earth now," Rain Old Man
said. "I have seen it from far away."

"And the stream is going dry," Deer Old Man said.
"It may be that the stream is going into the wound."

It might be that it was blocked by rocks upstream,
too, Night Hawk thought, but that amounted to the
same thing.

"Soon we will have no water," Healer Old Man
said. "And worse, there is a passage between the Upper World and the dead who live below."

All eyes widened, and Night Hawk shifted uncomfortably in his place by the fire. That was dangerous;
all manner of things might come out of such an
opening. The dead might come back for the people
they had loved. He shuddered. To be loved by the
dead was to die.

"The earth must be sewn up," Healer Old Man
said. "One of us must run along the edges of the
wound, and along the edges of our land, and sew it
back up before the dead come back to live with us."

"I will go," Wing Foot said. He looked proud of himself. It was dangerous—who knew what spirits and creatures he might encounter?—but he was the swiftest runner among the Kindred. The girls looked at him admiringly.

"No," said Healer Old Man.

"Why not?" Wing Foot was indignant.

"You must run for us and for the Turquoise Band, too, for all the Kindred. It must be one who has lived among both, and among the False People who inhabit the edges of the world. The runner must go beyond our hunting grounds. Therefore it shall be Night Hawk the Trader."

"I can outrun Night Hawk on one foot!" Wing Foot looked outraged.

"It is not a race!" Rain Old Man snapped.

Night Hawk stood up, dusting off his backside. He felt foolish for not having known what the Three Old Men were up to. He recalled saying that he always left matters of importance to them, but now he wished he could change his mind about that. Still, they must know. And if it was not done right, the world might end. "I am honored that the Three Old Men entrust me with this," he said.

"You must be purified first," Deer Old Man said. "And taught what you are to do."

Night Hawk managed to suppress a groan of protest. Being purified always meant being starved first. But he would do what they told him, for if the world ended, he would undoubtedly be hungry all the time.

The brush shelter was smoky, thick with the scent of resin from burning pine cones and green branches, shadowy with the darkness outside. Healer Old Man held up his hand like an apparition in the smoke. Pine sprigs crowned his head, and he looked like a tree walking. Deer Old Man chanted solemnly, antlers swaying up and down.

*"You will go, we send you out.*
*You will run far, we send you out.*
*You will come home, we send you out."*

Rain Old Man drew a stripe of wet red mud on either side of Night Hawk's face. His own face was entirely covered in it, a living mask of clay.

*"You will sew up the earth.*
*You will ask of the animal people,*
*You will ask of the gods,*
*You will ask of the earth*
*What it is they wish of us.*
*You will drive evil back within its dwelling,*
*You will sew up the earth."*

They led him to the door of the shelter, and it was like coming up from below ground. He took a deep breath of the clear, cold night air and began to run.

Hears the Night lifted a stone in his hands and set it to one side. He bent and raised another, his back aching. His hands were blistered raw, and he could see smears of blood on the stones as he set them down. The tip of his great tooth protruded from the pile of broken rock as if the whole of the creature who had worn it lay under there, too. What else might they find rising up from the stones as they dug? Wind Caller might come riding on its back, Hears the Night thought, seeing in his mind's eye a dark figure clinging to a monstrous form, fire springing from his fingertips.

The Yellow Grass People knew now that they had done evil. It didn't take Hears the Night to tell them. The earth had shaken, burying some of them, Runner and her child among them, and when they had begun to dig out, another cave had collapsed like a closing fist around Cat Ears and his wife, Silent. Cat Ears had clawed his way out as the roof fell in, but Silent had

not. Only Deer Shadow had not been touched. Caught
the Moon had run screaming out of her cave, stam-
peding away from the cliffs to huddle with the rest
on the dance ground, clutching one another while the
earth itself danced. When the ground had stopped
moving and she had crept back, she had found the
madwoman sitting perfectly still on her bed of hides,
not even a smashed grinding stone or an overturned
basket in the cave.

Hears the Night knew that to be shaman was to
have no defense against knowledge, even when the
knowledge that came was unwelcome—even if it said
you had done wrong and must somehow set it right.
The ghost of the one they had killed had come up out
of the ground. He must be placated or captured. Either way he must be returned to the ground. None of
the Yellow Grass People would go near the place
where Wind Caller's children had buried him, but it
was clear that the spirit was no longer with the body.
It roamed free now, broken loose from this world and
from the house of the dead. The Yellow Grass People
looked to him, to Hears the Night, to defeat it.

That seemed as hopeless a task as digging free his
great tooth. Hears the Night closed his eyes, praying
for a vision, but none came. He opened them again,
sighed, and took hold of the end of the tooth. He set
his feet against the stone floor and pulled. It moved
a handbreadth. A little trickle of rocks ran down the
pile that buried it. Hears the Night cleared them away
and rolled a few more after them, then tried again. A
shadow fell across the rocks, a figure with a flute to
its lips. Hears the Night spun around, looking behind
him at nothing.

"You can speak," Hears the Night said to Deer
Shadow. "You spoke to One Ball."

Deer Shadow's eyes narrowed slightly, but she
didn't answer.

"I have been wrong," Hears the Night said slowly.

"I tell you that so you will know I come to you in good faith."

She looked at him, and a tear slid out of the corner of her eye. She looked away.

"Your man has come up from underground for vengeance," Hears the Night said. "Or he has sent something," he added.

She looked at the empty space next to her, stared at it in what appeared to be a desperate concentration, as if trying to see through it or past it. When she spoke, her voice startled him.

"He isn't here now," she said sadly. "He's only here then."

"Tell us what we must do," Hears the Night said.

Deer Shadow shook her head. Her tangled hair hung loose over her shoulders. It caught her attention for a moment, and she combed at the knots with her fingers. Then she seemed to forget them, her eyes straying back to Hears the Night. She looked surprised to see him. "I don't know what you can do about what you have done," she said. "I would tell you if I knew."

She watched him leave and knew that he believed her. She wasn't sure she believed herself. It wasn't that she didn't know so much as that she couldn't know, could no longer see the Yellow Grass People clearly. She felt herself slipping away, like the stones in the earthquake, toward some other place where the Yellow Grass People would no longer be her concern. She looked around the cave and saw that it was growing transparent, as Wind Caller had done. Now, even when she watched him, she could see through him.

"There are more ways to make the world obey you," Spider said from over the door. She spoke with Listens to Deer's voice, and Deer Shadow looked up eagerly.

"I can't make him stay anymore," she said. "You must tell me how. The little shaman couldn't tell me how. He wants *me* to tell *him* things."

"Maybe you should have," Spider said.

"I don't know them anymore," Deer Shadow said. "What they are afraid of is what I want."

Spider hung upside down in her web. "They have good reason to be afraid. Shall I tell you a story?"

"Will it bring him back?" Deer Shadow asked her. She didn't care whether they were afraid.

"Not exactly," Spider said. "But you had better hear it."

*Well, once when the world was younger than it is now, there were two most magical people: a young man whose name was First Hunter because he never returned empty-handed from the hunt, and a woman named Morning Light, who wove the most beautiful baskets, baskets so magical that when they were filled with food they seemed never to empty themselves. Now, these were also the handsomest couple among the People, and it was no surprise to anyone that they sought each other out. Plainly they were favored by the gods. Everyone said so. And everyone expected them to marry.*

*But what everyone says has a way of turning out to be the truth in ways that you don't count on. Once they were married, they did not spend less and less time with each other like proper people, but more and more. Instead of finding food for his tribe, First Hunter spent all his time with his wife. When the hunters would call for him in the dawn light to come and run after the deer with them, he would shout at them to go away, and then he would climb back in bed with Morning Light. And as for Morning Light, when the women came to get her to go with them to dig camas bulbs and gather berries, she would be flat on her back instead. Everyone said it was disgraceful, but these two didn't care. When the shaman spoke to them, they laughed at him and called him bad names. When the chieftain called to them to come and be ashamed of themselves, they ran away.*

*Because they were behaving so badly, the tribe began to be afraid that the gods would be angry and something bad would happen. But First Hunter and Morning Light ignored them all, and like foolish lovers swore to each other that nothing would ever part them.*

Now, that is not a good thing to swear where Coyote may hear you, or any other of the gods who might be angry enough to take notice of bad manners.

The next thing that happened was that Morning Light fell sick, and no matter what the shaman did or how many times he tried to suck the sickness from her, nothing worked, and in three days she was dead. First Hunter's grief flooded the whole tribe. He refused to eat or even speak, and he sat by his wife's body talking to it until the shaman and the chieftain had to forbid him to stay any longer. They drove him out with sticks, and after that he wandered about the camp, disconsolate and calling her name, which made everyone in the tribe cross their fingers and hide.

It is hard to say who heard him, whether it was Coyote or Morning Light herself. But somebody did.

Now, at the end of four days, the spirit leaves the body, and that is when the body is burned so that the spirit cannot become confused and try to return. On the morning of the fourth day, First Hunter was skulking about the edges of the camp, weeping, when he saw a fire near a clump of greasewood bushes. He came closer, and there was Morning Light, combing her long black hair with a bone comb, in a fine dress of white deerskin, getting ready for her journey to the Skeleton House. Love makes men foolish, always, but none so foolish as First Hunter, who fell down weeping at his dead wife's feet and begged her not to leave him.

"I can't stay here," Morning Light said when he grabbed her hand. "I don't belong to this world now, and I won't be beautiful very much longer. The spirits will be angry with us."

"We promised each other that nothing would ever part us!" First Hunter said. "I love you! I will always love you. I refuse to let anything separate us."

"You are making a mistake," Morning Light said.

First Hunter grabbed her hand again. It was cool and smooth to the touch. "I won't ever leave you," he said.

"If you promise me that, you will have to keep it."

And First Hunter promised, so she gave in and let him take her back to their people's camp. When they arrived, the people were just going to the cave to get her body and burn it, and they were horrified when they saw her walking hand in hand with First Hunter.

The chieftain and the shaman and First Hunter's parents and Morning Light's parents all begged him to let her go, but he set his mouth in a stubborn line and said he wouldn't. He took her into their cave, and the rest of the tribe sat down to wait for the next awful thing to happen.

First Hunter and Morning Light began to lead their lives as they always had, making love to each other most of the day, and doing some work when they had to. But after a day or two, First Hunter began to notice that his wife was developing an unpleasant odor. Then her skin grew dry and gray. He began to spend more time hunting, and more time with the men of the tribe like a proper man. When he came home at night, though, Morning Light would cling to him and want to make love. He tried turning his back on her, and then when the odor became unbearable, he began going out on the dance ground to sit up all night. But Morning Light always joined him.

By now she was almost nothing but skin and bones, and the tribe would often see him racing past the midden or the maize field with Morning Light in pursuit. They shook their heads and crossed their fingers at both of them, and began to tell the shaman that something had to be done. To have dead people living among them was not right.

As for First Hunter, he was beginning to wish that he had never made any promises about eternal fidelity to Morning Light.

"I have to hunt today," he would tell her.

"I don't need any food to eat," she would answer him.

"*Come and make love to me instead, the way you said you would always want to.*"

"Well, I don't want to now," he had to admit.

"Coward!" Morning Light said. "You promised me. Now you don't want to keep your promise." Her skin was as thin as a film of water over her bones. Her eyes were sunk back in her head. Her teeth protruded. She smelled like the midden.

"I can't!" First Hunter wailed, agonized. He began to run away from the camp, and she darted after him.

That was when the shaman came out of his cave with two spears and his spear-thrower. He was having his morning stretch, loosening his back muscles on the edge of the dance ground, when First Hunter caromed into him.

"Oof!" said the shaman. "And where do you think you are going?"

"I am running from Morning Light," First Hunter said.

"There is only one place you can run away from the dead," the shaman said. "And that is up into the sky. I told you that something bad would happen. Why didn't you listen?"

"Just help me," First Hunter said. "Please. And I am sorry I didn't listen."

"Well, you'll have to climb on my spear, then," the shaman told him, "so I can throw you into the sky. There is no place you can hide from her here."

So First Hunter climbed onto the shaman's spear and held tightly, while the shaman nocked it into his spear-thrower and cocked his arm back.

"Please hurry," First Hunter said. "I can see her coming."

The shaman threw the spear, and the shaft went up into the air with First Hunter on it, piercing through the blue sky until it could no longer be seen.

"Well," the shaman said, dusting off his hands as Morning Light came flying onto the dance ground, her bones rattling. "And what do you want?"

"I am looking for First Hunter," Morning Light said. "He promised to stay with me always, and now he doesn't want to."

"Well, he's up in the sky now," the shaman said craftily.

"In the sky!" Morning Light looked at the shaman's spear and spear-thrower. "Will you throw me up there, too?"

"Certainly," the shaman said. He put Morning Light on his second spear and told her to hold on. Then he threw her up into the sky after First Hunter.

That very evening the People saw two new stars in the west. The first, very big and bright, began to run east across the sky, with the second, a little flickering star, pursuing close behind it. And they are there to this day, the bones of Morning Light chasing her still-living husband across the sky, and she is still dead, and now he cannot die.

"And," said Spider, pointing one long, jointed leg out the cave mouth to the west, "there they still are. Because they wouldn't accept What Is. If they had behaved themselves, they would have been together eventually where the dead people go."

Deer Shadow looked down at the empty space beside her. For a moment she thought she saw bones in it. "And is that what is happening to me?" she asked Spider.

"Maybe," Spider said. "I don't know what is going on inside you. Nobody does but you. And it is only a story. But I would be careful. When you ask Coyote for things, it is dangerous."

"Coyote, pah! I have no use for Coyote," Deer Shadow said. But she knew it wasn't true. She could smell him every time she tried to conjure up Wind Caller. "*He* tries to take him away from me."

"It doesn't matter," Spider said. "He is there, and you are playing with things you have no business with. There are rules. You have to follow them, or Coyote will own the world."

"I only want my husband back," Deer Shadow said plaintively, as if that were not unreasonable. "I wasn't through with him."

Spider made an irritated hiss through her teeth, and Deer Shadow could tell quite clearly that Listens to Deer was no longer there. This was Grandmother Spider herself, older than the world. "You can't have that," Spider said. "And you will unbalance the world if you go on trying."

Deer Shadow put her hands to her face. Grandmother Spider hung low in her great web, and her eyes were like two points of flame. In the corners of the Universe, where the web was anchored, four of her eight feet rested. Even Coyote cowered, flattened and cringing, on one of the moon-washed spokes of the great web.

# IX

# Sewing Up the Earth

Night Hawk was running. His feet slapped rhythmically at the hard, dry ground, making a sound like hands on drums. He had run through the red hills, and the tumbled yellow stone, danced among the hot springs whose waters bubbled bewildered from new holes. His path was the border between his people's land and the land of the Trespassers; maybe it would go beyond that still, if the tear in the earth led that way—maybe east to the land of the Buffalo Hunters or west toward the coast. Who knew where the hole in the earth went?

The Three Old Men had seen it from afar, but Night Hawk saw it up close—a deep, jagged snake-shape sunk in the ground. The little dry grasses whispered at its edges. *It is down there*, they said. When Night Hawk asked them, "What is down there?" they only rippled in the wind.

The dead lived beneath the flat waters of a lake in

the north. Everyone knew that, even the Trespassers. The rift in the earth ran south. But water could flow beneath the earth—Night Hawk had seen springs bubble from the rock, had seen a river flow away into the ground and come out miles away, had in curiosity once put a red-painted stick in the water to prove it. And if water could flow in subterranean paths, then why not the spirit people, they who needed no food or even air to travel? When the ground opened at the surface, would they not smell it, the clean air they no longer breathed but remembered? Would they not come, bones tumbling through the underground river passages, clattering in mysterious corridors, to rise through the rent in the earth?

*And what then*, Night Hawk thought, *when they are so many more than we, so powerful and angry?* For who would not be angry, living in that dim, cold world beneath the flat waters through which no one could ascend, knowing that above you the sun shone warm and the barewood trees had exploded in pink blossoms? They would find their ways through the earth and come out through this crack unless he, Night Hawk, sewed it up.

He traveled light, no more than journey food in the pack on his back, no greenstone necklaces to trade, no bone combs, no furs, no shells from creatures who swam the mysterious depths of the Endless Water. And even so he felt too burdened down to outdistance what might come leaping and buzzing and wailing through the rent in the valley floor. Night Hawk made himself slow his pace, resist the urge to sprint past his terror. His feet were a steady rhythm again now, slap, slap, like bone needle and sinew thread, sewing up the earth deep below where the walking mountains had pulled it apart.

Every so often the ground seemed to tremble under his feet as if the dead fought back against the slow closure of the earth over their heads. Night Hawk's heart would lurch, and he would peer down into the fissure, eyes wide, dancing on tiptoe, ready to flee whatever came out. But nothing did, and the rift grew no wider, and at last he came to the end of it, breathing hard.

From here the way grew more difficult, but his feet felt light away from that chasm, through which he might have dropped clear to the heart of the earth. He began to climb out of the valley, through yucca-dotted slopes and then oak and cypress and piñon pine. The ground here was tumbled, the deer trails obliterated with rockfalls that still slid beneath his feet and the bare roots of an oak clawing at the sky: trying to pull itself upright, Night Hawk thought, eyeing it uneasily. Upside-down things, inverted things, were dangerous; they had the power to turn the world the wrong way. The sky above the crest burned with a flat yellow disk of sun that threw the shadows of the tree's roots across a scree of loose stone, so that they looked like snakes writhing, burrowing through its surface. Around the sun the sky shimmered with a fierce whiteness, edging into blue. Everything seemed flattened and elongated to Night Hawk, and the hawk shape that rode the updraft above him winked in and out, a black speck in the dazzle.

His lungs burned, and he took slow, deep breaths as he started down the other side of the crest. This was familiar land to him, trails he had taken to trade with the Turquoise Band of the Kindred, and with the Trespassers. But it was out of its proper shape somehow, as if he were looking at it through water. A mouse shot out of the rocks under his feet, leaping like a grasshopper, and skittered down the slope. A little trickle of pebbles followed it. He came upon the spoor of a puma, and then upon a dead deer, ribs broken in the rockfall, belly half eaten away. He could see where the puma had tried to pull it out of the rockfall. The hawk screamed to another out of the blinding whiteness.

The way changed. The path steepened abruptly.

Night Hawk put his feet carefully. Sweat dripped from his brow into his eyes. He pulled a deerskin strap from his pack and knotted it about his temples as he ran. The valley below him shimmered in the heat, wavering the way the ground did at midsummer. His stomach lurched, and he shook his head, trying to rid himself of the sensation that *everything* was quivering. The stones slid under his feet, and the mountain rumbled. Night Hawk fought for balance, but the ground dropped away under him as if he had stepped from a ledge. He slid, rolling sideways down the slope, arms flailing for some handhold. The spiny branches of a thornbush tore through them. The ground heaved and buckled again and threw him, the intruder, from its breast.

Night Hawk felt himself falling, dropping through the bright air, and then there was a pain in his head and darkness. Strange creatures with gold eyes flitted near him, leaving glittering tracks, but none paused to investigate the interloper spread-eagled on their mountain.

Mocking Bird and his sisters dug through the rubble that had buried their brush hut a stone at a time, a full two days' work, weeping and cursing in their frustration while Bitch sniffed at the ruins and whined. Then they laid out their possessions in a battered row, to salvage the usable from the broken. Most of the baskets were crushed, and Mocking Bird's spear-thrower had cracked. When he hefted it, it bent suddenly in the middle, and he cursed it.

Maize Gone Away dug with the determination of a burrow dog until she had cleared the rubble from atop the storage pit and dug her hoarded seed from it. Others' Child collected the remnants of their life here, the cracked shell bowls, the hides and furs, the poles of Bitch's travois, the grinding stone that had just begun to take on the proper concave shape.

"We are leaving," she said fiercely. "We are going from this place. It is not a place for us."

The other two didn't argue. Their fear was already telling them to run. So the three hung their packs on their backs and left their valley and the stand of unripe maize, fleeing from the hole in the ground that Others' Child feared would swallow them.

They were near the chasm when the next tremor came, and they ran from its open mouth in stark terror. Others' Child had been right. The ground would eat them if they stayed here. The valley was no longer home but had transformed itself into a living predator, feeding on its inhabitants. When the ground stilled, they began walking toward the mountains.

The question of where they would go was in all their minds, but no one asked it. They would just go, and maybe a way would be shown to them. If they asked, there might not be an answer.

The buzzards, too, were waiting for an answer. The earth had tipped and left them many things to feed on, but now most of those things were gone, and the predators whose leavings they relied on had scattered in fear. The buzzards' great black-winged shapes rode the thermals, waiting somewhat less than patiently, their splayed wingtips wheeling black fingers against the sun.

"Look at them," Maize Gone Away said. "They've found something. Ugh."

"Everything eats something," Others' Child said, forcing nonchalance into her voice, but she didn't like the buzzards, either. Buzzard was an opportunist, not even willing to kill his own prey. That seemed to her to be cheating.

Mocking Bird watched the black birds settling in the distance. "At least they aren't following *us*," he said, trying to make a joke of it. Two more had joined the others, these still riding high on the thermals. As they watched, the first ones rose again to join them,

with ponderous flaps of their wings. "Not quite dead
yet," Mocking Bird said.

"Maybe they aren't really buzzards." Maize Gone
Away bit her lip. She had realized that their descent
into the next valley was going to take them beneath
the hovering shapes. "Maybe they came out of the
ground. They might be dead people, looking for a
way back in."

"Or looking for someone to take with them," Mocking Bird said harshly. "Don't talk about it."

"They are buzzards," Others' Child insisted, because she wanted to believe they were. "And whatever they are watching isn't dead yet. Maybe we can
eat it."

"We will go and see," Mocking Bird said, and
Maize Gone Away stopped arguing. Hunger was
growing greater than fear.

They moved cautiously down the slope and saw the
buzzards light again in the thicket of thornbush and
stunted oaks below them. From here the trail dropped
away sharply, torn off the mountain by the last
tremor, the exposed faces of the earth still damp. The
birds settled with a great flapping of wings.

"Go away!" Others' Child shouted, and threw rocks
at them. The three inched down the slope, sliding on
their backsides. Bitch scrambled ahead, her travois
bumping behind her, spilling all the packs. She
growled, and the buzzards flapped their great wings
at her and hissed. Mocking Bird and Maize Gone
Away ran after her, shouting, grabbing at the packs
and harness.

"Wait, you fool!" Maize Gone Away untied the harness while Bitch danced impatiently. As it slipped free
she launched herself into the flock and disappeared
in a maelstrom of beating wings. The three humans
threw more rocks, and in a few moments the buzzards scattered, lifting in lumbering flight. Bitch, a
feather clinging to her jaws, snapped after the last one
as it rose. Two more feathers spiraled through the air.

Others' Child pushed her way into the thicket and stopped. Maize Gone Away and Mocking Bird collided with her back.

"What is it?" Maize Gone Away demanded.

It wasn't an animal. "Sssh!" Others' Child said. "It's a man."

Bitch had gone behind her legs. Now she stuck her gray nose out far enough to growl.

"Is it one of ours?" Mocking Bird asked. "I mean, one of the People?"

"I don't think so," Others' Child said. She crept forward cautiously.

"Let me go." Mocking Bird shouldered her aside, spear in hand.

"No!" She grabbed his shoulder.

"I'm the man!"

"I'm the oldest. And he's hurt. I want to look at him, not have you run your spear through him as soon as he twitches." The man lay facedown under a stunted oak. She thought she could see blood in his short-cropped hair.

Mocking Bird took a closer look. "He's one of the Others!" he hissed. His hand tightened on his spear.

"We belong to no people now," Others' Child said. "And besides, I want to look at him." She had never seen a man of the Others close up. And this was the first human of any kind they had encountered since they had left the Yellow Grass People. Theoretically speaking, the Others weren't humans at all, but she found that hard to reconcile with the fact that she had been born to them. Perhaps they could become human, as she had done. And she wanted to look at this one.

Mocking Bird was sulking—he wanted to kill the man, Others' Child thought—but he stood back while she knelt in the dry foxtail grass and peered. There *was* blood in the man's hair, a lot of it. It was still sticky, and she could feel the cut in his scalp; enough to have knocked him out, she thought, but probably not to kill him. He was still breathing, making a harsh noise through his nose, which had most likely kept the buzzards at bay.

"You are lucky," she said to him. "They would have got tired of waiting pretty soon." She got her arms under his chest and tried to turn him over. His inert weight was heavier than it looked. "Come and help me."

Maize Gone Away shook her head, peering at the stranger fearfully. Bitch continued her singsong growl, the feather still dangling from her snout.

"He is too hurt to move," Others' Child said crossly. "How is he going to harm you?" She tugged again and managed to get him on his back. This time Maize Gone Away came forward and craned her neck at him. Mocking Bird stood with his spear ready in case the man got up.

He had a beaky nose, bigger than those of the People, and strange short hair like a woman at her initiation. He wore only a deerskin breechclout, yucca sandals, and the leather band around his forehead. They stared at him for a while before they noticed that his deerskin pack had fallen not far from him in the thornbushes. Others' Child got up and retrieved it gingerly. She upended it on the ground and found some dried meat and grass-seed meal and a pouch full of dried berries.

They snatched at the meat, stuffing their mouths with it. Bitch stuck her nose in between them and gobbled the scraps.

"At least he had food," Mocking Bird said, his chin smeared with berries.

"I don't think he's been here long," Others' Child said. "Someone may come looking for him. We can't stay."

"Take his pack," Mocking Bird said. "It may be useful."

"No!" Others' Child stamped her foot. "It is bad

enough to steal his food. I am going to see to his head so he doesn't die."

"Why?" Maize Gone Away said. It was a reasonable question. Bitch stuck her nose closer to the man and growled again. His eyelids flickered.

"Because I have been thinking," Others' Child said.

"And what have you been thinking, oh Most Wise?" her brother inquired. "That now we should rescue demons?"

"He isn't a demon," Others' Child said, irritated. "*I* am not a demon, and our people have traded with these people. Maybe with this one," she added. There was something a little familiar about him, but then the men of the Others all looked alike to her. Still, she had always taken notice of them, curious. "Get me my pack," she said over her shoulder to Maize Gone Away. "The one Bitch was carrying. With my medicine bag."

"Bitch tipped it off the travois. Trying to bite buzzards."

"Well, find it," Others' Child muttered, exploring the stranger's scalp again with careful fingers.

Maize Gone Away made a face at her and said, "Yes, oh Greatness." But she scrambled back toward the slope and found it. The contents were scattered in the grass. The herb bundle that was Others' Child's medicine bag was still closed, tied with a piece of sinew and a blue stone with a hole through the middle. It smelled like a combination of magic and the bitter tea that Mother had made them drink for coughs. Maize Gone Away stuffed the rest of the salvaged tools and clothes back into the pack and took the medicine bundle to Others' Child.

The stranger moaned and tried to move. Others' Child held him down with one hand. Now that she was that close, Maize Gone Away couldn't resist staring at him. His eyes tipped up a little at the corners, and his body was angular. He looked bony to her compared to the People. Maize Gone Away's gaze slid involuntarily toward her sister, all sharp angles of hips and shoulder blades as she bent over him.

Others' Child opened the medicine bundle and thought about its contents. Boneroot in a poultice was good for wounds, and so was mountain balm. She had those. First she would wash it and put ground lizard-tail root into it, she decided. That often kept a wound from going bad. She told Mocking Bird and Maize Gone Away to find her some water and bring her grinding stone, and whistled quietly between her teeth while they did, still thinking.

Maize Gone Away fetched the grinding stone. By the time Mocking Bird, grumbling, had spotted a stand of cottonwoods down the valley and loped off to see if they meant water—he refused to let Others' Child use the last of the water in their waterskin for the stranger—Others' Child had ground the dried lizard-tail root and set it aside in a turtle shell unearthed from another pack.

Maize Gone Away collected the rest of their scattered belongings and loaded them back on the travois, scolding Bitch while she did for being a dirty wild coyote. Bitch didn't seem to mind.

Others' Child felt a certain kinship with Bitch. She folded her legs under her and sat cross-legged, watching the man. This one was of her blood. The thought jolted her that he might even be related to her. Was this how Bitch felt when she heard the coyotes sing and bit through her rope at night to go with them? For the first time Others' Child wondered what her life might have been like had she not come to Found Water's clan. She tried to imagine that other life, a ghost existence parallel to her own, but the image eluded her. It shimmered on the edge of her vision, just out of sight. She stared at the man, wondering what would happen if he woke and talked to her.

Mocking Bird plopped the waterskin down beside her. "I brought us fresh," he said. "You can use the stale water on *him*."

Others' Child poured a little into her hand and dribbled it onto the cut on the man's head. It was a gash as wide as her palm, just over his temple.

"Hold his hair away from it." She poured water directly from the waterskin as Mocking Bird flattened the stiff dark hair back from the wound. The stranger said something and opened his eyes. She poured more water on him. The dried blood began to come away from the wound. It dripped across his face, leaving tracks on the dusty skin. Under the dust she could see fading stripes of red clay pointing upward from mouth to nose. The dark eyes looked at her for a moment and closed again.

Others' Child blew on the wound to dry it, hoping it wouldn't start bleeding again. Cuts on the head always bled horribly. Old Looks Back had said that was because you lived in your head, and so that was where you needed the most blood. Others' Child wondered if she ought to close up the edges with a thorn, but she was afraid the man would wake up again. So instead she dribbled the powdered lizard-tail root into the cut between her thumb and forefinger, and when no more blood welled out, used the empty bowl to make a poultice out of boneroot leaves and mountain balm and the rest of the stale water. It made a green gelatinous sludge, which she began to pack into the wound with her fingertip. Bitch came up and sat beside her, suspicious and protective. She had quit growling, but her ears were flat and her yellow-gray ruff stood up on the back of her neck.

"It's none of your business," Others' Child told her.

Night Hawk woke to find a coyote watching him. The gold-eyed creatures that had trotted through his dreams had coalesced into this one, and it looked very real. Where had the woman gone? There had been a woman before. She had held him down and done something to his head.

He tried to sit up, and the woman reappeared, her

face bent over his, a long fall of black hair brushing his shoulders. She said something as she pushed him back down, but his ears couldn't make sense of it. She might have been a ghost woman out of the rift in the ground, speaking a ghost language. He shuddered and hoped she wasn't.

She was putting something on his head, which hurt with a dull throbbing that dimmed his vision. Over her shoulder the coyote watched him, its yellow eyes as baleful as the low hum that came from its throat. Night Hawk closed his eyes, and the blackness behind them was spangled with gold lights like more eyes. His head felt as if he had spent a week drunk on cactus juice, and he wondered if he had, before he spun off again into that blackness, where all the glittering eyes came out like stars. Maybe that was where the coyote had come from, out of a skin of cactus juice.

He woke again in the dawn chill, with the sun just creeping over the top of the mountain. He was shivering, teeth chattering with the cold that came down at night in the high desert even in summer.

Night Hawk tried to sit up, and the sun and the mountains spun around him. His stomach heaved, and the pain in his head was pounding like a stone. He lay back and looked around him carefully. He lay in a thicket of scrub oak and thornbushes at the bottom of a rockfall. He knew he was on his back because through the twisted limbs of the oaks he could see the sky, turning a hard bright blue as the sun rose. He lowered his eyes, and when he saw his pack on the ground near his feet, a certain amount of memory returned. He had been stitching up the earth. Night Hawk groaned and sat up, successfully this time, although his head spun. He had been stitching up the earth and what—?

He could see the sheared-off face of the slope above him. Apparently the earth had protested the process of being stitched. Or the dead underneath it had. He wondered uneasily if *he* were dead now. Maybe the woman had been a ghost. She was beginning to come back into his memory. She wasn't anyone he knew, and her speech had been strange. Something odd about it; he couldn't think what. There had been a coyote. That wasn't a good sign.

Night Hawk moved his arms and legs gingerly. They seemed to work, but they were battered black and blue with bruises and abrasions. He remembered wondering if he had been drunk, but now he didn't think so. The Three Old Men had sent him out to sew up the earth, and they wouldn't have supplied him with cactus juice. He saw blood in the grass where his head had been. Night Hawk looked at the broken trail above him again and put his hand to his scalp.

It came away with something cold and clammy clinging to his fingers. It was green. Night Hawk sniffed it. Mountain balm, he thought. Maybe bone-root leaves. He patted his head again, but gingerly, and found the cold muck stuck to his scalp where it hurt. He felt in his hair and found dried blood. The mountain had tipped him off the trail, and the healer woman must have found him. In which case, where was she?

Night Hawk crawled on all fours to where his pack lay. Beside it was a turtle-shell bowl he had never seen before, filled with water. He picked it up and sniffed the water suspiciously, but it just smelled like water. His throat was dry, and his mouth felt as if it were stuffed with fur. He drank the water in two gulps. His stomach churned, and he wished he hadn't drunk so fast, but it stayed down. He pulled his pack into his lap and opened it, reaching for the dried meat. He swore and emptied the pack on the ground. Two spare spearpoints bounced out of it along with the empty bags his food had been in.

Night Hawk touched his head again. It had become reasonably clear what had happened to his food, and to his head. He didn't know whether the coyote had been real, but the woman had been, and she had had an appetite.

He crawled to his knees, and then, most carefully, to his feet. His whole body hurt. He looked around him for his spear and the spear-thrower that had been slung from his back. Had she taken them, too? He was beginning to wish she *had* been a ghost.

With a grunt of relief he finally found them, half covered with the earth that had buried the trail. He dug them out with his hands and saw that only the spear shaft was cracked. He could cut a new one with the knife that had been stuck through the waist of his breechclout (and that mercifully had not stuck through *him*) when he fell. He looked around for a suitable sapling and growled a curse he had once learned from a man of the coast—it involved a perpetually empty belly for someone. Thanks to the woman who had dressed his head and then eaten his food, he was going to have to hunt as he ran.

"We should have killed him," Mocking Bird said.

Others' Child cuffed at his head.

"But no, you left him *water*, and our bowl."

"Why should we have killed him?" Maize Gone Away asked. "You always want to kill things. And I wanted to look at him some more, too."

"*You* said we should kill him," Mocking Bird said accusingly. "And then you changed your mind."

"I changed my mind." Maize Gone Away shrugged.

"Yah, because it was a man, Shameless!"

"Shameless?" Maize Gone Away's eyes flashed. "I saw you with Sister! I threw a fish at you. I wish I had more!"

"Who would look at *you*?"

Others' Child spun around on the trail, fists clenched. "Stop it!" She stepped between them, pushing them away from each other. Her cheeks flamed. "Be quiet. The gods will hear you."

"He said—"

"I heard him." Others' Child bit her lip. "*I* wanted to look at the man, too." She *had* looked under his breechclout. She didn't tell them that.

"I've seen him looking," Maize Gone Away muttered. "Greedy eyes."

"That is what is wrong now," Others' Child said. "Us. Maybe that is why the gods shook the mountains, to tell us to be ashamed."

Maize Gone Away looked at the ground. Mocking Bird glared away from them at the red hills.

"We will talk tonight when we have made camp," Others' Child pronounced gruffly. "I told you I have been thinking. Be quiet and be ashamed of yourselves—as I am—until then." She set off down the trail again, following an old deer track, her shoulders set in fierce silence.

They followed her, feeling sick in their stomachs, for the rest of the day, until the deer trail came to a water hole. Others' Child put her pack on the ground and sat down. Bitch stuck her muzzle in the water and drank while Maize Gone Away untied the travois and dragged it under a willow tree. Mocking Bird found dry wood for a fire without being asked, and knelt over it with the fire drill. Others' Child didn't move, and nobody said anything. At dusk they ate the last of the food out of the stranger's pack.

Others' Child wiped her mouth with the back of her hand. "Now I will talk," she said abruptly.

"And why will *you* talk?" Mocking Bird said testily, but he softened it with a motion of his hands that said he would listen anyway.

"Because I know what has happened to us, and you don't. Because I am the oldest."

"I know what has happened," Maize Gone Away said. "I wanted to look at the stranger, and everyone got angry with me. You are like dogs with a bone."

"We are and you aren't?" Mocking Bird asked.

"It isn't looking at the stranger that was wrong," Others' Child said. She looked down at her lap now, not at the other two. "It is looking at each other."

"We always look at each other. Are we blind?" Mocking Bird folded his arms, deliberately misunderstanding her.

"We look at each other like men and women," she whispered. "It is evil, but I have thought and thought, and I see that it is not our fault. We are too much alone here."

"Are you saying that we should go *back*?" Maize Gone Away asked her. "Because we—? Well, I won't look anymore, then. I know it's wrong because we're kin. I don't *need* a man."

"Yes, you do." Others' Child chuckled. "That's why you were looking at the stranger."

"I don't understand any of this," Mocking Bird said. "I don't understand what you are talking about." He folded his arms more firmly.

"Yes, you do," Others' Child said.

"I don't think you should be talking like this."

"I have to."

"Well, I don't like it," Mocking Bird said uncomfortably. He didn't like the things she was making him think.

"That's plain," Others' Child said. "You look like Turtle."

Maize Gone Away chuckled. "Well, I won't go back to the Yellow Grass People. Not for anything. Not to the People at all." She folded her arms, too.

"No," Others' Child said. "We will go to the Others."

The two stared at her, mouths open.

"Now you look like Buzzard. We will go to *my* people," Others' Child said. "We will find mates and live the way we are supposed to. And we will take the maize with us," she added craftily, eyeing Maize Gone Away. "The maize needs to be planted and grow."

"Give it to the Others?" Maize Gone Away whispered.

"Maybe," Mocking Bird said. Others' Child could tell he was thinking. It seemed a daring thing to go to the Others—an adventure, and a spit in the eye for the Yellow Grass People. But the Others were the enemy, had been the enemy since their first memory.

"We will do something bad if we stay alone together!" Others' Child said fiercely. Mocking Bird flinched. "If we go to my people, we will have a belonging place."

"There will be people like the one we found," Maize Gone Away murmured. "But what if they don't want us?"

"They will give you a home if *I* come with you," Others' Child said. "I am theirs. I was stolen, and now I will come back." She said it flatly as if the matter were settled. The other two looked at her dubiously, but neither contradicted her.

When they were asleep, Others' Child sat a long time by the fire, thinking of the face of the stranger that was so like hers. These were her true people, and now finally she would belong somewhere. She imagined finding a man, not the bloodied stranger but a handsomer man with fierce eyes who would know her as his, who would love her in the ways that Hears the Night had not. She imagined her true mother, the woman from whose arms she had been snatched in a long-ago battle that she couldn't remember. Her mother would know her, too. And Others' Child would bring them maize and the deer magic that her foster mother had taught her (before she had turned her back on them), and she would no longer be Others' Child but Daughter Returned. Her people would be grateful. They would open their arms to her and honor her, and for her sake they would take in her foster brother and sister.

Others' Child stared into the heart of the fire and saw herself going home in triumph, the stolen returned.

# X

# The Old Women Who Remember

The ground was still shaking. Not very hard, but the Three Old Men had their heads together about it, and twice they had made the Dance to Release the Souls of the Dead, to remind any that might have ventured above ground of the way back.

Their gods would keep speaking in this way until Night Hawk came back, the Three Old Men said.

And where was he? The Kindred's water was going dry just as Deer Old Man had said it would, but they couldn't move on until Night Hawk came back. They couldn't ask the gods where else to go until the earth had been mended. That was what the gods had told them to do first.

Four days after Night Hawk should have been back, the Kindred gathered around the communal fire pit and waited, none too patiently. Four was a magical number, the number of the four directions. Surely he would come on the fourth day. And if he didn't, he would come on the sixth, Healer Old Man said sternly, warning against ill-advised assumption. Six was magical, too, when you included the directions *up* and *down*, zenith and nadir, into your compass. And certainly Night Hawk's journey had to do with the way down, from where the dead might emerge.

"The dead have taken him," Leaf Fall sniffled. "That's what has happened."

Wing Foot looked worried. His brow furrowed, and he squinted across the valley to the south.

"Be quiet, old woman," Healer Old Man said. "You are ignorant."

There was a wail from the youngest Rainmaker girl. "Aiee, the dead are coming for us!" She put her hands over her head.

"*Something's* coming," Wing Foot said.

The Rainmaker girl followed his gaze and shrieked. "It *is* them!"

"Hush," Leaf Fall said, getting her nerve back. "It isn't."

"There are *three* of them. And a dog. It isn't Night Hawk!"

"It isn't bone people, either," Wing Foot said. He was embarrassed to have secretly thought it might be. He watched them uneasily. And if they *weren't* bone people, what did they want?

Others' Child watched the people who had been hers at the beginning staring at her across the stones and dry grass. They were all there, with three men who must be chieftains standing in front of them. It was as if they had known she was coming. The chieftains carried tall staffs in their hands. One had a deer head on the end of it, another a dried snake, and the third a blue stone as big around as her fist, tied on with sinew and an eagle's feather. Plainly the staffs were magical.

The rest of the Others backed away a little as the newcomers approached, but the old chieftains stood their ground. Others' Child made a gesture of respect to them.

"They belong to the Trespassers!" Wing Foot said. "Look at the boy's hair."

"They are thieves, then!"

"I think they are bone people anyway," a man of the Deer People said. "Your hair grows after you are dead."

"Kill them!" someone else shouted. "They are what has angered the gods—bone people creeping around above ground!"

"You can't kill someone who's dead," Healer Old Man said irritably. He turned around and raised a bushy eyebrow at the Kindred. "Be quiet."

"That's a coyote!" someone hissed.

"No, it's not," another said scornfully. "It's a dog."

"It's a coyote. Do you think I don't know a coyote?"

"I think you don't know a dog."

"*Be quiet!*" Rain Old Man bellowed. They subsided, staring at him and at the strangers. "Night Hawk has not returned. It is most unpropitious to do anything before he returns to us. The Kindred must conduct no important business until his task is done."

Old Duck, who was the oldest of the Rainmakers, stepped forward and inquired, "Then just what are we going to do with them?"

"What are they saying?" Maize Gone Away whispered to Others' Child.

"I don't know. They are arguing." Others' Child furrowed her brow. Somehow she had not worried about that. She had been certain they would recognize her.

"How are they supposed to know who you are?" Mocking Bird said. "They probably think we're demons."

"*Sssh!*" The old chieftain with the snake staff shook it at them.

"See?" Mocking Bird said. "This was a bad idea."

Maize Gone Away stared at the sea of faces. The women were glaring at her, leery and suspicious. The men looked fierce with their cropped hair and harsh noses. But one was looking at her with a friendly face. He was beautiful, even with that nose. Maize Gone Away wanted to run over and hide behind him.

"It wasn't a bad idea," Others' Child said. "I just have to make them understand. It must have been like this when our father came to the Yellow Grass People."

"They nearly killed *him*," Mocking Bird said. "And our father helped the Yellow Grass People to kill these Others. What if they find that out?"

"Our father was a famous warrior," Maize Gone Away said. "They will respect him." She was sure that the beautiful young man would.

"Yah bah," Mocking Bird said sourly. The old man with the snake staff shook it at them again. Mocking Bird folded his arms and scowled uneasily. Going to the Others didn't seem such an adventure as it had before, standing here ringed by a circle of spears.

Others' Child watched the three old chieftains carefully, trying to find some familiar gesture in their movements or a remembered word in their speech. Once in a while she thought she almost caught something, almost understood, but it slipped away. They were arguing, she could tell that—in a dignified fashion, yes, but they were arguing. She stepped toward them, and they scowled at her for her presumption.

Others' Child touched her forefinger to her chest and then pointed at the Others, at all of them, peering between the shoulders of the men who had encircled them. "I am yours," she said.

A wave of incomprehensible chatter flowed through the group in response, stopping to be argued about now and then like a stream bubbling over rocks. The three old chieftains and the rest of the Others peered at her, uncomprehending.

Others' Child said it again. "I am *yours*."

"It is some kind of magic," an old woman of the Healers said. She made a circle between her thumb and forefinger to look through and bounced the curse back at the sender.

"She must be speaking the Trespassers' talk," a woman of the Deer People said. "She may be telling us something."

"If she is one of the Trespassers, she is telling us a curse."

"She doesn't look like one. The other two, yes, but not that one."

"We need Night Hawk," Wing Foot said. "He speaks with the Trespassers in their language. He can tell us who these are."

"If they haven't killed him," Leaf Fall said.

"It would take more than these three to kill Night Hawk. He has been to the coast where the Endless Water is. And anyway, two of these are women. What harm are they going to do?"

"If they are dead?" Old Duck shook his head mournfully at Wing Foot. "Dead women are even more dangerous than live women."

"They don't look dead to me," Wing Foot said stubbornly. He couldn't imagine the girl as dead, turning to bones in his arms. She looked too warm. He gazed at the animal sitting by her feet. "And that is a dog."

"Someone else is coming," Healer Old Man said.

Others' Child watched the young man who was arguing with the old one. He seemed to be defending them in some way, but it was hard to tell. He didn't appear to be angry or frightened of them. And he was so beautiful, as beautiful as the man of her imagining. She yearned toward him, one of her own kind.

The rest were still staring at them, suspicious. When

their expressions changed to elation, it took Others'
Child a moment to realize that it was not at final understanding of what she had been telling them. She
followed their gaze behind her and saw a man running toward them in the distance. A puff of dust rose
with every step. As he drew nearer she saw that he
had a pack and a spear across his back, a skin band
knotted around his forehead.

Maize Gone Away grabbed her arm. "Do you think
it's the same one?"

*Probably,* Others' Child thought, wishing they
hadn't taken his food. She squinted her eyes. She was
almost sure he was the same man. As he drew nearer,
she could see the scabbed-over scar on his head.

"I told you you should have let me kill him," Mocking Bird muttered.

"Hush! Maybe he'll help us. I mended his head."

"We left him without any food, too," Mocking Bird
said.

Night Hawk slowed as he approached the council
fire. While he was making respect to the Three Old
Men, his eye caught the strangers, and his brows went
up.

"*Have you sewn up the earth?*" Rain Old Man
chanted, making it clear that no strangers were to be
discussed before the proper ceremonials had been
sung.

"*I have sewn up the earth.*"

"*Have you asked of the animal people?*"

"*I have asked of the animal people.*"

"*Have you asked of the gods?*"

"*I have asked of the gods.*"

"*Have you asked of the earth?*"

"*I have asked of the earth as I stitched it up.*"

"And what have they told you?" Rain Old Man
asked him. The Kindred held their collective breath.

Night Hawk let his out slowly. "They have shown
me where we are to live," he said. He sounded star-

tled, as if he still found that implausible. He let his eyes rest curiously on the three strangers. He was certain that one was the woman who had healed his head.

A swift murmur of speculation rippled through the Kindred, the interlopers forgotten for the moment. "And how have they shown you this?" Rain Old Man asked him gently. People who had talked to the gods had to be handled carefully. Sometimes they went mad.

"When the ground shook again, I fell. I broke my head open." Night Hawk bent so they could see. "I spent a long time in dreamtime, and someone came and healed my head for me."

"One of the gods?" Healer Old Man asked him.

"I don't think so. It was a woman. I think it was that one." Night Hawk pointed at her.

"Aiee! She is one of the dead!" The Rainmaker girl put her hands over her head again.

"She wasn't dead. She ate my food!" Night Hawk said with a burst of laughter. It seemed a source of miraculous amusement to him now, after what had happened later. He looked at Bitch, whose nose stuck out from behind Others' Child's knee. "I remember the dog, too."

"What of the other two?" Wing Foot asked him. "We think they belong to the Trespassers."

"Hah! I do, too," Night Hawk said. Now the woman's speech made sense to him. He had just been too far into dreamtime to recognize it. "What are they doing here?"

"We don't know," Wing Foot said. "Old Duck thinks they are bone people, but I don't."

"Maybe *you* should talk with them," Leaf Fall said. "You can speak with the False People." She peered at his skull solicitously and said grudgingly, "She has done a decent job there. I would have used a thorn to close it, though."

"Later," Rain Old Man said. "Be quiet. We must

hear what the gods have told Night Hawk. That is more important." He thumped his snake staff and fixed his gaze on anyone who looked as if he was going to talk some more.

"It was because of the stranger woman that I found it," Night Hawk said. "She put a poultice on my head, but when I woke, she and the dog were gone. I thought then that it was a coyote, but I see now that it is only partly." He looked at Others' Child. "Like the woman, maybe. I don't know. But when I woke, they were not there, and the food in my pack was not there."

"Huh?" said Wing Foot.

"All the False People are thieves!" Old Duck announced, seizing on the only comprehensible element in this narrative.

"Hush!" Rain Old Man said, and the rest of them subsided.

"And it was because of that that I found where we are to live," Night Hawk said, trying to slow down and tell it in order. "I had to hunt for my dinner, so I went away from the path where the earth needed stitching, east into a dry valley, because I saw deer tracks there. I have been that way before, pack-on-back, but have never seen the deer people because there is no water. But now they go there, and I saw why: When the earth moved, it picked up the river and threw it, and now there is a lake there."

A long collective indrawn breath whispered through the Kindred. Night Hawk felt jubilant. He wanted to throw his arms around the sky and dance. The gods who had never before spoken to him had given him this honor, given it to him to lead his people to a new place. The Three Old Men must have known when they chose him. "Tomorrow we will leave," he told them.

"That is for us to decide." Rain Old Man harrumphed. He bent his head toward Healer Old Man and Deer Old Man, and, after they had talked, announced, "We will leave tomorrow."

"What about these?" Old Duck pointed at the four, the three humans and the coyote dog.

"I will speak with them," Night Hawk said. He owed the woman a debt. She might not be magical herself, but certainly the gods had used her for his benefit. Things did not simply happen. Lakes did not simply well up without supernatural help.

The older of the two women, the one who had dressed his head, was watching him warily. Every so often the boy's hand would tighten on his spear. When it did, the men ringed around the strangers would take a step forward. The Three Old Men would glare at them, and they would take a step back. It was like a dance.

The younger girl's gaze flicked between Night Hawk and Wing Foot, ranging from apprehension to interest. *Oho.* Night Hawk elbowed his way between Wing Foot and Old Duck and stood in front of the older of the girls. Not so very old, he thought. Younger than himself.

"You're the woman who took my dinner," he informed her sternly in the Trespassers' talk. "And I was on very important business."

She tipped her chin up. "It was pay for healing your head."

"My people want to know why you are here now."

"I belong to you," she said.

"I don't want you," Night Hawk said. "With respect." He backed off a little. Was this what happened among the Trespassers when they healed someone?

She flushed. "Not that way. I belong to your people. I was stolen by the Yellow Grass People. That is why I am called Others' Child," she added proudly.

Night Hawk looked dubiously at the other girl and the boy. The boy glared back at him. "Not them," he said with conviction.

"No," Others' Child said. "They are my foster

brother and sister. They are a gift for you. Because I have come home."

Night Hawk scratched his head. This was important business, and it was beyond him. He turned to the Three Old Men. "She says she belongs to the Kindred. She says she was stolen. It might be."

Speculation and argument erupted like a flash flood.

"I said she didn't look like the Trespassers."

"The other two do."

"They are bone people. They can look like anyone they want to."

"Has Night Hawk asked her if she's dead?"

"Maybe she's Leaf Fall's daughter. How long has it been since that fighting?"

"Too long. How should we know her?"

"Leaf Fall should look at her."

Leaf Fall spun around with a wail and buried her face in another woman's shoulder. "Noooo. It won't be her. She died in the fighting."

"Did you *see* her die, Old Aunt?" Night Hawk asked gently. He went to where she was wailing and tried to pry her face up.

"Did I need to see? A woman had her by the arm, and she had a knife at her throat." Leaf Fall put her fingers over her eyes.

Night Hawk threw up his hands. "It could be," he said again to the Three Old Men.

Deer Old Man scratched his head. "It was because she stole your food and you had to hunt that you found the lake where we are to go now and live?"

Night Hawk nodded. "Yes, Uncle." He also remembered how hungry he had been the first day. He supposed that hunger could have been a test. Nothing in that journey had been without purpose. But now he was out of his depth. He waited for the Three Old Men to speak.

"We will let the old women decide," the old man of the Deer People said finally. "They will know. You talk to her for them." He turned to the Kindred. "Go and get the Grandmothers."

Night Hawk waited impatiently while the oldest women of the Kindred stumped toward the fire pit. They were the repository of their people's memory, of turning years and marriages, clan relationships and ancient births and deaths. They were nearly toothless, but they commanded more respect than anyone in the tribe, maybe even more than the Three Old Men.

"Old Women Who Remember," Night Hawk said deferentially as they tottered forward. One of them, who in her youth had been Nightjar but was now Old Woman Many Grandsons, was carried on the crossed arms of two of her descendants. They set her carefully on the folded deerskin that their mother put down. Under Old Woman's watchful eye they backed off, away from matters that were not their business.

Two more settled themselves on skins, and a fourth stood leaning on her stick. She cocked an eye at Others' Child. "Ask her if she is dead," she instructed Night Hawk.

"Grandmother Snake wants to know if you are dead," Night Hawk inquired dutifully.

"Of course I'm not dead." Others' Child was indignant. She jutted her chin out at him. "Do I look dead?"

He tipped his head at her with a half grin. "No, but very dirty and much like a wild coyote."

"I am not dirty!" Others' Child said. "It was a dusty walk, but we are respectable people."

"What does she say?" Old Woman Many Grandsons demanded.

"She says she is not dead," Night Hawk said.

"Ask her if she is Leaf Fall's daughter."

"She says she doesn't know that. She was left behind in some fighting with the Trespassers. She was very small."

"Hmm!" Grandmother Watcher said. She was tiny, like a stick bird. "And where was this fighting?"

Night Hawk conferred with Others' Child again.
"The old grannies are trying to decide if you belong
to us. They want to know where you were lost."

"Where the Yellow Grass People live in summer.
Where they took the cliffs back from your people."

He relayed this information to the Grandmothers,
who put their heads together and muttered over it.

"And why wouldn't I belong to you?" she demanded while they debated. "This is what I was
told."

"You *could* have come from the Turquoise Band,"
Night Hawk said. "There are more of the Kindred
than just us. Or maybe from some other tribe of the
False People. How do I know what the Trespassers
are likely to do? Or you could be a demon, I suppose."

"I am not a demon." She glared at him to see if he
really thought she was. She suspected him of laughing at her.

Night Hawk shook his head solemnly. "It's very
hard to spot demons."

"Ask her who these are that she brings with her,"
Grandmother Snake said.

"They are my foster brother and sister," Others'
Child said. She faced the Grandmothers as she talked,
even if they couldn't understand her. She knew the
old women were important. She took Mocking Bird
by the arm. "This is Mocking Bird, son of my foster
mother and of my foster father, who did not belong
to the People but came from the south. And this is
my foster sister, Maize Gone Away. They are twins,"
she added, and she could see that the Grandmothers
were impressed. Twins were magical. They hardly
ever happened, and when they did, it was rare for
both to live.

"*Maize . . .*" Old Woman Many Grandsons seized
on the word when Night Hawk had translated it all
to her. The family relationships she tucked away in
their proper categories. Those were easy; she had a

whole tribe's genealogy in her head. But the strange word caught her ear. "What is the maize that has gone away from this girl?"

With some waving of hands, Others' Child explained.

"She *says* that it is the seed the Trespassers keep to themselves," Night Hawk said to the Grandmothers. "She *says* that her foster father brought it from the south, and that now she and her brother and sister have stolen it away because the Trespassers killed their father. She says that they have brought it to us, and now her sister, who plants the seed, will be called Maize Came, and she herself will be called Daughter Came Home." He cocked an eye at the Grandmothers, wondering how they were going to like being told that. It took some nerve to give yourself a new name in front of the Grandmothers. "It may be true," he said to soften their distrust. "I think it is."

It was odd that he should think so—Night Hawk the Trader prided himself on believing nothing that anyone told him. But this journey had changed that. He had seen the lake. He looked carefully at the woman. She was not as beautiful as her little sister, but to Night Hawk she was the more interesting. There was something wild about her, something feral like that half-coyote dog. He supposed it was because she was of and yet not of the Kindred. Oddly, it made him inclined to believe the things she told him.

"Tell her that we want to see this seed," Grandmother Snake said. Eyes snapping with curiosity, she stuck her long neck out toward Others' Child. Night Hawk almost laughed; it was so plain how she had got her name.

Others' Child conferred with Maize Gone Away, who took the bag of seed out of her pack. She held some out in the palm of her hand, and the Grandmothers poked at it, took kernels and bit them, or tried to—Night Hawk thought they might have four teeth between them.

"This is what the Trespassers were growing when Fire God and the Two War Gods told us to go and live in the yellow cliffs," Grandmother Watcher said. She sniffed with sudden suspicion. "And how do we know that the Trespassers will not be at this lake where you say the gods have told us to go and live?"

Night Hawk tried to make a connection between those things and couldn't. He looked helplessly at the Three Old Men. The Grandmothers were even older than the Three Old Men (whose title was a mark of respect and did not necessarily reflect their age), and sometimes they got confused. Grandmother Snake had been known to think that her grandson was her husband and to berate him periodically for unfaithfulness.

Grandmother Watcher took the hard kernel of maize out of her mouth and put it back in Maize Gone Away's hand. She turned her attention to Others' Child.

The four old women prodded her in the ribs and pulled at her hair. Old Woman Many Grandsons pulled Others' Child's jaws open and looked at her teeth. "Make them stop that!" Others' Child said.

"They want to examine you," Night Hawk replied.

"Ow!" One of them had pinched her arm. The last of them, Old Woman Tells Stories, hobbled forward and pulled Others' Child's eyelid down. She peered into the pupil.

"Tell them to leave me alone!"

"They want to make sure you're human," Night Hawk said.

The four old women put their heads together and counted on their fingers, arguing with each other. They counted again. They looked over their shoulders at the strange, wild girl and then at Leaf Fall. Old Woman Tells Stories nodded.

Old Woman Many Grandsons went and got Leaf Fall. She pulled her through the crowd and pointed at Others' Child. "She is the right age."

"She couldn't be," Leaf Fall whispered. Her eyes filled with tears. "They killed my baby."

"At the yellow cliffs, where this one says she comes from," Old Woman Many Grandsons said stubbornly. "She is yours. She is dirty from being with the False People, but she is yours."

"She has a look of Antelope about her," Grandmother Watcher said, squinting her eyes.

"What was she called?"

"Reed," Leaf Fall whispered.

"Well, now she says she is Daughter Came Home."

"No," Leaf Fall said. Her voice was louder, as if hope had entered it suddenly. "If she is mine, she is Reed." She came closer to Others' Child and peered at her, her lower lip trembling.

"Who is this?" Others' Child whispered uneasily to Night Hawk.

"The Grandmothers think she may be your mother," Night Hawk said. "And if you are not kind to her, I will make you sorry," he added.

Others' Child stared at Leaf Fall. She touched her own face with her fingertips, wondering if she looked like this plump, strange woman. She had only seen her own face reflected in a still pond, so it was hard to tell.

Leaf Fall slid another step closer. They were nearly the same height. She stared back at Others' Child and whispered something to Night Hawk.

"What is it?" Others' Child asked, anxious. Mocking Bird and Maize Gone Away were watching round-eyed.

"She says that if you are Reed, you have a pale spot on your behind," Night Hawk said. "She wants to look at it."

"What?" Others' Child clapped her hands over her backside.

"Go with her," Night Hawk said, laughing.

"I don't have to go with her," Others' Child said. Her face was flaming. She could hear giggles from the people nearest them. "I have a spot there. You can ask my sister."

"Have you seen it?"

"Of course I haven't seen it. How could I see it?"

"Then Leaf Fall wants to see it."

Leaf Fall tugged at her hand suddenly as if she had just found the courage to touch her. Others' Child looked over her shoulder at Mocking Bird and Maize Gone Away. "Stay here," she said with heavy dignity.

The cave that Leaf Fall took her to was small and dark, the kind that a woman living alone would be allotted. *If this is my mother*, Others' Child thought, *I will make them give her a better one. If I call the deer for them, then we will have power*. But the cave was swept clean, storage baskets and grinding stones neatly stacked, and no leavings strewn about the fire. Leaf Fall pulled her into the center of it and pointed at her hide skirt. Others' Child unknotted the thongs that laced it and pulled it down over her hips. Standing very straight, she turned her back to Leaf Fall and the light from the cave mouth. Bending over like that in front of someone was an insult. Why had she assumed that she and her mother would know each other? And why had she not wondered about her father? There seemed to be no man here, and for some reason she had not expected one.

Leaf Fall scurried around in front of Others' Child, eyes wide, mouth stretched in a smile that looked as if it had been startled out of her. She put her hand to her heart. Then she began to talk, very fast, in words that were beyond Others' Child's grasp.

"I don't know what you're saying," Others' Child protested. "Are you my mother?"

*"Mother."* Leaf Fall grabbed her by the arms. It seemed that their words for that were similar. Leaf Fall said it again, her hands clasped together now, dancing clumsily around her newfound daughter. *"Mother."*

*   *   *

"You belong to us now," Night Hawk said to Mocking Bird and Maize Gone Away. "When the Three Old Men have made all the proper ceremonies, you will be adopted. You will be people of the Kindred." He looked at them as if they were bound to like that.

Mocking Bird glanced warily about him. The Kindred, pretending to be going about their business, were all watching the newcomers with sly interest, all the more evident for its studied nonchalance. Three girls who were tying bundles of spoons and tools into a hide for the journey observed him from the corners of their dark eyes and giggled when he caught them doing it. He smiled at them in spite of himself. Their bare breasts hung loose under necklaces of seed pods and feathers, tips golden brown, smooth as warm sand. Now they caught *him* looking, and he jerked his head away, embarrassed.

Maize Gone Away was sitting cross-legged on a stone, listening attentively to Night Hawk the Trader, but *she* was watching the young man who sat beside him. A very beautiful young man, much too pretty for Mocking Bird's liking. *Girls*, he thought, suddenly disgusted.

"You must learn to speak as we do now," Night Hawk said. "So I won't talk to you in the Trespassers' speech anymore."

"How will we understand you?" Maize Gone Away wailed.

Others' Child wondered the same thing. It had been many years since she had been among her people, and she had barely begun to talk when she was stolen. Leaf Fall had taught her a few words already, but she talked so fast.

"It won't be hard. I learned your speech," Night Hawk said. "You will learn."

"Not by people jabbering at me," Others' Child said. "My ears hurt. And I cannot understand my mother. I asked her where my father was, but I couldn't make her understand me at all."

Night Hawk shrugged. "He was killed by the Trespassers. At the same time that she lost you, I think. I've heard he was a lazy man, though, and did her no good."

Poor Mother, Others' Child thought. She wondered why Leaf Fall hadn't taken a different husband, then thought that after the Yellow Grass People made war on them, there must not have been many men left. The Yellow Grass People had trapped them in a canyon, her father had told her, and many had been killed.

"Then she will have me now, and I will see that someone hunts for her," Others' Child said. "Now she will have me to care for her when she is old."

"And how do you know no one cares for her?" Night Hawk said. He was beginning to feel this girl pushing him from his place.

"You?" Others' Child said, surprised. "If you have cared for my mother, then I am grateful." She made it a courtesy. "But now I am home."

Night Hawk grinned. He didn't think the boy had wielded much power among the three. He was reasonably sure he knew who had been in charge. "Very well, Woman Who Knows All That Is Important," he said, lapsing into the Kindred's speech. "Go and find your mother. She will be looking for you to scrub the Trespassers off you." Leaf Fall had gone away with the Grandmothers and the Three Old Men once she had brought Others' Child back to the Kindred, but now he saw her coming across the flat sandy strip where the Kindred made the Deer Prayer.

"Reed!" Leaf Fall beckoned imperiously to her daughter, but her eyes glowed with love.

"That is your name," Night Hawk said when Others' Child looked blank. He translated it into the Yellow Grass People's language.

"It is not," Others' Child said with conviction. "I am Daughter Came Home. I dreamed it."

Night Hawk shook his head, chuckling. "Not if Leaf Fall says you are Reed." He thought this new woman had too many opinions.

"I don't want to be Reed."

"It becomes you," Night Hawk said softly. "Let her call you what she wants to. She is not so old as the Grandmothers, but she has missed much in this life."

Others' Child stood up from the warm stone where she had been sitting listening to Night Hawk. What he said might be important, and she couldn't talk to anyone else to find out. "Reed." She turned the foreign word over in her mouth, seeing the slender stalks that it stood for, bending in a ripple of air along the riverbank. They danced, in the right wind. Maybe it was not a bad name.

Leaf Fall held her hand out, and Others' Child put hers in it. Reed walked away with her mother.

But the name didn't cling the way it should. She felt it fluttering in the breeze outside her skin; it wouldn't sink beneath the surface. Maybe it took time. There were other things to think about. Leaf Fall took her down to the dying river and stood approvingly while she washed herself in it. They walked back to the caves, her bare brown skin drying in the sun, and Leaf Fall combed her hair and braided it the way the Kindred's women wore theirs. She chatted all the while, cheerfully, incomprehensibly, and several times she turned serious, telling Reed important things that Reed couldn't fathom. They ground meal together and packed their mutual possessions for the next day's leaving. Night Hawk had told her that he had found a lake on his magical journey—now she understood the purpose of that running—and that the Kindred were to go and live there. *A lake*, she thought. Once she had seen a lake, but not in the dry years.

Magic seemed everywhere around her, and things were meant to be, like the last perfectly shaped stone sliding into place in the lining one built inside a storage pit. She felt that she herself might be three or four people at once.

Mocking Bird had been given a place among the young, unmarried boys, and when they reached the lake, the Three Old Men would decide whether he and Maize Gone Away should be Rainmakers or Healers or Deer People. Maize Gone Away would not be a daughter in Leaf Fall's house, in any case, but have her own dwelling, as befitted one who had brought the Trespassers' magic food to the Kindred.

Reed, on the other hand, found her place already made for her. She had been given to the Healers as a baby and would be reinitiated into their society with the new babies in the fall. There were other initiations, too, to take her back into the tribe of her birth. The Grandmothers came to Leaf Fall's cave as they were bundling their belongings and conferred, heads together, not bothering to bring Night Hawk to translate for Reed. Reed began to sense that her thoughts on the matter would carry no weight anyway.

*Let them do what they want*, she thought. Proper ritual was not to be neglected. She smiled and nodded when Leaf Fall explained it all to her, and wondered how different it would be from her own girlhood initiation into the Yellow Grass People. For the first time since she had come here she thought of Deer Shadow and then deliberately put the thought aside. Deer Shadow had gone away; that was Deer Shadow's choosing. Reed had to go somewhere.

The Grandmothers watched as Reed knotted the straps on her pack and tied the rest of her bundles on Bitch's travois. They eyed Bitch dubiously, and she returned the courtesy. They clucked their tongues when the knots came loose and had to be retied. They inspected Reed's hair and the baskets she had brought with her and the blue stone on a thong that she wore around her neck. When she knelt to poke the coals with the quick gesture of respect that the People always gave to fire, they rolled their eyes and muttered.

When she strapped her spear and her throwing-stick to the bundles on the travois, they burst into conversation with Leaf Fall.

Finally they went away, and Reed curled herself on her bed of dried grass and whistled Bitch up onto it with her. She wrapped her arm around Bitch's neck and buried her face in her coat.

Leaf Fall watched her, eyes vaguely troubled. Of course she couldn't know things. The Grandmothers were right. She would have to be taught everything. It seemed a daunting task, with a grown daughter. Antelope had grown up knowing, but this one—it was as if she had been dipped in a pool of the Trespassers' taint. Everyone knew that all their ways were wrong ones. How could she scrape them off Reed?

# XI

# Always Water

The Kindred followed Night Hawk down the deer
trail, a new trail only recently begun to be trodden
out under the prints of endless sharp hooves through
the foxtail grass and stands of oaks. There had been
no water before where they were going, but now the
river, one of the many tributaries that flowed south
into Water Old Man, had moved, a new channel cut
with the rending of the earth, and where the old dry
valley flattened out, there a lake had formed.

Already, so Night Hawk said, there were fish in it.
The Kindred walked behind him, chattering, exclaim-
ing anxiously each time they crossed a ridge, looking
for the lake.

"It will be blue, with silver fish in it," Old Duck
said to himself. He had said the same thing over and
over all during the journey, and Reed thought that
perhaps he had known a lake like that in his youth
and yearned for it.

She walked at the head of the band with Night Hawk because he was the only one who could understand her. He wouldn't speak the Yellow Grass People's speech to her, but he slowed his words, and when she lapsed into her old tongue, he understood her. The air was bright around him. It lit his hair with flashes of sun luminous as feathers, his skin spotted and dappled with the shade of the oaks. Her feet felt light, as if she moved a little above the warm earth. Mocking Bird and Maize Gone Away were behind her with Leaf Fall and Wing Foot, Night Hawk's friend, and two girls of the Kindred. The girls' voices rose in the warm, sweet air like bird calls, and Mocking Bird had pulled out his flute and was making it sing as he walked.

"I feel strange," Reed said. "Almost like someone else."

"You are someone else," Night Hawk said to her. "You took time and turned it in your hand. Now you have the life you would have had if you had not been lost. I think you have done a magical thing. I hope you are going to like it," he added.

She turned to him, dark eyes shining. Her hair was braided in heavy plaits down her back and threaded with cedar twigs that gave it a sweet pungent odor. Her long legs kept pace with his, flashing in and out of the live oak shadows. Her pack hung from a sling over one shoulder, and between her breasts hung three eagle feathers on a thong that Leaf Fall had given her. "Why should I not like it?" she demanded.

"I don't know," he said. "There was a girl from your people. I think my people took her when there was the fighting, when you were lost. She was young, like you, but she never was happy with us. I remember her. She used to sit and stare at the horizon, and then one day, oh, years later, she was just gone."

"Gone? Where did she go?"

"Home, maybe," Night Hawk said. "I think that

was what she had been looking toward all those years."

"Not if she was looking for us," Reed said. "She never came home to us."

"Ah, well, there are many trails out there, and most of them eat their travelers. I am not surprised."

Reed was silent a moment. It could have been herself and Mocking Bird and Maize Gone Away that the earth had eaten. Looking back on it now, she was frightened at the idea of what they had done. They were too young to have known how easy it was to die, like the girl who had watched the horizon. Here among humans again, she wanted most to burrow into that warm companionship and not fear the wild lands again. So she said, "I am not like that. And I was of the Kindred at the first, so why should I not be happy among them?"

"I don't know." Night Hawk shrugged, his hawk-nosed face thoughtful. "I like them most fondly in small visits, but that is because I am a restless man. Perhaps you are more settled." He looked uncertain.

"If the trail is likely to eat you, then it is foolish to be restless," Reed said firmly, to show him that she was neither. "That is no life for a man, being among strangers."

"That is what your mother says."

"Then my mother is right." Reed smiled at Leaf Fall over her shoulder and at Wing Foot walking beside with Maize Gone Away. "What makes this one so restless?" she asked Wing Foot, to show how much her knowledge of his speech had grown.

"He has no sense," Wing Foot said, smiling back.

"A hawk flew up in his mother's face when she was carrying him," Leaf Fall said. She clucked her tongue disapprovingly. "I could tell it meant no good."

Reed smiled. She had understood that well enough. Words that she had not known ten days ago at the start of their journey sang in her ears now like strange, newly discovered insects.

Night Hawk stopped abruptly, and she nearly walked into him. "There," he said, stretching out his hand, and the Kindred crowded around him on the crest of a shallow ridge whose slope flowed downward through the oaks into sage scrub and then whispering grass—and finally the silver flash of water, almost too bright for the eyes.

Two deer stood ankle-deep in the lake. As the Kindred watched, they lifted their heads and bounded away, leaping in graceful arcs, the spray hanging in the air behind them.

The Three Old Men had bustled forward as soon as Night Hawk raised his hand. "There is soft stone at the foot of this slope," Night Hawk said to them. "And shallow caves. It will take only a little digging. If you wish it, I will tell the Turquoise Band to come and help when I go to them next."

The Three Old Men put their heads together quickly. Healer Old Man harrumphed in his throat and said, "The Turquoise Band has as many hungry mouths as we do. We will do our own digging."

"You are going away?" Reed said to Night Hawk, and they frowned at her.

"I am always going away," Night Hawk said. "That is what I do."

"But we don't know how to talk yet, my brother and sister and I." Reed looked around her, feeling abandoned. She was used to him.

"The best way to learn is to have to," he said.

Leaf Fall dragged her daughter away by the arm. "Not now. You cannot talk to him while the Three Old Men are talking to him." Reed understood most of that and frowned. Leaf Fall pulled her farther away.

The Three Old Men finished conferring with Night Hawk, and the Kindred picked their way down the slope to the shining water. The children bounced excitedly on and off the trail, scattering in the scrub like turkeys, whooping and leaping. There would be a great deal of work to be done by everybody now, even more than at the autumn moving-on, but also anything might happen, particularly while the adults were distracted with making camp and with weighty matters such as pacing off ground for the Deer Prayer. That could not be made just anywhere, and already Deer Old Man and Rain Old Man were arguing about it. The children ran into the shallows of the lake, flailing it up with their arms.

The Kindred dug out the cliffs with stone adzes and bone picks while the children carted away the rubble in baskets and the women cut brush for journey huts. It would take days before the cliffs were livable, but Night Hawk was right—the stone was soft and already partly eroded by the wind or some old water that had gone and now come again. Already berry vines were sprouting from the ground, and new greens grew by the lakeshore. There were turtles and snails and cool, spicy cress in the stream that fed the lake, so Night Hawk said. Rabbits would come to the lake, too, and waterfowl, and in time there would be flowers, and bees, and honey. It would be a good life beside the lake.

Reed marked out a spot for herself and Leaf Fall and began chipping at it despite dark looks from the Grandmothers and another harrumph from Healer Old Man. Leaf Fall looked anxiously at the Three Old Men and at the other women and then went and helped her.

"Now you have me to take care of you," Reed said. She wasn't sure whether her mother understood her or not, because her speech was clumsy and involved much gesture, but she went on stubbornly. "You will have a—good place. Food. I can hunt, too, besides my brother, who will hunt for us."

Leaf Fall might have understood that. She waved her hands at Reed, frantic shushing motions, looking over her shoulder at the Grandmothers. When Night

Hawk strolled by, she pulled at his arm.

"Women don't hunt," Night Hawk told Reed after Leaf Fall had jabbered at him. "You will make a scandal."

"Women hunt if they're hungry enough," Reed said, still stubborn. But maybe that would make trouble. She felt unsure. "And who *will* hunt for us, then?"

"Your brother," Night Hawk said. "Your husband, if you don't make any more scandals and someone will marry you."

She decided he was teasing her and ignored that.

"Women hunt with slings and throw sticks, maybe," Night Hawk said. "But the Three Old Men make sure that everyone is fed. Women who have no man get a part of every hunt."

"Yah, and I know what part," Reed muttered. She dug her adze into the soft stone. "*My* mother will not eat leavings."

Night Hawk shook his head. He went on toward the lake, whistling between his teeth like Mocking Bird's flute. He didn't seem to be doing any work digging out the cliffs.

In the morning Night Hawk came to Maize Gone Away. He made a deep gesture of respect and called her Maize Came, and the people who gathered outside her brush hut whispered it after him. He said that Rain Old Man and the Grandmothers told him that it was time to plant the food she had stolen from the Trespassers. He held his hand out as if to help her up from her bed.

Maize Gone Away scrubbed her eyes with her fists and yawned. She saw the Kindred gathered behind him, and she sat up slowly, deliberately, pulling her new name around her like a blanket, thinking hard. Maize was power. Father had known that. Power and danger. She stood unsteadily.

"I am Maize Came," she said slowly, trying out the new language, letting Night Hawk prompt her in a whisper. "I have brought food that will make the Kindred powerful, but the Kindred must listen to me." She stared hard at them until she was sure that they were. There would be no one like Cat Ears among these people. If there was, she would see that they killed him.

"There are proper times and proper ways to plant, and it must be done as I will show you," she said. "And the maize must be kept watered if there is drought again. The Yellow Grass People did not believe and do this, and thus they lost the maize. That will happen also to the Kindred if they do not listen."

"We listen," Rain Old Man said solemnly.

Maize Came knelt and pulled the sack of seed from her pack and hefted it in her hand. She held it up to them, balanced on her palm. "This is all there is," she said fiercely. "The rest was lost when the mountains walked. We will plant some of this, but not all. *Always* there must be seed held back. Who among you will dispute this with me?"

She stood and watched them implacably while Night Hawk repeated her question, but no one spoke. *Good*, she thought. *It will not come to me as it did to Father. They will be afraid of me at the start.*

Aloud she said, "I will show you how to burn off the field. If you do as I tell you, the Maize God will come to live among you. But it will take much work and water carrying. It is late in the season."

"We will work," Wing Foot said. His face was eager. "If Maize Came shows us, we will do as she has said."

"The warriors of the Kindred will listen to Wing Foot," Maize Came agreed solemnly.

Night Hawk repeated that testimonial, and the women looked admiringly at Wing Foot. He noted Reed among them and smiled sardonically at her. She flushed and turned her face away.

Maize Came nodded to the Three Old Men, giving them her respect, and they nodded back. Satisfied, she set out for the lakeside, the Kindred trailing behind her in awed procession.

"All the girls of the Kindred will be jealous if you wink your beautiful eyes at Trespasser women," Night Hawk whispered to Wing Foot as they followed her.

"I'm not winking my eyes at anybody," Wing Foot said, but he put no force in the statement. He looked cheerful and bemused.

"If you marry the Maize Girl you will be important," Night Hawk murmured, "but the other one has more power."

"I haven't said I am marrying anyone," Wing Foot said uncomfortably, but the feeling seemed to be momentary. In two more strides his face had brightened again, watching Maize Came's graceful back and bare feet gliding past the silvered water. The sun, flaming suddenly over the mountain, stained the far shore pink.

"You never listen to me," Night Hawk said.

"Why should I?" Wing Foot asked cheerfully. "You never give me good advice."

Maize Came stopped a short distance from the shore, and the Kindred fanned out around her. She began to pace the field off, and Night Hawk nodded. He had seen the maize fields of the Trespassers. She would burn the grass and scrub bushes off, and then when it was cooled, they would dig holes in the earth and put the seed in them. There was more than that, of course. This was grave and serious magic, but that was the part ordinary people could know.

Then, unless it rained, they would pour water on the buried seed, and in ten fingers' worth of days it would come up, tiny green shoots poking from the ground. Night Hawk had tried to slip away and look at the Trespassers' maize field once, but the men of the Trespassers had caught him and made it clear with a spearpoint that going too close to the maize was forbidden. And that had been in a good year, before the drought. *We are an important people now,* he thought, feeling satisfied because it was in some way his doing that the Maize Girl was here.

His eyes slid to the sister. He was certain that it was his doing that *she* was here. The coyote dog sat at her heels, scratching behind one ear, while Old Aunt Leaf Fall watched it with dislike. Night Hawk grinned. He wasn't sure why Reed had come home, but there was something in her that would stir the Kindred into some new mixture. Leaf Fall had got more than she had bargained for in this returning daughter. Calling her Reed, tethering her to a time when nothing had been shifted or shaken, wasn't going to change that.

The next day Maize Came planted her seed. When they had watched, awed, the hunters made the Deer Prayer and went out to learn the new ways of the deer in this valley. In the afternoon they came home with three, eyes wide with their success. Their dogs, sated with the entrails, loped beside them.

Mocking Bird had taken Bitch out, but she had fought with the Kindred's dogs and spoiled his aim, and he had not brought down the deer he had wanted. There would have been four to bring home if he had. He went and squatted irritably by Leaf Fall's hearth while the women butchered the kill. He had let the men cut his hair, too, and now his head felt strange.

There wasn't even anyone to talk to. Reed and Maize Came were with the rest of the women, and Night Hawk had gone off somewhere with Wing Foot, who *had* brought down a deer, by himself. At least there would be a feast tonight. And the Three Old Men were to say to what affiliation the newcomers should belong. Mocking Bird wanted to belong to the Deer People. They were the ones whose business it was to talk to the deer. Everything to do with hunting or making war was influenced by them, by their prayers and rituals. The Healers, and the Rainmakers, who were in charge of the sky and the earth and things that grew in it, seemed to him unimportant by comparison. The People had not been warriors, but Mocking Bird was a warrior's son. His father's people were fierce and gave their enemies to their gods. It was right that Mocking Bird should belong to the warrior society.

The smell of fresh meat cooking began to thicken the air. Mocking Bird pulled his flute from his belt and sauntered down toward the newly built fire pits. He perched on a stone that was left over from the building and played quick little notes like birds fluttering. A Rainmaker girl—who had decided he was not bone people after all—smiled shyly at him, and two others, bolder, cut a piece off the carcass they were supposed to be minding and brought it to him. He put the flute down and gobbled it, wiping the warm juice off his hands onto their bare flanks when they tickled him teasingly. One pulled away, but he held on to the other, a girl about his own age with bright eyes and a crooked tooth. It made her look somehow raffish, and when he held her by the wrist and pantomimed spanking her backside with his other hand, she grinned at him and stuck her tongue out. Then she twisted free and ran off giggling with her friend.

As the sky darkened and fell into night, the Kindred settled around the fire pit. There were boiled summer greens, camas bulbs packed in mud and roasted in the coals, and fish cooked on hot stones. Rarely had the Kindred been this well fed, and they looked with growing respect at Maize Came. The seed she had planted had brought food already. *Like brought like.* Everyone knew that, and it was clear that Rain Old Man thought so. He gave her the best place at the fire and sat down next to her, gnawing a rib bone, the juices running down his chin.

"Rain Old Man wants another wife," Old Duck cackled.

Rain Old Man only said, "Hah!" at him and went on eating.

There were interested murmurs. Everyone knew that when Rain Old Man was angry he could send lightning into the belly of whoever had been unfortunate enough to annoy him.

Maize Came bowed her head at Rain Old Man in a proper gesture of respect, but when Wing Foot sat down on her other side, she smiled. There were more murmurs, and jokes that Mocking Bird could figure out without knowing the language.

Rain Old Man stood up. "Tonight the Kindred will take the woman who is Maize Came into the Squash Band." He paused while everyone paid attention to him. "She will be a woman of the Rainmakers," he added grandly.

There were whoops from the Rainmakers, and someone drummed his fingers fast on a skin drum.

"Her twin brother, thereby part of her, will be a Rainmaker, also," Rain Old Man added. "Tonight they have eaten of our kill. By this we make them ours, ours to us."

*But I don't want to be a Rainmaker*, Mocking Bird thought. He stood up to protest to Rain Old Man, but he had turned away. Mocking Bird saw Deer Old Man and ran after him instead.

"With respect, Uncle—" Mocking Bird lurched in front of Deer Old Man, feet stumbling over new words. "I want to be Deer People."

Deer Old Man raised a bushy eyebrow at him. "You are Rainmaker."

"But I do not want to be."

"You do not choose," Deer Old Man said pointedly. He eyed Mocking Bird's cast-down face, the angry mouth. "Get Night Hawk to explain it to you," he said gruffly. "You do not hear well enough to listen to me."

*I won't*, Mocking Bird thought. Night Hawk would just tell him to do as he was told. And then he would tell Wing Foot, who thought he was such a fine hunter, and Wing Foot would laugh.

The last of the twilight flowed into the trees, and then there was only the red fire and the thin horns of the moon. The Rainmakers kindled torches at the fire, and the Kindred began to move toward the ground where they made the Deer Prayer, with Maize Came at the center of them. Her dark hair became shadow, and her red skin looked as if it were pieces of the fire.

"Come along," Wing Foot said, clapping Mocking Bird on the shoulder. "You, too."

Mocking Bird shrugged his shoulder away from him. They followed the Kindred silently, but Wing Foot didn't appear to notice that anything was amiss.

The Rainmaker girl who had smiled at him ran back and took Mocking Bird by the hand. "Come on!" She tugged him forward.

All the Kindred who belonged to the Rainmakers were gathered at the center of the ground where the Kindred danced their Deer Prayer. Night Hawk stood among them, and he beckoned to Mocking Bird. "Bring him over here, Blue," he called to the girl.

Mocking Bird went grudgingly. It was clear they weren't going to listen to him when he said he didn't want to be a Rainmaker just because his sister—his *sister*!—was going to be one. He scowled at Night Hawk.

Night Hawk didn't appear to notice, either. Rain Old Man lifted his snake staff, and a hush fell over the Kindred. Rain Old Man's face was masked with strips of snakeskin, and when he shook his head, the rattles buzzed and hummed. They made the hair stand up on Mocking Bird's neck.

*"We bring this girl to live among the Rainmakers."*

They moved closer, encircling Maize Came. He saw her disappear, leaving him standing outside the circle in the night. Weren't they taking him, too? They had said they were.

*"We take this girl to live among the Rainmakers."*

The low chant went on. He couldn't understand most of it. Night Hawk had moved away with the rest and left him standing there. The other Kindred, those who weren't Rainmakers, ringed the edges of the dance ground, watching. Mocking Bird thought of just walking away if they were going to treat him thus, but he was afraid to. He didn't know how to talk to them very much yet. He couldn't make them understand things.

A hand closed around his arm. He jerked his head up and saw Rain Old Man looking down at him through the snake mask. The rattles hummed.

"Come."

Mocking Bird saw the circle open to let Maize Came step through. In her hands she held a gourd dipper full of water, and she poured it out as she walked, a thin stream lit red and silver by the moon and the torches. Night Hawk walked behind her with a torch so that she was silhouetted by fire, her body outlined with a thin aureole of flame. Mocking Bird gaped like the rest of the Kindred, and then he felt Rain Old Man tug him forward, past his sister, into the waiting circle and felt it close behind him.

*"We bring this boy to live among the Rainmakers,"* Rain Old Man intoned, and the rest of them repeated it. Their voices hummed like the dry rattle that comes from under a rock.

> *"To all that is in the sky will you speak.*
> *To all that grows from the earth will you speak.*
> *To all that lies beneath the earth will you lend*
> *   your voice.*
> *The old men will teach you.*
> *The old women will show you the way."*

They poured water down his back. He could feel its cold current slide along his spine. The drops splashed back from the ground against his heels. Rain Old Man gave him a dipper of water and closed Mocking Bird's fingers around it. "Learn from the old ones and be wise," he said.

*"We take this boy to live among the Rainmakers."*

The Rainmaker people crowded around him until he could feel their breath in his face. Then they stepped backward, opening the circle, and Night Hawk whispered in his ear, "Pour the water out as you go. Make it last until you get to the edge of the dance ground. Then throw the dipper as far into the lake as you can."

"Why?" Mocking Bird demanded.

"Because that is the way it is done," Night Hawk said reasonably. "Usually it is babies coming to us, and the parents throw the gourd. It fills with water, and that way there will always be water for you to bring."

"I didn't want to be a Rainmaker," Mocking Bird blurted.

"Oh, you don't get to choose," Night Hawk said. "And anyway, we are very important people. Now go." He gave him a little push toward the lake.

The outer circle of the Kindred opened before him, and Mocking Bird could see Maize Came on the shore of the lake now, empty-handed, waiting for him. He walked carefully, pouring the thin stream of water out, feeling the cold drops spatter his feet. Why didn't he get to choose, especially something that important? Among the People, he would have had a vision that told him what kind of person he was going to be, and what his totem was. That wasn't a matter for other people to decide.

He spilled the last of the water out on the lakeshore while he grumbled in his head. Maize Came smiled at him and touched his shoulder. Her fingers were damp; he could feel the lake in them. Mocking Bird drew his arm back and heaved the gourd out over the water. It fell with a plop and a lifted spurt of spray, bobbed for a moment, filling with water, and vanished in the dark.

"Now we belong," Maize Came said. Her voice sounded light, like the splash when the gourd hit.

"I didn't want to be a Rainmaker," Mocking Bird said, but he kept it under his breath. No one was listening to him. The ceremony was over, and the Kindred walked back toward the warmth of the fire pits, torches bobbing above their heads with the smoke streaming out behind. Wing Foot appeared—he was much too easy to find, Mocking Bird thought—and Maize Came leaned toward him as she walked, almost leaning *on* him, laughing and trying to talk to him.

Mocking Bird saw the girl with the crooked tooth. He took his flute from his belt. It went to his lips of its own accord, the way it always did, and sang to him in his head. It sang to him the song it wanted to play, and he blew into the hole, and the notes bubbled up.

The girl with the crooked tooth skipped up to him. She was called Thorn, for the tooth, but she was very pretty. "I saw you throw the dipper," she said. "It went *way* out. You'll always have water."

Mocking Bird didn't understand much besides "water" and the admiration in her voice. She looked nice in the torchlight. It tipped her breasts with a rosy glow and made him think of cactus flowers. She was slender around the waist and wide-hipped. He felt himself getting stiff under his breechclout. His cheeks felt hot. "Do you want to walk?" he said. He gestured at the lakeshore.

The girl thought about it quickly. "All right," she said. Her eyes gleamed with mischief, and she shot a swift glance over her shoulder.

Mocking Bird started to walk away with her, hoping that it wasn't her father or an older brother she

had been looking for. The girls of the Kindred seemed
fairly free, but he didn't know the rules yet. There
were always rules. He remembered listening to the
People's Grandmothers talking about them endlessly
at the Gathering: who could go with whom, whose
mate might leave whom over which transgression.
Only the incest rule was an absolute taboo. The rest
were social, and as far as Mocking Bird had figured
as a child, the adults had broken them regularly. If
there were not three or four scandalous stories to
come out of a Gathering and tell over the winter, the
People did not consider it to have been interesting.

He eased her into the shelter of a pile of wind-
eroded stones that stood like a sentinel beside the new
lake, water lapping at their feet. Behind, on the other
side, there was a stone that was cupped at the top,
making a seat just wide enough for two. It hadn't
taken any of the Kindred's young, unmated ones long
to find it; it was the perfect courting site. Mocking
Bird was cheered to find that no one was there before
them.

They scrambled up the lower stones, and the girl
snuggled against him. They could see the stars clearly
now, a spatter of them blazing behind the thin moon.

He tried out his few words. "You are—pretty," he
said.

The girl laughed. She pointed at his flute. "Make it
sing."

Mocking Bird put it to his lips and made a sound
like bright crickets. The girl watched him. He wondered if she wanted the other girls to know they were
here.

"We had a man who could play a thing like that,"
she said. "Night Hawk the Trader brought it from
somewhere, maybe from the Trespassers, even. But he
didn't make it sound like you do, and anyway he died
last spring."

Mocking Bird looked at her over the flute. He
caught maybe one word in ten and remained baffled.

She didn't seem to notice, talking chattily to him while he played. Slowly she stopped, though, after the music had whispered against her throat for a while and sung in her ear, a sound as sinuous as water. She licked her lips. Her breast felt hot against his ribs where she leaned against him. The cold night bit him on his other side. He laid the flute beside him on the stone, and she wriggled closer, and his hand ended in her lap.

After a time, when he pushed it deeper, she scooted away with a laugh. She began to climb down the stones. He leaned after her, his fingers burning, trying to think how to make her come back.

"Mother will be looking for me!" she called back up to him.

He understood that. "I will come and talk to your mother," he said. He knew love, wanted only the girl with the crooked tooth, wanted her now, tonight. His body was quite clear about that.

She laughed. Her laughter floated on the air the way the flute notes had. "You are too young! Mother will smack me if I don't go with someone who will make a good husband!" She waved to him and dropped to the ground.

"When will I be made a Healer?" Reed asked her mother. The Grandmothers were coming this morning to wash her again, as they had done every morning since she had come back to the Kindred. Maize Came and Mocking Bird were members of the Rainmakers now, and of the Kindred as well, and Reed found herself rebelling.

"When you have been made clean," Leaf Fall said earnestly. "All that time with the Trespassers, with dirty people, that has to be washed off."

"My brother and sister are not washed every day!" Reed had learned enough of the Kindred's speech to be argumentative.

"They are Kindred now because the Three Old Men

have said so. But you were born Kindred. It is different." Leaf Fall nodded her head, agreeing with that, with the Grandmothers.

She bit her lip. She hadn't thought it would be like this. She looked at Leaf Fall twisting yucca rope on her thigh, fingers rolling it expertly, palm slapping up and down in unbroken rhythm. This was her mother. Love for her clutched at Reed's chest. But she didn't love the Grandmothers, she thought sourly, bottom lip pushed out.

She poked at the water basket full of yucca leaves and wood ash to see if the fibers were soft yet. Leaf Fall had announced this morning that their cave was big enough and they could stop chipping out stones and dirt like gophers. Now they were going to make rope all day. They had a new hearth to heat the stones to boil the yucca in, and Leaf Fall had found a fine yucca patch to cut young leaves from. They needed new sandals and new everything else, too, after their long trek from their old place. And Leaf Fall would teach Reed the proper way.

"I know how to make rope," Reed had said, but Leaf Fall had just shaken her head. The Kindred twisted rope a little differently, it seemed, and the right way was theirs.

Leaf Fall jerked her head up now and put her rope down, tying off the end with a quick knot so it wouldn't untwist. "Old Women Who Remember," she said, making a respectful gesture at Grandmother Snake, who stood in the cave mouth.

Grandmother Snake came in with Old Woman Many Grandsons behind her, and Grandmother Watcher and Old Woman Tells Stories behind them. With an air of purpose they set down three baskets and a skin bag.

Grandmother Snake cocked her head at Reed. "Hmm!" she said.

"Stand up, child," Leaf Fall said.

Old Woman Tells Stories examined Reed's hands

and feet and sniffed at the yucca leaves boiling in the basket. "Too much ash," she said.

Grandmother Snake held Reed by the wrist while Old Woman Many Grandsons rubbed something out of the skin bag on her. It smelled like deer fat that had gone rancid, and Reed wrinkled her nose and tried to pull away.

"We are pulling the Trespassers' dirt from your skin," Old Woman Many Grandsons said. "Stand still. And why have you not been to the Women's House yet? It is almost a moon since you came to us."

"I haven't bled yet," Reed said.

"Are you pregnant?" Grandmother Watcher demanded angrily. "Did we not tell you that you may not go with our men until you are clean?"

"I am not pregnant," Reed said. "I just haven't bled."

"Tsk. Then you should have come to us for sage tea."

"I know how to make sage tea," Reed said between her teeth.

"Your daughter is disrespectful," Old Woman Many Grandsons said to Leaf Fall.

"She is learning," Leaf Fall said. She looked at her feet. "It is hard."

Grandmother Watcher began to chant, and the other Grandmothers turned away from Leaf Fall and circled Reed until she could feel their dark eyes crawling over her skin. The grease itched, and she wanted to scrape it off, to roll in the sand and then go into the lake with a ball of soap.

*This woman has lived wrongly among bad people,* Grandmother Watcher intoned. She looked at Reed through slitted eyes.

*We make her clean again. We pull wickedness from her.*

The Grandmothers pressed around her, and Old Woman Many Grandsons lit a piece of resin in a turtle shell and filled the cave with smoke.

*"We teach her how the true people live, for she is ignorant."*

They said it again several times, and then the Grandmothers packed their deer-foot rattles and their skin of rancid salve back in their bags and baskets and stumped away.

Leaf Fall looked at Reed, her mouth trembling. When she was sure the Grandmothers were out of hearing range, she said, "I have not taught you properly. It is my fault."

"You have taught me," Reed said. She poked at the grease on her skin with disgust. "But I don't know how to change to please them. I don't remember to do things the new way. Why does it matter that some things were different among my foster people?"

Leaf Fall looked shocked. She picked up her rope again. She looked into its twine as if the taboos of the Kindred might be twisted in its fibers. "We are a people of tradition," she said. "Old, very old. The Grandmothers remember tradition for us. Because you are unclean, everything you do they will watch. If you do it differently, they will think it is *because* you are unclean, and everyone will say you have been ruined by living among the False People."

"Yah, that is what I heard Juniper Who Minds Others' Business say to you yesterday, is it not? *Her* daughter looks like a buffalo cow," Reed added.

"Juniper's daughter has made a good match with the son of Deer Old Man," Leaf Fall said.

"Yah, and I may not go with a man until the Grandmothers tell me to. Maize Came, my sister, has all the men of the Kindred following her like dogs, but *I* may not!"

"Be patient," Leaf Fall said. Her eyes welled with tears. "Please, because I ask it. The men will wait. It is important that you not seem to make eyes at them and go against the Grandmothers. The men will not want you if you do. They will think you are bad luck. Always the Kindred will remember that you were gone from us. But I will teach you the right way, I promise. But you, you must remember how it is important to be careful, to do things properly. Please." She looked at Reed pleadingly. This was her baby, miraculously returned to her. How was she going to live happily, to find a man who would marry her, if she wouldn't obey the Grandmothers?

"And when will I be clean?" Reed said. "Bah!" She rubbed at the grease on her skin with water from the cooling basket of yucca leaves.

"At the autumn, when the Healers take you back." Leaf Fall bit her lip. "If you don't offend the Grandmothers."

Reed's eyes filled with furious tears. They spilled down over her cheeks, and Leaf Fall went to her and took her in her plump arms. "The ways of the Kindred hold the world together," she said. That should be obvious, but perhaps Reed hadn't known it. Leaf Fall patted her and crooned baby talk, trying to comfort Reed as she had when Reed was young. But Reed had been little, soft and accommodating, not this angular, stubborn person who drew ants in the ground. Leaf Fall had seen her do it, had seen the ants' nest under Grandmother Snake's bed where one had not been before, because who could miss a nest that big and put their bed over it?

She was terrified that Reed would do it again.

Mocking Bird found Reed by the lake, scrubbing her skin with sand and then yucca soap and then sand again. "What are you doing?" he said, looking vexed himself. Reed's expression was sullen.

"I am washing," she said. She rubbed fiercely at her calves. There were raw spots on her knees and arms. "If you want to help, clean my back." She handed Mocking Bird the ball of soap.

"Phew, what is that on you?"

"Nasty grease the old Grandmothers put on me. They say I am not clean."

"Well, this isn't going to change that." Mocking Bird held his nose. "You smell like a dead bear."

Reed looked over her shoulder at him with narrowed eyes. "Just get it off me."

"Yes, Most Important," Mocking Bird said, but he scrubbed at her back with the soap. "Go in the lake now."

Reed waded into the muddy water. The lake was new, and the bottom had yet to settle. She could still feel grass under her toes, and bubbles of bad smell rose where she churned it up. She waded out until she could swim and then dived under the surface, muddy or not, letting the water cover every inch of her. Her skin was raw from scrubbing, and the water stung like the Grandmothers' dry fingernails. She swam back to shore and wriggled her shoulder blades until she felt their touch sliding off her.

Mocking Bird was waiting for her, arms folded on his chest. "I do not like it here," he said.

"Yah bah, and why should you not like it?" Reed demanded, shaking wet hair out of her face. "You are Kindred now. It is me that they spread with nasty grease and say I am not to go with any men until they tell me!"

"It is different for you, I suppose," Mocking Bird said, shrugging, intent on his own grievance. "But I do not like being of the Rainmakers like Night Hawk the Trader. I am a warrior's son and a hunter, and I wish to be of the Deer People."

"It doesn't matter," Reed said. "Everyone hunts and fights, if that is what you are worried about. It is an honor that Rain Old Man wanted you."

"He wanted Maize Came," Mocking Bird said sourly. "And I am tired of being that one's twin and having to cut my hair when everyone pays attention to *her* and brings her snails and cress and a quail's liver."

"Who brought her a quail's liver?" Reed asked, momentarily distracted.

"Wing Foot." Mocking Bird kicked at a stone at the water's edge. "I don't like him."

Reed didn't say anything, but she bit her lip.

"I want to be Deer People," Mocking Bird said. "If you make the picture magic and call the deer for these people, they will let us be what we want. Why haven't you done that?"

Reed shook her head. She began to pull her skirt on, tugging it over her wet skin. In a few moments she would be dry. The sun was hot and baking the sky a bright blue.

"I want you to do that," Mocking Bird said again.

"No." She shook her head from side to side, and water flew out of her hair in drops that smelled like dead grass.

"Why not?"

"I mustn't be different from anyone else," Reed said between her teeth. He could hear angry mockery in her voice. "If I am different, they will say that I am still not clean."

"But you have the picture magic!" Mocking Bird said. "Like Mother."

"I don't want it," Reed said angrily. She wrung the water out of her hair.

"You could show them!"

"I will not show them anything if they think I am dirty." She set her mouth in a thin line.

Mocking Bird could tell by looking at her that she had made some other picture elsewhere. He thought that she loved old Leaf Fall, but if he were the Grandmothers, he would look where he sat down. He tried to think of some other way to convince her to make the picture magic, but she wasn't listening.

"These are my people," she said wearily after a moment. The mockery had vanished from her voice, and she just sounded resigned. "I have to learn to be like them." She turned and walked determinedly back toward the cave where her mother was waiting.

# XII

# The Maize Girl

Being blessed among the Kindred did not excuse the Maize Girl from an ordinary woman's work. The Grandmothers made that clear. But Maize Came was happy with that arrangement and quite willing to seek the Grandmothers' advice. The Grandmothers pronounced her a praiseworthy person of much virtue and power.

Maize Came *liked* grinding meal and drying meat, liked scraping and tanning hides when there were other women to chatter with, and when Wing Foot just might happen by and stay to tell her about the day's hunt. It would be an honor for her, of course, if she were to marry Rain Old Man—a girl so young. The Grandmothers all agreed. But who could blame her if she took the young one instead? Wing Foot was also an important man, the fastest runner and the best hunter among the Kindred, and certainly fine to look at, the Grandmothers said, chuckling, their heads together.

Maize Came heard it all and pretended not to, but it was good to know that she had the Grandmothers' approval. They were the true power in the tribe, very much as the old women of the Yellow Grass People had been. If you knew that, life became easier; you could fight the men if you had to. That was where Mother had made her mistake, Maize Came thought. She had always rebelled against the old women, and they wouldn't come to help her when the tribe wanted to kill her husband. With a sigh Maize Came thought that now Reed was doing the same thing, but after worrying because she thought she ought to, she forgot Reed. Worrying about other people was hard when you had love for the first time, when you had found this wonderful thing you had been longing for and had not even known it all those years of living alone.

Today the women were in a meadow half an afternoon's walk from the camp by the lake, gathering seed, and Maize Came found that she could think of Wing Foot and work at the same time with no trouble. Her basket hung down her back by a sling across her forehead, and she bent over the waving stalks of pale grass knowing that she looked industrious and graceful, beating it with a rawhide paddle. The seed fell into the basket in her left hand. Beat and fill the basket; straighten and with a practiced movement tip the seed over your shoulder into the carrying basket on your back. Bend and beat the grass some more, moving through the field. There was always time to think, to dream away an afternoon until her cheeks were hot.

At the far side she stopped with the other women, hands on her hips, stretching out her back. There was a light breeze. If it held, it would be just right for threshing. This was what Maize Came liked, this being part of the whole, of having a place, honored by the other women, too, so long as she remembered not to act lordlywise. Very likely Wing Foot would hap-

pen to be crossing the meadow when they came home
to the lake. He would have a pair of rabbits dangling
from one hand, and somehow, unaccountably, be lag-
ging behind the other men.

Maize Came smiled, a secretive curving of her lips
that held the pleasure of that inside so that she could
taste it. She walked through the ripe grass swinging
her gathering basket by one hand, feeling the weight
of the harvest basket on her back. Not such good seed
as maize gave, but it would be a while before the
maize grew them enough to eat. A season and a season probably. Maybe longer. She would make the
Kindred obey her and keep most of the seed back to
plant. But she would show him—anyone who happened to be interested—how finely she could grind
meal when she ground this grass seed.

Wing Foot was waiting, pretending to relace his
sandal, on the edge of the meadow under a scraggly
willow. "Ho," he said, with a sly grin. "Would you
like to practice talking?" Maize Came understood
nearly everything that was said to her now, except
when she didn't want to. It was a game they played.

She tossed her head at him, being careful not to slip
the sling loose. She stood very straight under its
weight. "I have work to do, not like lazy men," she
told him.

"Then I will help." He slipped the basket off her
back before she could stop him and hefted it onto his
shoulder. The rabbits dangled from his other hand,
three of them. "We had a fine rabbit drive," he said.
"Maybe I will find you some skins to warm your feet
this winter."

She flushed, knowing that the other women were
watching him carry her basket for her. She swung the
little basket in her hand again. "It's a fine thing to
stay warm in the winter," she said solemnly.

"Two are warmer than one," Wing Foot said to no
one in particular, looking at the trees.

Maize Came suppressed a smile and sneaked a look

at him out of the corner of her eye. Her heart thudded
in her chest. It did that every time she looked at him,
or thought about him touching her, which was
mostly.

He followed her to the camp, talking about how
they had killed the rabbits, circling them and driving
them in on each other with noises and shouts until
they could hit them with their throw sticks. When she
set her little basket down outside her cave, Wing Foot
put the big basket down beside it and squatted on the
ground while she got her threshing tray. Maize Came
poured the seed into the tray and began to pound it
with a blunt stick. The little breeze made her hair
dance in fine tendrils about her face.

Wing Foot sniffed the air. "Fall is coming," he said.
"Soon it will be time for moving again."

"Moving where?" Maize Came tossed the seed in
the threshing tray, and the loose chaff lifted in the
wind. It whirled around her face, and she sneezed.

"After the deer," Wing Foot said. "There won't be
browse this low. Don't your people move in winter?"

"Oh, yes." Maize Came tossed the seed again. The
fine hulls whirled away in the wind. "We are much
like you. I didn't believe Mother when she told me
that the old soft man had said that to her, but it is
true."

"That is what Night Hawk always said," Wing Foot
agreed. "I never believed him, either."

They looked at each other with complete satisfaction.

"I think my sister was angry when Night Hawk
went away," Maize Came said.

Wing Foot shrugged, uninterested in her sister. "He
goes every spring."

"Well, it was hard, not to have anyone to talk to."

"You have me."

She put the threshing tray down and stared at him
blissfully. He stared back. "That is why the gods have

done all this," Maize Came said with conviction. "So that we would be together."

"That is what my totem says. Badger is my totem, and I asked him," he assured her solemnly.

Maize Came sighed, spinning out happiness. She pounded energetically at the threshing tray.

Mocking Bird glared at her from the edge of the rubble pile where the Kindred had thrown the dirt and rocks they had cleared from the caves. Thorn, the girl with the crooked tooth, wouldn't walk with him again, and the other girls who would treated him as if he were a baby. They let him fondle them, but nothing much else. Yah bah, his twin sister was old enough to marry, with ugly old men courting her, but he was not, and how was that?

Men had to be older, Thorn had said with a giggle, or they weren't steady; the mothers wouldn't approve of them. Who wanted a husband who was off throwing skipping stones in the lake when he should be at the Council Fire listening to the Three Old Men?

Mocking Bird flung the flat stone he had been playing with away from him, and Bitch lifted her ears with mild interest, but she didn't chase it. Bitch didn't chase sticks, either. If she couldn't eat it, she didn't see the use of it. Instead she cocked her head at Wing Foot's rabbits, lying carelessly next to Maize Came's hearth.

Even his sisters had no time for him, Mocking Bird thought angrily. Reed was truculent and fierce with him when he talked to her. Mocking Bird didn't think Reed liked any of these people except Leaf Fall, but she kept trying to be one of them. She was crosser still since Night Hawk the Trader had gone, pack-on-back, and since Handsome (Mocking Bird shot a caustic glance at Wing Foot) was courting Maize Came. Why couldn't he want Reed instead? *She* wanted *him*. And then he would leave Maize Came alone.

Mocking Bird folded his arms angrily. There had

never been a time—until they had come *here*—that he had not known everything his twin was thinking, like one person in two bodies. He turned his back and scowled out at the lake, conveniently forgetting why they had come here in the first place.

Bitch considered the situation. She lowered herself onto her belly and began to ease toward the hearth, where the humans were ignoring their rabbits.

When Maize Came looked up, Wing Foot was still staring at her happily, and Bitch was disappearing into the rubble pile, one of Wing Foot's rabbits bumping along the ground between her forelegs.

Maize Came yelped and pointed, and Wing Foot jumped to his feet and floundered in the rubble.

*"Drop it!"* Maize Came yelled. Bitch looked back at her and disappeared over the top of the rubble. Wing Foot sprinted after her. In a few moments he came back with the rabbit in his hand, dust and sticks in his dark hair. He ran his fingers through it, rocking back on his heels.

Maize Came put her hand over her mouth.

"Most funny," he said severely, and they both burst out laughing. "I am going to take these rabbits, which are not mine, to the cooking pit before your evil dog eats them." He lifted a hand to her and strode along the trail, well worn now, that ran along the low cliffs where the Kindred had dug out their caves. Maize Came watched him go with a sigh and a smile.

"Yah, I have killed many rabbits," Mocking Bird said sourly, and she jerked her head up.

"You let Bitch steal that rabbit!" Maize Came accused. "You were right there, weren't you?"

"What if I was? That one's importance is too great. Yah, he was funny, falling about in the rocks."

"And what were you doing hiding in them, spying on me?"

"Only waiting for a chance to talk to you," Mocking

Bird said sullenly. "But you are always talking to Most Handsome."

"I am not."

"You are."

"And you are spying on me, like that one, skulking around rubble piles." Maize Came jerked her chin at Bitch, whose gray nose poked around the rocks.

Mocking Bird guffawed. "Yah, he was funny, chasing a dog! *Wait! Wait! Come back! Come back!*" He pranced, mimicking the chase.

"He caught her, too," Maize Came said, her eyes narrowed. "*You* can't catch her."

Mocking Bird bent down to glare at her. "And what else has he caught, Most Promiscuous? I see the way you walk when he's watching you."

"The way I walk is none of your affair," Maize Came said furiously. "And neither is Wing Foot."

"Yah, and the old man, too? Rain Old Man with no teeth? What do you let *him* do to you?"

"Go away!" Maize Came shouted at him. She balled her hands into fists and pounded them in the threshing tray so that the chaff flew up and scattered. "Who gave you the right to own me? I am not your woman!"

"You are my sister," Mocking Bird said. "My sister who was not a dirty person before she came here, wiggling her backside for men, letting men touch her like . . . like . . ."

Maize Came jumped to her feet, upsetting the threshing tray. "Go away!" she screeched. "Go away out of my sight. *You* are the one who is dirty! Dirty like that dirty coyote!" She glared at Bitch. "I've seen you with the girls. How dare you talk about me and mine?"

Mocking Bird's mouth twisted. "I only . . . They . . . It is different with you." His voice was low now, miserable. "You are not just sister. We were always like one person, the two of us. There was never anyone between us before, not even Reed. Is this how it will be, here?"

Maize Came's face softened. She held her hand out to him. "I have to marry. You will marry. Is that so bad? We will still have each other."

"Not with that one," Mocking Bird said stubbornly. He put his hands behind his back, deliberately holding on to his anger.

"Wing Foot is a good man," Maize Came said.

"He thinks too much of himself. He preens like a turkey cock."

"He doesn't," Maize Came said. "You are jealous."

"All right, so I am jealous. Of that one. I don't like him. I want you to stay away from him."

Maize Came's lip trembled. "But I love him. We are one person, too. You can't ask me to do that."

"You would do it if you loved *me*," Mocking Bird said.

"No!"

"Yah, you are different. You are spoiled. You are someone else besides my sister."

"*You* are not my father," Maize Came said, stung and getting angry again. "You are not allowed to give me orders. Besides," she added smugly, "I am the Maize Girl. You will get in trouble. I will tell the Grandmothers."

"Your father is dead. I am your brother. You will listen to *me* instead of those old women."

"No." She stuck her chin out at him, lips compressed, stubborn.

"I am telling you to stay away from him." Mocking Bird's voice was furious again.

"Tell your backside," Maize Came said.

"Are you going to obey me?" he shouted at her.

She put her hands on her hips. "No one obeys babies," she said, calculating the insult carefully. "Go away, Born After I Was. I don't have to listen to you."

Mocking Bird jerked his chin up. His face blazed. "You stay away from him! You do what I say or you

will be sorry!" He spun on his heel and stalked off,
ignoring the interested faces that turned from other
fire pits to stare at him. After a moment he realized
that Bitch wasn't with him and whistled for her angrily. She stuck her nose out from behind the rubble
pile, eyed him, and disappeared again. He shouted at
her, but she didn't come. He thought he heard a stifled laugh. Face flaming, he walked on.

Amused voices followed him, Wing Foot's at the
center of them: "Ho, try whistling the dog to heel before you try it on the women!"

Mocking Bird clenched his fists until the nails dug
into his palms.


Reed dragged the heavy water basket up from the
lake, the sling around her forehead biting into the
skin. Around the Council Fire she could see Wing
Foot with the other men, and she slowed, watching
him wistfully. He looked just the way she had imagined the man in her daydreams, the man that Daughter Came Home would find. But she wasn't Daughter
Came Home; she was Reed and forbidden to men until the equinox and maybe after that, and how would
he know that she loved him?

She had seen him walking with Maize Came and
turned away angrily because it wasn't fair that the
Grandmothers liked Maize Came. Maize Came was
the Maize Girl and holy, and Reed was somehow always bad or wrong. Night Hawk the Trader had tried
to explain it all to her, but she hadn't liked his explanation.

Reed dumped the water basket down by Leaf Fall's
hearth, sloshing water over the top. The Grandmothers might be watching, she thought sourly. Let them
mark that down on their tally sticks.

"It is because you were one of us," Night Hawk
had said to her, sitting by the lake the day before he
left. "It is easier to take something that has never been

ours and make it so than to reclaim that which was once ours."

"Why?" Reed said.

Night Hawk chuckled. "Because the Grannies think it is," he said. "That's what most ritual amounts to, if you want my opinion. But then, that is why I am not one of the Three Old Men."

"You found the lake," Reed said. That had been holy business, and they both knew it.

"That was different." Night Hawk looked a little more serious than usual, the way he did whenever he thought about the lake. "That was the gods' doing. I heard them speak. This is just tribal matters. It is whatever the Grandmothers say it is."

"Then why do the Three Old Men let them say?" Reed asked indignantly.

"Because it is easier that way," Night Hawk said. He cocked his head at her. They were sitting by Leaf Fall's hearth so that everyone would know this was a respectable visit and only for talking about how matters stood with the False People. A trader needed to know that. "If there are no little rituals, and patterns that everyone follows, and rules for things, then no one knows how to be, and may do anything. It is the little rules that make it certain that we will follow the big ones."

"I am tired of their rules!" Reed said. "I am tired of being different and not clean. I *am* clean!" She held out her hands to him, palms up, indignant.

"You look clean to me, Quarrelsome," he said. "So why do you want to stay here?"

"It is my place," Reed said, baffled by the question. "Where else would I go?"

"Foot-on-trail," Night Hawk said. "There is much to be seen out there."

"I have seen it, many thanks. We saw it for nearly three turns of the sun, my brother and sister and I. We have seen it enough."

"That wasn't seeing. That was trying to stay alive.

Did you *really* see? Maybe I should show you the cat bones."

"What cat bones?" she asked him suspiciously.

"I saw them once," he said. "After a big storm. I could find them again, I think. It was a cat bigger than any *I* have ever seen, as big as a buffalo, and it had two fangs as long as my arm in its mouth."

"From the Old Days," Reed breathed. "From the Cold Time, before the Great Game went away."

"You know about the animals of the Cold Time?"

"The shaman of my foster people told me. He had a tooth from an animal, too—as long as a spear shaft, but it curled. The shaman who killed my father has it now," she added bitterly.

"Then you should come with me," Night Hawk said, "and find the cat again, and scare the magic out of the new shaman with it."

Reed chuckled in spite of herself. "That would be very fine. Tell me more about what you have seen."

"Red and blue birds with hooked beaks. Spotted cats. Herds of buffalo. White sand so bright it hurts your eyes. The Endless Water."

"You have *seen* the Endless Water?" *Where the world ended?* Reed's eyes opened wide.

"Once." Night Hawk looked to the west, thinking. "I was gone two years, but it was worth it. I saw the sun go to lie down far out in that water, and the water turned to fire."

"I will never see anything like that," Reed said sadly.

"You could. I could take you."

It seemed too fantastic an idea to contemplate, like thinking that he might teach her to float in the air. She chuckled ruefully. "*Then* what would the Grandmothers say?"

Night Hawk drew his knees up and put his arms around them. "You aren't thinking about it the right way," he said, wondering at the same time why he was talking to her like this. Did he want a wife? No.

And yet . . . Something in this one saw things differently, maybe thought about things differently. None of the other women of the Kindred, or the men, for that matter, could do that. Like the Grandmothers, they knew what was what, and don't bother them with giant cats or what was beyond the Endless Water. Something was beyond it, he was pretty sure of that. The People Who Lived at the Coast didn't think so, but it had been Night Hawk's experience that there was always something beyond anything. "You aren't thinking about it properly," he said again. "If you went foot-on-trail with me, the Grannies could say anything they felt like, and why would you care?"

"I care that they say I am dirty," Reed said forcefully. "I should like to see those birds and the sun falling into the Endless Water, but this is my belonging place. I looked for this place. It is home. It is a place to enfold me. I *want* it. So I have to care what the Grandmothers say because they will not let me be here if I do not." She explained it to him carefully, so as not to insult him. Night Hawk did not seem to care what anyone thought, but it had been her experience that most men were insulted when you didn't agree with them.

"That is up to you," Night Hawk said. Maybe it was just as well. But he said, slyly, "I heard that the Grannies have decided you aren't allowed to go with a man until the equinox." And so why was he bringing that up? There were other women, and prettier.

"Yes," Reed said stiffly.

He grinned. "The equinox is a long time."

"I don't mind," Reed said, irritated.

"The Three Old Men will go out and look at their sun stone every morning," Night Hawk said, "and the sun will *crawl* toward it, until you are an old woman before it gets to the sun stone."

"I can wait. And men are not such a fine thing as women are told," she added, goaded.

Night Hawk hooted with amusement.

"You've been going with the wrong men," he suggested.

"I only went with one," she said, before she could stop herself from telling him her business.

"And how was it?"

Her face flushed. "Short," she said between her teeth, and he hooted again. With dignity she said, "I meant that it didn't take very long. And it isn't your business, anyway. He went to sleep afterward," she added, aggrieved.

Night Hawk put his hand over his mouth. "Definitely you have been with the wrong man."

"Well, I'm not going with you!" she snapped.

"I didn't ask you. Rattlesnake," he said.

"You asked me to go foot-on-trail. Aren't you interested in girls?"

"That would be different. But you won't come with me."

She still wasn't sure if he was serious, but it didn't matter. "I can't," she said again. "I have to be here. Here is where I am supposed to be." She sounded very determined about it.

"Then I had better go. Before the Grannies are outraged."

"Tell me one more thing about the trail. About what is out there."

She *could* see it, he thought. That twist that made the world a different place every morning. She just wouldn't let herself. "I saw a snake as big around as my leg once," he said. "And long enough to reach from here to the next fire pit. It was eating a dog whole. That would be a fine thing to scratch under Grandmother Watcher's bed."

Reed's head flew up, eyes wide. "I don't know what you mean," she said unconvincingly.

"You know, I told Wing Foot that your sister is important, but you have more power," Night Hawk said. "I am sorry it didn't do any good."

Reed flushed and looked at her toes. They were

dusty, and her sandal laces were loose. She fiddled with them.

"You don't want him," Night Hawk said gently. "You are smarter than he is."

"He's your friend!"

"I know. That's why I'm telling you that. You wouldn't suit each other. Let him go with the little Maize Girl."

"You don't know anything about what would suit me," Reed said.

Night Hawk wondered if he did. He thought he would suit her. Did that mean that he did want a wife? It was an uncomfortably new idea, one he wasn't used to. And, anyway, she was mooning over Wing Foot and didn't seem inclined to satisfy her yearnings with him. He stood up. "If I find the cat bones, I will bring you a tooth," he said.

And then he had gone, and she hadn't seen him again. When she asked, Leaf Fall said he was pack-on-back and wouldn't be there again until late autumn. Maybe until winter. Sometimes he came to the winter shelters, she said, traveling on snow shoes just when everyone thought he was dead this time. And she didn't have time to worry about a wild boy, she said, when there was so much to be done to get Reed ready to be made part of the Kindred again at the equinox.

Reed watched her sister walk by with Wing Foot. It was almost time to harvest the maize. Maize Came had a kind of glow on her face, as if she were ripe, too. In a few more days the equinox would come. Reed wondered suddenly how the Three Old Men would know the equinox when their sun stone was at the old place. Maybe they had kept a tally stick and would make a new stone. She longed to ask—the notion interested her—but that wasn't women's business. After the equinox the Kindred would go from the lake to their winter place, and then in the spring to meet with the Turquoise Band in their communal hunting grounds, and then to the lake again.

Reed watched Maize Came and Wing Foot disappear in the direction of the lake. She ladled water into a cooking basket for soup. Maybe in the spring it would be different.

Mocking Bird saw his sister and Wing Foot going toward the lake, too. He turned his back angrily. *Let her go with Most Handsome, then.* He went back toward the cave where the young men slept together, planning to finish chipping the new spearheads he wanted. He had already cut the blanks from the core stone. He would finish them tonight. Maize Came had been rude and disrespectful to him—and he didn't care what she was doing with *him* by the lake; that was her business. She had said so. They were probably sitting on the stone by the rock tower, he thought, scowling. Watching the moon and making stupid talk. Touching each other.

His steps slowed as he came near the young men's house. It was darkening fast, and he could see the fire's glow behind the hide that hung at the front. Shouts of laughter came from around the fire. The young men had made cactus liquor, even though it wasn't a festival. They were shouting jokes at each other, advice about hunting and women. Mocking Bird thought about being part of that group, telling lies about deer run down and great fish caught, about girls bedded, while his sister was with *him*. It made him a little sick to his stomach.

He turned away from the noise and the laughter and looked around him for Bitch, but she was away, too, hunting, maybe, or sleeping by Reed's fire. It seemed that even his dog divided her loyalties. Why, then, should he expect a woman to be different? He said it out loud, in a sour voice, but no one heard him or offered any agreement to assuage his feelings.

Mocking Bird looked toward the lake and decided to walk there a little. There was no law that said he could not. What other people might be doing there was not his fault.

He walked along the shore, brooding in the deepening twilight. The faint murmur of voices came to him from the lapping, shallow waters. He could hear soft splashings and laughter from the courting couples who favored the lake. His cheeks began to burn, and he hurried, walking faster, looking straight ahead.

Maize Came's voice came lightly to him over the water. He stiffened. How dare she make a fool of him like this, cavorting in the lake with a man whom the whole camp knew he had forbidden her to see? The fact that she had defied him and made no promise to stay away from Wing Foot only made matters worse. They were deliberately making a fool of him. He knew they were. He could hear them laughing.

*I don't care what she is doing,* he thought, but he went toward the sound, slipping into the scrubby oaks that grew above the water line, shielding himself from eyes on the lakeshore. He peered through the trees and scrub brush.

They were in the shallow water, in a finger of the lake that ran between two low ridges and made a secluded cove. Manners said that you didn't go in that cove if someone was already there. Mocking Bird eased closer, ducking behind a nearer tree. It was hard to see in the darkness, but he caught the glimmer of moonlight on the calf-deep water and his sister's skin. She was naked. He stumbled over her hide skirt on the bank. He fell, clinging to a bush, but they didn't notice him. They were too busy with each other; silver ripples spread away from them on the water each time they moved. Mocking Bird could see moonlight on wet skin and Wing Foot's hands on his sister's breasts.

"Dirty bitch!" The anger washed over him like scalding water. He pulled his belt knife out and splashed down the bank into the moonlit shallows.

He grabbed Wing Foot by the shoulder and spun him around.

"Don't you touch her! She isn't yours!" The knife blade caught the light. Mocking Bird lunged at Wing Foot, aiming for his throat.

Maize Came screamed. Wing Foot stumbled backward in the roiled water and put his hand up to hold off Mocking Bird's knife. He was naked, too, his knife and breechclout left on the shore. He grabbed Mocking Bird's wrist, and his fingers bit into the tendons as Mocking Bird hacked at him with the knife, struggling to get at Wing Foot's face.

"Stop it!" Maize Came circled her brother and Wing Foot, screaming. "Stop it!"

Other voices called to them from the lake, the men's voices angry, the women's high and frightened. Maize Came heard brush being trampled as they began to move toward the cove.

Mocking Bird writhed in Wing Foot's grip, the obsidian blade nearly in Wing Foot's eyes until Wing Foot stuck a leg between Mocking Bird's and hooked his ankle from under him. Mocking Bird went down flailing, and Wing Foot twisted Mocking Bird's knife hand hard behind his back.

"Drop it or I'll break your arm." The breath in his ear came in hard, fast pants.

Mocking Bird gritted his teeth. His eyes stung with the pain. Splashing and shouts came from all around them.

"Stay away," Wing Foot said to the men who were coming after them. "This is mine." He tightened his grip on Mocking Bird's arm and pulled. Mocking Bird yelped, and his fingers opened. The knife splashed into the water. Wing Foot let go of Mocking Bird and dived for it fast. He brought it up dripping, gleaming like the dark water. Wing Foot went after Mocking Bird with it.

"No!" Maize Came splashed after them. A handful of men stood on the lakeshore, and she could hear others in the distance. "Stop him! Please!"

"He came after me with a knife," Wing Foot said. Mocking Bird had retreated to the shore and was scrambling up the bank. Wing Foot went after him.

"He's my brother!"

Mocking Bird got to the top of the bank, and two men grabbed him. Maize Came climbed after them, hiccuping and sobbing.

Wing Foot had the knife to Mocking Bird's throat now. Mocking Bird glared at him with slitted, venomous eyes.

"It's my right," Wing Foot said furiously. "Let him go and let me have him."

Maize Came pulled at his arm. "He's my brother. He is bad and wicked, but he is still my brother. Send him to the Three Old Men." Her face was tear-streaked, and her teeth were chattering.

Mocking Bird looked at her furiously. "This is your fault!" he told her.

Wing Foot put his hand around Mocking Bird's throat and snarled down into his face, "If you say another word to my wife, I will chase you down and cut your tongue out."

"Yah, you can try," Mocking Bird said.

"You keep your mouth shut!" Maize Came said. She slapped his face. It left the imprint of her hand on his cheek. "You are a fool and you are making a fool of me and I will not forgive you. But I won't have my husband kill my brother. It will poison our lives. Do you hear me?" She shook Wing Foot's arm.

Wing Foot lowered the knife. Grudgingly.

"Shall we take him to the Three Old Men?" the others asked carefully—Wing Foot might be about to lose his temper again. "It is better that they kill him for you."

Wing Foot unclenched his fists. "Because you ask it, Heart," he said shortly to Maize Came. Everyone nodded their heads. That was sensible.

* * *

By the time they reached the Three Old Men, the whole camp knew what had happened. Torches flared back and forth along the path that bordered the caves, and everyone had come out, wrapped in furs, to stand at a respectful distance around the Council Fire and see what the Three Old Men were going to do about it.

Reed ran out to meet them when word first began to whip through the camp. Two men were dragging Mocking Bird between them, but they wouldn't let her near him. Maize Came was sobbing as she walked, and Reed put her arms around her.

"Go away from her!" Wing Foot said roughly, turning on Reed. "You brought him here with you. This is your fault."

*We came together*, Reed thought, stung, but she didn't say it. Maize Came was sobbing on her shoulder and wouldn't let go of her. Wing Foot gave Reed a look of loathing that made Reed's stomach shrivel into a miserable knot. Everything had turned bad somehow. As they passed Grandmother Watcher, Reed saw her nod to Old Woman Many Grandsons as if to say, *There, I knew she would make trouble.*

The Three Old Men looked very solemn. Reed didn't know what the law was, but she was suddenly terrified. They made way for Maize Came to stand beside the Council Fire, but Wing Foot pushed Reed away, and the men who had come from the lake with them moved in front of her.

"Why do you bring this one before the Three Old Men?" Healer Old Man asked.

"The law is broken," Wing Foot said angrily. "By this one. He raised his knife against me."

"Why is this?" Healer Old Man looked at Mocking Bird, who stood between two men, his arms twisted behind him.

"Does it matter?" someone said angrily. "This is the law!"

"Everything matters," Healer Old Man said.

"My sister is not for him!" Mocking Bird blurted. He knew he had gone over the edge, done a thing that could not be undone. He would show them he didn't care.

"It is not law that you may forbid your sister the man she chooses," Healer Old Man said.

"It is law that it is death to raise a knife against a man of the Kindred!" the same voice shouted again.

Rain Old Man looked bitter. "We have taken in Rattlesnake and trusted him not to bite us."

Reed tried to push her way through the crowd in front of her, but they wouldn't move. Leaf Fall grabbed her by the arm. "Come away! You may not speak now!"

"But that's my brother!"

"And you are my daughter, and they will blame it all on you, very likely, for bringing him here! Come away!"

"What about my sister? They are glad enough to have *her*," Reed spat.

"She is different," Leaf Fall said. "She is holy, and so it doesn't matter where she came from. It is right that she is not of us." She pulled at Reed's arm again.

"No!" Reed jerked free. She ran away from Leaf Fall and circled to the other side of the crowd to listen.

"It is law," Rain Old Man was saying. "This one was told of the law when he was taken into the Rainmakers."

"We didn't know!" Maize Came wailed from inside the circle. "We didn't know the proper speech of the Kindred then. We didn't understand!"

"Nevertheless, the Maize Girl has not broken any of our laws," Healer Old Man observed.

"Then let me speak." Maize Came took a deep breath and tried to stare them down. "This one is twin to me. He is part of me. He has been wicked, but he is still my brother. What must I do to buy his life?"

"That cannot be done," Healer Old Man said. "That is the law."

"Am I valuable to the Kindred?"

"You are Maize Girl," Healer Old Man said. "You are holy."

"Then I will leave if you kill my brother." Her teeth began to chatter again. *Leave Wing Foot?* "My brother is part of me. Tomorrow when we harvest the maize, you will find it withered in its husks if you kill him. And I will go away and not come back. I am the Maize Girl, and I say this."

Healer Old Man looked troubled. "What does Wing Foot say?"

"I have already said that I would not kill him," Wing Foot mumbled, as though embarrassed to have promised that. "Let the Three Old Men decide."

The Three Old Men looked as if they did not much want to. Law was law, but the transgressor was the Maize Girl's twin. It was complicated.

"We will not have him among us!" someone shouted. "He has broken the law!"

"And what then should the Kindred do, if we cannot keep him and cannot kill him?" Healer Old Man asked solemnly.

"Let him go back to the False People!"

"Drive him away!"

"No!" Maize Came held her hands out to Mocking Bird.

Wing Foot grabbed her arm. "That is the best you can do for him. Will you go with him?"

She looked a long time at him, eyes wide. "No," she whispered.

Wing Foot let his breath out. "Let him be driven away," he said to Healer Old Man. "I am the injured, and I ask it."

Healer Old Man bent his head. "It will be so."

They wrestled Mocking Bird forward, and the crowd parted in front of him. Someone gave him a shove.

"Not without his spear!" Reed screamed. "Give him his belongings! We are respectable people."

All the Grandmothers turned as one to admonish her, and Leaf Fall put her hands over her own mouth.

"This one is *not* permitted to speak to the Three Old Men!" Grandmother Watcher snapped.

But Healer Old Man held up his hand and, looking solemn, spoke in a low voice to the men who had been holding Mocking Bird. They waited while Mocking Bird's spears and pack were brought out from the young men's house. While they waited, the Kindred picked up rocks. Mocking Bird eased his weight from foot to foot, his eyes wide with fear. The men came back and hung his pack on his back and gave him his spears.

"Be seen by the Kindred no more," Healer Old Man said.

The Kindred began to throw their rocks. The first one hit him in the shins.

Mocking Bird ran. He plunged past Reed with his mouth set, not looking at her now or at anyone. Reed whistled for Bitch to follow him, but she didn't come.

A rock thudded into Mocking Bird's back, and he ran into the darkness.

# XIII

# The Dance

Reed ran to Maize Came, pushing away the people around her. Maize Came's face was streaming with tears. Wing Foot stood behind her, protective. He glared at Reed.

"Where will he go?" Reed wailed.

Maize Came scrubbed her eyes with the back of her hand. "That is not for me to decide," she said angrily. "And I do not care."

"Yes, you do," Reed insisted. "He is your twin."

Maize Came's lip trembled. Wing Foot took her arm. "You have the Kindred," he said into her hair. "You are of us." He put both arms around her, cradled her.

Maize Came leaned into his shoulder, weeping. "I didn't mean him to be angry at you. I didn't know he would."

Wing Foot looked at Reed over Maize Came's head. "Leave her alone."

* * *

Reed shivered in her bed. The fire had burned low, and Bitch hadn't come home. Unless she was sleeping with Maize Came, Reed thought. Maize Came didn't need her. Maize Came had Wing Foot to warm her bed. Reed snuffled dolefully. Leaf Fall was snoring on the other side of the fire. She had worried herself to sleep, fretting over whether Reed would be blamed for Mocking Bird's lawbreaking.

Reed stared groggily into the embers of the fire. It didn't matter. They blamed her for everything else, as if it were her fault that they had lost her in the first place, and her fault that she had survived.

Reed tussled with that notion and decided she had hit on truth. It hadn't come to her clearly at first; it had been lumpy and cloudy like the lake water, unwieldy to put in its place. But now she could see it and name it the way Night Hawk had seen those bones and known them for a cat. The Kindred had patterns and rituals for everything. Their life had layers of complexity that would have baffled the Yellow Grass People. Reed had not behaved according to the pattern, and for that they could not forgive her. Ever. Night Hawk had known it because he did not fit the pattern, either. Maybe that was why he went away.

But what was left? To be alone again? Reed closed her eyes, shutting that out. No road she had taken had brought her home. And she had squandered all her magic, hiding it from the Grandmothers. Maybe she should have called the deer for Mocking Bird when he asked her to, she thought dismally. Maybe she wouldn't be able to do it now, and no people would want her.

"Have you tried lately, and not spent it making ants in people's beds?" a soft voice inquired above her.

Reed opened her eyes warily. A big gray spider hung in the space between the hide flap and the cave mouth. The spider folded four of its eight arms and shook its head. "Humans never learn anything," it announced. Reed's mouth opened too, in a round *O*.

She sat up, looking nervously over her shoulder at Leaf Fall. She knew who this was. Anyone would know. It was Grandmother Spider herself. But it was also the soft man, she thought, the one who had talked to Mother.

Reed thought about that and knew without asking that Deer Shadow was dead. Spirits like Listens to Deer didn't come to more than one person at a time. She closed her eyes again and tried to squeeze out tears, but they wouldn't flow. Maybe Mother was happy now. And what had Reed ever done to make either of her mothers happy? She sniffled, feeling more desolate than ever.

"You'll wake up that one," the Spider said, pointing at Leaf Fall.

"Hush, then," Reed hissed. People shouldn't see other people's dreams.

"She can't hear me," Spider said. "But you keep thinking about her. That's what will wake her up."

"I can't help it. Who will take care of her if I leave?"

"Oh, are you leaving?"

Reed knew that she was. It was something else that simply was, without having to be questioned. "I don't belong here anymore."

"No." Spider shook her head in agreement.

"But where do I belong?"

"Don't you know?"

"If I did, would I be asking you?" Reed said crossly, too miserable even to worry about insulting Spider.

Spider shifted a little in her web, and Reed could see that it was a very large one, its ends anchored far away in the stars. There were a few things hanging in the spokes that she decided not to look at too closely. "My brother went away," she said. "Should I follow him? Should we live alone?"

"No!" Spider said. "You would be like Rock Water Boy and his sister Wood Rat. You know why you came out of the wild lands to these people."

Reed hung her head.

"There are many things that want my attention," Spider told her irritably. "There are still mountain chains to stitch together, and nets to weave to hold the stars in place, and Coyote always just behind me undoing it all. I do not have time to think up things that you ought to think of for yourself."

"What about my mother?" Reed said.

"This one?" Spider said. "She hasn't had you very long. She can get by without you again."

That seemed heartless, but Spider was not in the business of making everyone happy. Spider was there to keep the world together, to weave the great pattern that overlay all others, the pattern within which the rituals of the Kindred were a small and insignificant knot.

Reed wanted to ask Spider about her mother, Deer Shadow, but she knew that Spider wouldn't answer. Spirits didn't come to bring the latest news. They came when a person needed guidance and that need had called them. Unfortunately what they thought someone needed to know might not be what you asked. Reed knew that if you didn't ask the proper question, they might not give you any answer at all.

Reed scratched her head, which was spinning. She thought she saw Coyote sitting in the door just under the web, but it could have been a shadow on the hide. A coal tumbled down and split in two on the hearth, sending a shower of sparks into the blackness above. (And now that she thought of it, why could she see Spider when it was so very dark?) The sparks lit what looked like a pair of yellow eyes, the gleam of a white tooth.

"Am I to go into the wild lands again?" she asked fearfully. "Without my brother? Grandmother, I want to belong to somebody."

"You belong to me," Spider said succinctly, and Reed shivered.

"We all do, Grandmother," she said respectfully. If

she had been afraid of the Kindred's Grandmothers, it was nothing to what she felt for Grandmother Spider, even softened by the presence of Listens to Deer. "But I want to belong to human people. Is that so wrong? That is how we are made."

Spider considered. "Then you must decide if it is worth it, being with human people, to stay here with people whose ways are alien to you. Are you happy?"

Reed sighed, but she knew better than to lie. "No. And I don't think I will be, ever. But maybe it is not their fault. Night Hawk tried to tell me that."

"That is generous of you," Spider said. "There is the possibility that you are learning."

Coyote—he *was* there—yawned and clicked his teeth together with a snap. "Maybe you are trying to teach an egg to walk," he suggested to Spider. "You can't teach humans. You have to let them do things."

"*You* certainly haven't taught them anything," Grandmother Spider said. "Except how to tell lies and copulate with each other's mates."

Coyote scratched his ear. "I know better than to try to teach them anything else. That was all they wanted to know. I just give them new things. I gave this one's mother the picture magic, and great doings will come of it in the future, believe me. Do you want to see?"

"No!" Spider snapped. "It is very bad for humans to do that."

"Unless of course *you* decide they should," Coyote suggested.

Reed listened, interested. She had never heard spirits argue with each other. She thought Coyote was a little afraid of Grandmother Spider, but Reed was more afraid of Coyote. Grandmother Spider had more power, but Coyote was unpredictable. He stood for the wildness at the heart of things, the wildness that Grandmother Spider could weave into her web one thread at a time, and still never tame it. Coyote made Reed want to get up and run with him, howling and singing into the night, making the Kindred afraid.

She gripped the deer hide that covered her bed as if it would anchor her.

When she woke before dawn, Grandmother Spider and Coyote were gone, but their argument lingered in the air. Reed could see the words like colored smoke over the fire pit. Leaf Fall was still snoring, and Reed tiptoed to her pack and stuffed her belongings into it. She still had the spear that the Kindred's Grandmothers had muttered over, and she made sure she took that, too. She put as much journey food in her pack as she thought Leaf Fall could spare and filled a waterskin from the basket by the door.

Reed looked uncertainly at Leaf Fall, loss settling like a rock in her stomach again. Was there some way to say, *I love you but I cannot stay with you, with your people?* She pulled off the blue stone she had worn around her neck since she was a baby and laid it on the bed by Leaf Fall's hand. Maybe Leaf Fall had given it to her in the first place. It seemed a shame now, Reed thought, that she had never seen Antelope, who was her blood sister and lived with the Turquoise Band of the Kindred. She would have seen her in the spring, if she had stayed.

*Yah, and been her shadow,* Reed thought, her mouth twisting. *Her unclean sister.* She shrugged the unknown Antelope away and, with her, the name she had never been able to be. *I am Others' Child,* she thought. *Always Others' Child. Someone else's. Then I will be so.*

Outside the cave, there was just enough light to see by, misty and thick, the trees and the stones of the fire pit darker shadows in the gray morning. Others' Child set out past the Council Fire in the direction that Mocking Bird had gone. As she passed the first stand of trees, a dog came out of them and trotted at her heel. It put its nose in the palm of her hand.

At first Others' Child thought it was Coyote. She

sucked her breath in to scream, and then she saw it was Bitch.

"Where have you been?" Others' Child demanded. "Sleeping warm with my sister and her husband? We are going away again, Mocking Bird and me. Are you coming?"

Bitch didn't answer. Others' Child hadn't really been expecting her to. Then she would have known it was Coyote. She didn't want to take a trip with Coyote.

She went on talking to Bitch anyway. There was no one else to talk to. She told her to find Mocking Bird, and Bitch put her nose to the trail, so that was a sort of answer.

They were on the trail that the Kindred had followed when they came to the lake, but after an hour, Bitch branched off on another, older trail that ran south. No one seemed to use it now, human or animal, and it was almost completely covered in leaves, but Bitch seemed to be certain of it, with the stubbornness of Coyote when he wants something. Others' Child followed.

At midmorning they scrambled down a steep slope with a scree of tumbled rock from the earthquake, and Others' Child saw a footprint clear in the dust at the bottom.

"Very well, you were right."

Bitch lifted her head and whined. Then she changed to a low growl. Others' Child looked where Bitch was looking, and her heart thudded. Someone was coming back the way that Mocking Bird had gone, but it wasn't Mocking Bird. He had a big pack on his back, and he walked with a stick. At first he was only a shape in the trees, humpbacked and ominous. Then he came closer, and she let her breath out. It was Night Hawk. She smacked Bitch's nose in irritation for frightening her.

"Be quiet, No Manners."

Night Hawk looked surprised to see them. He

raised both eyebrows. "You are early and far away."

"And going farther," Others' Child said. She told him angrily about Mocking Bird, told it in her own speech, shaking away the Kindred's tongue along with the name that had sat so uneasily on her skin.

Night Hawk scratched his head. His hair had not been cropped in a while, and it hung on his shoulders. He was dirty with trail grime. "That might be him I passed on the trail back a ways," he said.

"You saw him?"

"I didn't see, no. But someone was there, in the brush. I didn't know how many someones, so I got my spear out and went along looking too dangerous to touch. So I hoped." He grinned. "If it was Mocking Bird, he didn't want to see me, either."

"He was afraid," Others' Child said defensively.

"So he should be. He broke enough rules to keep the Three Old Men busy for a full moon. And why do you have to go with him?"

"Because I was wrong." Others' Child dug her toe in the dirt. "I can't stay with these people. I thought that I could, but even Wing Foot blamed me for Mocking Bird. They will blame me for anything, and I will never belong."

"I told you already that you are smarter than he is." Night Hawk furrowed his brow at her. "And where will you go?"

"I will go home," Others' Child said heavily. "To the people that the Kindred left me with. Maybe they have become better since we were gone."

"And maybe they are just like they always were," Night Hawk said.

"They are no worse than the Kindred!"

"No worse. But better?" He shrugged. "They are humans. And do you know how to go home again?" He looked around them at the half-buried trail, the tumbled stones, the skyline in the distance that was not as it had been before the earth moved. On the high slopes, too, the leaves were turning gold on the aspen trees. "If you will come back until spring, I will take you there if you still want to go. Or . . . you could go pack-on-back with me. I will show you the cat."

Others' Child shook her head. "No. And my brother is out there."

"The more fool he," Night Hawk said unsympathetically. "And because he was greedy-eyes for his own sister and tried to stab my friend, I should feel sorry for him?"

"He wasn't," Others' Child said, offended. "They are twins. It is different."

Night Hawk raised an eyebrow at that.

"It is Maize Came getting all the honor," she said, exasperated. "Nothing that happens can touch her, yet I am still dirty, and my brother is laughed at by the girls because he is young. He only wanted to be important. We were important among the Yellow Grass People."

"Being important is dangerous," Night Hawk said. "Your father found that out."

Others' Child hung her head, embarrassed. "It wasn't just that, not truly. It was that somehow they took Maize Came away from us. I didn't know that would happen."

"Your sister is gone from you," Night Hawk said. "She is holy now to the Kindred, and there won't be any changing that."

"Then I *will* go away," Others' Child said. "I am not holy. They won't miss me."

"What about Old Aunt?"

"She will miss me," Others' Child said. "Will you take care of her?"

"I took care of her before you came," Night Hawk said. He sounded angry. "I will do so again, Thoughtless."

"I am not thoughtless!" Tears stung her eyes. "I can't live among your people. I tried. You said yourself that I should go and see the world instead."

"I didn't say you should go back to the False Peo-

ple," Night Hawk said. His voice softened. "I saw
how it was hard for you. I will tell Old Aunt that you
love her. But in the spring, when I come to trade with
the Trespassers, maybe you will come away from
them again."

Others' Child shook her head. "I will be important
to my people now. I will not be able to leave them."
If Deer Shadow was dead, there would be no one to
call the game. Odd, how when she had first gone
away, she had wanted nothing more than for them to
starve.

"You can always leave anywhere." Night Hawk
shifted his pack straps on his shoulder. "I will tell Old
Aunt where you are gone."

She watched him climb up the trail. She bit her
lip—what would she want with a man like that, sar-
castic and opinionated? What did she want with any
man after Wing Foot had held *her* to blame, as if
everything were some woman's fault? And Mocking
Bird, who couldn't keep his hand on his temper and
couldn't let his sister have a man when it was none
of his business, twins or not. And now he would be
like a man with an arm bitten off, driven away from
her.

Others' Child compressed her mouth into a flat angry line. Men seemed worth very little to her just now,
and it was Deer Shadow who kept bumping her presence about in Others' Child's memory, as if her spirit
hadn't gone away yet. Others' Child felt the hair lift
along her arms and kept looking around her, but
there was no one to see. Night Hawk was out of sight,
gone now. The mountains seemed empty, as if the
Great Mystery Spirit hadn't put the animals on them
yet, except for the hawk floating high up in the cold
sky. Whatever was traveling with Others' Child was
inside her head.

She turned in a circle, looking again at the emptiness. It was cold today, even though the sun was
climbing. She pulled her deerskin shirt from her pack

and shrugged it on. In a few days the Yellow Grass People would leave the Gathering and go to their winter place. She and Mocking Bird would have to catch up to them before the first snow. She hoped that was where Mocking Bird was heading. There was no telling what he would do in a temper. Others' Child turned south again, toward the trail that Night Hawk had come by. She gave Bitch a shove along it.

They caught up with Mocking Bird at noon. Others' Child didn't think he had gone very far the night before, just far enough to be well away from the Kindred, probably. She imagined him spending a miserable night in the trees, afraid to light a fire. Now he was sitting morosely on a rock, eating a quail raw. There was a pile of feathers by his feet. She and Bitch had slowed their steps and crept forward, and now she could see him clearly through a sage bush. He looked so miserable that she left out the things she was going to say and just called his name.

His head jerked up, eyes wide, and he dropped the quail. "Sister?" He flung himself at her, buried his face in her shoulder, and she could feel hot tears on her skin. In a moment, though, he was pretending he hadn't made them.

"Where did you find that one?" Mocking Bird gestured scornfully at Bitch, who hadn't come when he had called her last night.

"She came as I was leaving," Others' Child said.

Mocking Bird wiped his nose. "Is . . . Maize Came with you?" He looked over Others' Child's shoulder into the bushes.

"No," she said wearily. "Our sister is holy to them now. We made a mistake, you and I. I didn't know they would take her."

"She could have left them anyway!" Mocking Bird said indignantly.

"And left her man, too? No, she is holy there, and

she will have a good life. Our people might not take
her back, for stealing the maize."

"Is that where we are going?" Mocking Bird asked.
He scrubbed his nose with his arm again. "I didn't
know where I was going. And we stole the maize,
too."

"No, it was hers. All the People knew that. She was
Follows Her Father."

"Yah, and who says they will take *us* back?" Mocking Bird said, suddenly argumentative, remembering
his grievances against them.

"They will take *me* back," Others' Child said with
certainty. "I can call the game. Also, our mother is
dead."

"What? Did the trader tell you that? I saw him go
by and hid from him. Was he coming from the People?"

"Maybe. The Gathering is a good place to trade. But
he didn't say anything. The old soft man who was
our mother's friend talked to me in the dreamtime."

"Did *he* say?"

"No," Others' Child said, exasperated. "But he
would not have come to me if she had been alive.
Listens to Deer was very old and holy, and he only
talked to our mother." Others' Child thought it might
be all right to name him now. She had never known
him in life, and if he came in Spider's form, then he
was a spirit and not an avenging ghost. And anyway,
after a time the dead ceased to be angry about it.

"Then what did he say to you?" Mocking Bird demanded.

"It was *my* dream," Others' Child said. How could
she describe Spider and Coyote, and the way their
words had still been in the air this morning? She
didn't understand it herself. And she didn't want to
think about Coyote. "I just know."

"Women think they know everything," Mocking
Bird said bitterly. He did look as if a piece of him had
been torn off, and Others' Child felt sorry for him

again. Maize Came had her new husband; she wouldn't be thinking about her twin now.

"It hurts, doesn't it?" Others' Child asked him. "Maybe it will get numb in a while, like an old scar. Old Aunt from the Yellow Grass People used to say that after she lost her finger when she was small, after a while she couldn't feel the place where it had been anymore. It took a long time, though."

"How do you know this?" Mocking Bird said. "How do you know what it is like to be twins with someone?"

"Because I am not stupid!" Others' Child snapped. "Always you have had someone you belonged with." She turned her head away from him. "Because I have never had it, does that mean I didn't know it? And want the same?"

"You had us," Mocking Bird said.

"And without Maize Came, am I enough for you to have? Bah! I will take you to the Yellow Grass People again, where we both belong."

"You will take me?" Mocking Bird stuck his chin out. "I am not a child. I am nearly three years a man, even if *those* women did not think so."

"We will go, then. We will call it what you want to." Always some man wanted to call things by a different name, so that they would be what he wanted them to. "There is no doubting you are a man," she growled under her breath.

It was getting cold, and the way to the high caves where the Yellow Grass People wintered was not easy. The mountains had changed, and Mocking Bird and Others' Child stopped often, puzzled. They carried also the weight of their anger, dragging it uphill like a rock they couldn't put down. Mocking Bird bitterly described the lies and the worthlessness of women. Others' Child brooded on her hurts.

The Yellow Grass People would assuage those, Others' Child told herself. They were stupid and wrong, but they were *her* people. It didn't matter whom she had been born to. She would go home and call the game for her people as her mother had done, her mother who was dead and burned bones now. She would go home and most magnanimously forgive them.

They came to the winter place at the end of a cold day, gray sky above gray fog, so that the fires in the cave mouths looked to Others' Child like wet red pools, like flowers under the cold water. The men had come in from hunting. The two hid in the brush and saw Magpie and old Cat Ears, and Wakes on the Mountain, and Hears the Night, who looked older now and had a furrow between his brows. The hunters had very little meat between them.

Others' Child stood up. "Come on," she whispered to Mocking Bird and Bitch. "Now."

They showed themselves, looming out of the fog like avenging spirits, and Magpie screamed. The others turned to look where she pointed.

"Are you ghosts?" the shaman demanded. Everyone else got behind him.

"I was asked that the last place I went to," Others' Child said. "Do I look like bones?"

"Where have you been, then?"

"She's come to curse us because that one died," Magpie said fearfully.

Others' Child looked where Magpie was pointing. A woman lay on a bier. She could tell without going closer that it was Deer Shadow. That loss was three years old, but now its finality came to her. She bit her lip, but the tears tried to come out of her eyes anyway.

"Ghost, how did you get here so fast otherwise?" Hears the Night asked her. He held his eye stone out at her to keep her magic at bay.

"When did she die?" Others' Child asked him.

"Yesterday."

Yesterday? Yesterday they had been on the trail.

Others' Child shuddered. Grandmother Spider always knew what was going to happen before it was woven into the web. "We walked from the lake where the Others live, because you will need me now."

"There is no game to call," Cat Ears snarled. "Unless you can make it from fog."

"Be quiet!" Hears the Night snapped, and Cat Ears clamped his mouth shut.

*They are afraid of us,* Others' Child thought, and she saw that Mocking Bird had seen it, too. The people were thin and ragged, as if something had chewed on them. The camp looked shabby, even though they must have barely settled in for the winter. Leavings of bone and torn baskets, the peeled rinds of dried squash, skittered across the frozen ground. When Cat Ears spoke, she could see that his teeth were black and almost gone.

"Yah, the Yellow Grass People have become starveling dogs." She managed a sneer, but for some reason her heart lurched in her chest. She was sorry for them.

"The game has been scarce," Hears the Night said. He lowered the eye stone and made a show of braving her magic. "The maize is no more. We have begged seed from other bands of the People, but there is not enough rain. It does not grow."

"You have brought this on yourselves," Mocking Bird said suddenly. He was a presence now, immediately, counterpoint to Others' Child's sympathy. He stepped between Hears the Night and Wakes on the Mountain and stared scornfully at the rest of the Yellow Grass People. He looked uncannily like Wind Caller in this light, and Others' Child heard a little indrawn hiss of breath from Wakes on the Mountain.

"You brought this on yourselves when you killed my father," Mocking Bird said. "He has taken your food away from you and given it to the Others." One of the women wailed, and Mocking Bird looked satisfied. "The seed you beg does not grow, either, because my father has cursed it and you. Yah!" He spat at them. "Nothing will grow until you have the true seed back again."

"And where is the true seed?" Wakes on the Mountain asked. He looked bone-weary and desperate with trying to feed his people. Others' Child thought he was ready to listen to anyone, even a deserter who came home out of the fog to curse him.

"Maize Came, who used to be Follows Her Father, has taken it and given it to the Others!" Mocking Bird said angrily. "And that is your fault, too!" Now he would be hungry with them, he thought, because the Others had driven him off.

A murmur rippled through the Yellow Grass People, a sound half angry and half frightened, like bees. Should they listen to these vengeful children of the man they had killed? Hears the Night said that they had been wrong to kill him and that was what had brought starvation on them, worse than before. Now this boy said it, too. They looked expectantly at the chieftain or the shaman to tell them.

Wakes on the Mountain looked at Mocking Bird. He could find very little room left to hold his pride. The other chieftains at the Gathering had said game was scarce since the drought and the earthquake; but this year they had seen better days, and the Yellow Grass People worse. The other chieftains had shown him handfuls of the maize they had grown. The seed would not sprout for the Yellow Grass People, even when they cleared another field away from the old one. Hears the Night said that a curse radiated out from the grave where Wind Caller's children had buried him, but everyone was afraid to dig it up. Wakes on the Mountain thought Hears the Night was afraid to, as well.

Old One Ball pushed his way through the little crowd past Wakes on the Mountain and stood in front of Mocking Bird, his feet planted wide and determined. "Tell us what we must do," he said gruffly, ignoring Wakes on the Mountain. The rest of the people surged around him, echoing, pleading.

Mocking Bird watched them begging him—men who had killed his father with rocks and a spear! It gave him an enormous satisfaction, something hot and gratifying that he could hold to his chest. Others' Child had been right. Traveling here was worthwhile.

"How may the seed come home?" the shaman asked.

Mocking Bird didn't answer him.

"What must we do?" Wakes on the Mountain asked it this time. He made a gesture of respect with both hands, though Mocking Bird knew that his teeth were gritted.

"Propitiate my father," Mocking Bird said savagely. He pushed past Wakes on the Mountain and Hears the Night and went into the cave where Deer Shadow's bier lay. He sat down beside it with his back to them. The people looked at each other uneasily, but no one wanted to follow him. After a moment they heard his flute.

The notes were thin and desolate. The people converged around Others' Child, who stood her ground.

Magpie looked as if she wanted to put her hands to her ears to stop the sound. She glared at Others' Child and said, "This one has taken our maize to her own kin. We should have known better than to trust one of theirs."

"It was my sister who did that," Others' Child said. They were as willfully stupid as only people who are starving can be. "I will speak with your shaman. I will not speak to *you* until it is time to call the game for you." She narrowed her eyes at Magpie.

"Let it be so," Hears the Night said. When Magpie opened her mouth again, he said, "Go take the meat and cook it. We are hungry."

When Magpie looked as if she still might protest, Wakes on the Mountain gave his wife a push. Then he picked up his spear and his dignity and went into the darkness of his cave. It was the shaman's job to wrestle with ghosts, if that's what they were. If they were humans, they would have to be taken back into the affairs of the Yellow Grass People, and his wife would have to bite her tongue. That was the law. Wakes on the Mountain scratched his head. And would that lessen the curse? How had the Yellow Grass People gone so far from the right path? he wondered. Everything they had done had seemed to be right at the time.

It was getting dark quickly, and the air was dank with fog. The crisp cold that brought snow and made the deer and the rabbits easy to track had not yet come—might not come if they were truly cursed. The Yellow Grass People huddled around their fires, wrapped in furs and hide blankets, and listened, teeth on edge, to a flute that sounded unpleasantly familiar in the fog.

Mocking Bird sat over his mother's bier and played for her. Her face looked old to him, as ragged as those of the living, but blank, as if she had never really been inside it. Certainly she was not there now. The Yellow Grass People didn't need to fear Deer Shadow, Mocking Bird decided. She had drifted away from them slowly. She wouldn't want to come back.

Mocking Bird wondered if, now that she was in the Skeleton House with his father, his father would take the curse away. If it *was* his father's curse. Their mother had cursed her people, too. Or it might have been their own anger that had done the damage and not a curse at all, Mocking Bird thought. That wouldn't surprise him. Anger was more powerful than almost anything else. He had found that out when he had pulled a knife on Wing Foot. The anger had become the knife, and the knife the anger, until the idea that he should kill Wing Foot had made the most sense. It had still made sense to him as they had begun to throw rocks at him, but it had dulled a little by the time Others' Child found him on the trail. Now

he saw why that had been a bad idea, but the anger
was still there, a hot little ball in his chest, hotter and
smaller than his anger at the Yellow Grass People.

Hears the Night looked as if he were not sure how
to properly invite a ghost into his cave. If that was
what she was. "Would She Who Returns to Us wish
to sit by the fire?" he suggested.

"I am Others' Child," his unwelcome guest said.
"And I do not wish to be remade with a new name.
I think that Coyote gave me this one, and I have had
ill luck when I have tried to change it." She sat down
by the shaman's fire and laid a hand on Bitch's head.
Bitch plopped down on her haunches beside her.

Hears the Night looked at them both as if he were
weighing their probable origins.

Others' Child suppressed an urge to frighten him
and scatter curses on the ground like dry leaves. It
would be very satisfactory to do so, but wicked. She
knew what Spider would have to say about it. "I have
come back from the Kindred," she said. "The people
I was born to, whom you call the Others."

"Is that truly where you have been? Among the
Others?" Hears the Night looked skeptical.

"Our sister is still there." She wouldn't come back,
either. "She is the Maize Girl now, and holy to them."

"If you have truly lived among the Others, then
you have much to tell us." Hears the Night closed his
eyes. His fingers rubbed the spiral of his great tooth.

"Many things," Others' Child said. She thought
about the cleft in the ground and Night Hawk's cat
bones. Would the earthquake have sucked them in
again, or let more loose?

"Are these humans?" the shaman asked her.

"I think so," Others' Child said.

Hears the Night looked skeptical again. "It might
be that you would know," he conceded. "You knew
when your mother went Away. That is a gift."

Others' Child looked him in the eye. "I would

know. And we are not ghosts. It is my father's ghost you need to worry about."

Hears the Night sighed. "We have done wrong," he said, nodding to himself. "The gods are angry with us. Your mother cursed us, and your father's spirit haunts us. How may we be free of them?"

The last piece of the old bitterness slid away, like a coal breaking open in the fire. He looked old with worry, and he cared more for the Yellow Grass People now than he did for his pride, she thought. And he hadn't wanted to wash the skin off her for learning other ways. She thought he might even wish to hear about them.

"I will show you," she said abruptly, catching at that hope. "I will do it now. I must have a stick to draw with, and there must be torches to see by." It was odd how swiftly she could forgive. She wouldn't have thought so, but it had come as swiftly as the hatred had. This *must* be her home, she thought, not among the Kindred. She willed it so.


"This must be done also at the caves where you killed him, or they will not be fit to live in," Others' Child told the circle of faces that stared through the torchlight at her. The people nodded, eyes wide. The shaman had given her a drawing stick, sharpened and hardened in the fire. Others' Child knelt before the first cave, which was Wakes on the Mountain's and Magpie's, and began to mark her father's likeness in the frozen ground. Magpie yelped.

"Make that one be quiet," Others' Child said.

"He will come here!" Magpie howled.

"How did the chieftain come to marry a stupid wife?" Others' Child muttered to no one in particular, and there was a stifled snort of laughter from a young woman newly married here from the Smoke People. Magpie gave herself airs and was not best liked. The older women turned around and glowered at the new woman.

"He is already here," Others' Child said to Magpie. "He has his teeth in your belly. If you want him to go away, you must give him honor." She proceeded with her work. Magpie laid her hands on her belly, frightened.

The dancing figure moved along the ground with the flickering torchlight, one foot lifted, flute to his lips. On his back she drew the hump of a pack, heavy with the maize seed. "Bring home the maize," she told him in a whisper. The little figure fluttered in the light.

Others' Child stood and moved on to the next cave and the next, drawing him outside the shadows where Deer Shadow's bier lay. Mocking Bird didn't turn around. They could hear the flute notes floating above his head. In the shadows his strangely cropped hair looked like the looped braids his father had worn. The dancing figure leaped and spun outside the door.

Others' Child marked her father's likeness outside each cave and then four times on the dance ground, at each corner the likeness of the stranger who had come with gifts and been killed by the people he served. They would remember him always, she thought. He would dance through their rituals forever until the dance overpowered remembrance of death.

When she was done, she stood up, arching her back, and looked at the sky. The fog was lifting, leaving a splatter of bright stars against the black. Torchlight flickered in the edges of the cuts she had made in the ground, and she saw her father walking between the torchlight and the stars. Others' Child heard, or thought she did, a second flute twining its notes with Mocking Bird's. The hair lifted briefly on the back of her neck. Something had happened. When she looked up at the stars again, she could see him clearly.

# XIV

# How War Came

They were to burn Deer Shadow's body on the fourth day, and miraculously they had meat with which to make a feast for her. Others' Child called the deer, and they came to honor Deer Shadow, crunching across new snow, their delicate tracks like dark words spoken on the ground.

The hunters came home with three deer, one of them a great buck who was old and wily and whom Cat Ears called Old Man Clever because he had seen him before and never caught him. This time the buck had stopped in its tracks and lain down under the hunters' spears, the young men said breathlessly, and after that even Cat Ears gave Others' Child the place of honor at the fire.

Deer Shadow's body lay on its bier in her cave while the people ate their fill in her honor. No one had seen her die, Hears the Night said. She had just left, as if it was time. Others' Child tried hard to remember what her mother had been like alive, when she had been joyful, before the bad time. The memory came in fragments, like broken ice, bright slivers here and there pooling in the sun. Deer Shadow had left a long time before she had really died, Others' Child thought. It made it hard. She had loved her husband more than her children. That was all there was to it, and it wasn't fair to blame her for that. Would *she* feel that way about Hears the Night if she married him now? Others' Child wondered. She tried to imagine it and couldn't. Hears the Night was most certainly touched by the gods, but not with her father's fierce fire. She couldn't see him walking among the stars.

Others' Child sighed, staring into the fire, sated finally, a greasy bone in her hand that she was keeping from the other dogs for Bitch.

Next to her Cat Ears sighed heavily, and she looked at him.

"It's the end of the Time of Magic," he said, "with your mother and father gone. Everything will be different now."

*You killed them*, she thought. Maybe Cat Ears didn't like to think about that now. "Different?" she asked him.

"I can't say we were friends. Not so you would call it that. But I had a soft spot for your mother. I did." He grinned sneakily. "I'd have married her. Don't tell Silent."

*He's drunk*, Others' Child thought. Silent was dead. There was a gourd of fermented berry juice at his feet, unsteadily propped against one fur boot.

"She should have married me," Cat Ears said dolefully. "It was a mistake to marry him. The two of them together made too much power. That's what killed him." He took a swallow from the gourd. "It made a light, though, you know? Like a little sun somewhere behind them. We won't see their like again."

Disgusted, Others' Child got up with her bone and

went to look for Bitch. She found her with Mocking Bird and the other young men. He looked drunk, too, she thought irritably. She gave Bitch the bone.

"Where have you been?" Mocking Bird asked her.

"Listening to Cat Ears maunder. He is old and soft in the head, and he thinks now that he didn't kill our father."

Mocking Bird grunted. "He gave me the place next to his when we drove the deer."

"And what does that mean?"

"That I will be the next chief of the hunters," Mocking Bird said. "It was good to go away from here for a while so that they could see our worth."

Others' Child stared at him, baffled. Men had never made much sense to her, and tonight they made none.

"When the spring comes, there will be more to hunt than just the deer," Mocking Bird said, and the other young men nodded solemnly, drunkenly, in agreement.

"Yah, you are as stupid as slugs." She got up angrily and stood with arms folded while Wakes on the Mountain and Hears the Night came out of the cave carrying her mother's bier. She kicked Mocking Bird, and he stood up.

They laid the bier on the pit they kept for burnings and piled dry brush around it. The fire leaped up in the icy air, a flock of flame birds flushed from the brush. Hears the Night put more on top of the body to make it burn faster. Others' Child heard a doleful sniffle beside her and saw Cat Ears again, morosely drinking from his gourd. Hears the Night had already opened the skeleton road for Deer Shadow's spirit to travel along. When the burning was over, he would close it again, with a chant and three strokes of his tooth, and the bones would be put in a crevice in the rocks so that she would not be tempted to come back to them. Tonight and for a long time after no one would speak her name, lest that call her back, too.

Others' Child watched for her mother's spirit

launching itself onto that dark road, but she could only make out a few whirling flakes of snow. Maybe Deer Shadow had already gone. Others' Child tried to imagine her mother, transparent as the snow, under the lake with the rest of the dead. She looked at Mocking Bird, but he had done his mourning and was talking again with the young men. Her sister was gone, too. Only Hears the Night and drunken old Cat Ears were there to talk to. Others' Child felt the blackness of the night cup around her like a hand. Was this what her mother had felt when she realized she was alone?

Hears the Night stepped back from the bier and lifted both arms. The people turned their faces to him.

"The deer have come to us again," he said.

They murmured agreement to that, and Others' Child felt the aloneness encircle her again. Would she be holy now, like Mother—enclosed?

"Now that the deer have come, now that the Deer Woman's magic has returned to us, I can tell you how it must be," Hears the Night said. "We must atone for our wrongdoing by making all things as they were. As they have been. The earth has stood on end to tell us this, because the maize is gone from us. Only by bringing it back again will we make the world straight, and please him who brought it to us."

They crowded around him, shouldering past Others' Child, doing her honor with bowed heads and cupped hands, but pushing on past her to hear the shaman.

"He who was killed taught us first to make war," Hears the Night said. "With war we must bring back his gift."

The hunters shouted and stamped their spear shafts on the ground. Others' Child stared at them.

"We must take back the maize and bring home the Maize Girl, or we will wither with the drought again. I have seen this in a dream," Hears the Night explained, though no one doubted him. The hunters yipped and shouted, and Mocking Bird smiled, arms folded on his chest. "This one, the son of He Who Brought Us Maize, knows the ways of the enemy. He will lead us to them." The shaman put his hand on Mocking Bird's shoulder. The hunters yipped again triumphantly, and old Cat Ears grinned a broad grin.

"He is only trying to get you killed," Others' Child said furiously to her brother. She filed a bone needle on the grinding stone as if she were trying to grind sense into his head, or dangerous notions out of it.

"I'm to be chief of the war band," Mocking Bird said stubbornly. "That is right. My father was a warrior. Not like these people."

*These* people, Others' Child thought, were all in their caves making more spears so that they could fight the Kindred. "And what do you know about leading a war band?" she said, but he wasn't listening. *Yah bah,* she was the magic Deer Woman, who made picture magic for the tribe, and what did that earn her but the chance to hear the men tell how fierce they were and how they would make war on the Others and bring Maize Came home whether she wanted to come or no, and Others' Child knew she did not.

She had said so to Cat Ears, and he hadn't listened. She had said so to Wakes on the Mountain and Hears the Night, and Magpie had scolded her for arguing with the men. And her brother was bigheaded with being a warrior and fighting the Others.

"We are to have the maize," Mocking Bird insisted. "He Who Brought Us Maize wishes it to be so."

"How do you know what he wishes?" Others' Child inquired scornfully. "Did he *speak* to you? This is our father you are yammering about!"

"*My* father," Mocking Bird said. "That is why I am to lead the warriors."

"You are to lead the warriors because old Cat Ears thinks you will get killed. Cat Ears doesn't love you any more than he loved Father."

"Hah! I am to be chief of the hunters after him."

"The Kindred will kill you if you go back there," Others' Child said. "And it won't make Maize Came want to come home. Why must you make war? We can get seed now from the Smoke People or the High Rock People."

"It won't grow," Mocking Bird said. "We must take back the true seed."

"Because you say so. Because you want to make our sister come home. Yah, you are spiteful!"

"She ought to come home." Mocking Bird folded his arms across his chest. "She should marry a man of the People. That is who she should marry."

Others' Child tested the needle against the palm of her hand. Mocking Bird had brought her a hide to tan, and she knew that he expected her to make him new leggings out of it. Since his blood was so hot, he wouldn't need them, she decided in silent anger. She would make herself a warm dress instead. Bitch, who needed no clothes, lay with her belly to the fire and listened to the two-legged people argue.

"Well, she should," Mocking Bird said. "Cat Ears says it will be a great fight, and the People will sing songs about us afterward forever."

"They will sing about your backside," Others' Child said suddenly. "Go away. I don't want to talk about this anymore."

"It isn't talk for women anyway," Mocking Bird said, stung. He left her and went away to the Young Men's House, where they all wanted to talk about war. Cat Ears was right, he thought. That was why women were not chieftains.

Others' Child stared after him feeling as bewildered as she was angry. This was not what was supposed to happen. The way she had imagined it had all been different, just as the way she had imagined her return to the Others had been. She jabbed the needle into her palm and sucked the drop of blood she inadvertently drew. The needle was sharp enough. She put it away in her mother's sewing basket. Caught the Moon had come to the cave and shown Others' Child how she had kept all of Mother's things safe. Caught the Moon had been proud of that. "She wouldn't have known it if her bed had disappeared, let alone her needles and things," Caught the Moon had said. "So I kept them. Things will turn different now that you're here." She had beamed, apparently taking personal credit for that.

But there was nothing different, not from how it had been, and not from the Others. No one listened. No one thought. They only wanted to fight and take things from each other. She sat cross-legged by the fire and pounded her fists on her knees. Her father hadn't been any different, either, she thought. Mocking Bird was right about that. Maybe only she was different, because she belonged to both—and neither. The back of her neck prickled. She knew who was present in contradictions like that one. She stared at the hide that hung over the cave mouth, willing him to materialize.

The smoke from the fire stung her eyes, but nothing happened. She concentrated intensely. There was only Bitch, on her back now, snoring. Others' Child's eyes began to stream. Finally she dipped a cupped hand in the water basket and washed them out.

She should be working, she knew. Women should always be doing something. There was the hide to finish tanning, and soap to boil, and the deer meat smoking over the communal fire to tend to. Rebelliously she curled up instead on the bed next to Bitch where it was warm. The wind was howling outside again, and her feet were icy in her boots. She curled in a ball and poked them under Bitch's belly. She had enough power so that no one would come in to fetch her if she didn't come out. She still had that. Unless Caught the Moon decided she must be sick.

*I am not sick,* she thought at whoever might be outside. *Go away.*

Of course that was when he came. Coyote only came uninvited. He wasn't Bitch this time. Bitch lifted her ears and looked at him interestedly. "Shameless!" Others' Child slapped her nose. Bitch bared her teeth at Others' Child, and they glowered at each other.

Coyote hung his long tongue out, amused. He had come along a trail that Others' Child could just see running away into the hide that hung over the door. It was hard to tell where it ended. She thought that if she stood up, she could probably walk along it wherever it went. She didn't. She had heard of people doing that, and they hadn't come back.

"Ho, children," Coyote said. "Haven't you fixed me anything to eat?"

"There isn't anything," Others' Child said.

"There is meat smoking outside," Coyote said, insulted that they would try to keep it from him.

"I can't give you that," Others' Child said, certain that she couldn't. "You'll have to get it yourself."

"Bear is watching it," Coyote said. "Isn't there anything else?"

Others' Child saw that there was a bone in the ashes of the hearth, so she gave him that.

"Thank you for your kindness," he said and cracked it open with his side teeth.

"All the men are going to make war in the spring," Others' Child told him while he gnawed the bone. "Did you start this?"

"Certainly not," Coyote said, and she knew that he had. "Human people don't need encouragement to make war."

"There was no war before you thought of it."

"Oh, no," Coyote said. "That was the ant people, that wasn't me. But war is necessary." He ran his tongue down inside the bone, licking out the marrow. "Without war, everything would stay the same. And if it stayed the same, it would just stop, *thoomp*, like that."

"What would stop?"

"Oh, time," Coyote said. "Things like that."

"There must be other ways besides war to keep time moving," Others' Child said, dissatisfied. Coyote's answers were never in a straight line. They were always bent in some way, so that you had to turn yourself upside down to follow them.

Coyote licked his muzzle and sat up straight, curling the brush of his tail around his front toes. The tip of it was black from the time he had flown with the ravens and fallen out of the sky so fast that he had caught on fire. His eyes were yellow and glowing. Others' Child found herself looking into them. Something clenched and loosened and clenched again between her legs, a not unpleasant sensation. For a moment, she was inside Bitch, drinking in his smell, eyes wide to the night, wild and graceful in her skin. Hairy paws itched to leap across the crusted snow with him. His penis jutted out bright pink.

It was only for a moment. She fell out of Bitch so hard that she hit the dirt floor with a thump when she landed. Coyote's yellow eyes gleamed at her, and she knew that he could put her back into Bitch if she asked him to, and then she would have no ungrateful people to look after.

Others' Child pulled her human skin back around her. She wondered how she could stop Mocking Bird and Cat Ears from fighting the Others without stopping time. Coyote heard her thinking.

"I don't stop things," Coyote said. "I set them rolling, like pushing a big rock down a slope. After that it isn't my affair where it goes."

"Well, that sounds like inventing war to me."

"It isn't," Coyote said. "It's just the Universe. But I will tell you about war if you like. About how it started."

*It was the ant people that began it, because they were the first people to think of work. That was all they did.* (Coyote stretched his feet to the fire, spreading his toes wide, and looked scornful.) *Work was Why-They-Were. They never thought of anything else, like chasing butterflies in the spring, or seeing if they could make a liquor out of cactus fruit, or climbing to the top of Sleeping Chieftain Mountain when it snowed and sliding down it. They only worked, and when they slept at night, they only lay still with their eyes open, and dreamed an endless dream of work.*

*And so the ant people were the first to build anything, and because of that they were the first to own anything and the first to make war over it. They never thought that there might be more ant people. They kept to the hill they had built by shoving dirt up it one grain at a time, and to their gathering ground, where they found food and dragged it home, each ant carrying a piece bigger than he was to feed the new ants that were always being hatched from the eggs that the Ant Mother laid endlessly. They were sufficient to themselves, and they needed no one, except the occasional leavings of someone else's kill, which was all well and good* (Coyote was not above that himself) *except that it is shortsighted to think there is no one but you in the world.*

*But beyond the anthill are many more things than ant people know. And so one day a scout for First Ant People, who had thought that they were Only Ant People, discovered a scout for Second Ant People, and both were very much astonished. They looked each other in the eye and saw columns and hills belonging to Other Ant People.*

*And so each scout told his chieftain what he had learned. "I have seen long columns of—" he would say, and then he would have to stop and make up a word, because they had no word for that yet. And the word that they made up was a new one, and it sounded like something that tasted bad, and it was* enemy.

*And each ant chieftain did something new, too. He*

made up a word to match the new word enemy, and
that word was kill. By those two words, the ant people
changed the world. First Ant People fought Second Ant
People, not for food but just to kill them because they
were not First Ant People and therefore might be dangerous or want First Ant People's hills. And Second Ant
People fought First Ant People for the same reasons.

So now the chieftains were called chiefs of war, and
now there was yet another new word. And the world
was filled with suffering and a very bad smell, and the
bodies of dead ant people covered the earth. And because
of that a fourth new word came into being of its own
accord. The chieftains didn't have to make this one up;
it just came. That word was death.

The human people watched the ant people at first with
puzzlement, and then with horror, and then slowly with
interest, wondering if they ought to be like that. It
seemed very important to the ant people. First Man
moved the people away from the ants, but wherever he
took them, they could still smell the bitter odor of the
ant war. The smell poisoned the air so that the human
people began talking among themselves about how some
bands were different from others and so might be dangerous. Those who lived on the coast grew suspicious of
those who lived on the mountain, and those who lived
by the river began to distrust those who lived on the
plain.

When Earth Mother saw the disharmony and the danger to the earth from what was happening, she felt very
sad, because the ants were her children as much as the
human people or the deer or the birds. But something
had to be done. The human people were learning too fast.
And so she made a great fire that would consume all the
ants who were fighting, and she told the human people
to hide inside the mountain. They did this, and Earth
Mother set the world ablaze and fanned the flames high
up into the sky until the fire roared with a voice louder
than Storm Wind. The ants stopped fighting and looked
at the blackened earth, and felt their jaws unhinge and

*their arms and legs break free from their bodies, and then
an orange cloud of flame swept them up and turned them
to ash.*

*The ash lay all over the earth, and the odor of the
burned ants hung in the air long after the ashes had
blown away or sifted back down into the ground. The
human people came out of the mountains and began to
clean up, setting things right, and for a while the deeds
of the ant people, and the new words they had made,
were nearly forgotten.*

*Earth Mother thought then that it was going to be all
right, that war had been stopped, and she was happy
with the way the world was going. But the human people had learned too much. After a while the words came
back up out of the ground, because when you make new
words, you can't unmake them again. And the human
people took them and used them for themselves.*

"So you see," Coyote said, "humans will find a use
for anything you teach them. And they imitate others
dreadfully. I don't think you can stop war now."

"Can't you teach them *not* to make war?"

"That's not my business. War keeps everything
changing. I told you. And besides," Coyote said skeptically, "I don't think anyone *could*."

"You could try," Others' Child demanded.

"Why should I want to? It doesn't do *me* any
harm."

"To help people," Others' Child said.

"Oh ho, are you confusing me with Spider? Why
should I help people?" Coyote lifted his hind leg and
scratched behind his ear. "Tell me, why were you left
behind with these people to begin with?"

"In the fighting," Others' Child said.

"Why was there fighting?"

"Because the Others wanted our summer place, and
they came and took it away."

"And why did your people fight them?"

"To take it back, of course. It was ours!"

"Well, then," Coyote said. "Now they think the maize is theirs."

"But it's not!"

"Because you say so? It is too complicated for me." Coyote stood up and shook his fur out. Others' Child saw the snow in it, like stars, clinging to the guard hairs. He bent down, stretching, paws in front of him, back concave. "That's why I never meddle in war. You can have my daughter there." He straightened and turned his head toward Bitch. "She's faithful, comparatively speaking."

Others' Child blinked at the blank place where he had been. She scrubbed at her eyes. Bitch whined at the hide flap, ears flattened. She got up on the bed and turned around three times and lay down.

Others' Child never saw him again through the winter. No one came to her in dreamtime, although she asked desperately, pleadingly, angrily, pounding her fist on her knee, for them to. In the meantime, Mocking Bird and the rest of the men made spears and spear-throwers, and talked around the fire at night of how many of the Others they would kill, until the women were sick of them.

Hears the Night said Bear had told him that the maize belonged to the Yellow Grass People, and that He Who Brought Us Maize had told Bear this. The women all agreed with that. They had no difficulty in maintaining ownership; they were merely tired of listening to men. In the winter the men had very little to do except make new spears and hunt when the weather broke, and the rest of the time boast about old hunts and enemies yet to be killed. But the women had clothes to make from hides tanned in the summer, food to cook—someone was always waiting to be fed—and children to mind and hope to see through the winter alive.

Others' Child went to Mocking Bird one more time, to try to tell him to leave Maize Came alone. But he went to Hears the Night, and Hears the Night came and lectured her, and she lost most of her newfound sympathy for him. Deer had become plentiful this winter, whether because of shifting weather patterns or her own magic, and the piñon nuts were fat and full of oil. For once the Yellow Grass People were not hungry, and did they give her thanks for it? No, it made them bigheaded and ready to fight.

"It is not for the Deer Woman to tell the men when to make war," Hears the Night said to her. He sighed, vexed. "You have much power and magic. I know this. I think again that you would make a good wife."

Others' Child froze, watching him warily.

"But we must take back what is ours to please He Who Brought Us Maize. You will see this if you think about it. When we have done this in the spring, when we have brought back the magic seed and the Maize Girl, and killed the enemy, then it will be time for the shaman of the Yellow Grass People to have a wife." He coughed and looked important. "I may not do so until then. My magic will be needed in the fighting, and I may not dilute it with woman magic."

Others' Child made a gesture of respect. "The shaman is wise," she said.

"Indeed," Hears the Night said. He was standing in her cave mouth, backlit by a low sun. She looked at him carefully and seemed to see the ant body under the skin, the feelers seeking the next thing to own, the next reason to fight to defend it.

# XV

# Battle and Magic

At the solstice the men went into the secret caves and turned the sun around. Others' Child still hadn't found a way to tell them they were fools and have the message stick. Mocking Bird went around lordlywise now that the Yellow Grass People were giving him his father's due. Others' Child finally acquitted old Cat Ears of wanting him killed. Now that Wind Caller and Deer Shadow were both dead, they were receding toward the status of gods, of magical spirits, and Cat Ears derived both pride and power from having known them. It was only right that the son of these should come after him as chief of the hunters. That, too, gave Cat Ears status.

Others' Child gave up trying to talk to the men. The women would have been happy enough to welcome her into their friendly, gossipy circle, accord her honors for her magic, and marry her off—Hears the Night was the obvious candidate, and Magpie, motherly now, spoke seriously to her about his virtues. They did not want to cleanse her or purify away all taint of the Others. They were happy to have her call the deer. And if they suspected that there might occasionally be ants in someone's bed that would not have been there otherwise, if that someone had been insulting, well, that was to be expected. The woman who carried the picture magic in her would command respect. So she had a place now.

And seemingly didn't want it. She grew irritable with the gossip and the endless stories of the last Gathering, of who had married whom, who might be a witch, and who would be chieftain next of this or that band. To Others' Child their voices were a flock of squawking birds who knew little and were convinced they knew all. They assured her that beyond the western mountains was nothing but a deep hole where the sun went to lie down at night, when Others' Child knew there was the coast and the Endless Water. They maintained that Hears the Night's tooth had come from a ghost animal, a spirit of the Great Game that the old shaman had called forth from the air, when Others' Child knew about the cat bones buried in the ground. The things that Night Hawk had told her did not impress them. They did not argue with her so much as act as if they hadn't heard her speak.

Finally Others' Child edged away from the women as well, and kept herself alone until they said she no doubt thought herself Most Important, and more important than the picture magic warranted. Her mother had been like that, now that they thought about it. Magpie grew suspicious and critical again.

The last snow fell, a luminous, magical snow such as comes on the edge between winter and spring, and everyone knew that when it melted there would be spring greens and the lower meadows would be carpeted with beeflowers, and the ducks and geese would come overhead in dark rushing streams. There would be new fawns among the deer people, and the lean coyotes would come looking for them, their patchy winter coats sticking to the bushes in tufts of yellow-gray fur.

All that would come up from under the crystalline snow that blanketed the night as far as Others' Child could see. The moon was only half full, but she could see colors by its light in the reflection of the snow. She could see the russet brown of her deerskin dress and the red feathers, her mother's, tied to the tops of her fur boots. The men were chanting the Going to War Chant that they hadn't even known before her father had come among them, and checking the bindings on their spears. War would come up from under the snow, too.

"Yah, they are stupid ant people," Others' Child said to Bitch, but Bitch pricked her ears toward the men's chanting and looked interested.

"No!" Others' Child caught her by the scruff of the neck and towed her away, floundering across the deep, white, magical earth.

Five mornings later, when the men were ready to go to the Others and take the maize back from them, Mocking Bird couldn't find Bitch.

"Where is she? Where is the dog when I want her?"

"I don't know," Others' Child said, not looking up from the piñon nuts she was roasting. They were the last of the winter store, the cones that had fallen green and been kept to ripen in the storage pits. The women were not going anywhere this morning, only the men. After Mocking Bird had led them to the Others and they had taken back the maize and the Keeper of the Maize, then they would come back for the women. "I haven't seen her this morning," she said, uninterested.

"Yah!" Mocking Bird threw his hands up and stomped off, cursing all dogs. The other hunters— they had taken to calling themselves the warriors—

were gathered by the winter dance ground with their dogs and their spears and the small boys running after them, pleading just once more to go, too. They were very fine in their fur cloaks and their best shirts and leggings, with feathers and amulets sewn to their spear-throwers. They had painted their faces with red mud and charcoal.

Others' Child, squatting sullenly and poking her roasting pine nuts, watched the warriors set out (without Bitch). When they were out of sight, she got her gathering basket and slipped around the knot of chattering women who stood at the top of the trail telling how many of the enemy each of their husbands would kill and how many fine things they would bring to their wives.

In the other direction, higher up the mountain, there were small caves, just big enough to crawl into, that the people used for winter storage. Others' Child scrambled up the slope to them, out of sight of the women below. She put her basket down and tugged at the stone that nearly blocked the opening to the largest cave. A furious growling answered her on the other side.

"Be quiet," Others' Child said, tugging at the stone. "Oof, this is harder to roll away than it was to push in. And if you bite me, I will leave you there." She staggered back a little as the stone began to move, and fell on her back. It rolled on her foot, and she cursed it. Bitch stuck her snout through the widening hole, teeth bared.

Others' Child got up again and pulled the stone the rest of the way out. She wasn't surprised to see that Bitch had already chewed through the rawhide thong that Others' Child had used to tie her up while she pushed the stone over the cave mouth. She grabbed at its trailing end. Bitch flattened her ears and growled again. Others' Child grabbed the spear and the pack she had hidden there, too, and held on to Bitch.

"Bah. I have brought you almost the last of the meat, to make up for it." She handed Bitch a strip of dried deer meat. Bitch cracked it between her teeth but kept up her singsong growl.

Others' Child sat cross-legged on the ground, watching her eat. "We are going foot-on-trail, you and I," she said finally. "Coyote told me you were mine. That's why I shut you up, in case you forgot that and went with the men."

Bitch lifted one ear. She had the strip of meat between her front paws like a bone and was cracking it with her side teeth. Her yellow eyes were still baleful.

"We are going to get there before they do, too." Others' Child didn't know what she would do then, but maybe someone would tell her, if she were audacious enough to go without waiting for answers. She had seen the white deer again, just a glimpse of it against the snow that night the moon had been so bright. She was pleased to think that it was her mother, but she knew it might have been anything. It had lifted its head and looked right at her out of glowing eyes. It might have been Coyote in a deer hide, too.

When Bitch had finished her meat, Others' Child stood up and whistled her to heel. Bitch came, running her tongue over her muzzle, but her stiff-legged walk and the set of her ears were a sure sign that she was still in a temper. Others' Child set off through the brush, away from the caves where the women still were, and down the wet mountain slope to get to the trail the men had taken. She left the gathering basket sitting in the mud in front of the cave where she had tied Bitch.

The way was still sloppy wet, but the men were anxious to catch the Others before they settled into their summer camp by the lake. They would wait for the Others by the lake, the Yellow Grass men decided, and take them by surprise. It might be that the lake would make a fine place for the Yellow Grass People to live if the deer did not come back to their old trails near the tufa cliffs. It might even be that they were meant to have the new lake. The Yellow Grass men agreed among themselves that surely the gods would not have given such a fine place to the Others on purpose.

Traveling alone, Others' Child and Bitch made good time even on the muddy ground, and they caught up to the men by midafternoon. The war party was easy to track. "Yah bah, it is a good thing no one is trailing them but me," Others' Child said disgustedly.

Bitch whined when they got close enough to smell Mocking Bird, but Others' Child smacked her nose, and after that Bitch seemed sulkily content to stay at Others' Child's heel. Once she had spotted the men, Others' Child kept herself and Bitch well back on the trail until night. At dusk the men camped and made a fire and cooked the journey food the women had given them—piñon nut gruel and dried, powdered meat mixed with deer fat. Others' Child crouched in the wet sage bushes and listened to their talk for a while. Then she slid backwards on her stomach to where she had left Bitch waiting for her. They slipped through the brush past the men without so much as a growl from one of their dogs, and Others' Child chortled silently at that.

She felt less pleased with herself when they stopped over a ridge from where the men were and made their own fire and cooked their own journey food, and the night seemed to lean in on her over her shoulder. *And I have been in the wild lands myself alone before*, she thought, *and all places are very much the same to me*. But that had been with Mocking Bird and Maize Came, not truly alone like this; with the weather warming, things would be out hunting. She sat with her back to a big rock and laid her spear across her lap.

In the morning they moved on, going more slowly

now and taking pains to hide their tracks. Mostly they
kept to the scrub and the chaparral, with an ear out
for Rattlesnake, who was also waking up.

If she got to the lake before the men, Others' Child
thought, and before the Kindred, maybe she could do
something to stop them from fighting. She looked for
the white deer again but didn't see it. The suspicion
deepened that it had been a supernatural trick of the
light, some otherworldly prank. Maybe Maize Came
would know what to do.

When the journey food ran out, Others' Child
found snails in the river and a bank where camas
grew and loaded her pack with those. She set snares
for quail, praising herself for having got ahead of the
men. There were enough in their band to run down
game together, and they were noisy in their travels.
If she had been behind them, there wouldn't have
been a bird or a rabbit left in a day's walk.

The sun had warmed, and now was the time when
the animals who ate plants, humans included, foraged
for their keep with little trouble. Behind them came
the meat-eaters, still winter-thin with winter appe-
tites. The humans had their place in those ranks, too,
a fact that afforded Others' Child a certain grim
amusement even while she kept her back to a cliff or
a cave wall at night.

Bitch caught mice to supplement her diet, and one
night she caught an owl that had been hunting the
same mouse. Others' Child heard a flapping of wings
beyond the fire, and a yelp from Bitch and then a
furious growling tussle. Bitch came back with feathers
on her muzzle and the dead owl dangling from her
jaws, her nose and throat raked open in long, bloody
scratches. The owl's talons, like curved knives, had
fur and skin in them.

"Foolish, it is a wonder you didn't lose an eye,"
Others' Child said. Bitch ignored her, biting at the owl
and spitting out feathers. Others' Child inspected the
talon marks. "I will put yarrow in those," she mut-

tered, standing up and looking at the sky, which in
the open seemed limitless, the stars retreating into dis-
tances unimaginable. "We are too far away," she said
to Bitch, "to take foolish chances fighting owls." But
too far from what?

As the air warmed she could feel winter sliding off
her like a dank robe, and the sense of being too far
from some belonging place intensified. She yearned
for something she wasn't sure of, not the Kindred or
the Yellow Grass People, but something, some wild
streak in the spring air that beckoned, that fluttered
just over her head like Butterfly Boy, teasing, telling
her to follow him, to spiral upward on the air currents. *No*, she told it. *I have a thing I must do. I must
stop the foolish ant people.* But she saw a line of ant
people marching across the sand and wondered how
she could do that.

In the meantime, she grew scruffy with trail dirt,
and her sandals wore out, and she felt like a resent-
ful ghost dodging the men's band, camping always
behind a ridge or hidden in a canyon, always hungry, always looking over her shoulder, while
something inside her said, *Come away, come away into
the soft air.*

In another handful of days she came to the lake
ahead of the men and dropped flat on her stomach in
the brush because there were fires along the lakeshore. The Kindred had moved from their winter shelters early. So much for Mocking Bird's large talk that
he knew the times of their wanderings. He knew only
one year, and in that one they had been delayed by
the earthquake and by waiting for Night Hawk to
come back.

Now what to do? Others' Child wondered. The Yellow Grass men would see the fires, too, and likely
they would not attack the Kindred tonight but would
stop and think about it for a while. She put her hand

around Bitch's muzzle to make her be quiet, and they eased forward in the dusk. The Kindred were moving around their fires, boiling spring greens and cooking fish from the lake. The smell bit into Others' Child's nose, and her stomach cramped hungrily. She saw Maize Came go by with a bundle balanced on one hip, talking earnestly with old Leaf Fall. Maize Came was big-bellied as a cooking basket, and old Leaf Fall kept grinning at her toothlessly, patting her arm and belly.

Others' Child bit her lip, annoyed and jealous. Well, she couldn't go to Maize Came, not when she could see Leaf Fall mothering Maize Came now, and with Wing Foot about, too, no doubt.

A familiar profile crossed between the fires and the bushes where Others' Child crouched, smelling the fish. Night Hawk. She held her breath as he went to the lake to wash. The sky was darkening overhead. When she thought it was dark enough, she slipped toward the lakeshore, too, but she couldn't find him. Giggles and splashes came from the shallows under the trees, and she ignored them. If he was there, she was certainly not going to interrupt him, and if the men of the Yellow Grass People came and killed them all, it would be his fault for lying in the mud with some slut when he should be worrying about important things. She washed the dirt off herself, resentfully, and hid in a tree until the camp was still.

When all the fires had burned low, she slid down out of her tree and told Bitch, who was lying under it, to stay. Bitch whined and paced back and forth from Others' Child to the tree in an uneasy circle, but Others' Child shook her head. Bitch would have all the dogs of the Kindred in an uproar; she smelled too much like a coyote.

Others' Child slunk along the edge of the trees and then along the cliff face, hoping that Night Hawk slept in the same cave as last summer, and that he slept alone. What if he didn't? And what if she fell over the Three Old Men instead? That thought halted her at the cave mouth, but there was something familiar about the breathing she could hear inside. There was only one pair of lungs, she could tell that, and this cave was too small for more than one person. She slipped past the hide flap and scooped a coal out of the fire with a bone spoon that she found there, in the hope that it would give enough light to see by.

She held the spoon next to his face, her big toe throbbing because she had stubbed it against a rock by the fire pit. His mouth was open, and the cropped hair hung in his eyes. It was Night Hawk. She put the spoon down carefully.

"If you are stealing anything," he said, "I will tear your arms off and put them up your backside."

Others' Child sucked her breath in hard, her voice catching in her throat. A hand closed around her ankle. She struggled for balance. "Hush!" she managed to say. "Be quiet! Be quiet!"

Night Hawk sat up, still holding her ankle. "Reed?"

"I am not Reed," she said crossly because he had scared her. "I told you."

"Then I will call you Rattlesnake. Rattlesnake, don't bite me." Night Hawk tugged on her ankle. "Come down here."

Others' Child sat down.

Night Hawk kept his hand on her ankle. His fingers kneaded it with interest, as if it were some new appendage. "Why are you in my cave? Was it not so fine among the Trespassers as you thought?"

"Mocking Bird has told them that they must take the maize and the Maize Girl back from you," Others' Child said. "All the men have come to do that."

Night Hawk blinked. He seemed to be trying to wake up now. "All the men? The Trespassers' men? They have come here?"

"They are camped away a little, waiting, I think. They will likely come tomorrow."

"To make war on the Kindred?"

"Mocking Bird told them that our father has cursed them and that he won't be placated until they have taken the maize back. Mocking Bird is still angry over Maize Came."

"And why are you with them?" Night Hawk inquired. "Do the Trespassers let their women fight for them?"

"When they have to," Others' Child snapped. "And they do not know I am here. They would not listen when I told them it was not a right idea, and so I came after them."

Night Hawk scratched his head. "To do what? To warn us? Then we will just kill your men."

"To warn Maize Came, I thought, but then I decided that that wouldn't work."

"Not if you want to stop them from fighting," Night Hawk agreed. "Little Sister hasn't your audacity." He scratched his head. "So you came to me." His smile was sleepy and pleased.

"I tried to catch up to you at the lake," Others' Child said stiffly. "But you were playing in the water with some—"

"I went to wash," Night Hawk said.

"Oh."

"And what business is it of yours if I wasn't?"

"None."

He put his hand on her ankle again.

"Are you going to help me think how to stop this?" Others' Child demanded.

"Yes, but we have until morning to think. I think just now that I am glad to see you. I told you that you would not be happy with the Trespassers again." The hand slid up her leg and under her hide skirt. "You are winter thin."

"There was plenty of food," she said, "but I have been on the trail."

"Alone?" he asked. His hand stopped at her knee.

"Yes. Bitch and me."

He shook his head, apparently marveling. "And now you want *help* with stopping this war? Someone who came here foot-on-trail by herself?"

"Are you going to help me? Or are you going to play stupid games with talk?"

"I am going to go and steal you the maize," Night Hawk said. He stood up.

"What?"

"There is seed to be planted this season. Maize Came threatened to curse all the Kindred the way she cursed the Trespassers if we didn't save it. If we give your people half, there will be no need for fighting."

"You don't want to fight them?" Others' Child had thought she would have to convince him.

"No, because you don't want it," Night Hawk said.

"Oh." Others' Child looked up at him dubiously. "They will still want to take Maize Came."

"That is another matter. They can't do that. We will tell them so, you and I."

"That is more dangerous than letting them fight," Others' Child said. "They will all throw spears at us instead."

"No," Night Hawk said. "Maybe not. And you wanted a plan. That is the only one I have."

"How will you get the seed? Maize Came will have it."

"Wait for me."

"Here?" She envisioned Night Hawk caught with his hands in wherever Maize Came had her store of seed, uproar in the camp, the Three Old Men and the Grandmothers pointing to her, quivering in Night Hawk's cave. "Are you going to tell her?"

"Not unless she catches me."

Others' Child thought that might be wise. Maize Came belonged here now. Before she could ask him anything else, he had gone, leaving her alone in his cave.

It seemed a very long time before he came back. Long enough to listen to an owl hoo-hooing in the

trees and imagine that it was some vengeful spirit
here to foretell death because Bitch had eaten its mate.
Everyone knew that owls told you about death. It was
probably bad luck to eat one. And would Bitch stay
where she had left her, or go looking for Mocking
Bird? It was all very well that Coyote had given Bitch
to her, but Bitch wasn't biddable.

Others' Child wrapped her arms around her knees
and shivered by Night Hawk's banked fire. After a
while she crawled into his bed and pulled his blankets
over her. What was he doing? She listened for sounds
of argument or shouting, for footsteps in pursuit, but
the only noise was the owl and the roar of a cat on a
distant hillside. The sound lifted the skin along Others' Child's spine, and she thought again of the bones
Night Hawk had told her of. They seemed to her to
signify something, some power beyond what could be
seen on the surface of the world, as if the cat bones
had stretched, maybe, and cracked the earth open. She
pulled the blanket tighter around her.

Night Hawk slipped past the hide flap with a basket under one arm and dropped onto the bed before
he saw that Others' Child was in it. "Hoo, that was
not a nice thing to find. Give me some of my blanket.
My courage wants warming. The Maize Girl doesn't
trust us. She has been keeping Rattlesnake in the hole
with her seed."

Others' Child wriggled over, frightened. "Are you
bitten?"

"Would I be here if I were, instead of yammering
for Healer Old Man and the Grannies? No, I pinned
him down with a stick while I filled my basket, and
then I left him alone."

"What about Maize Came?"

"She is sleeping, unless Rattlesnake has told her,
and I doubt it. He was only one of Rattlesnake's children, anyway. They don't talk often. In the morning
we will go to the Three Old Men and wake them up,

but we won't give them time to dance the Warriors' Dance. That may stop them from wanting to fight."

Others' Child silently blessed the Kindred's endless affinity for ritual.

"Of course it won't help if your people attack them first," Night Hawk said. "And it might be useful if you came with me."

"To the Three Old Men?" Others' Child imagined a ritual that they would dance before they threw her off a cliff. And when they found that Mocking Bird was here . . .

"It would also help if your brother kept his tongue between his teeth," Night Hawk said. He shivered, still unnerved by Rattlesnake. The shiver turned to a yawn. "That is a lot of people to expect good sense from, I suppose." He moved closer to her, and she found that his hand was on her leg again, fingers moving lightly against her thigh. Her skin quivered.

"We can't do anything until dawn," Night Hawk said. "It's dark outside."

"I'm cold," Others' Child said.

"I know." Night Hawk's other hand rested on her breast. Even through the deer-hide dress the hand felt warm, and so she leaned into it. His fingers closed tighter. His breath blew hot on her neck. His eyes glowed yellow in the faint reflection of the fire. "Warm," he whispered, pushing his hand higher between her legs.

This, she saw suddenly, was what the spring air had been talking to her about. She leaned into his other hand, felt fingers exploring her and thigh muscles go slack. This time was for coming together, even with the maize and the Yellow Grass men looming behind her shoulder. It was for coupling in the warm darkness. Night belonged to Coyote, and here was her trail into his wild lands, not alone but hand in hand, so that she and Night Hawk could frolic there impervious and not be eaten. That was how it was done.

Night Hawk tipped her under him on the bed and tugged at the ragged laces of her hide skirt with his teeth. His hands moved against her skin like warm rain. The knowledge had left her breathless, and she splayed her legs apart under the rabbit skin while he pulled his leggings down and took out his penis. It stood straight up and seemed to salute her, all that pent-up desire. She yearned for it. He had stopped talking, stopped cajoling. His breath was heavy now, and his body had an odor that made her groin ache and her breasts tingle. He pulled her splayed knees apart and pushed himself into her, breathing hard.

It was like having Coyote inside her, irreverent and impudent, playful and hard, maybe even a little dangerous, and not the way it had been with Hears the Night at all. She wrapped her legs around Night Hawk's back, clinging to him, and saw the wild, disorderly land billowing around them, with the Endless Water in the distance.

Afterward they lay, breathing hard, entwined under the rabbit skin with his hand still between her thighs. She clamped them together around it, wanting to enfold it. He stroked her with his palm, fingers moving inside her, knowing that if he kept it up, he could make something happen. They had pulled off her hide shirt, and he put his other hand over her breasts again, rubbing the nipples with his fingertip until they stood up taut, in a dark engorged ring. Others' Child arched her back, howling and mewing, and felt her flesh explode like birds' wings.

"Hush," he said, laughing. He put his mouth over hers. "Hush."

"What was that?"

"I don't know," he chuckled. "It is just something that happens."

"It was not like that with Hears the Night," she said frankly.

He laughed again, pulled her into the hollow of his arm. "Good."

* * *

She hadn't thought she would sleep. Every night sound seemed to be the Yellow Grass men coming with their spears, with Mocking Bird in the front, just to be sure and get killed. But Night Hawk was bending over her, and she could see the faint streak of gray that outlined the hide flap.

"It is morning, Sleep," he said. "It is time to talk to the Three Old Men and your most foolish brother."

"Oh." Others' Child scrubbed at her eyes. She sat up and reached for her clothes. "The Grannies will know we did that," she said dubiously, looking at the torn laces on her skirt.

"The Grannies know everything. We'll be gone, you and I, to see the cat bones and the red and blue birds and the giant fish that live in the Endless Water, and we won't care." It seemed he had a wife now, he thought, bemused. He hadn't had to tumble her last night. He had done it on purpose, so it must be meant. He stretched and watched her putting on her clothes, and wanted to do it some more.

When she was dressed and they had combed their hair and were respectable and not like two people who had been legs-in-the-air all night, they slid out of the cave and through the sleeping camp. Night Hawk scratched at the rock outside the cave of Rain Old Man. The maize was the Rainmakers' province, and besides, Night Hawk was a Rainmaker.

"What do you want?" Rain Old Man asked him gruffly as he came out of the cave, and Night Hawk told him. Rain Old Man's eyes widened when he saw Others' Child.

"I thought Coyote had eaten that one."

He had only swallowed her, Others' Child thought, looking at Night Hawk's profile in the false dawn. It wasn't so bad.

"We will give the Trespassers back half of the maize," Night Hawk said.

"Why will we do that?" Rain Old Man demanded.

"And the Maize Girl will tell them that she wishes to stay here. We will do it because it is better not to fight with the Trespassers again, and see our men killed when there is good game and water this year and no need to."

"There might not be next year," Rain Old Man said practically. "If they want to fight us, we should let them. Then there will be fewer of them."

"Who found the lake?" Night Hawk said sternly.

"Night Hawk the Trader," Rain Old Man conceded.

"The lake was given to us so that we might live in peace and always have game and water. I was told this."

"Hummph!" Rain Old Man said. "I will talk to Healer Old Man and Deer Old Man." He stumped back inside his cave. Over his shoulder, he said to Night Hawk, "Also, I will tell the Kindred to pick up their spears. In case."

The Yellow Grass men came up over the ridge above the lake with the sun behind them. There had been a small argument over whether Mocking Bird should lead them, since he had been wrong about the Others not being at the lake yet, but Cat Ears had said that that didn't matter. Strangely, Cat Ears seemed to feel a kind of foster father's pride in Mocking Bird. To Cat Ears, there was power in the association with a powerful spirit's son. That he had been at odds with that spirit while it was in the flesh did not matter now.

"We will surprise them while they are asleep," Mocking Bird told the Yellow Grass men. "Where my sister is, the maize will be, and we will bring both home where they are meant to be, and then my father will take the curse from us."

Wakes on the Mountain nodded. He raised his spear, and Cat Ears and Hears the Night waved theirs. With the sun at their backs, they made a line of black figures along the ridge, uplifted spears not

unlike the waving antennae of the ants. The sun
bounced off the rock face below, splashing itself back
into their eyes, gleaming off the lake waters so that
the whole valley shimmered. The men of the Yellow
Grass People poured down the ridge.

They were running hard, spears notched into atlatls, when Others' Child and Night Hawk came out
of the caves and stood between them and the Kindred. Bitch had been whistled from the woods and
sat at Others' Child's heel. Her yellow-gray head was
cocked sideways as if she could hear the angry words
spattering on the air. Behind them, the Kindred stood
leaning on their spears.

The Yellow Grass men skirted the lakeshore, and
Mocking Bird slowed, uncertain. He pointed at Others' Child, and his brows drew together in a frown.
Others' Child stepped closer to them to be absolutely
certain they could see who she was, wondering at the
same time whether, if they were angry enough at her,
it would make any difference. The Yellow Grass men
bunched behind Mocking Bird.

Others' Child raised her cupped hands and held
them out. Out of the corner of her eye she could see
Night Hawk doing the same. "There is seed enough,"
she shouted. "It is not necessary for the People and
the Kindred"—she used the polite word, the Kindred's own word for themselves—"to fight each other
over it."

The Kindred muttered behind her as if they might
not be certain of that, either. Maize Came was clinging
to Wing Foot's arm. The Kindred and the Yellow
Grass men eyed one another across the open ground.

"And what is the Deer Woman doing among the
Others?" Wakes on the Mountain demanded in an
awful voice.

"These are the people I was born to," Others' Child
said. She looked at Night Hawk sideways again. "But
I do not belong to them now, nor to the Yellow Grass
People. I will go my own way now, but it is not right

that my people and my people kill each other."

"The maize belongs to the Yellow Grass People," Wakes on the Mountain said. The Yellow Grass men shouted their agreement. "He Who Brought Us Maize has said so."

"I am daughter of He Who Brought Us Maize. So is she who was Follows Her Father." She pointed at Maize Came. "We say it belongs to all." She was not at all certain Maize Came felt that way. "The gods did not send it for us to look greedy-eyes on it. The more that is planted, the more seed there will be."

"That is very fine," Wakes on the Mountain said, "but you were not asked. The maize is not your affair."

"And Follows Her Father must come home," Mocking Bird said angrily. "She is ours. The Maize Girl must come home."

"No!" Maize Came said. She spoke in the Yellow Grass People's language to be sure they understood. "Yah, you are dirty thieves who killed my father. I will go nowhere with you. That is why I have taken the maize and brought it to the Kindred. My brother should be ashamed to have returned to you."

The Kindred took a tighter grip on their spears. They were uncertain what was being said, but the tone was plain enough. The Three Old Men had had trouble persuading them not to fight in the first place. Wing Foot had wanted to, and he and Night Hawk had argued fiercely over it, their friendship barely intact.

"We had best give them the seed quickly," Night Hawk said in Others' Child's ear, "before your fool of a brother gets stubborn." He took a careful step toward the Yellow Grass Men.

"It would have helped if she could have kept her tongue behind her teeth," Others' Child muttered. "That is half the problem. They are twins. They must love or hate."

"She has not been of a particularly even tempera-

ment lately," Night Hawk said with a rueful grimace
that might have been half a grin, his head turned from
the men. It was obvious that the baby was due soon.
"And disinclined to look kindly on men in general,
even her husband and my fine self." Another step.
Bitch kept pace with them, whining.

Hears the Night eyed them with disapproval, the
Yellow Grass men ranged behind him. "And why do
you bring a man of the enemy?" he inquired of Others' Child.

"To prove good faith, Uncle," Night Hawk said in
the Yellow Grass People's tongue, giving Hears the
Night proper respect.

"I do not approve of that," Hears the Night said.
He narrowed his eyes at Night Hawk. "I remember
you. You are the wanderer who brings red dye to
trade."

"And greenstone and blue bead necklaces and
shells from the Endless Water and many other excel-
lent things, O Uncle," Night Hawk said.

"You do not have any business with this woman."

"To the contrary," Night Hawk said, suppressing a
smile. "She has business with me. It is thanks to her
that your people and my people need not kill each
other." He held out both hands, cupping the maize.
A few seeds dribbled onto the ground at their feet.
Cat Ears made a grab at them, and Bitch growled at
him, muzzle pulled back above pointed teeth.

"Shame!" Mocking Bird shouted at Bitch. He
picked the kernels up himself, and Bitch looked
abashed. He stood up and glared at Others' Child.
"You had no business coming to these people. We
will take you home with us when we have killed
them. You and the Maize Girl who belongs to us." He
grabbed Others' Child's arm and pulled her toward
him, jerking her hands apart so that the maize went
flying, a little shower of golden seed.

Cat Ears lunged at Night Hawk.

"Stop!" Others' Child screamed.

Night Hawk flung the maize from his cupped hands into Cat Ears's face. It brought Cat Ears up short for a moment, and his spear slid out of its thrower. Cat Ears grabbed for the spear and for Night Hawk. Night Hawk cuffed at him and, weaponless, took to his heels while Others' Child writhed in Mocking Bird's grip. Cat Ears flung a spear after Night Hawk. The Kindred roared and spilled across the ground toward them, spears raised.

Others' Child elbowed Mocking Bird hard in the ribs. "Stop them!"

"Hold still!" Mocking Bird shook her. "Hold still and go back there and bide in the trees till we are done. I should beat you for coming here!"

"Yah, you can try!" Others' Child gasped. She kicked Mocking Bird in the shins.

The Yellow Grass men drew closer to the Kindred. A spear flew past Wakes on the Mountain's ear. Night Hawk had reached his people and seemed to be arguing with them. He waved his arms. Wing Foot grabbed him by the shoulder and shouted in his face.

Bitch looked from Others' Child to Mocking Bird, puzzled. She took a step toward them uncertainly, and then a step back. She began to whine, a low singsong of worry.

Something in Bitch's gyrations caught Others' Child's eye. She stopped struggling with Mocking Bird and tried to stand still. He was still pulling at her. "Be still! I am not fighting you!" she said, pinching his shoulder between her fingers. For a moment he stopped, surprised. She put her feet flat on the ground and felt for movement. Bitch was spinning in a circle.

"Stupid ants!" she shouted suddenly. "Stupid ant wars! The gods will open the earth under you because you haven't learned anything!" She pulled away from Mocking Bird, who was still surprised, and ran after the rest of the Yellow Grass men. She could hear her brother's furious feet behind her.

"I will open the ground again!" she shouted, pushing her way through the men, hoping the Kindred would stop throwing spears—and hoping that Bitch was right. "The gods have given me the power to do this because I belong to both people and no people and because my father brought you the maize. I will do it if you fight each other! I will open the ground!" She faced them, hands on her hips.

From where he stood in the midst of the Kindred, Night Hawk shot her a glance that seemed to imply that she had better be able to back that up.

Cat Ears lifted his spear again. "We are warriors! Do we listen to women?"

Others' Child stamped her foot. "If I stamp again, Cat Ears, you will listen from a hole in the ground. Shall I do it?" The trees seemed to be tilting in the distance, she thought. The eyes of the rest were elsewhere, caught in their desire to fight one another, to make themselves great and the enemy less. They couldn't see the trees shimmer.

"Kill them!" Cat Ears screamed.

"Kill them!" Mocking Bird shouted, loping at his side. Spears flew from spear-throwers, and a man of the Kindred fell.

The ground trembled, and now they felt it, suddenly, terrifyingly. It swayed, and Cat Ears staggered. Wakes on the Mountain spread his feet apart and stared wildly at the mountains all around them. The world heaved and rocked. Night Hawk looked at Others' Child with wide eyes.

The women outside the Kindred's caves were screaming. The waters of the lake rolled back and flung themselves onto the shore. The warriors reeled and fell, their spears snapping when they tried to lean on them.

Others' Child lurched, trying to keep her feet, and regarded the chaos around her with frightened satisfaction. She wondered what would happen if the ground didn't stop moving. Would they expect her to be able to stop it? She imagined guiltily that some god had heard her boasting of nonexistent powers and might decide to teach her a lesson. She staggered toward Wakes on the Mountain—who was chieftain, *not* Cat Ears—and as she got nearer, the ground subsided.

"And is it not as I said?" she gasped.

Night Hawk shouldered his way through the Kindred until he was standing beside her. "The gods have spoken," he said. "Take the maize and go before we are all sucked under into the house of the dead!" He looked very much as if he believed it.

"That is how it will be," Hears the Night said abruptly. He looked as if *he* had thought twice about wanting a woman who could cause earthquakes. Some forms of power would burn even a shaman's fingers. But he looked at Night Hawk with the obvious hope that he would be the one to get burned.

"My sister must come with us," Mocking Bird said stubbornly. He was afraid, but he was angrier than he was afraid.

"No," Others' Child said. "That is what started it, wanting to make people do as you say."

Maize Came waddled across the trampled ground, and Wing Foot pushed his way out of the crowd of warriors and caught her by the arm. She argued with him for a moment, then pulled away from his hand and came within a few paces of her brother. Wing Foot scowled after her.

"I can't go back with you," Maize Came said softly to Mocking Bird. "You can't stay with me. You made that happen. Now it is."

"You are my twin. I have Father's flute, and you have his grain—we are part of the same thing."

"I have to stay here. I live here."

Mocking Bird looked from his twin to Others' Child. "That is not right. We are supposed to be together."

"No. We *were* together. Now we are not." Others' Child felt her eyes sting. It didn't matter how mad you were at someone. If you loved them, you always felt sorry for them. She could tell that Maize Came did, too. "You are important to the Yellow Grass People now," she said, trying to soften it. "You don't need us."

Mocking Bird compressed his lips. His glance strayed to old Cat Ears. "I will be the next chief of the hunters," he said, as if that meant he should have what he wanted.

Maize Came nodded. "That belongs to you," she said sadly. "I don't. You can't have everything."

Maize Came belonged to something new now, Others' Child suspected, thinking about it later—to some place in the workings of time and space, some perhaps particular spot on the web. Night Hawk sat beside Others' Child on the rock that shadowed the lake, and she leaned her head against his shoulder, surprised at how easy that felt.

The Yellow Grass men had collected the maize and taken it away with them, prepared to tell their wives that they had been through battle and magic for it.

"Did you really do that?" Night Hawk asked Others' Child. "Did you make the ground shake?"

"I hope not," Others' Child said. "I saw Bitch turning circles. She knows when the ground is going to shake. I don't know how."

"What would you have done if it hadn't stopped?"

"I don't know. I was afraid it might not. What if the gods *had* heard me?"

Night Hawk chuckled. "Maybe they did. Spider has a heavy footfall."

"Don't joke about it. That isn't respectful. It isn't safe, either," she added.

"The world is a joke," Night Hawk said after a moment's thought. "It seems that way to me. Otherwise, why do we laugh?"

"Maize Came doesn't laugh," Others' Child said thoughtfully.

"She takes herself seriously. She has to. She is important."

Once Maize Came had been afraid that the Maize God had taken her father and might take her. He *had* taken her, Others' Child thought now, but she had taken him, too. Changed him. The Maize God wouldn't want blood anymore, she decided. It seemed very complicated and beyond her reckoning.

Old Leaf Fall didn't seem to mind. She had Maize Came for a daughter now and was happy with her status as Wing Foot's mother-in-law. *I only worried her*, Others' Child thought. She didn't know what she could do about that. She had too much of a taste for looking over a precipice. She peered sideways at Night Hawk.

"Where will you go now?" she asked him.

"Where do you want to go?"

Others' Child thought a moment. "I should like," she said, "to see the Endless Water. I don't have to see the cat bones. I know about them."

"They are on the way, anyway," Night Hawk said.

# Epilogue

The old woman's head nods forward on her chest. She is almost asleep herself by the end of her story. Enfolded in it like a blanket, she knows these ghosts, these luminous inhabitants of the old times, so well that she can dream their stories out loud.

"What happened to them after that?" a young woman of the cliff people asks her. She is fourteen and a romantic. She doesn't want the story to end.

"They went to see the Endless Water," the old woman says, dismissing the young woman's desire for details. She thinks how Spider told it to her first, folding all of her eight arms in resignation at Others' Child's impatience. "The young always want to know everything," Spider said, or says now—sometimes the old woman can see her in her corner under the roof. Sometimes she is in her, balancing on her web, holding the world. That is when she is young again herself.

"But after that?" the girl persists.

The old woman shakes her head. How can she explain that Others' Child and Night Hawk are a ripple, one of many, spreading from the heart of the world to the people here now in this room? "Look," she says, and shows them the reflection in the fire:

There is Wind Caller, standing on a streambank, admiring himself. His pack is on his back, and he holds his flute to his lips. His image, reflected upward in the rippling water, is the one that Others' Child marked in the ground outside the caves of the Yellow Grass People. It will reflect down the years, moving through Night Hawk and Others' Child, into and through all the other travelers, the wanderers who come, pack-on-back, to bring strange wares. The cliff people have painted its reflection on the red canyon walls.

"They are part of the dance," she says softly, and chuckles suddenly because she can see Coyote now, dancing behind them, prancing on his hind legs, stars streaming from his tail. They don't see him, but he is there. He will always be there. Wherever There is, Coyote was there first.

# Afterword

Native American myths appear in infinite variety, each storyteller fashioning the next version to suit the audience or the lesson being taught. The stories in this book, of the ant people, of Butterfly Boy, of First Hunter and his Morning Light, have been adapted from tales recorded in *American Indian Myths and Legends*, edited by Richard Erdoes and Alfonso Ortiz, and *Tunkashila* by Gerald Hausman. I am indebted to both.

Thanks are also due to Nancy Collins and Lynn Erwin of the Hollins College Library for helping to track down hard-to-find material; to Pamela Lappies and Elizabeth Tinsley of Book Creations and Ellen Edwards of Avon for first-rate editing and plot suggestions; and to my husband, Tony Neuron, for three A.M. story conferences. I am grateful to them all.

If you enjoyed
*The Deer Dancers, Book Two:*
*Wind Caller's Children,*
sample the following excerpt
from the captivating sequel,
*The Long Walk,*
coming in September 1996
from Avon Books.

The caves where the Kindred spent the winter were high in the red sandstone mountains. Up there the low sun warmed the rocks for a few hours, and the piñon pines made fat, oily nuts when the ground was covered with snow. Every year, when the browse began to die, the deer moved up the slopes after the nuts, and the Kindred followed the deer.

That was when Night Hawk the Trader and his wife would come home, if they were not wintering elsewhere among monsters and False People—this according to the old Grandmothers of the Kindred, who knew that all that was real and true fell within the borders of the Kindred's hunting grounds and the bloodlines of the Kindred. Night Hawk's wife had been born to the Kindred, but then she had been lost to the Trespassers in the south, and anyone could see what had come of that. She was not called Others' Child by both peoples for nothing. As for Night

Hawk, that one had been footloose since a hawk had
flown across his mother's path when she carried him.
The Grandmothers told one another this with em-
phatic nods and gestures, toothless lips compressed.

Winter was the slow time, the digging-in time, like
rabbits into burrows, when the women made clothes
from the hides tanned in summer and fall, the Three
Old Men talked to the gods about the Sun, and the
other men gossiped, and hunted if the weather was
good. When the weather was not good, which was as
often as not, the Kindred lived on stories told around
the fire pit to still their rumbling stomachs. In winter
no one was ever really alone, not even if he was dying. The caves were smoky and cramped and your
neighbors knew all your business, and you theirs.

Now it was the third moon after Turn of the Year,
and the mountains were wet with melting slush that
made the faint new green of the aspens look like
leaves of ice. Night Hawk was sharpening his spears
and mending his pack and his dogs' travois, and
when he looked up from that, his eyes went over the
horizon.

In winter, the Kindred could see south down the
red mountains to the high blue peaks beyond, with
the river valley in between, and farther yet the black
desert, leavings of a time when fire had come out of
the earth and melted the stone. Everyone knew that
country—they hunted over it. But behind them to the
north lay the high desert and the land where the dead
lived under their lake. In the east, the buffalo hunters
lived on the plains, and the tall grass went on for
miles. And beyond the high mountains to the west
lay the coast where the Endless Water lapped at the
shore and the people lived on strange, spined fish.
The Grandmothers didn't know about any of those
last, nor did they wish to be told.

Others' Child was making yucca rope, twisting the
fibers on her thigh, rolling them expertly against her
deer-hide leggings with one flat palm. They always
seemed to need more rope by year's end, and rope

making was not something you could do in one evening, on the trail. The late winter air had a bite to it, and the wind had picked up, whipping the cold damp off the melting snow and flinging it at them like a wet hide, puffing up the smoke from the hearth in gray clouds. She coughed, and her eyes streamed. The Grandmothers flapped their hands in front of their faces. When they peered through the smoke at her, they looked like the wrinkled masks that the Three Old Men put on to tell the future.

"It is going to be another boy." Old Woman Many Grandsons poked a finger at Others' Child's thickening waist. "I can tell. You should stay here until it comes. Otherwise it will be unlucky, like the last one."

For a fleeting moment, Others' Child yearned to. Then she saw the other old grannies watching her with tooth-sucking disapproval, and her own sister, Maize Came, bouncing her fat son and daughter on her knee, and she rebelled. "The last one was not unlucky," she said. Little Brother was sitting by the fire pit, fanning the smoke away from his mother and her visitors with a deer-hide fan. They had only come to tell her what she ought to be doing. That was never what she was doing, according to the Grannies. Others' Child had grown up with the Trespassers, and so she was tainted and forever suspect.

"Unlucky is finding death in your trail," Grandmother Snake said.

"Coyote will get it like the last one," Grandmother Watcher said.

Others' Child put her hand on her belly. It was too soon to feel the new one moving, but she willed it to give her some sign, something to counter the Grandmothers and their vociferous disapproval of all that she did. They didn't cluck their tongues at Night Hawk, her husband, she had noted. He was male, of course; his wanderings didn't tie knots in the rituals the Kindred had devised for themselves. There was a proper way to do everything, from making snowshoes to boiling soap, and Others' Child's ways were all wrong, primarily because she wasn't penitent, did not regret sufficiently the years she had been separated from the Kindred.

"They mean well," Maize Came said when the Grandmothers had been fed with mush and dried meat and had consented to go on their way again. Maize Came smoothed back the sleek bands of her black hair from her round, beautiful face, and smiled affectionately at Others' Child.

"They are stupid," Others' Child said. "That is not the same as meaning well."

"How you can talk like that about your own people!" Maize Came was shocked. Since she had married, Maize Came had grown very orderly.

"Your people," Others' Child said. "They are your people." Which was ironic, because Others' Child had been born to the Kindred, and Maize Came had been born to the Yellow Grass People, which was the true name for the Trespassers. But Maize Came had brought the great gift, the maize. She was holy now, whereas Others' Child was only willful. Others' Child fingered the angular bump in her nose, and the abrupt jut of her chin. It didn't matter what she looked like; she wasn't theirs.

"You think everyone is stupid," Maize Came said astutely, "when they don't agree with you."

"No one has to agree with me," Others' Child muttered. She wrapped her fingers around the yucca rope she had been plaiting and jerked vengefully on it, straightening out the kinked coils. She wished she could straighten out her life that easily, just shake it and give it a good yank. "I only wish they would stop telling me how I should do things, and what I have not done that I ought to do, and how my husband will hardly stay with his people over winter now—as if that was my fault."

"That one had a wandering foot when you met him," Maize Came said placidly, with the contentment of a woman whose own husband was important in the councils of the tribe. "They are only vexed because they said that no one would marry you, when you came back to them and weren't biddable, and then he did."

"Well, that is stupid," Others' Child said stubbornly. "They didn't want him to marry one of their women and take her foot-on-trail. Me, they could spare."

Maize Came giggled. "Well, you don't listen to them. Why should they love you? They are old. All they have to enjoy is making people listen to them. One day you will be like that."

All women were, Others' Child thought. It was the only power they had. "I will not," she said defiantly. She would make trouble instead. The Grandmothers could wait and see.

If Spider had asked Others' Child, when she first went to sleep in Night Hawk's cave, what she wanted, Others' Child would have said just this—not to have to listen to the Grandmothers. Nor yet to the elders of the Yellow Grass People, who had raised her and then killed her father with rocks because they thought he was a god and thought he had taken his magic away from them again. She would have said, "I will go foot-on-trail with my husband," and meant it— even though she had done that three turns of the year with her brother and sister, between the Yellow Grass People and their coming to the Kindred. With a husband it would be different—with a man who made her skin ache when she looked at him. But now the ground was harder than it had been, and one of her knees hurt when she climbed.

Others' Child snuck a look at Night Hawk while Little Brother paddled in the stream at her feet. She saw how even the curve of her husband's back was familiar to her now—she would have known him by that one line, bent over his snare, the vertebrae making little knots in his russet skin. The shoulder blades were a sharp angle to either side. She could close her eyes, too, feel the bones under his flesh, and know him. It was only the country behind him that changed, yanking her out of one place into the next.

Just now he was silhouetted against towering peaks of gray rock, as angular as bones and capped with snow. There were still teeth in the air, and they should still be with the Kindred in their winter caves. But this year Night Hawk had been ready early. Budding like the willow tree, Others' Child thought, with a green urge to be gone.

He looked up from his snare, his cropped hair hanging in his eyes, and beckoned to Little Brother. Brother hopped up and padded through the reeds to him, his mother forgotten.

"This is how it is done," Night Hawk said, and Brother watched solemnly as he knotted the line.

"Duck?" Brother said hopefully, watching the sky.

"Ducks. And then maybe we will have green feathers to take to the people at the Endless Water."

"Yah bah," Others' Child said to the turtle shell she was cleaning in the stream. "This many years ago you were going to show me the Endless Water." She held up five fingers to Night Hawk's back. "So far I have seen strangers' villages and too much empty country." She sighed, because at first she had loved that. It was easy to remember but not to bring back the joy of it.

There were things that the other women of her people had never seen that Others' Child had walked up to and touched—tall, needlelike spires of rock towering above her, raised fingertips of stone. Bones half buried in a riverbank that once had been a cat longer than twice her height with fangs the length of her forearm. She had seen its skull, and the ribs protruding from the clay, and her heart had hammered in her own ribs for an hour afterward.

All that had been before the babies had begun to come. Before Elder Brother. Before this new one in her belly had left her slow and waddling again. Before she had found that she couldn't go like Bitch and have them by the trail and raise them rough and leave them to fend for themselves in a year.

Night Hawk came up through the reeds with Little Brother on his shoulders. "I have a mind that we'll trade with the buffalo hunters this season," he said. "There has been rain, and the grass will be tall. They will have hides to trade for that greenstone we brought from the south last year."

Others' Child scratched the outline of a duck in the mud on the riverbank for good luck in the snares, and stood up stiffly. The dogs' gray heads popped from the grass beside her, out of their trampled-down nest. Thief and Gray Daughter were Bitch's pups, and three parts coyote, product of one of her expeditions into the hills, her last litter before she died. Too many deaths, and all of them badly scabbed over, even a coyote dog's.

They walked up the twilit riverbank to their camp. Others' Child could hear the coyotes in the hills begin their hunting song, wild yips that reverberated down the canyons and coalesced into an undulating howl, reaching up to the thin buffalo horns of the moon. The two at her heels ignored them. The other pups had scattered to the wild, but Thief and Gray Daughter stayed; Others' Child wasn't sure why.

Night Hawk had built a spring house, a journey hut of newly leafed branches, beside the river. He was good about that since the babies came. They didn't sleep in trees anymore, or in strange caves where Rattlesnake might be living. Every night he cut fresh brush for a shelter while Others' Child made fire with the fire drill if the coals they carried packed in mud had gone out. Life had been simpler when he had been alone on the trail, but each year when they wintered with the Kindred, he never suggested leaving her behind. She wouldn't have stayed. Now . . . no, not with the Kindred, but . . .

"The buffalo hunters live well," Others' Child said while she poked at the hot ash in the fire pit to see if the fish she had wrapped in leaves and buried there was done.

"They do." Night Hawk sat down by the fire and stretched his legs. "Meat all year. I would get fat and lazy. Imagine not hunting but once a moon."

"They run them off a cliff," Others' Child said. That always killed more than the hunters could eat. It struck her as wasteful, and she shook her head disapprovingly, forgetting that she was trying to entice him, lure him toward a life among the buffalo hunters.

"It is something to see," Night Hawk said. "I saw it once. They are like thunder come alive. Once they start there is no stopping them. I saw a man caught up with them and killed. They found him at the bottom."

Others' Child tried to imagine that, to feel herself lifted on the great furry backs, rolled among the thundering hooves, flung surprised outward into empty air. To drop in an instant of wonder as if you were Hawk, and then to smash. She shuddered. It seemed too easy for that to happen. Elder Brother had gone that way, lifted on the fever to some place she couldn't reach. And then he had dropped suddenly, clear out of life. Others' Child's eyes filled with tears, and she poked angrily at the fish.

Night Hawk watched her, puzzled. It had been nearly a year. The child didn't occur to him.

A tear splashed into the coals and spat back up at him. "What is it?" he said. Maybe it was the new baby. Pregnancy made women odd, there was no denying that. He supposed it would make him odd, carrying someone else around inside himself.

"Maybe if we had been with the buffalo hunters, I could have saved him," Others' Child said mournfully.

"No, you couldn't," Night Hawk said, figuring

things out. He had loved the child, too; Elder Brother had been his firstborn, but he knew Death when he saw it. Elder Brother had gone away because Death had held out something that he wanted, like a shiny stone. That was all there was to it.

"There are healers among the buffalo hunters," Others' Child said. "I am not a healer, that is plain." She wrapped her arms around herself and rocked back and forth while Little Brother stared at her.

"It wouldn't have made a difference," Night Hawk said, exasperated. "It wouldn't have mattered if you had had a healer."

"It would not have all been me!" Others' Child said. "And what about this one?" She pointed at Little Brother, who was pounding a stick on the rocks by the fire pit. "Who is going to raise him?"

"We are," Night Hawk said. What had happened? She had been happy to be a hawk with him, and now she was a thornbush, trying to put down a taproot.

"Indeed?" Others' Child glared at him. It had become easy to fight over this. They were neither of them malleable people, and now they seemed to have hardened in just a few moments into their respective shells, like turtles. "And who will help me with them? Where are the aunts and grannies who watched you when you were small?"

"You don't like the Grannies. You are rude to them."

"Some grannies. Other grannies. There must be some place for us to be." She patted her belly. "How will they grow up, knowing no proper people, no proper way to be? Who will they marry?"

"I don't know." Night Hawk grinned and bent over, nose to nose with Little Brother. "Who will you marry when you are old enough?" His hawk-nosed profile was lit by the firelight, and his eyes gleamed.

"You have not thought about it, have you, Most Scornful?" Others' Child said.

Night Hawk sat back on his heels. "No," he said.

"Things happen that we don't arrange for. Hush and think about those things, and don't talk to me like Rattlesnake. I am your husband."

"I am afraid," Others' Child said. She spread out her hands so that he could see she had no courage hidden in them.

Night Hawk came around to her side of the fire and put his arms around her. He rocked her the way she had rocked herself, silently, back and forth, his breath warm in her ear. After a while he could feel the stiffness loosen itself from her arms, flow away down them like water. She leaned against him limply. Little Brother crawled into her lap and stuck his thumb in his mouth.

"It will be all right," Night Hawk said in her ear.

"How will it be all right?" she answered wistfully. "Foot-on-trail with a lapful of babies?"

"Cuddle up with this one," Night Hawk said, "and I will take the fish out of the fire before he is charcoal." And what husband of the Kindred would touch a cookfire? But Night Hawk had cooked his own meat long before she came down his trail.

Others' Child curled on the bed of grass he had cut for them and watched him bewildered. When he brought her the fish in a turtle shell, she ate it, digging her fingers into the hot flesh hungrily, picking out the bones. Brother opened his mouth like a magpie's baby, and she fed him pieces she had cleaned the bones from.

Night Hawk opened his pack for the flute that he had learned to play from Others' Child's brother, Mocking Bird, who was Maize Came's twin. He put it to his lips and made it sing a little bouncy song that Brother would go to sleep by. The world outside the brush hut was settling into twilight. The curved moon hung in a pink and turquoise sky, and a nightjar boomed over the valley beyond the clump of cottonwoods.

Others' Child closed her eyes. Brother was a sticky

bundle curled in the hollow of her knees and belly. Thief sat by the hut door, looking out at the twilight, and Gray Daughter turned around three times by the fire and flopped down in the dirt. Thief stood up, stretching, nose to paws, his back bent into a concave line, his black-tipped tail erect. He yawned, his teeth white as the cat's bones in the twilight, jagged snow mountains upside down in the pink and turquoise sky.

He cocked an eye at Others' Child, and she could see that he was smaller than he had been, and his gray nose longer. The ruff across his chest was matted, and there were feathers clinging to it. He licked his muzzle.

"Many thanks for the fine duck," he said to her. He nosed among the ashes in the fire pit, too. Night Hawk didn't seem to notice him.

"That is my husband's snare," Others' Child said indignantly.

"That is why I knew you would want to give me the duck," Coyote said. "After all the fine things I have done for you."

"Hah!" Others' Child said. "What have you done for me?" She knew it wasn't wise to insult Coyote, but you could argue with him. Coyote liked to see who could get the better of whom.

Coyote scratched vigorously behind one ear before he answered her. He was thinking. "I found you a husband," he said. He lolled his tongue out. "I will take him away again if you want me to."

"No!"

"You don't like him. You want to go live in a warren with rabbits. Why don't you give him to me?" He looked at her sideways, a yellow gaze that set the hair up on the back of her neck.

"I am very happy with my husband," Others' Child said. She looked at Night Hawk, playing the flute. Was it her imagination, or did he look paler, as if she could look through him? "Go away."

"If you were happy with him, I wouldn't be here."

"I am happy." She looked at Night Hawk, terrified that he would somehow hear, that thinking about him would pull him into the dream with her. Dreamtime was as real as waking time, and sometimes more dangerous. It was dangerous to fall into another person's dream. You were like the buffalo falling off the cliff with no way to stop yourself.

"Do you want my advice?" Coyote said.

"No. Go away."

"There is a great deal of dissatisfaction with you in certain quarters." Coyote grinned. She could see the iridescent green feather that clung to his nose. "Spider was saying so only the other day."

"Tell Grandmother Spider that I am sorry if I have offended her," Others' Child said carefully. Coyote was capricious, but he forgot to be angry with you when the next thing distracted him. Spider never forgot.

"You are disturbing harmony," Coyote said. "There is no balance because you are trying to want four things at once. It is mixing everything up. Just last night, a mouse spoke back to me, and Bat came out in daylight and flew into a rock."

"You should have known I couldn't go foot-on-trail with babies," Others' Child said. "You and Spider didn't tell me that."

"Oho, are we supposed to tell the puma to eat rabbits?"

"My baby died."

"If nobody died, the world would be filled up with people, bumbling about on top of each other like a gourd full of fishing worms. We have death to keep you from bumping into each other."

"He hadn't got started yet."

"Did we promise you a certain number of years? This woman is specially exempt from death? Different from all the other people?"

"You didn't say my babies would die," Others'

Child said stubbornly. "My mother and my father both died. That should be enough for you, Hungry."

"Thank you, I believe I will." Coyote nosed in the ashes again, found the remains of the fish, and ate it.

"That is my breakfast." She started to say, "Also, it has bones in it," but she supposed a bone in his throat wouldn't hurt him.

"You are most kind." Coyote looked thoughtful for a moment, gagged, and coughed up a fish bone.

In the morning, Coyote was gone, as he always was; and, waking, Others' Child was never sure whether he had been there or not. The fish was gone, too, but Thief had ashes on his nose, and he wasn't named Thief for nothing. Others' Child sighed and went down to the snares by the stream. There were feathers on the ground, and a pair of duck feet, sad and flat-looking, tangled in the snarled lines.

"I will wait by the snare with rocks next time," Others' Child said to the stony hillside above the stream. Nothing answered her, and she shrugged uneasily. When a spirit came to you in dreamtime, it was important, but dreams were often ambiguous, keeping meaning just out of reach. All Coyote had told her was what she knew already, that life was chancy. The duck had found that out, too.

"Something got your snare," she said to Night Hawk.

Night Hawk prodded Gray Daughter with his toe. "Lazy. I will tie you by the snares if you don't keep better watch."

Gray Daughter looked at him balefully. She knew what had come in the night, Others' Child thought, but she wasn't saying. Others' Child wasn't sure she could say, either. She looked at Night Hawk, who seemed untroubled by dreams or untoward visits from spirit people or even the urge to find a resting place, and sighed. She made the sigh loud enough for him to hear.

It didn't do any good. For two moons they tramped through a countryside that changed like the shifting terrain of a dream, from red rock bluffs and canyons striped yellow and brown and blue-black like birds' wings, to dry washes tangled with old, tumbled stone and alive with the sudden buzz of snakes; and then finally through a flat river valley choked with reeds. The water flowed sluggishly there as if it, too, was reluctant to go any farther, and a white heron stood on one foot in it with a still-wriggling fish in its beak. When it saw them, it lifted itself in a sudden flapping of wings, legs trailing like a wasp's, and sailed up over the cottonwoods into the sky. Others' Child wondered what it would be like to lift that easily from the ground instead of tramp across it.

Beyond the river they came to the camp of the buffalo hunters where the tall grass grew. The grass seemed to go on forever to the east, like a flat lake of green and yellow, whispering in its rippled stalks. The buffalo hunters lived in skin shelters on the prairie and lived easily, Others' Child thought. She spoke a little of their language, but Night Hawk spoke it fluently, and she watched with envy the women that he bartered with—fat, comfortable women with babies on their hips and baskets balanced on their heads, held lightly with one hand. They pressed around him, prodding with their fingers at chunks of red dyestone, turquoise beads and deer-bone flutes, shell fishhooks that had come from a man who had gotten them in the west. They spread their own wares out for Night Hawk to inspect—soft buffalo robes with the curly fur brushed and shiny. *I am lucky if we stay in one place long enough to tan a deer hide*, Others' Child thought.

She put her hand on her belly and arched her back, trying to take the ache out of it. The shaman saw her and solemnly pressed his fingers on her backbone and belly. He wore a horned headdress that looked like a low moon riding on his brow, but he had a kind, wrinkled face and thick, tufty brows like an old badger.

"I had another baby," Others' Child said to him on impulse. "He died of a fever. How could I have saved him?"

The shaman shook his ponderous head, horns swinging against the red sky. "The sickness has to be sucked out," he said. "It was in there in his skin."

"Could I do this?"

The shaman shook his head sorrowfully. "No."

The chief's woman came up and took Others' Child by the arm, tugging her toward the fire pits where meat was roasting, a whole carcass. Little Brother padded after them, following the smell.

"This would be a fine place to live," Others' Child said at night, when she lay down with Night Hawk, bellies full of meat and mouths greasy, in the hide shelter that the buffalo hunters had given them.

"Oh, most certainly, Puts Down a Taproot," Night Hawk said. He looked at her scornfully. "I could listen to old men tell lies around the fire, with their buffalo growing bigger every tale, until I die of boredom and disbelief."

"Men tell lies like that everywhere," Others' Child said. "And it isn't their buffalo that get bigger with the telling. These are no different. They are a good people. We would be welcome here."

"Heart, they are no different from the Kindred." Night Hawk rolled over and closed his eyes, head pillowed on his arm.

They *were* no different from the Kindred, Others' Child thought, but they had a shaman who could suck out sickness. The conviction that that would have been enough to save Elder Brother lingered. She looked at the smooth hide walls and imagined staying here inside them, wearing them like a turtle shell, imagined that she belonged to these comfortable people.

In the morning they moved on, with the buffalo hides lashed to the dogs' travois.

# SUE HARRISON

"A remarkable storyteller...
one wants to stand up and cheer."
*Detroit Free Press*

"Sue Harrison outdoes Jean Auel"
*Milwaukee Journal*

## MOTHER EARTH FATHER SKY
71592-9/$5.99 US/ $7.99 Can

In a frozen time before history, in a harsh and beautiful
land near the top of the world, womanhood comes
cruelly and suddenly to beautiful, young Chagak.

## MY SISTER THE MOON
71836-7/ $5.99 US/ $7.99 Can

An abused and unwanted daughter of the First Men
tribe, young Kiin knows that her destiny is tied to the
brave sons of orphaned Chagak and her chieftan mate
Kayugh—one to whom Kiin is promised, the other for
whom she yearns.

## BROTHER WIND
72178-3/ $6.50 US/ $8.50 Can

# BARRY LOPEZ

**DESERT NOTES: Reflections in the Eye of a Raven and
RIVER NOTES: The Dance of Herons**
71110-9/ $9.00 US/ $12.00 Can

"Barry Lopez is a landscape artist who paints images with sparse, elegant strokes...His prose is as smooth as river rocks."

*Oregon Journal*

**GIVING BIRTH TO THUNDER,**       71111-7
**SLEEPING WITH HIS DAUGHTER**    $9.00 US/ $12.00 Can

In 68 tales from 42 American Indian tribes, Lopez recreates the timeless adventures and rueful wisdom of Old Man Coyote, an American Indian hero with a thousand faces—and a thousand tricks.

**WINTER COUNT**      71937-1/ $7.00 US/ $9.00 Can

Quiet, intoxicating tales of revelation and woe evoke beauty from darkness, magic without manipulation, and memory without remorse.

**FIELD NOTES:**       72482-0
**The Grace Note of the Canyon Wren**    $9.00 US/ $12.00 Can